Invincible

Piercing the Veil, Book 2

C.A. Gray

www.authorcagray.com

Copyright and Disclaimers

Invincible
By C.A. Gray

Published By:

Wanderlust Publishing
Tucson, AZ

Cover Art By:

Jayme Kelter, Copyright 2013, Klarite Photography

All Rights Reserved

http://www.klaritephoto.com/

ISBN: 0-991-1858-1-1

Acknowledgements

Thank you Lord, for helping me get another book "out there," and helping me through the sometimes discouraging and always challenging process of writing and editing, and for the diligence to keep going when it would have been easier to give up. I love you.

Once again, a huge thank you to my mom, Cyndi Deville—my primary editor and biggest support. :) Your suggestions are gold!

To my other editors, Lindsay Schlegel, Tamara Murphy, and Jim Strawn—I couldn't have done this one without you! Thank you for all your excellent, specific suggestions to improve the story and characters.

Jayme Kelter, your photography skills are unparalleled. Thank you so much for the use of your amazing work for my cover!

Menna Bevan, thank you once again for your help in editing my British-isms! I'd look like such a fraud without you… ;) (Although I made a lot of edits since you read it, so, uh, please forgive my slip-ups…)

Anna Bastrzyk, thank you again for your excellent and efficient graphics work.

Clive Johnson, thank you again for your very professional formatting!

And to my readers, thank you so much for your support and encouragement. I definitely couldn't do this without you!

Praise for "Intangible," Book 1 in the "Piercing the Veil" series

"I really love this book. I enjoyed the adventure and the story, which i think was a cool interpretation of King Arthur's legend. The twists were awesome and exciting. The revelation at the end was just the perfect intro for the next book.... I would definitely recommend this to all YA and fantasy readers out there." —Fire Fairy Book-A-Holic Reviews

"I don't want to give too much away, but I will say this was a page-turner. This is a book that will appeal to young and adult alike. I gave this book 5 stars." —Book Referees

"Five fantastical stars for Intangible by C. A. Gray! ...I really loved this story. I was skeptical when I saw that the mythology of King Arthur played into it. I've read so many retellings of the Camelot stories. Very few of them are original, but this one definitely is. C. A. Gray has so many things going for her in this story; originality, good writing, engaging characters, and this author is smart. In order to write a story like this, you would have to have a solid grasp of physics. She really impressed me... C. A. Gray knows her stuff!" —The Readiacs

"I was very excited to start reading this book and I must say that I was not disappointed!... The story is fast paced and full of plenty of action and twists and turns. I was so engrossed in the story that I didn't want it to end. I can't wait for #2!" —The Book Lover's Attic

Out of Northumbria there rises a king,

Born of a union that rent the nation.

His sword, Excalibur, was forged in Avalon

Whose blade can sever body from spirit.

He shall take it up from the stone,

And cast it away into the depths,

Bearing with it the spirit of the Shadow Lord.

For seven ages and eight,

It shall pass out of all knowledge.

In the days of the Child of the Prophecy,

The Shadow Lord shall rise once more.

The child shall come from the line of the King,

The firstborn of his surviving heir,

Born in the seventh seven less eleven,

Under the sign of the Taijitu.

Nearest kin shall be locked in mortal combat.

Both shall fall

Yet the one who holds the blade that was broken

Shall emerge victorious.

Prologue

A stealthy pair of eyes scanned for any sign of life on the banks of the Lake of Avalon. Although the Fata Morgana and most of the footbridge had been destroyed in the battle, there would still be penumbra guarding the lake. The Watchers had long believed that both Excalibur and Sargon were somewhere in the depths of this water….and now so was Kane. Hidden amongst the trees in this world-between-worlds, Achen peered through the fog hoping for evidence that Kane has survived.

An eerie light from the distant world of men dappled the water through patches of fog. *Come on, Kane,* Achen thought, *give me a sign that you made it!* At just that moment, Achen caught a flash of gold from the lake.

He caught his breath. Was that just the reflection of the light on the water? Or was that… could it be…*Excalibur*?

Another roll of fog passed over his hiding place

just at that moment, and Achen decided to risk it. He morphed, sprouting wings, and very cautiously followed the roll of fog as it meandered over the water, hoping the penumbra would not see him.

He lowered himself as close to the water's surface as he dared, peering down below as he skimmed across it. Wreckage from the former Fata Morgana littered the bottom of the lake, but he saw none of the bodies killed in battle. It was as if those that had fallen into the water had simply vanished from existence. Achen tried not to shudder at the thought.

At last he reached the spot where he had seen the gleam of gold, and bit his lip to keep from crying out. It had not been a mirage after all: he *had* seen Excalibur.

Then, beyond the sword, Achen saw Kane.

Suspended near the bottom as if a weight had been tied to his feet, Achen saw the frame of a skinny teenage boy with white-blond hair billowing out around his head. A jagged scar marred his right cheek. His skin was pallid, and his body limp. But then Achen realized that Kane's open eyes were *moving.*

"Kane!" Achen hissed as loudly as he dared. "Kane!"

There was no response. The glassy eyes appeared fixed on something invisible to Achen, and Kane's expression was beyond terror.

Forgetting stealth, Achen hissed again, "Kane! Come on, look up at me!"

Then, for the first time in his immortal life, a sharp pain pierced Achen between the shoulder blades. At first, he registered only surprise. Whipping around, he saw a sentry poised above him, ready to attack a second time. It was a penumbra with the head of a man and the body of a bird, its talons outstretched. On instinct, Achen summoned and thrust a ball of light towards the belly of the shadowy enemy. It ducked, opening its mouth and letting out a terrible cry like a falcon as the bolt struck home. From the banks, four other penumbra sentries instantly alighted to join the battle.

Achen steeled himself, casting one more glance below him.

"Hang on, Kane," he whispered. "I'm coming!"

Chapter 1

Peter Stewart lay face up, staring at the blood-red canopy of his bed on the third floor of the Watcher Castle. For those few seconds before he opened his eyes, he kept hoping to find himself in his blue bedroom at home in Norwich, at the top of an exceedingly narrow staircase. He hoped Carlion had only been a dream, and that he would return to his usual and rather mundane existence as the nerdy kid at King's Secondary School, who spent half his time in the headmaster's office for accidentally setting things on fire.

Five days had passed since the accident in the Jefferson's BMW, and when Peter thought of how much had happened in those five days, it made his head spin.

So it turns out there's an Ancient Tongue after all. In his mind, Peter heard his dad's voice saying, *Just remember, in the not-so-distant future, I will be in the enviable position of saying, I told you so!*

Peter groaned and rolled over, facing the frosted glass windowpane. Even in his head that sounded annoying.

And there really were penumbra. And they influenced everybody to varying degrees.

Except Peter. And his dad. And Lily.

Nobody controls Lily, Peter thought wryly.

And a group of Watchers had been stalking him his whole life because apparently he was both a descendant and a doppelgänger of King Arthur.

And he might be the Child of the Prophecy, destined to destroy the Shadow Lord. His stomach turned over at that. What a horrible idea.

And apparently his dad had been in on the whole thing from the beginning.

Oh, and he had a twin brother. Who might be dead. *If he isn't dead, that's probably worse,* Peter added to himself.

He sighed deeply, feeling his lungs expand to the limit and then fall back again, like deflating a balloon. He knew he'd have to get up and go down to breakfast in a few minutes. Isdemus had given Peter and his companions, Brock, Cole, and Lily, three days to recover from their horrific adventures at the Fata Morgana. Last night after dinner, though, Isdemus had said it was time they went to school in Carlion, since they couldn't go back to Norwich. Peter wished desperately that he didn't have to go. He wished he could just pretend none of this ever happened.

Peter swung his legs over the edge of the bed and let them dangle there, resistant to the fact that the moment he let his feet touch the floor, it would be time to start his day. Finally his soles made contact with the cold stone, and he pushed himself upright with his arms, striding towards the little bathroom connected to his room. He had to prime the pump in order to draw a bath, but when the water began to flow out, he was grateful that at least it was hot— the fire specialist had evidently already made his rounds that morning.

While the bath filled, Peter glanced at himself in the mirror over the wash basin just enough to see that at least the reflection had not changed: he was still extraordinarily pale and pinched-looking, his blond hair rumpled from a night of turbulent dreams. He stripped off the gray t-shirt and shorts he slept in the night before and gingerly stepped into the bath, wincing that the fire specialist had done such a very thorough job.

When he was clean and dressed in the clothes that Gerald the servant laid out for him the night before—a maroon sweater with odd little poufs here and there on the front, as if it had been made in the 1970s, thankfully paired with nondescript jeans—he slipped out into the hallway, trying not to feel jittery that today would be yet another first.

***

Lily Portman hadn't slept a wink all night.

She sat on the window seat in her chamber and rested her cheek on her hand. Waves of exhaustion rolled over her from time to time, but she warded them off with subsequent bouts of nerves.

Today, she would start at yet another new

school. Paladin High would make thirteen new schools since she was six years old.

Usually the story went something like this: she'd show up and keep her mouth shut for awhile, so everyone just thought her quiet and a little weird. Slowly, she'd make a few acquaintances. Then a few weeks to a few months down the line, she'd slip up and respond to her acquaintances' penumbra, instead of to the person. Everyone would freak out and avoid her after that, and eventually the teachers would find out about it too. The teachers would tell her foster parents that they suspected Lily was psychologically disturbed, and her foster parents would sigh and say, "We know, her social worker told us…"

Pretty soon after that, Lily's foster parents would either pull her from the school and send her somewhere else, or else they'd send her back to the system for a new set of foster parents. Or both.

Lily sighed. *But then, everything changed.*

At King's Secondary School, Lily met Peter, and his existence turned everything she thought she knew upside down. He didn't have a penumbra. That fact alone was like… she tried to think of an analogy. *It was like thinking I was the last person on earth, and then I met another survivor.*

But she'd had no idea how to act around him, so she'd made a complete idiot of herself. And the worst part was, even when she knew she was being an idiot, she couldn't help it because she wanted to be around him so badly. And at the same time, she wanted to slap him for having the audacity to be so bloody *scientific.* Of all people, the *one* guy on the planet that didn't have a penumbra *had* to be a pragmatist...

Then the accident happened, and Carlion. She finally had proof that she wasn't crazy. She and Peter weren't the only ones after all.

Then Dr. Stewart got abducted, and Brock too, and she found out about the prophecy...

The prophecy. Her stomach turned over at the thought of it. The idea that *she* might be the subject of a prophecy that was written 1500 years ago... but she stopped that thought cold.

Probably it would turn out to be Peter after all. Wouldn't that make the most sense? She had nothing like Peter's abilities. It was Peter who looked like King Arthur. And he was a boy. And everyone thought it was him. Of *course* it would be.

She sighed. Then, just to complicate her life even more, every now and then against her will, she found herself imagining what it would be like to kiss him.

That was probably bad.

But she didn't need to think about all of that right now. Outside, the birds chirped, the sky was golden, and it was time to get ready for another first day of school... but this one promised to be different. For the first time since she was six years old, Lily had hope that she might actually belong somewhere.

***

"Peter!" Lily called when she saw him in the corridor. "I was just coming to find you. Gah, what are you *wearing*?"

Peter made a face and said, "I know. I guess it'll take Gerald awhile to get used to our tastes. But you look—" he groped for something nice to say as he surveyed her outfit— "decent." She wore a brown square-necked frock reminiscent of *Alice in Wonderland*.

"I'm wearing an apron dress the color of mud, Peter."

Peter pursed his lips, amused. "Serves me right for trying to compliment you."

Lily fell into step beside him, turning away so he couldn't see the beginnings of a blush. "You're trying to compliment me and the best you could come up with was 'you look decent'?"

"Well, I mean, look what I have to work with," Peter said before he could stop himself. His eyes widened and he backpedaled, "I mean, the dress! Because of Gerald. Not because of you, in the dress…"

Now Lily's cheeks burned. "Just… stop."

Peter kicked himself mentally, and groped for another topic as they walked in silence for a few minutes. He had a hard time coming up with anything because he was so confused by the fact that he'd made her blush. "Er," he said at last. "Did you sleep all right?"

"I hardly slept at all," she admitted. "I've been to a lot of new schools in my life, and most of them have been dreadful. But I'm actually excited about this one," she confessed almost timidly.

"Because it's a school full of Seers?"

"Yeah. I can actually say what I think here!"

Peter smiled wryly. "Because usually you're so reserved." His initial impression of Lily had been that she was weird, and possibly insane—but certainly not shy. That seemed so long ago, though; it was odd to think that he'd actually only met her two days before the accident, or exactly a week ago. Between the accident and the Fata Morgana, things had happened so fast that he really hadn't had time to think about Lily one way or the other, except to be alternately glad for her help and irritated at her cheek. Now that things had calmed down a bit, though, Peter had actually been wondering what he thought about Lily quite a lot. Somehow they didn't seem as comfortable around each other now as they had at first, but he didn't understand why.

Lily replied, "Well, yeah, but here I can say what I think and I won't get judged for it. There's more than that too, though. I'm trying to think how to explain it." She thought for a minute and then went on, "Have you ever been somewhere or done something where you just felt, 'this is it'? Like, this is the thing I was meant to do, or the place I was meant to be?"

"Yeah. Studying physics," said Peter automatically. "Never about a place, though."

"Me neither, but I guess I've always believed that it exists somewhere, and when I find it, I'll just *know*, in that way you just know things…"

"Intuition or whatever?"

Lily frowned at him. "You don't have to sound so condescending about it, Peter."

"I'm not!" he protested. "I believe in intuition!" He crossed his fingers behind his back when he said it, and she raised an eyebrow at his hidden arm.

"Uh huh," she said, not buying it.

He laughed, chagrined. She smiled back, and he dropped his eyes, suddenly self-conscious.

I do not *fancy her,* he thought stubbornly. His dad kept insinuating that he did, and it irritated him—because of course he still liked Celeste, his crush of the last three years. Intentionally, he recalled Celeste's long dark hair and heart-shaped face... but he couldn't help remembering what Lily had said about Celeste's penumbra, which was apparently a really big snake. *That might make her slightly less attractive.*

"Pete! Lily! Wait up for us!" Cole bounded down the stairs above them trying to catch up, with Brock following behind. "Pete, what are you *wearing?*" Cole said when they got close enough.

"Yeah, yeah, all right," Peter grumbled, and then he sized up Cole, who wore a fairly reasonable white polo shirt, but trousers that looked like they could have fit three of him. He'd cinched them about the waist with the drawstring, and he looked like he was wearing a burlap sack. "You should talk. My sweater and your trousers together would be a sight..."

Brock wandered up behind Cole, and he met Peter's eyes briefly, then looked away. Brock had been Peter's arch-enemy at King's, but hadn't been nearly as horrible to him in the three days of tenuous normalcy since the Fata Morgana. Instead, they seemed to have traded their open animosity for oppressive tension. Neither of them knew how to act around the other anymore. Peter figured he should try to make friends with him now, but he really, really didn't want to.

"Er," said Peter. "Morning, Brock."

"Morning," Brock replied stiffly, looking off down the hall.

Peter sighed, and fell into step beside Cole as they headed towards the Great Hall. *At least I've got Cole here,* he reminded himself. Even just one person with whom he still had a straightforward, familiar relationship was better than none at all.

Chapter 2

Breakfast was overwhelming. A cornucopia of breads, eggs, sausages and bacon, fruit, yogurt, tea, coffee and milk spread across the table in the Great Hall, and the sounds of cheerful chatting and quiet laughter mingled with cutlery scraping porcelain plates. Some sixty or seventy Watchers ate, and a couple of the bodies around the table glowed in various humanoid forms. The nimbi did not eat, but they chatted animatedly to make up for it. Peter had met almost everyone in the room at some point in the last few days, but only briefly, and he couldn't remember most of their names.

"Come in, sit down, tuck in," said Isdemus when he saw Peter, Lily, Cole, and Brock. Isdemus sat at the head of the table wearing robes that made him look as if he were swathed in a sunrise, and although his voice was quiet and gravelly, it carried, with forceful authority.

"There aren't any seats," said Lily, frowning.

"Here we are!" said Bruce, who sat towards the head of the table around Isdemus, along with Jael, Sully, and Dan. He stood up and produced four empty chairs from various parts of the table where other Watchers had finished their meals and abandoned their plates, and managed to squeeze them all in.

"Where's Mum?" Cole asked brightly.

"She finished her breakfast and decided to help with the cooking for the rest of us," Isdemus explained, gesturing for the four teenagers to have a seat.

"Mum, cooking?" Cole choked. "Does she even know how?"

"I heard that!" Mrs. Jefferson said in a mock-scolding tone, batting Cole on the back of the head with her elbow as she replaced an empty platter of sliced bread. "I may have burned a few things here and there, but oh, it's so exciting in the kitchen! There's steaming and cracking and sizzling and laughing and chatting and gossiping, and—my goodness, why did I ever hire a maid back home? They don't have gas stoves or electric or anything, they just have Mary Beth, who's a fire specialist, and she goes around heating everything while everybody else follows the recipes and mostly they make them up, and did you know, they make the biscuits with real fresh buttermilk here, which is absolutely disgusting if you drink it straight"—here she made a face—"but the biscuits are delicious once Mary Beth is done with them, aren't they?" She went on prattling about her domestic adventures, but the kids only half listened.

Isdemus reclined in his high-backed chair, enjoying a steaming mug of tea and grinning fondly at Mrs. Jefferson as she bubbled over with enthusiasm. Meanwhile, the other servants came and went, bearing fresh platters from the kitchen and removing plates, occasionally stopping to have a conversation with Isdemus or one of the other Watchers.

"Better than toast and jam, eh?" said Bruce to Peter with a wink. Peter sat down and picked at his food. He tried to smile back at his dad, but it came out in a grimace.

"I'll say!" exclaimed Cole to Peter's dad. "I just hope Paladin High is half as incredible as this breakfast!"

Peter shook his head. "I don't think I've ever met anybody as enthusiastic about food as you, Cole."

Cole eyed Peter's meager plate and said, "Yeah! What's the matter with you?"

Peter shrugged. "Not hungry, I guess." He glanced over at Lily, who nibbled on a sausage and stared at the fire behind Isdemus, her eyes wide and vacant, as if she were somewhere else. Apparently she felt the same way.

Peter glanced over at Dan, Sully, Jael, and Isdemus. He noticed they were all relatively silent, compared to the rest of the Watchers in the Great Hall. Every now and again they whispered something to one another with serious expressions and tones too low for him to overhear.

Peter nodded in their direction at his dad, and whispered, "What's going on over there? Are they plotting something?"

"Oh, you know," Bruce shrugged with a grin. "They're always plotting *something*." He dabbed the corners of his mouth with his napkin and said, "I suppose this is as good a time to tell you as any, though—we'll be leaving just after breakfast."

"Leaving?" Peter repeated, frowning. "Just for the day, you mean? Where?"

"Well, I told you that Isdemus didn't think it would be a good idea for me to go back to the university for awhile, or anything associated with my normal life in Norwich," Bruce explained. "But I have to do *something* with myself, so I volunteered to go along with these jokers." He jerked a thumb in the direction of the other three Watchers with his goofy, lopsided grin.

"You didn't answer the question," Peter frowned, setting his fork down.

"Didn't I?" Bruce said vaguely, and pushed his sellotaped glasses further up the bridge of his nose.

Across the table, Gladys, whom the teens met on their first night in the castle, stacked dirty plates, along with a plump jovial woman in her mid-forties named Alice and her daughter Mary Beth. They chatted with each other as they cleaned. Every so often, Gladys took the opportunity to glance furtively in the Watchers' direction, but she never attempted to address them directly.

"You're going on a quest!" Cole accused Bruce, his eyes lighting up excitedly. He spoke loudly enough that Jael, Sully, and Dan all looked up also. "Aren't you?"

"I am sending them on an errand for me," said Isdemus calmly, sipping his mug of tea.

"Well, what are you questing for?" Cole persisted.

Lily's eyes focused and she sat up, tuning in to the conversation. "Isn't it obvious? They're looking for Excalibur."

"Shh!" Cole admonished, glancing in the direction of the Watchers with an expression of horror.

Lily rolled her eyes. "Cole, it's not like Excalibur is a big secret here."

Brock swallowed a mouthful of poached eggs and interrupted, "How can they go looking for Excalibur when they already know it's at the bottom of the Lake of Avalon, though? And it's not like they can get down there." He directed his question partially to Lily and partially to the Watchers, who ignored him and resumed their whispering. Then he added with a shudder, to no one in particular, "And I'm sure there are still loads of penumbra there. Even if there was a way to get at Excalibur, the place is probably overrun."

"But they've got to go back to rescue Kane," Cole guessed loudly, unperturbed. Lily kicked him under the table, and he said, "Ow, what was that for?"

"Be a *little* sensitive," Lily hissed under her breath. "Kane isn't something to joke about!"

"I wasn't joking about him," Cole protested, hurt. "Of course they're going to try and rescue him… he is Pete's brother, after all!"

Suddenly there was a loud clatter of plates behind them, and everyone jumped and turned to see what had caused the commotion. Gladys, who had just removed a plate from the table, stooped to collect the shards. Her hands trembled, and her normally sallow face was bright red. "Excuse me," she muttered, loudly enough that everyone could hear. "So sorry… excuse me… sorry…"

"Not at all, Gladys, not at all," said Isdemus graciously, but Peter noticed that he watched her with a curious intensity after that.

"What's with her?" Peter whispered to his dad.

Bruce shook his head. "She's always been a little strange, hasn't she?" he said rhetorically. But his expression was suddenly grave, and drained of color.

"You're *not* going back to the Fata Morgana, though," Peter whispered to his dad again, returning to the previous subject. He looked anxiously at Isdemus for confirmation and said, louder this time, "Right?"

"I am afraid that where they are going is none of your concern," said Isdemus, mildly but sternly.

"Isdemus forbade me from going there, actually," Bruce told Peter under his breath, his voice taking on a hard edge.

Peter's eyes widened. "Well, good! But why would you *want* to?"

"Cole is right. Your brother is down there. And he *might* still be alive. Maybe it's not likely… but it's possible." He swallowed, looking away from Peter. "But Isdemus is in agreement with Brock that the place is likely overrun. He sent Achen as soon as we got back, and he seems to think that's all we can do." With an effort, Bruce's expression seemed to clear, and he looked back at Peter with forced cheerfulness. "All I can do is wait for news, like everybody else."

"So you're going on a quest to distract yourself," Peter guessed. Bruce shrugged at him, which Peter knew meant yes. He frowned at his dad. "Do you have to go away *today* though?"

Bruce looked surprised. "Why not today?"

"Because!" Peter wanted to say, *because it's my first day of school,* but that sounded much too childish. He probably wouldn't have said it even if they were alone, but certainly not in front of Brock.

Apparently his dad knew what he'd meant anyway, though. Bruce's expression softened, and he rumpled Peter's hair across the table, earning him a scowl as Peter tried in vain to fix it back. "You'll be fine! This isn't like Norwich, you'll be a celebrity here! By now the whole city knows about what happened at the Fata Morgana."

"That's what I'm afraid of," Peter muttered.

Bruce shrugged apologetically, pushing back from the table a bit as he slid his empty plate away from him. "Sorry, kid. Not my decision. They're leaving today, and if I'm going with them, I've got to go today too."

Peter turned back to Isdemus and asked, louder this time, "Is it safe, this mission?"

"They will be perfectly safe, I assure you," Isdemus answered, but something about his tone forbade further questioning.

"Then why is it a secret?" Peter challenged, turning back to his dad. "Can I come?"

"No!" said all five of the Watchers at once. Peter was taken aback.

"What we mean to say," said Sully quickly, "is that there is no need. What's most important is that you get your education."

"Oh, come on!" Peter protested, "I never learn anything in school anyway! I spend most of the time making up experiments and trying not to get caught or blow anything up. You'll be doing the headmaster at Paladin High a favor if you send me away. Tell 'em, Dad!"

"It may be true that you have learned everything that King's Secondary School could teach you," Isdemus replied, "but I promise that is not true of Paladin High. On the contrary," he added, with a twinkle in his eye, "as an outsider, you may find that you are in need of remediation."

Peter opened his mouth and closed it again, not sure what to say to that.

"Might not know everything *here*, hot shot," Lily translated under her breath, earning her a sour look from Peter.

Cole stifled a laugh in his napkin, and while he still pressed it to his lips, Mary Beth snatched it from between his fingers and plopped it in the center of the plate in front of him. Then she removed both without so much as asking Cole if he was finished, still jabbering away as she worked.

"So what *are* they gonna teach us at Paladin High?" piped Cole. Then he added, imploring, "*Please* tell me we're gonna merge minds with the fish…"

"And learn geography by porthole?" added Lily hopefully.

Isdemus shook his head. "I'm afraid not that,

unless they're taking you to Carlion's sister cities, where there are no penumbra. Remember how recognizable you four are to the penumbra in the outside world now." Isdemus had told them when they had first arrived that there were other cities like Carlion spread throughout the world.

Peter stared at the fire behind Isdemus, a weighty feeling of gloom descending upon him. *Remember how recognizable you are.* The words echoed in his mind. *Remember how they all want you dead.*

"So they're gonna teach us how to get better at our gifts then?" Cole persisted.

Dan, who had just ended a whispered conversation with Jael and Sully, looked over at Cole and grinned. "They'll just teach you how to get more precise. Observe." He turned to his water goblet, staring very intensely at the liquid as he began muttering under his breath. Slowly tentacles of water rose like steam, except they remained in their liquid form, curling about like clay beneath the fingers of a master sculptor. Each tentacle wrapped itself around the others until it became obvious that he was shaping the petals of a rose. Once the water glass was empty, with a command from the Ancient Tongue, suddenly the fluid froze, and he plucked the ice rose from the glass, and handed it across the table to Jael, who blushed like a schoolgirl but took it reluctantly, pursing her lips and refusing to look at him. Peter raised his eyebrows at this and looked at his dad quizzically, who returned an expression as if to say, *Yeah. I know.*

Cole's eyes widened. "Cool! I want to do that!"

"Your equivalent, Cole, would be to understand

the nuances between healing the layers of tissue in a wound and healing various diseases," said Isdemus. "It takes very different skills to heal blood dyscrasias, cancers, and infections, for instance. They can't all be done with the two simple words I taught you just before we went to the Fata Morgana."

"*Stad fola*?" Cole said eagerly, as if to prove that he still remembered them.

"Right. Those words tend to work well in acute trauma, because they essentially mean 'stop bleeding.' Chronic illness is trickier, however. You have to understand the physiology and know exactly what has gone wrong in order to tell the body how to get better. That is why healers are so well-respected in Carlion. It's not an easy task."

"Wow…" said Cole, his eyes round as saucers as he sat back in his chair in wonder.

Peter had hardly listened to most of this. He felt a sickening dread growing in the pit of his stomach. He felt like he'd already had enough of Paladin High, and he hadn't even been to school yet.

Abruptly he scooted his chair back and walked away from the table without explanation, although he could feel everyone's eyes on him as he left. He didn't care; he just needed some air.

Bruce watched him keenly, scooting his chair back too. "Excuse me," he murmured, and followed Peter.

Bruce caught up with him just as Peter reached the main hallway lined with tapestries and torches, which at this moment were rendered unnecessary by the broad daylight streaming through the castle windows.

"What's up?" Bruce asked, slinging an arm around Peter's shoulders.

Peter shook his head and didn't answer, folding his arms over his chest.

"Oh, come on," Bruce chided. "What are you, six years old?"

Peter snorted and shrugged himself out from under his dad's arm, ducking into an empty sitting room with a few oversized velvet chairs before yet another crackling fire and an enormous arched window. Books lined every available centimeter of wall space.

Bruce sighed, following him. Peter sat down in one of the chairs facing the window over the grounds, and Bruce sat in another, opposite the round little coffee table decorated with a globe set in precious stones. "All right, go ahead and sulk. I'll wait," he added, eyes twinkling. This got a smile out of Peter, somewhat against his will.

After another long pause, Bruce prompted, "You don't want to go to school, is that it?"

"I don't see why I have to!" Peter burst out. "It's bad enough at King's where everybody ignores me or makes fun of me, but here I'm a celebrity! It's... it's embarrassing!" Peter knew that wasn't really what was bothering him, but since he couldn't identify the real issue, it seemed a reasonable surrogate.

"That doesn't have to be a bad thing!" Bruce insisted. "Peter, you're a hero to this city. Think of that! You know how everyone treated Brock back at King's? That will be *you* here!"

"Except I might not even be the Child of the Prophecy," Peter retorted, "for all we know, it *is* Lily."

"Even so," Bruce argued, "*you're* the one that blew up the fortress, not Lily. That story is already larger than life."

"I did not, *you* blew up the fortress!" There was a half beat of silence. "I just..." Peter trailed off. "I just think something familiar would be nice, for a change." Peter rested his chin on his fist as he looked out the window. He wanted to change the subject to something that made him seem less pathetic. He remembered the rose Dan had made for Jael and his dad's knowing expression, and decided that was as good a topic as any.

"What's going on with Dan and Jael, anyway?" he asked reluctantly.

Bruce shook his head with a groan. "Looong story."

Peter looked up, interested now. "Tell me."

With a sigh, Bruce said, "The short version is, Jael's husband died. He was another Watcher, died on assignment about fifteen years ago. She changed after that—she didn't used to be as cold and gruff as she is now."

"Huh," said Peter.

"Dan's been crazy about her for years but she'll have none of it. We all kind of figure it's because she's afraid to get hurt again. But Dan doesn't give up. Hat's off to him for that."

"Huh," said Peter again, sympathetically this time. "Maybe she just doesn't like him, though?"

"Maybe," Bruce shrugged again. "The question

is whether Jael's capable of liking anybody that way anymore."

Peter clucked his tongue sympathetically. A few seconds later, though, his thoughts returned to his own predicament, and the fact that he'd soon have to face a new school where he was famous. He lapsed back into gloomy silence.

"Wait, I have an idea!" said Bruce, changing the subject. "What if I ask Isdemus to go and get Newton?" Their cat was still in their house in Norwich. "That might make you feel more at home, huh?"

Peter blinked, and looked at him hopefully. "You think he would do that?"

Bruce shrugged. "I don't know that Isdemus will be able to spare one of the Watchers for that, but I can ask him." Peter's expression was so unabashedly eager that Bruce laughed. "Before I go I'll talk to Isdemus about sending someone to go and get him. Maybe Vanessa, she's a space specialist and I think she's otherwise between assignments right now. Happy?"

"I guess so," Peter murmured, sinking back into the chair morosely as he stared out the window.

There was half a beat of silence. Then Bruce said, "Are you trying to be difficult on purpose?"

A small smile curled the edges of Peter's mouth against his will. "Maybe."

"Suggestion?" asked Bruce.

"You're gonna tell me anyway."

"True," Bruce conceded. "Think about Lily."

Peter looked up sharply. "Huh?" His cheeks grew slightly warm. He didn't want to have this conversation again.

"Seriously," Bruce went on, though he didn't seem to notice Peter's blush. "This has got to be much harder for her than it is for you. Right?"

"I don't think you need to worry about Lily, Dad. She thinks this is all fantastic, being in a place where people finally don't think she's nutters."

"It's to her credit that she sees the best in situations, but this is hard for her too, depend on it," said Bruce. "Even in Carlion, Lily is still an orphan with only a few friends, who mostly focus on their own problems." He said this last bit pointedly. "If you focus on how uncomfortable she is at yet another new school, and with her history, you won't be thinking so much about yourself."

"I think you just called me self-centered," Peter said, raising an eyebrow.

"Well, you *are* fourteen." Bruce gave him his signature goofy grin.

Peter sighed. "I really wish you weren't going today," he admitted at last.

"I know, kid. But you really will be fine. After all, you faced the Shadow Lord and lived to tell the tale. How bad can a new secondary school be?"

Chapter 3

Achen beat his wings furiously over the deadly water if the Lake of Avalon, whipping a lasso of light around his luminous body. The four penumbra sentries hovered just out of reach of his whip, waiting for an opening to attack. Finally one snarling creature dove for Achen's chest, talons first. Achen reversed his swing, and his lasso of light collided with the penumbra's neck. In a flash, the penumbra vanished.

Achen took advantage of the flash, and morphed into the form of a flea. He wished he could call for reinforcements, but he knew if he did that, he might never find Avalon again. The only reason Isdemus had been able to send him back after the battle was because Achen had only just left, and the island had not drifted very far yet.

Careful to maintain the cover of fog, Achen flew as fast as his now-tiny wings could carry him, perching instead on the branch of a tree once he got to the banks. Then he resumed his usual form just long enough to inspect the wound between his shoulder blades. He didn't know what it meant that he had been hurt; how bad was it? Since he'd never been wounded before, it was impossible to tell. He felt weaker than he normally did, though. Was it only a temporary setback, or would he be wounded forever?

When Achen saw the other four penumbra circle back and spread out, obviously searching for him, he morphed back into the form of a flea, effectively vanishing once more. He knew he was safe from discovery for the time being—safe enough to contemplate what he had seen.

Kane was alive, although he seemed to be in some kind of suspended animation. He was also right beside Excalibur… which meant perhaps he had not been quite as crazy to jump into the lake as they had all assumed. Perhaps it had been an act of bravery after all, rather than an act of lunacy. It also meant that Achen might be able to both save Kane and retrieve Excalibur at the same time.

But one very large problem remained: how to get them out, without destroying himself in the process?

***

Kane couldn't feel his body. He wasn't even sure if he had a body anymore.

The world around him was a perfectly geometric, crystal clear nothingness, like being trapped inside a prism. If not for his memory of what had just happened in the Fata Morgana, the last vestiges of

Avalon, he would have no concept of where he was.

He remembered the battle raging all around the Fata Morgana, and the Watchers running towards him to rescue him as he fought off penumbra from all sides. Then, at the last second, he'd locked eyes with Peter, realized that he would never get to Excalibur by summoning it... and he made a devastating decision. He dove into the churning waters of the Lake of Avalon.

Are the others still alive? And if they are, do they all hate me for deserting them? Kane wondered desperately. But he had no answers. *How long have I been here?*

To Kane's shock, another voice replied to his last question. It was high and cold, and chillingly familiar.

That question has no meaning, it said. *Time is different here.*

Kane jumped—or at least he would have jumped, if he'd been able to move. *Who's there?* he demanded. It sounded like the voice was coming from inside his own head.

I am in your head.

Kane felt a flutter of fear. *This isn't happening. This can't be happening.* Why *did I jump in?*

I was wondering the same thing, said the voice casually, but with an edge of curiosity that seemed almost dangerous.

Without warning, Kane felt like he was being ripped open from the inside.

Kane's memories overtook him like a flood. At first they were a random cacophony of images and sounds, much too fast to identify. But then the scenes began to coalesce into a theme—of Peter.

Kane watching Peter from afar as he studied alone on his porch, sipping lemon squash as Newton wound his fluffy white body between Peter's legs.

Kane getting soaked to the bone as he peered through the window on a stormy day to see Peter eating a sandwich at lunch with Mr. Richards.

Kane following an older version of Peter as he trekked through the fallen leaves at King's towards the headmaster's office after yet another science experiment gone awry.

Permeating each memory was a gnawing sense of loathing, Kane's fingernails biting into the palms of his hands, and his jaw aching as he ground his teeth. Peter had robbed him of his birthright and destiny, and Kane hated him for it almost as much as he hated the Shadow Lord. Even in this wasteland of nothingness, Kane could taste the acrid bile rising in his throat at the thought. Kane would *force* Peter to reveal his own unworthiness. Then Isdemus and the Watchers would be forced to admit they had been wrong about Peter—*wrong, wrong, wrong!*—and they would all see that Kane had been the true prodigy all along.

The memories evaporated just as suddenly as they had come, leaving only the geometric prism of the lake.

You envied him, the voice concluded, amazed. *You despised him!*

Kane didn't answer.

You wanted to be the Child of the Prophecy instead of Peter, the voice surmised. *That's why you despised him, because all the Watchers believed it was him and not you.*

Kane still didn't answer, but something inside him trembled.

But why did you jump into the lake? mused the voice.

Kane felt the beginnings of the gutting sensation again. but before it could force him to reveal the answer he cried out, *Stop!* Sargon relented, and Kane snapped, with more courage than he really felt, *I saw Excalibur, here at the bottom of the lake. I may not be able to see it now, but I will find it, and I will destroy you!*

So you dove in to get the sword, knowing you may never find your way back out again, concluded the voice, with a tinge of admiration. *That was very brave, Kane.*

Kane knew he was being patronized, and fell into an indignant silence.

I understand how you feel, Sargon continued sympathetically. *Passed over. Rejected. Always second best.* There was a long pause. *But you don't have to be, you know.*

I don't have to be what?

Second best.

Kane knew he was being baited. He tried to resist, but it seemed so pointless. After all, the Shadow Lord knew his every thought.

Ask me to show you how.

The need inside Kane was so primal that it overrode all sense of reason.

Ask me.

Kane tried to resist, but it felt like bench pressing

a weight that his muscles simply could not support.

Fine! Show it to me!

*

The moment he thought the words, Kane felt the gutting sensation again, only now in reverse: he knew in a flash that he was inside Sargon's memory now, seeing through his eyes.

Kane's chest nearly split apart with agonizing pain.

He was on a battlefield, gazing into a pair of sea green eyes flecked with gold. Kane knew those eyes as Peter's, but crow's feet lined the skin, streaked with mingled sweat and blood. Sharing the mind of Sargon, Kane could feel his own stomach tie in knots as he recognized King Arthur.

He watched as Arthur fell to his knees, Sargon's blade protruding from his abdomen, even as Arthur's sword lodged into his own chest. Despite the pain, Sargon gloated, and Kane felt himself saying, "I have defeated you, Arthur. Nothing now remains between me and world domination. Knowing this, despair and die!"

But Arthur gave him a grotesque smile, lodging his blade deeper still into Sargon's chest. "You did not defeat me," Arthur croaked, "because the sword I hold is Excalibur!"

Sargon wheezed in surprise and fury, feeling his lungs fill with blood as his eyes fell upon the sword. He saw the golden glint, and knew that Arthur spoke the truth. This was the very sword that had been prophesied: the one that would prevent him from taking another body once Mordred's was dead.

Still, he managed to choke out venomously, "No

more than a setback! Your bloodline still ends here, Arthur, with the death of your only son! One day, when I destroy that sword, I will return, more powerful than ever. And there will be no one left to stop me!"

Dimly, he heard Arthur laugh, and then the words, "You are too late!"

Sargon's head fell back upon the ground, wondering what Arthur meant even as he felt his life draining away. There could be no Child of the Prophecy now. The moment he died, Arthur's bloodline *would* end.

Wouldn't it?

Kane knew the moment when Sargon's spirit let go completely: it felt like snapping off a particularly tenacious rubber glove.

So that's what death feels like, Kane thought, as he shared Sargon's last breath. It didn't seem so bad.

For an interminable period of time after that, Sargon had no eyes, no senses, and no concept of time. He was bound by the sword itself.

Then suddenly there was a flurry of color, like stepping into the sunlight after endless ages inside a darkened cave. Kane knew this was the moment when Lancelot had taken Excalibur from the battlefield and

"...cast it away into the depths,
Bearing with it the spirit of the Shadow Lord.
For seven ages and eight,
It shall pass out of all knowledge."

The moment the sword entered the lake, Sargon's world became the prism of crystallized light to which Kane now also belonged. And glittering before him now was Sargon's captor.

Excalibur.

Something inside Kane swelled to bursting when he saw it, shimmering in the void just beyond his reach. It was exactly how he'd always envisioned it, how he'd seen it in the stories of the secret library. The blade shone with purest gold and two entwined dragons curled about the hilt, their eyes set with emeralds. Engraved in the blade were the characters of the Ancient Tongue. One side, he knew, said "Take Me Up," and the other said "Cast Me Away."

It's the only way out, Sargon whispered. *The world has awaited this moment for thousands of years, when Excalibur would again fall into the hands of the Child of the Prophecy.*

A deep longing swelled in Kane's chest at the words. The fulfillment of all of his fantasies was right there for the taking.

Oh yes, said Sargon, *you must be the Child of the Prophecy. You know that now, don't you? How else could you and I end up here, side by side, at the end of all things—just you, me, and Excalibur?*

Something compelled Kane that was almost primal, and he reached for the hilt again and again—but he still could not move his body. The sword glimmered before him like a delicious mirage.

Excalibur traps us both here, Sargon whispered. *If you want to fulfill your destiny, first you have to destroy it. While it exists you can never escape.*

Kane rallied with one last surge of violent effort. *If I destroy it, then you will be free, too! Never!*

You are the hope of mankind, Kane, Sargon insisted, his thoughts soft and lilting, like a lullaby. The whisper flowed into Kane's mind like a noxious gas penetrating through the cracks of a closed door. *You know it, and I know it. Isn't it time the rest of the world knows it too?*

Kane felt himself begin to crack. Was there any point in resisting?

You must destroy it, Sargon repeated.

The fissure in Kane's soul deepened. He despised himself... but in his mind's eye he saw himself holding the golden sword, defeating the Shadow Lord.

How? Kane thought desperately. *I can't touch it! Even if I could, I have no tools here. It's made of metal; I'd have to melt it down...*

To his surprise, Sargon laughed. *You cannot melt Excalibur! No tool conceived by man could ever leave so much as a scratch. No, Kane. There is only one way to do it, and you know what that is.*

Kane found that he did know: it was the only weapon he had left in this place. *The Ancient Tongue.*

Yes.

Then why don't you *say it? You know the Ancient Tongue as well as I do!*

I know it far better, Sargon corrected, *but I cannot touch the sword. I am bound by the curse of the prophecy. I cannot touch it, Kane, but you can. Of course you can. It is your destiny.*

Kane had no arguments left. Sargon's flattery was nearly irresistible.

Only speak the words, Sargon whispered. *It can all end right here, right now.*

Chapter 4

When Peter emerged from the sitting room with his dad, he found that Cole, Brock, and Lily were almost at the castle gate; he had to jog to catch up. Cole heard his footsteps and turned around to wait for him.

"What was that all about?" Cole whispered.

Peter shrugged. He didn't want to admit to Cole that he was afraid to start at Paladin Secondary School, so instead he said, "Dad's gonna see if we can bring Newton here."

"Oh yeah!" Cole exclaimed, "I forgot about Newton! Who's feeding him, then?"

"Nobody right now, but Dad said he'd ask Isdemus to send another space specialist to get him." Peter paused for a second and dropped his voice. "Honestly I wish I could just go myself, though."

"How come?"

"I dunno…" he trailed off. Cole waited for him

to answer as they exited the castle. They both squinted as they emerged into the sunlight, and the cheerful sound of the splash of water in the fountain shaped like a pair of dragons filled the courtyard. Finally Peter ventured tentatively, "Isn't any of this... bothering you at all? How new everything is?" He gestured around them with his head, and added, "Being here?"

Cole was quiet for a moment. "Well..." he chewed his lip. "I guess I hadn't really thought about it."

Peter cast him an incredulous sidelong glance and shook his head. "It must be nice, being you."

Cole said vaguely, "Yeah. It's okay," like he had no idea what Peter meant by that. Then he shifted his attention to Brock and Lily. They were up ahead of Peter and Cole, but Lily walked very fast, purposely out of synch with Brock.

"So my brother's a total stranger now," Cole muttered.

Peter gave a short laugh. "Seriously. No offense, but if I could have picked the people to get stuck here with, he definitely would not have made the list."

"What do you mean, 'stuck here'?" Cole exclaimed. But before Peter could answer, he went on with a sigh, "Honestly I'm not sure if he'd have been on my list either. But I really do think he's trying not to be... well... *him* anymore. I think something really happened to him in the Fata Morgana."

"Yeah, he almost died," said Peter bluntly. "That sort of thing can make even Brock Jefferson reevaluate his priorities." He saw Cole wince. "Sorry."

Cole shrugged. "It's okay. Not like he doesn't deserve it for being a prat to you for all those years. I mean, he's kind of been a prat to everyone."

"Not to you?" said Peter, surprised.

Cole thought for a minute. "No, he just ignored me. I'm only his clumsy kid brother. Not like I ever helped his status any." He gave a short, bitter laugh which took Peter off guard. He'd never heard Cole talk about Brock that way before.

"Is it any different now?" asked Peter.

"Well…" Cole watched Brock and Lily obviously each trying to pretend the other was not there. "Yeah, but I don't know how to describe it. I mean, he's still ignoring me, but it feels different now. I don't know."

"Like he's ignoring you for a different reason?"

"Yeah. I mean, not like status matters here, right?" Cole snorted.

Peter fell silent for a moment, lost in thought as he watched Brock from behind. Then he ventured, "Has he said anything to you at all? About what happened to him at the Fata Morgana before we got there?"

"Of course not. He doesn't talk to me," said Cole. He added as an afterthought, "I don't know if he talks to anyone, actually."

"He talked to my dad," Peter said. "I guess he tried to confess to him or something. You know, just in case they bit it in the end."

"Really?" asked Cole, interested. "What did he say?"

"Dunno. My dad keeps secrets really well, unfortunately."

Cole snickered. "I wonder how long it takes for the Schism Response to wear off," he mused, referencing the stages of denial newcomers to Carlion tended to experience before they accepted that the world was not the way they had originally believed it to be.

Peter shrugged, and admitted, "I'm not even sure it's worn off for me yet." He was on the verge of confessing how badly he wanted to go back to Norwich, where at least life had been predictable. But they reached the stables, and eight-year-old Eustace trotted around the corner to meet them, his vibrant red hair glinting in the sunlight. Eustace dragged the reins of two horses behind him, and another stable hand, a skinny boy about Cole's age, brought out two more.

"Peter!" cried Eustace, bursting with excitement. "We saw you comin'! I heard all about your adventures, everybody in th' castle's talking, but you haven't come out since you got back and I've been just dyin' to hear... so it's *true*, then? You *are* th' Child of the Prophecy?" Peter opened his mouth uncomfortably and glanced at Lily, trying to decide how to respond. But before he had a chance, Eustace went on, "I go to Paladin Secondary School too, I just came out here to feed th' horses before I go, and I'll come back early, o'course, 'cause my lessons aren't as long as yours, but I bet I'll see you there, Peter—" Eustace handed around the reins, prattling without coming up for breath. The second stable hand stared unabashedly at Peter, hardly blinking, but said nothing. While Eustace jabbered, everybody managed to mount their horses after a few tries. Lily mounted awkwardly in her knee-length dress, looking around to make sure she didn't flash anyone.

Finally Peter cut Eustace off mid-stream, since there seemed to be no other way to shut him up. "Well, thanks for the horses, Eustace." He nodded in the direction of the other stable hand, who continued to gape back at him, but did not otherwise return the acknowledgement.

"I'll see you at school, maybe, Peter!" Eustace called after him hopefully.

Once they were far enough away that Eustace could not see, Cole turned around to smirk at Peter.

"Shut up," Peter muttered.

"Wonder what he'd say if I told him I fit the prophecy too," Lily mused crossly.

"Please do," said Peter. "Tell everybody. In fact, *I'll* tell everybody—"

"Nobody will believe it isn't you, Pete," said Cole flatly. "You look the part."

Lily pursed her lips and said nothing.

Traffic on horseback jammed the dirt road from the castle into town. The citizens of Carlion were dressed just as garishly as the last time the teens had ventured into town, wearing capes, feather headdresses, burlap sacks tied with rope, ruffled poet blouses from the seventeenth century, and any number of other mismatched fashions. The din of chatting and thudding hooves against the dirt forced them to raise their voices to hear each other.

"This is worse than the motorway," Brock

grumbled.

"Quit being so negative," said Lily sharply.

"Quit being so u—" Brock started to retort, but he cut himself off just before what sounded like the beginning of the word *ugly*. He bit his lip instead.

Lily laughed scornfully. "How did that taste going down?"

"Hey!" called a boy on a dappled horse who joined the traffic jam from an adjoining road. He had brown hair cut in the shape of a bowl, glasses, and a chubby face. "You're him, aren't you?" he said without preamble, looking at Peter.

"Er," said Peter, looking over his shoulder. "Who?"

The other boy rolled his eyes and sidled up next to Peter's horse. "Everybody's talking about the outsiders who came to Carlion, and one of 'em looks like King Arthur and blew up the Fata Morgana. Obviously that's you."

"Oh, yeah," Peter said awkwardly. "Hi."

"Your name is Peter Stewart, right?"

"Um, yeah."

"I'm Anthony Hutchins." He stuck out a hand, and Peter hesitated, repositioning his hands on his reins so that he could shake it without losing his balance. "You're headed to Paladin High, aren't you?"

"We all are," Brock cut in, sounding a little annoyed that he was not the object of attention.

Anthony turned in Brock's direction when he spoke, and his eyes grew wide. "You must be the earth specialist!"

Brock blinked, and his eyebrows shot up.

"Yeah…"

"Aren't you the one who made the ground appear in the Fata Morgana so everybody could get out?"

Brock sat up straighter, and his voice deepened a bit as he replied, "Yeah. Yeah, that was me."

Peter rolled his eyes at Cole, who tried not to laugh. Lily did laugh.

"How'd you know about all that?" Cole asked Anthony.

"It's all over town!" Anthony said again, nodding enthusiastically. "I guess one of the top Watchers told Jim Garvey the whole story right after you got back, and then Jim told his wife Brenda…" He stopped and made a reeling motion with his hand, like that was explanation enough. Then he turned to Cole and said, "So which one are you?"

Cole looked momentarily perplexed, so Peter helped him out. "I think he means, what's your gift."

"Oh! I'm a healer!"

Anthony frowned at him. "Healer is a profession, not a gift. You must be a eukaryote specialist, then."

"A what?" said Cole.

"Eukaryotes," Peter explained. "Cells with a nucleus."

"Oh," said Cole blankly.

"Means you specialize in stuff that's alive," Peter translated.

Anthony pointed at Lily. "And you're the only girl, so you must be the one who made the force fields. You have the same gift as me, then—

electromagnetism! So you read minds, right?"

Peter nearly choked. "*What?*" and Lily repeated, confused, "Read minds?"

"Well, not *read* them exactly," Anthony amended. "Most people don't think in words, they usually think in pictures, or sometimes in feelings. So I guess most of the time it's more like being able to read feelings."

"Oh," Peter groaned, and then reluctantly explained aloud, mostly to himself, "That makes sense, actually. Thoughts are a form of electromagnetic energy…"

Anthony went on, looking at Lily, "I'll bet you've always been good at reading people even in the outside world, right?"

"Yeah," Lily hedged, "but that's because I'm a Seer. I heard everybody's thoughts, but it wasn't really *their* thoughts, it was just the suggestions from their penumbra—"

Anthony waved a hand dismissively. "But even with other Seers, couldn't you pick up on their feelings pretty easily?"

Lily glanced at Peter reflexively, and she looked away almost as fast. "I didn't meet many Seers before coming here," she said evasively. "And I'm… not really sure if I can read their feelings or not."

Peter felt his cheeks begin to burn.

"Oh, don't worry," Anthony assured her with a grin, "after a couple sessions in Ancient Tongues when we all practice our gifts, you'll be able to read anybody like a book!" Peter's stomach turned over. Anthony went on, winking at Lily mischievously,

"Which comes in handy for me, I must say. I pretty much always get what I want."

Under his breath, Cole leaned over to Peter and said teasingly, "She'll be able to read you like a book! Won't that be nice, Pete?"

Chapter 5

Dan, Sully, Jael, and Bruce headed down the flight of stairs leading to the Commuter Station, each with a sack lunch over one shoulder. They had not bothered to pack more than one meal ahead, because Isdemus told them they would be received as guests in Carlion's sister city in Egypt, called Ibn Alaam.

"So, I don't understand," said Bruce as he jogged to keep pace with the other three. "I know we're after the Philosopher's Stone. But why are we going to Egypt?" The Philosopher's Stone was the object Morgan le Fay had sought so diligently, because its possession would grant her the unlimited power of the Ancient Tongue. If the Shadow Lord managed to inhabit a human body and found the Stone before the Watchers did, not only would he have that power, but all the penumbra who had sworn allegiance to him would have it, too.

"Shh!" said Jael, turning around to look at him

with exasperation. "Do you want to announce it to the whole castle?"

Sully slowed down and fell into step with Bruce, and Bruce obediently dropped his voice to a loud whisper. "Shouldn't the Stone be somewhere in England?" Bruce persisted to Sully. "I know it supposedly ended up in France in the thirteenth century. But I thought the last known historical figure to have possession of the Stone was Isaac Newton, and he was British! How did it find its way to—"

"Newton never had the Stone," Sully interrupted in a similarly loud whisper. "He was just a Watcher famous in the outside world for other reasons, and he was so obsessed with finding the Stone that it was connected to him even in pop culture."

Bruce almost stopped walking. "Newton was a Watcher?"

"Come *on*!" Jael hissed impatiently, tucking her short graying hair behind her ears.

"How did I not know that?" Bruce went on, looking at Sully. "All this time, I've been studying physics as a Watcher myself... we even named our cat after him, for goodness' sake!"

"I can't believe you never saw his painting hanging in the portrait gallery," said Sully. "You of all people..."

"I'm sure I must have seen it, I just guess I didn't know what I was looking at..." Bruce muttered, shaking his head. "All right, then. If Newton never had the Stone, then who was the last known person who *did* have it?"

"Morgan le Fay," said Sully. "Far as we know, it

was never used again after the Fata Morgana incident."

"Morgan le Fay was also in England, though," Bruce pointed out.

Dan and Jael reached the entrance to the Commuter Station and waited for Sully and Bruce to catch up. When Bruce got close enough to Jael that she no longer had to shout in order to be heard, she said, "Isdemus says that after Morgan le Fay used the Stone, one of the penumbra probably returned it to its previous hiding place."

"And they think Morgan le Fay originally found it in Egypt?" Bruce returned, trying to catch his breath as Jael pushed open the door to the Commuter Station. With a day job as a physics professor, he was significantly less fit than the other Watchers, who made it a point to stay in shape so they would always be ready for battle.

Sully explained, "According to Isdemus, the Pyramid Texts of Ancient Egypt referenced alchemy. He said the references were obscure and written in hieroglyphics, which I guess is why nobody ever looked into them much before—plus, according to the translations known to the outside world, those references all refer to the translation of the pharaoh's body from earth to heaven."

"Which doesn't mean much necessarily," said Bruce, tracking.

Sully nodded. "But Isdemus thinks the texts might actually be talking about the Stone. If they are, it might mean that le Fay found the Stone in Egypt originally."

"But to figure out where in Egypt, we'll have to

decipher the texts," Dan chimed in, walking down the narrow hallway of the Commuter Station, looking for the appropriate painting. "And in that case, the library in Ibn Alaam is the place to be." He stopped in front of a painting of a brook meandering beneath a bridge somewhere in the old English countryside. Beneath it was a totally inappropriate label that read, "Ibn Alaam, Egypt."

"What if the Pyramid Texts weren't talking about the Stone at all, though?" asked Bruce, frowning.

"Well, then we're no worse off than we started," said Jael. Before anyone had a chance to respond, she moved towards the painting and disappeared. Dan was right behind her, and Sully and Bruce followed.

When he emerged on the other side, Bruce blinked in confusion. "Wha—?" he began. He could barely see a foot in front of his face. Everything was white, although very loud, like the bustling and shouting of a crowded thoroughfare, and the air smelled like fish and exotic spices mingled with the stench of rotting produce and unwashed bodies. He was so befuddled that he forgot to move out of the way, and Sully bumped into him as he emerged in exactly the same spot.

"*Oof!* Sorry…" said Sully.

"Oh!" said Bruce with relief, stepping forward and stretching out his hand towards the white barrier. "It's a sheet!" Sully gave him a wry smile as Bruce pulled it aside, and at once the sights matched the sounds and smells. The four Watchers found themselves in the bustling center of the city. Bruce blinked again and turned around to look at the others, all of whom now looked as confused as he was. "I don't understand."

"Why did the porthole take us *here*?" asked Dan aloud, voicing Bruce's thoughts. "I expected we'd show up in the castle…" But they merged with the flow of pedestrians, blending in.

The buildings were many stories higher than those in Carlion, with scaffolding hanging off the upper stories where stone and masonry specialists had abandoned their attempts to refurbish the ancient, crumbling stone. Sheets hung in lieu of awnings in order to shield merchants from the scorching sun. Clothes hung from metal rungs bolted to the walls just outside of the windows and balconies above street level, suspending cotton garments in the wind.

"Looks like Cairo," Sully nodded, smiling as he looked around. He had been stationed in Cairo as a recruiter for the Watchers on and off for two decades.

"Is that a good thing?" Jael made a face. She watched as stray dogs tucked their tails between their legs and loitered in door frames and in between the booths of street vendors, feeding on half-eaten and discarded falafel infested with flies. On either side of the street, raw shanks of meat hung from cords to entice the buyer, and behind the butcher's cart, still-live goats bleated and chickens clucked, awaiting their turns for slaughter.

Sully shrugged and looked over his shoulder at Jael. "Good is relative. It's all about what you're used to. This feels like home to me."

Everything about the place seemed busy. All sorts of people mingled in the crowd: women in gallebeyas, men with mustaches or full beards, and children in rags weaving in and out of the crowd as if playing tag with one another between the legs of strangers. Although the occasional nimbus moved through the crowd as well, most of them took a humanoid form, and would have blended in completely if not for their telltale glow.

"This is almost like a regular city in the outside world," Bruce frowned.

"Are you kidding me?" Dan gaped, gesturing all around them. "I'm in culture shock over here! This is nothing like the western world!" Then he mused, eyes wide as he took in the sights, "I've never been to the near east before…"

"Well, it's not like a regular city in *England*, of course," Bruce amended. "But I barely see any evidence here of the power of the Ancient Tongue."

"How can you know that already?" Dan asked, frowning. "We only just got here…"

"Look at their faces," Bruce pointed out, still frowning. "They seem… downtrodden. Don't they? Like they don't have any sense of personal power. Like the world just happens *to* them."

"Well, this is a larger city than Carlion. Maybe that makes it harder for everybody to work together, using their gifts," said Sully, shrugging as they threaded their way through the crowds towards what they could only assume was the main road. "If they can't combine their efforts, then it would look essentially like nobody had any gifts at all, right?"

"True," said Bruce thoughtfully. "Once I moved to Norwich, though, if it hadn't been for the fact that I'd spent so much of my life in Carlion, I'm sure I'd have stopped believing in the Ancient Tongue altogether. The outside environment has a way of sucking all the faith out of you." His frown deepened. "It looks like that's what happened here."

"Yes, but this isn't the outside world," Jael said. "These people should know better." She stopped a woman dressed in a skirt and blouse that might have been ordinary in the Western world around the 1960s. "Excuse me," she said gruffly, and without further introduction she demanded, "What's your gift?"

From the woman's expression, it was evident that she understood English well enough to be surprised.

"Jael!" Dan scolded, pulling her hand away from the woman's arm. "I'm sorry, she doesn't know how to be polite," he smiled apologetically. "It's just that... we're here from Carlion, and we're trying to find the Watcher Castle. This *is* Ibn Alaam, isn't it?"

"Yes," said the woman, looking suspiciously from Dan to Jael and then behind at Bruce and Sully. Her eyes settled on Jael again at last, and she said, "What do you mean, what is my gift?"

Dan and Bruce exchanged a wary look, and Dan said, "Your gift. In the Ancient Tongue." When the woman still looked blank, he said incredulously, "You mean you don't know about your gift?"

She shook her head slowly, and said, "I am afraid I do not know what you mean."

"What's the point of this city, then?" Jael demanded.

"Well, there aren't any penumbra here. That's something," Sully muttered.

"Look, can you tell us how to get to the castle, please?" said Dan soothingly.

The woman turned and pointed up the street, still looking slightly alarmed, as if she hoped they would go away and leave her alone.

"Thank you," said Dan, and began to move down the crowded street in the direction she had pointed.

"Well," said Sully finally, falling into step beside him, "Carlion does have very little contact with Ibn Alaam, less than many of the other sister cities. Perhaps Isdemus simply did not realize how vastly their philosophy differs from ours…"

Bruce hesitated, and then said to the others anxiously as he caught up, "Wait a minute. Don't you think we should tell that woman she has a gift? We can't just leave her like that…"

"That's not why we're here," Jael said matter-of-factly. "Once we've found the Philosopher's Stone, perhaps we can talk to Isdemus about setting up a training program here. But that's not the priority at the moment."

Bruce scowled at the back of Jael's head.

"Duck!" Sully said sharply.

Thinking Sully meant that there was a duck waddling about at his feet somewhere, Bruce looked down, only to be smacked in the face by the slimy body of an enormous fish as a vendor tossed it to one of his employees for packaging. It fell to the ground in a *poof* of dust.

"Wrong kind of duck," Dan remarked, suppressing a smile.

"Ugh," said Bruce, making a face and wiping the cold slime off his cheek with one hand. The employee scrambled over to pick up the fish and throw it away, apologizing profusely in Arabic.

"Jael doesn't mean to sound heartless," Dan said to Bruce softly enough that only he could hear. "She's just very task-oriented. That's what makes her a good Watcher."

"I disagree," Bruce said, disgruntled. "Good Watchers exist for two reasons: to protect the line of the Child of the Prophecy, and to teach anybody who will listen about the power they always suspected but never knew they had. And I think it's part of our job to instruct a member of a sister city that doesn't even know about her gift!"

Dan waffled his head side to side, considering. "For the most part, I'd agree that that's true. But at this particular moment in history, I'd say preventing the Shadow Lord from returning to a physical body and creating an army of penumbra with godlike powers is also *fairly* high up on the priority list."

Bruce smiled wryly and conceded, "Touché."

When they reached the edge of the city, Sully approached a stable and asked the stable hand in Arabic if they could hire four horses to get to the Watcher castle.

"You mean camels?" the boy replied in Arabic.

Sully looked at the others, but they stared back at him blankly. "They want to know if we want camels instead of horses," Sully translated.

Dan answered with a shrug, "Sure, I… guess."

Once the boy disappeared, Dan leaned towards Sully and whispered, "How do you ride a camel?"

"Probably the same way you ride a horse," said Jael. "You get on its back, and…"

"Yeah, but I mean, how do you get *up* there?" Dan pointed down the road to a couple of other travelers who had just come into view, entering the city on camelback. The camels were indeed quite tall, and the saddles did not have any stirrups.

Just then the boy reappeared, pulling the reins of two camels behind him, while another stable hand followed with the other two. Sully smiled gratefully, and just as he was about to try and figure out how to mount, the boy said expectantly, still in Arabic, "That'll be fifty sheikhs."

Sully stared at him, and then turned back to look at the others. "I think he just told us we owe him half a hundred wise men."

"Sheikhs are our currency in Ibn Alaam," said a soft voice, in English, but with a thick accent. They all turned to see an attractive woman with dark skin and eyes the color of a milk chocolate bar. She wore a simple white linen tunic and matching trousers that set off her dark skin perfectly. She smiled at them in greeting and stepped forward, handing the boy a handful of coins. "One more camel for hire to the castle, please," she added.

The boy bowed to her and ran off to the stables for another camel, and she turned around, pushing a curtain of long dark hair away from her face. "I was sent to meet the Watchers from Carlion. Our leader, Bomani, told me you would be coming. I assume that must be you four?" she asked, extending a hand towards Sully, since he was the closest. "I am Masika, a member of Ibn Alaam's branch of the Watchers."

"We are from Carlion," Sully confirmed, shaking her hand. "Sully," he introduced himself, "and this is Jael, Bruce, and Dan." Masika took each of their hands in turn, but both her fingers and her gaze lingered on Dan a moment longer than the others. She lowered her eyelashes and smiled. Dan smiled back, oblivious. Jael looked from Masika to Dan and frowned.

The stable boy returned with the fifth camel, and Masika gave the boy a nod of thanks. Then she pulled the camel's reins towards the ground, and he obediently sat down so that she could straddle his back.

"So that's how you do it!" said Dan, and pulled on the reins of his own camel, trying to emulate her. But the camel refused to budge.

"Animals can tell when you are not confident," said Masika with a smile. "You must tug like you mean it."

Dan pulled on the reins a little harder, and although the camel cast him a reproachful look, after a moment's hesitation, he knelt on the ground. Bruce and Sully copied him, and their beasts also obeyed. Jael yanked on her camel's reins, but the beast continued to stare with wide, vacant eyes, as if it didn't even notice her presence. She scowled at it and yanked harder, like a threat.

"Once you are on, grip the camel's flanks with your knees so you do not fall off when he stands up," said Masika. "Camels move a bit differently than horses when they walk, and you may find it difficult at first to get used to."

"Ha!" said Dan triumphantly, grinning at Jael as his camel stood up with him still perched on top.

"Show-off," Jael rolled her eyes, as her camel jerked its head away from her stubbornly.

"Very good," Masika said to Dan, favoring him with an indulgent smile. "I will show you all the way to the castle if you would like. Ibn Alaam is not easy to navigate."

"That's not necessary," said Jael quickly, at the same moment that Dan said "Thanks!" and Bruce said, "That would be excellent," though he was distracted, trying to maintain his balance as his camel stood up. At last Jael managed to crawl aboard her camel as well, with some huffing and a lot less cooperation from the camel.

Once they were all successfully on their way, Masika guided her reins towards Dan. Dan smiled politely and said, "Thank you for helping us. We had all expected that the porthole would take us straight to the castle, instead of into the heart of the city. I'm not sure what we would have done if we hadn't run into you."

"We'd have managed," Jael muttered, but she was too far behind Dan and Masika for them to overhear. Sully was farther away too, but Bruce heard, and smirked at her.

Bruce sped up then, and fell into sequence on Masika's other side. "Tell me," he began, but then he faltered, not sure how to ask his question without seeming rude. "Er, we were talking about the gifts here in Ibn Alaam. You do know the Ancient

Tongue, don't you?"

Masika looked momentarily shocked, but then she smiled haughtily. "Of course we do not know the Ancient Tongue. No one has spoken it since the last of the original Knights of the Round Table passed away. I thought that was common knowledge."

Bruce was stunned to silence. He looked around at the others, who returned his expression of incredulity. "You're kidding," he said at last.

"You mean the Watchers don't teach the citizens of Ibn Alaam about their gifts? What do you *do*, then?" Jael demanded.

Masika had to turn around to see her, and she arched one perfect brow in Jael's direction. Then she cleared her throat and said, "Like the other members of the Watchers from Ibn Alaam, I spend most of my time in the outside world, recruiting."

"What is your job in the outside world?" Dan asked Masika, his tone placating.

"I am an anthropologist."

"An anthropologist!" Dan repeated, looking at the others as if he couldn't believe their luck. "Well, that's perfect! We're—" he glanced up and down the road to make sure there were no other travelers near enough to overhear, and then lowered his voice, "—You might already know this, but we're here to investigate the historical references in your library to the last known locations of the Philosopher's Stone. I'll bet you know them inside and out!"

Masika looked confused. "Well, of course I do. But why are you interested? Bomani told me that you were here because you wanted to access some of the information from our library, but you must already be aware that the Stone has been lost for millennia. What we *do* know about its previous whereabouts is more mythological than historical…"

"Of course we know that," Jael said flatly. "But unfortunately, this is the only lead we've got."

Masika shook her head. "I am sorry, I do not understand. Lead for what? The documents in our library, cryptic as they are, have been in our possession for centuries. Why are the Watchers of Carlion interested in them now?"

Sully, Dan, Jael, and Bruce all exchanged a significant look, and Sully said, "When we get to the castle, we'll tell you the whole story."

"Not that you'll believe it," Jael muttered.

Sully ignored her and continued, "By the time we're done, however, I suspect you'll wish we hadn't told you after all."

Masika frowned at him. "Why is that?"

"Believe me," said Bruce ominously, "I'd forget it if I could."

Chapter 6

The crowd thinned as Peter, Cole, Brock, and Lily approached the main thoroughfare of the city, before Anthony told them to turn off. "It's at the bottom of the hill here, see?"

"That?" said Peter incredulously. "It's enormous!" The closer he got to the structure, the more apprehensive he felt about an entire school full of people who were bound to stare at him.

"Well, there are about fifty thousand people in Carlion, and this is the only secondary school," Anthony shrugged.

"Fifty thousand?" Cole gaped at the same time, and Peter said, "How in the world can that many people disappear from England without anybody noticing?"

"Well, Isdemus told us that they don't disappear, remember?" Lily said. "Most of them were born here, so I guess that means…"

"According to the outside world, most of us

don't exist," Anthony finished with a grin, his dimples deepening. "But that makes sense, since according to the outside world, this city doesn't exist, either."

"Didn't Isdemus say there were other cities like this one all over the world?" Cole asked excitedly.

"Yup. Far as I know, Carlion is the largest, but they're all over," said Anthony.

Peter and Cole exchanged a look of awe as they pulled up to the hitching post outside the enormous brick building. There was a queue to get to it, and Peter's horse Charger stamped his feet impatiently. Peter sympathized with him, feeling equally apprehensive. The queue inched forward, and Charger practically pranced in place. It gave Peter an idea.

"Er," he said to no one in particular, "I, um, I think Charger needs more exercise. There's something I want to check out in Carlion anyway. I'll be back in time for the second class."

"What?" said Cole, looking perplexed. "What do you have to check out?"

But Peter pretended not to have heard him. "I'll see you soon," he promised, galloping off before the others could reply. He overheard Lily in the background huffing, "Honestly! What's gotten into him?"

Peter broke away from the queue of students and headed back onto the main road into Carlion. As Charger galloped, Peter felt the wind in his hair and on his forehead, evaporating the beads of cold sweat that he only just then realized had accumulated on his face as he neared Paladin High. He felt like he could breathe again for the first time since he'd woken up that morning.

He almost merged onto the main road, but as he approached it, he saw a few of the townspeople point at him and stare. He pursed his lips, redirecting Charger down a narrow side street. Presently he realized the road he had chosen meandered towards the crops in the field.

After he had been riding for about ten minutes, quite off the beaten path, suddenly there appeared a dark cloud in the crystal blue sky. Peter had to steady Charger to keep him from spooking at the clap of nearby thunder. The sky above grew black and ominous, though it only seemed to be raining in the distance.

A few minutes later a squat, middle-aged, and very incensed-looking man galloped up the road, took no notice of Peter, and guided his horse through the fields as quickly as he could in the direction of the spontaneous rainstorm, splashing mud as he went. Seconds later, two more very official-looking men galloped along behind him, though with somewhat less vehemence. One of them did at least deign to tip his hat in Peter's direction on his way towards the storm. Curious, Peter urged Charger in the same direction.

When he caught up, the first incensed little man was yelling at the farmers, waving his finger back at the other two more dignified-looking persons behind him. "I brought the magistrates," he huffed, "just to prove that you've been mucking about with the weather when you know good and well that it's clearly my jurisdiction. Do you know how difficult it is to clear up a storm when I've been commissioned to maintain sunshine for the entire fortnight?"

The farmer who looked as though he was the foreman, or at any rate the person in charge, drew up to his full height in an effort to intimidate the angry little weatherman. "We have been asked—by *Isdemus himself*," he added with importance, "to double our yield by the end of the quarter. Our population is growing quite rapidly, he says. And crops need watering." He glanced at the ministerial officials behind the red-faced precipitation specialist. Nobody seemed to pay any attention to Peter for once, who stood a pace away, looking on curiously.

"Then why didn't you call Jim Garvey? That is what you agreed to! Jim can pull the water from the river and run it to your bloody crops without all this ruckus." He waved his hand angrily at the clouds.

"Jim Garvey and his wife are otherwise occupied with desalinating water from the Channel," said the foreman haughtily. Jim was the irrigation specialist in Carlion, Peter remembered.

"Well, he has an apprentice, dun he?" demanded the weatherman.

"Kenny is only fifteen and practically a menace. He's hardly honed his gift well enough to be trusted with something like this."

The weatherman looked back at the magistrates in desperation. It was then that he noticed Peter, and his gaze lingered with a flicker of interest on Peter's face. Peter gave him a little halfhearted wave, after which the weatherman turned his attention back on the problem at hand.

"If I recall, John," said one of the magistrates in a rather disinterested tone, "you *did* sign an agreement promising not to tamper with the weather without written consent from Horace." The little weatherman, whose name seemed to be Horace, puffed his chest up and shot the foreman named John a dirty look that said, *so there.* "Under the circumstances and given that agreement, you will kindly refrain from creating thunderstorms, and will contact either Horace or Jim Garvey and associates if you wish to plant and water new crops where irrigation is not yet in place."

John, whose pride seemed to be wounded more than anything else, turned a peculiar shade of puce (or perhaps it was merely the shadow cast by the storm clouds) and protested, "But Isdemus—"

"—requested more crops, and said nothing of the methods used to get them," said the second magistrate. "That being the case, you will comply with his wishes while operating under the previously agreed upon terms."

With a self-satisfied smile in the foreman's direction, Horace looked up at the sky and said in an authoritative tone, "*Coinníollacha imíonn! An ghrian Scairt an ghrian ar!*" Within seconds, the storm evaporated and the sun returned to its full vigor.

"Now what are we supposed to do?" John cried angrily. "We've just planted, and the crops must be watered!"

"Ask me nicely," Horace said smugly.

The foreman looked as though he'd prefer to

63

punch him in the nose. But the magistrates stared him down, unblinkingly, if disinterestedly, and he knew he had no choice. Through gritted teeth, he said, "Horace, will you please send some water for our crops?"

With exaggerated politeness, Horace said, "I'd be delighted to, John!" He turned back to the sky and said with an obnoxiously soothing voice, "*Bairille báisteach earraigh!*" And in place of the previous angry storm, a gentle spring rain began to sprinkle from nearly imperceptible clouds. Peter was not directly under them, but he felt the moisture of the mist carried towards him by the wind. It felt wonderful.

"Our work here is done," said the first magistrate, and he and his companion turned and cantered back through the now sad-looking fields.

John's eyes flashed in Peter's direction and he snapped, "What are you looking at?"

Peter held up his hands. "Nothing! Sorry, I just…"

"Hullo there," said Horace cheerfully, eyes wide as he stared at Peter's recognizable face, "I know who *you've* gotta be!"

"Sorry, didn't mean to meddle," Peter said quickly, tugging on Charger's reins to turn around and go the opposite way.

"Wait a minute!" cried Horace. "Aren't you the Child of the Prophecy?"

Peter dug his heels into Charger's flanks and galloped away as fast as he could.

After he'd merged back onto the main road, Peter presently heard another set of hooves behind

Charger's. He assumed it was someone late for work and didn't turn around until he heard a voice call out, "Pete! Wait up!"

He closed his eyes and sighed. *Cole.* At least it wasn't Lily. She probably would have lectured him.

"I said I'd be back after the first class!" he called, trying to hide the irritation from his voice.

"But where are you going?" Cole persisted. Peter slowed down enough that Cole could catch up with him. "Aren't you excited about school?"

Like a sharp stick in the eye, Peter thought. But aloud he said, "Sure. I just wanted to go check... um... something."

"What did you want to check?" Cole asked, falling into a canter beside Peter.

"Um..." Peter drew a blank. Then he sighed. "Fine. I just didn't want to go. Happy?"

Cole stared at him, puzzled. "Why would that make me happy?"

"You are so literal sometimes," Peter murmured, more to himself than to Cole.

"I don't get it, Pete. Why wouldn't you be excited about Paladin High? Especially since you're the hero everybody's been waiting for!"

Peter looked away. "I'm not a hero," he muttered.

"But Pete—"

"I'm not, okay?" He pulled Charger's reins up sharply to face Cole.

Cole shook his head, still trying to understand, his horse stamping in place as well. "Everyone thinks you are, though. And with the accident, and the Fata Morgana—"

"I don't *want* to be the Child of the Prophecy, all right?" Peter burst out. "Why can't everybody just leave me alone?" Peter immediately regretted the last statement when he saw Cole's stung expression, but he set his jaw and stared at his friend defiantly anyway.

"I'm sorry," Cole said meekly. "I'll just... go back then."

Peter sighed. "Cole, wait." Cole turned back around and looked at Peter expectantly, his previous remark already forgotten. One thing Peter loved about Cole: he never held grudges. Now Peter *had* to tell him the truth, though—and only right that second did he even know what the truth was. "Cole... what if..." He swallowed hard. It was difficult to say this out loud. "What if I fail?"

Cole blinked at him. "Fail at what?"

"Saving the world!" Peter spluttered, his intensity renewed. He shook his head vigorously. "Let Brock do it, he's perfect for the job. Or Lily! She wants it to be her anyway! But I..." Suddenly Peter felt short of breath and stopped talking. He didn't know how to finish the sentence anyway. He deflated and his shoulders slumped. He could feel Cole staring at him, looking almost terrified at his outburst. "What if I can't do it?" he whispered at last. "What if I let everybody down?"

Cole didn't move or speak for a long moment. Finally he said in a tiny voice, "Do you still want to go back to get Newton?"

Peter blinked at him, trying to understand how Cole got from the speech he had just made to this. Then he remembered their conversation that morning, when he had said he just wanted something familiar around him.

"I'll help you get him if you want," Cole offered again, his tone meek.

Peter started laughing incredulously. That was the last thing in the world he'd expected Cole to say, but he understood that his friend was trying to offer him comfort in the only way he knew how. When he recovered himself, he said simply, "You know we can't be seen, though."

Cole shrugged. "Maybe we can get Anthony to help us. He seems cool."

"He seems like the sort of kid who gets in a lot of trouble," Peter countered. Without discussing it, both he and Cole steered their horses around and headed back in the direction of Paladin High.

"Exactly!" Cole grinned at him.

Chapter 7

When Peter and Cole arrived back at Paladin High, there was no longer a queue at the hitching post, nor were there many available spaces. Peter finally found two near the water trough, and he and Cole tied up their horses.

"How are we supposed to know where to go?" asked Peter, looking around as they herded themselves through the doors.

"I saw where Anthony went before I came after you. Follow me."

"But you're not in sixth form," Peter pointed out. "Should we even be in the same classes?"

"Brock told everybody we're twins," said Cole, and then added ruefully, "Although if we're twins, then I definitely got the short end of *that* stick."

When Cole opened the door to the classroom, Peter realized that there was one thing worse than being a celebrity at a new school, and that was being a celebrity at a new school and arriving late.

All the other students were seated already, and the professor stopped mid-sentence when she saw the latecomers, her attention fixed on them.

Peter was momentarily distracted from his own discomfort when he caught sight of the professor. Her face lit up in a broad plastic smile as her eyes settled on Peter's face, and she minced her steps as she walked, arms delicately suspended from her side as if she were a bird. Her blond hair was almost wig-like, plastered perfectly and enormously into place. Her cheekbones were unnaturally prominent, her curves exaggerated, and her fingernails so long as to seemingly preclude all possible utility.

"Well! I wondered if I'd have the pleasure—!" she exclaimed in a voice like bubble gum, looking Peter up and down and making him feel even more uncomfortable, if that were possible. "Hello, Peter Stewart!" She clapped her hands together and gave a little titter. Peter felt his cheeks burn, and he immediately spotted a couple of empty seats next to Anthony in the back, as if he'd been saving them. Peter tried to thread his way towards Anthony, but the professor stopped him.

"Wait, wait, wait!" she declared, and then added theatrically, "Class, you may have noticed that we have a celebrity among us!" Everyone *had* noticed, staring at Peter curiously and whispering. Peter begged Lily for help with his eyes, but she suppressed a smile and shrugged at him.

The professor fluttered her absurdly long eyelashes at Peter, but gestured to Brock and Lily also. Cole still stood beside Peter, midway to the seats Anthony had saved. "I would like all of our new students to stand up and introduce yourselves to the class, and tell us one interesting fact about yourselves!"

"Do we have to?" Cole said before he could stop himself.

"Why wouldn't you want to?" the professor exclaimed brightly. "Here, I'll go first! My name is Candice 'Candy' Vane—but that's Professor Vane to you," she tittered again with a little wink, "and this is nutrition class. But I also teach drama— *which is my favorite subject.*" She added the last bit in a stage whisper, and tittered again. Peter caught sight of a few students at the other end of the class, who mimed a gagging motion.

"Shocker, that one," Cole muttered in Peter's ear. He stifled a laugh.

"Now, your turn!" cried Professor Vane, and turned an open palm towards Cole like she was leading a cheer.

"Er, okay…" Cole said uncomfortably. "I'm Cole Jefferson, and I'm from Norwich…"

"And something interesting about yourself!" Professor Vane prompted in a sing-song voice.

"Um, I'm…" he floundered for a moment. Finally he blurted, "And I'm best friends with Pete Stewart!"

"I hate you," Peter hissed to Cole, his face roughly the color of a tomato. Cole shrugged at him with wide, apologetic eyes.

Professor Vane skipped Peter, although her eyes glinted at him for a moment before she moved across the room to Brock, who stood up with a lazy, arrogant grin, like he'd been waiting for this.

"I'm Brock Jefferson, Cole's brother," he said, in an absurdly deep voice, "and I'm the earth specialist who saved everybody in the Fata Morgana."

Peter saw Lily's mouth drop open and she shook her head with slow incredulity as the females in the class burst into spontaneous applause.

"Oh, wonderful!" cried Professor Vane, clapping along with them. "How splendid! I'm sure when you get to Ancient Tongues, you'll dazzle everybody with a reenactment!"

Peter saw Brock flash the professor a devastating grin as he sat down.

Next Professor Vane moved to Lily, extending her game-show-host palm as she invited her to stand.

"I'm Lily Portman, and… er…" she also cast a look at Peter across the room. "And I once fought in a competition with a *bokken.* That's a bamboo sword."

"And? Did you win?" asked Professor Vane.

"Of course I won," said Lily haughtily, tossing her hair over her shoulder as she sat down.

"And now," Professor Vane cried with relish, clapping her hands together, "what I know you've all been waiting for—" She extended one set of claw-like nails in Peter's direction, as if displaying the grand prize. "Peter Stewart! Would you please tell us something interesting about yourself?"

The whole class turned to face Peter again. "Er," he said. "Hi, I'm Peter, and I like physics."

Professor Vane blinked at him. "Something *interesting*, dear."

Peter shrugged and said just a bit resentfully,

"I'm not very interesting, I guess."

She made a reeling motion with her hand and prompted, "Do you have any secret hobbies? Any hidden *desires?*"

If possible, Peter flushed even redder and scowled at her.

"Any pets?" she added with a note of irritation.

"I have a cat. Named Newton. Because I like physics," Peter added stubbornly. With that he pushed the rest of the way towards the seats next to Anthony and sat down, Cole at his heels. After a moment of confused hesitation, the class clapped politely. A redheaded girl sitting in front of Peter turned around and smiled shyly at him over her shoulder. He pretended not to notice.

When the applause died down, Professor Vane turned around and wrote on the blackboard. Peter wondered how she managed to hold a piece of chalk with those nails. He absently glanced at Anthony, who opened his notebook and began to doodle a cluster of grapes beneath the title "Nutrition."

Peter frowned back at the blackboard, and read out loud, "What's 'The Doctrine of Signatures'?"

Anthony waved his hand dismissively. "Don't worry about it. I can tell you everything you'll need to know about nutrition in ten words or less. Eat foods that look like what they're supposed to do." He ticked the words off on his fingers. "Hey, all right! That was exactly ten!"

Cole and Peter exchanged a look. "Huh?"

"So for instance, what do walnuts look like?" Anthony said.

They both stared at him, stumped.

"A brain, of course!" He mimed breaking a walnut in half, demonstrating both hemispheres. "So walnuts are brain food. Like that. If someone looks a bit too pale you give them more reds to build up blood. If someone looks a bit doughy," he poked his own belly, "they should probably lay off the bread. Et cetera."

"What if you're normal?" Cole asked.

"Then you eat all the colors, or else you'll end up out of balance." He shrugged. "The end. You can ignore the rest of the lecture now."

Peter took him at his word.

"Professor *Vane*. I get it," Cole murmured, studying the professor critically. "She looks sort of... wrong, somehow. Doesn't she?"

"She's had a bit of work done," Anthony whispered.

"What does that *mean*?" Cole whispered, perplexed. "I thought in Carlion people didn't get surgery like they do on the outside..."

"Yeah, the healers here are eukaryote specialists—oh, you would know," Anthony added offhandedly, remembering Cole's gift. "So they can interfere with people's bodies directly..."

"But what about the law of conservation of matter?" Peter said, frowning. "If they don't implant stuff, where does the extra... er, material come from?"

Anthony leaned across Peter so Cole could hear too and explained, "Healers can only take the cells that are already there and make 'em swell up."

Peter stared at Professor Vane incredulously, who was waiting for the class to settle in with a vacant smile on her face. "So her cheekbones…"

"Are like sponges, yeah." Anthony sniggered. "I've always wanted to ask her if I can poke them. I'm so curious…"

"Shh!" hissed the Asian girl who sat beside the redhead in front of Peter.

They stopped whispering for awhile, listening to Professor Vane lecture. She sounded so affected, it was almost mesmerizing.

"So," Cole whispered to Peter at last, looking at Anthony pointedly.

Peter caught the look, and gave a little cough. "Um, Anthony?" Anthony looked up at him with one eye, though he didn't stop doodling. "How are you at…" He tried to think how to phrase the request. At last he settled on, "…breaking and entering?"

Anthony let out an incredulous staccato laugh, setting his pen down. "I like you already!"

Chapter 8

Kane thrashed about in his mind, looking for any means of escape. Surely there had to be a way for him to get out of the Lake of Avalon without destroying Excalibur.

You are being short-sighted, said Sargon. *If you were to destroy the sword, don't you realize what that would mean?*

Yes, I would set you free!

True, technically, Sargon replied, as if it were a matter of complete indifference to him. *I would be free to reenter a human willing to offer me his body.* Even though he did not say the next words, Kane could feel them in pictures as clearly as if he had.

I know what you're thinking, Kane accused. *But you have to get my permission. I know how it works! I'll never give you permission, never!*

Well, that's up to you of course, Sargon said, his tone something like a shrug. *But I suspect your position on that subject is based largely on ignorance.*

You could offer me all the power you want, and I'll never give you my body! I'd rather die!

Oh yes, I know that. You are very brave, Kane, Sargon replied. Then he paused long enough for Kane's curiosity to overwhelm him.

At last it worked. *If you weren't offering power, then what did you mean?*

You seem to be laboring under a false impression that when I take over a person's body, that person disappears completely, and I take full ownership. That is not true.

Kane hesitated.

Both of us coexist in the same body at the same time, Sargon went on. *Souls have substance. They can't just vanish. They have to go* somewhere. *If the person's body isn't dead, there is nowhere for the soul to go. It stays with the body as long as the body remains alive.*

What are you saying? Kane demanded suspiciously.

The reason the kings of old were willing to yield their bodies to me was because they, too, could enjoy absolute power through me. But there was a flip side to that. If they wanted, they could have turned against me. They simply chose not to.

The seconds that passed after that statement were interminable. *You're telling me that when you're inside my body...*

You could kill me if you wanted to, said Sargon nonchalantly. *Of course, you'd be committing suicide in the process. Minor drawback.*

I don't believe you, Kane said flatly. *If I killed*

myself, you'd just take somebody else's body.

Not if you killed me with the newly destroyed fragments of Excalibur, said Sargon. *Doesn't the prophecy say that 'both shall fall, but the one who holds the blade that was broken shall emerge victorious?'*

Kane thought about this, suspicious. *If that were true, why would you tell me?*

Because I believe that once you join forces with me, once you let my mind merge with yours and see how unstoppable we can be together, you won't want *to kill yourself anymore.*

Kane didn't reply.

I can touch your mind right now, Kane. I can see your desires. You long to be the Child of the Prophecy, the One who finishes me off, but you want it not because you consider it to be right. You want the glory.

He paused long enough to let that sink in.

You see, Sargon went on when Kane did not respond, *there are two ways to look at this. The first is that, if you were to give me your body, you could kill me, and thus become the One, if that is what you really want. It would be your hand, and not Peter's, that would finally do me in. You would die too, of course, but you would die a martyr's death, as a hero.*

On the other hand, once you see what we can be together, once you see that you can achieve glory and honor by other means, and live to enjoy them, I believe you will choose to join me.

I am not evil! Kane shouted. *I will kill you without hesitation!*

Sargon replied with supreme nonchalance, *But you see, either way it makes more sense for you to offer me your body. If you really intend to kill me, I promise you will find that nearly impossible if I have taken over a host willing to cooperate with me. I will be unstoppable, and you will still be merely human. In that scenario, you would die trying to kill me, and I would live on. So you see, Kane, if you are determined to kill me, you would die either way. But if you offered me* your *body, you would take me with you.*

Kane had a funny sensation that his throat was constricting, except he knew he wasn't breathing oxygen in the first place.

Sargon's words made sense.

And yet, Sargon would never tell him this if he didn't really believe Kane would ultimately side with him. Sargon was inside his mind, and Kane could not seem to keep him out. He knew Kane as well as Kane knew himself. He could see into his soul, and apparently what he saw made him so confident that Kane would choose to join him rather than die a hero that Sargon offered him the means of his own demise on a silver platter.

What kind of a monster must I be?

Sargon replied in a bored tone, *Your existential conflicts are touching, but really I don't see how you can be surprised. Haven't most of the Watchers suspected as much all along?*

Isdemus didn't! Kane insisted. *Isdemus believes that there is good in me...*

Isdemus raised you as a son, Sargon pointed out. *He could not bear to think that, with all his wisdom, he could still raise a child who would grow up to be the polar opposite of everything he stood for.*

Kane tried with all his might to shut out Sargon's voice, but it was no use, and he knew that before he tried. *He knew me better than anyone else, and he still thought I was good! Isdemus believes in me!*

He thought you were good because his own ego would not permit him to think otherwise, said Sargon, with the blasé that implied he was speaking the obvious. *But consider Isdemus's actions, Kane. Whom has he spent nearly all of his time and energy trying to protect? Whom has he invested in the most? Whom has he believed to be the future salvation of mankind? Was it you?*

STOP! In his mind's eye, Kane saw himself crouched in a trembling ball, arms over his head, in a futile attempt to shield himself from words that felt like being bludgeoned with a bat.

Sargon left him like that for a brief few moments, and then said quietly, *You can see, can't you, why I am willing to stake my existence on your ultimate allegiance?*

Kane forced himself to uncoil from his protective mental posturing. The sword still floated in the sea of colors before him, gold and glinting in the kaleidoscope of motionless crystal, as if waiting for him. Sargon was silent too, and all Kane could hear was the thunder of blood in his ears.

He knew he was going to do it. He had known from the first moment. He was merely delaying the inevitable.

You've underestimated me, Kane said quietly. *You think I'm not brave enough to die if it means destroying you in the process?*

Oh, I know you're brave enough, said Sargon. *I simply don't think you have the will to do it.*

Quite a gamble you're willing to take.

I've dominated the known world by gambling with high stakes and winning.

You're not going to win this one.

I have your permission then? Sargon asked the question indifferently, but Kane could feel the edge of eager desperation just beneath the surface, and that edge gave him the last rush of courage that he needed.

You have it, he thought, gritting his teeth. And then, with a tremendous effort, he opened his mouth, not just in his mind, but in reality, against the inertia of the lake that was still as death. His tongue felt swollen and stiff, as if it hadn't been used in a hundred years. But still he managed to speak.

"Scrios claíomh!"

Chapter 9

Lily caught up with Peter, Cole, and Anthony after the nutrition lecture ended, forcing them to end their conversation about how to get back to Norwich. Cole noticed Lily's approach last and kept whispering, until Anthony shot him a pointed look. His eyes widened and he bit his lip. Fortunately, Lily did not notice.

"Oh, Peter?" called Professor Vane in a singsong voice, waggling her fingers at him when they were almost to the door.

A groan escaped Peter's lips before he turned around. "Yes?"

"Are you by any chance of the *dramatic* disposition?" she crooned. "I'm casting *Romeo and Juliet* this afternoon, and I think you would just make an *excellent* Romeo…"

"Sorry!" Peter cut her off forcefully, turning red. "No!"

Lily, who fell into step beside him, stifled a

laugh. "Oh, c'mon, Peter," she teased, "I think you'd be a natural…" Peter shot her a warning look, and she pursed her lips harder, barely concealing her mirth. "You never know, you might have the gift of… what would that be, entertainment? Is that a gift here?"

Undeterred, Professor Vane called out, "What about you, Brock? *Oooh*," she squealed like she could barely contain herself at the thought. Then she glanced at Lily conspiratorially and gushed, "Can't you just *see* him in the role of the romantic hero, Miss Portman?"

Brock glowered at Lily, daring her to reply.

"You know something," said Lily as seriously as she could muster, "I actually think I could!"

"Auditions are right after class in the auditorium!" clapped Professor Vane, bouncing up and down a little. "Brock, I will look for you, and *please,* bring your friends!" she added, looking pointedly at Peter.

A few of the other girls who lingered in the classroom exchanged secretive glances with each other with winks and giggles, a silent pact to vie for the chance to read Juliet opposite Brock. One of them was the pretty blond whom Brock had sat next to during class.

When they entered the hallway, Lily, Cole, and Anthony all burst out laughing, and Brock cast a seething look at Lily, who held up her hands innocently.

"I was being serious!" she protested before he could say anything. "I actually think you could pull it off! You love being the center of attention, don't you?"

The three girls exited the classroom behind them, mostly staring adoringly at Brock, but periodically glancing at Peter as well. One of them, the redhead who had been sitting in front of him, said breathlessly, "Do you think you'll come too, Peter?"

Peter blinked at her, and flushed. "Uh."

"Sure he will!" Lily said for him, elbowing him in the side.

The redhead blushed a little too, to Peter's great confusion, and grinned. "Me too! I… I hope I get to read with you!" Then all three of them dissolved in giggles and bounced off, the blond girl watching Brock over her shoulder as the others pulled her away.

Peter grew redder by the minute, and wheeled on Lily. "What did you say *that* for?"

She giggled wickedly as Anthony led the way to their next class. "Maybe I like watching you squirm."

"I can't go after class today, anyway," Peter said before he could stop himself, and his eyes widened when he realized what he'd said. *Why do I have no filter at all?*

"Why not? Where are you going?" Lily asked suspiciously.

"Here we are," Anthony interrupted, and opened the door. "This is Professor Crane's classroom." Peter ducked inside before Lily could ask him anything more, shooting Anthony a look of silent thanks.

Some of the students in Natural Sciences were

from Professor Vane's class and some were new. Professor Crane's face lit up when he saw the newcomers.

The professor was bald on top, allowing the gray hair above his ears on either side to grow in wild, wiry tufts that stuck straight out like wings attached to his head. His kindly eyes and mouth creased permanently into an enormous grin. This, combined with the high magnification of his glasses, gave the overall impression of a very cheerful insect.

"Peter Stewart!" he cried excitedly, clapping his hands together when he saw him. "We meet at last!"

A hush fell over the room at the sound of Peter's name. All of the other students stopped talking, and those who had not been in nutrition with him already turned to get a better look.

"I don't think he looks like King Arthur," said one girl critically, regarding him with a frown. She had mousy brown hair pulled back in a ponytail. "He's much too red in the face."

"That is because he is blushing, you idiot," said an Indian boy next to her in a hushed tone, although everyone heard him due to the silence in the room. "He wasn't that red a second ago."

Peter's face deepened to a frightening shade of maroon, and he looked at his feet.

Brock scowled, apparently annoyed that Peter was the center of attention instead of himself. He stepped forward, his scowl instantly morphing into a gallant grin as he addressed the whole class. "I guess you know who we are already too, but just in case, I'm Brock Jefferson." He paused, waiting for the eyes to focus on him. Once he had them, he basked for a moment, and then added like an afterthought, "This is my brother Cole, and this is Lily Portman."

Despite Brock's manner, Peter still felt a rush of gratitude towards him for taking the spotlight off Peter long enough that he could regain his normal color.

"Well, hello, Brock," said the professor, stepping forward to offer a meaty hand, which Brock shook. "I am Professor Crane, and this is Natural Sciences." Even as he pumped Brock's hand, though, he peered over his shoulder at Peter. "I am very curious to see how you perform in my class, Peter! Perhaps your father mentioned that we were childhood schoolmates?"

Peter started, surprised. "No, sir, he didn't!" He liked Professor Crane better already.

"Oh, yes! Always got in loads of trouble together, he and I! He tells me you're just the same—much too brilliant for your own good, eh?"

"Er," Peter muttered, not knowing what to say to that.

"It's true," Cole cut in. "Bit annoying, really."

Professor Crane laughed. "I imagine you will all find this course to be a bit different than you're used to in Norwich."

"It certainly *looks* different," said Lily to Peter, looking around. The classroom was almost bare, except for the blackboard and the desks. There were no textbooks, no plaster skeletons of the human body or anything else to indicate that it was a science classroom except for a poster of the earth that read, "Gravity: If the world didn't suck we'd all fly into space." In front of the classroom, a poster stood on an easel next to Professor Crane, depicting a bazaar with hanging carpets that looked like they might be able to fly. It seemed a very odd choice.

"Most days we go on field trips," Professor Crane went on. "Today we are going no further than the Enchanted Forest. Right then! I think everyone is here. Line up, line up," he said, and the students obeyed, lining up in front of the mercantile picture. Most of them still chatted with each other in whispers and cast furtive glances at Peter and Brock, and to a lesser extent, Cole and Lily.

"The picture must be a porthole," Brock surmised to no one in particular.

"'Course it's a porthole," said Anthony matter-of-factly. "Otherwise we'd never get there and back before our next class."

"I never understood why they don't just use photos of the place where they're going," Lily whispered. "It's awfully confusing."

Anthony replied, "Sometimes they do, but most often people just use whatever they happen to have lying around when they go to see the space specialist."

"So what he just happened to have lying around was a poster of an Indian mercantile?" Lily whispered back rhetorically.

"Trust me, that's far from the most random thing about Professor Crane," said Anthony with a dimpled grin.

"In you go! I'll follow behind; don't wander too far!" said the professor, and the first brunette girl disappeared into the picture. The next followed after her, a short and slightly chubby-looking boy with a Scottish accent.

Peter and Cole looked at each other and shrugged. "Shall we?" said Cole.

"Here goes nothing," Peter murmured back. He stepped forward until he felt himself cross the threshold of the event horizon, and suddenly felt the familiar, disorienting sensation of a hook locking on to his center of gravity somewhere in the middle of his intestines, compelling him forward.

The next thing he knew, he found himself standing beneath the impossibly thin tree trunks of the forest, with the expansive canopy bursting from their stalks overhead. The sunlight filtering through made the forest look cheerful and radiant, and cast everything in shades of green. A cluster of students stood a few paces away, their chatter blending in with the song of the birds in the trees.

Peter turned around to see where he had come from, and all he saw was more forest. Then, suddenly, Cole appeared out of thin air.

Lily appeared next, and then Brock and Anthony, followed by a steady stream of other students. Last of all came Professor Crane, who stood rigidly in place. "Somebody give me a really good landmark!" he cried. Then he said, "Oh, I know," and he took off his vest, a strange brocaded thing, and dropped it where he stood. "There we are. When we finish today, we have only to find my vest to find the entrance to the porthole."

"Are you saying unless you leave some sort of marker, you wouldn't know where the porthole was?" Lily asked, a bit apprehensively.

"Well, the nimbi of the Enchanted Forest have a tendency to rearrange themselves, so we can't very well use them as landmarks, now, can we? There now!" He took a few steps forward, and the rest of the students circled around him. "Today's lesson is going to be on finches." A little cheer and excited chatter went up from the students, and Professor Crane smiled, but held up his hand so he could continue. "I've promised Professor Lambert that I would have you all back in time for Ancient Tongues, so I want you to come back here by half past, so we can get you reoriented to your human selves. Got it?"

"Our human selves?" Brock repeated incredulously.

"But sir," said a petite Asian girl anxiously, "how will we know it's half past if we're finches? We won't have watches, of course."

There was a snicker behind her from a tall, black-haired boy. "But sir, but sir!" he mocked in a tone low enough that the professor could not hear, but Peter could. He scowled at him. The boy returned an easy, arrogant grin.

"You'll be able to tell by the position of the sun, Ms. Kwan. Don't worry about it now; I know you can't see it down here in the forest, and you can't interpret its position as a human, even if you could. But I promise that once you're a bird and can rise above the canopy, you'll know exactly how to read the sun by instinct."

"*Psst!*" said Cole to Peter excitedly, "This is even better than merging minds with fish!"

Peter felt apprehensive, but said nothing.

Professor Crane stuck two fingers in his mouth and whistled. Suddenly the trees, which were already alive with sound moments before, swelled to epic proportions, as if they were standing in the middle of a menagerie. Peter looked up; the branches looked like they were on verge of giving way with the weight of the finches the professor had summoned.

Professor Crane smiled broadly again, and Peter thought the grin was directed at him, to gauge his reaction. "Now, everyone needs to come forward and stand within my field of sight," he said.

The students obeyed, and suddenly Peter noticed that Lily was beside him. Professor Crane lifted his arms in the air as if to encompass them all with his words. In a loud voice, he cried dramatically, "Nonfat milk! Butternut squash! Six slices of smoked TURKEY!"

The students stared at him blankly, and Anthony leaned over to Peter and whispered, "Told you he was weird."

Professor Crane chuckled at his own joke. "Just kidding, for real this time. Ready? Here we go! *Aigne chumasadh leis an glasán*!"

Peter had a sensation much like what he experienced going through the porthole, and yet not at all the same. His field of view changed, as if his eyes had moved laterally to the sides of his head— which, as it turned out, they had. The trees suddenly seemed taller and the forest expanded in either direction. Somehow his vision became clearer, and the colors seemed brighter. He tried to wiggle his fingers and toes and lifted a few centimeters off the branch below him before gliding back down. That was when he realized that he was in a tree instead of on the forest floor.

"Whoa! Look down!" came a chirp beside him, which Peter instantly recognized as Cole's. He glanced up in the direction from which the voice had come, and saw that Cole was covered in brilliant sunshine-yellow feathers.

When he recovered from that shock, he did look down, and saw the bodies of their entire class lying below, motionless. It looked like they had all simultaneously collapsed.

"This has got to be the weirdest feeling ever..." Peter murmured. He turned to look at the branch on the other side of him and recognized Lily. She was covered in rose-brown colored feathers. Brock, beside her, had a vibrant blue head and a full breast of downy white and black feathers.

Peter looked down at his own feathers in muted colors of brown, gray, and black. "Figures," he muttered to himself. Then he turned to Cole. "Hey," he said, "How is it that we still know English?"

"We're not speaking English," said Cole, "Listen!"

Peter realized he was right: his mind interpreted the words in English, but they spoke something else entirely. "What are we speaking then?"

Cole ruffled his vibrant yellow wings, enthralled. "Finch language, I guess?"

"How come we can understand it?" Lily interjected, craning her neck around Brock to see them.

"We're inside the finches' heads. I guess we

know whatever they know!" laughed Cole, his laughter sounding like an eruption of song. Enamored of the sound of his own voice, he went on laughing until the others joined in like a chorus.

"Right then!" cried Professor Crane musically. He now had bright red feathers and a long hooked beak, and he fluttered up to a higher branch to make it easier for all the students to see and hear him at once. "The first thing to do is to learn how to fly. Technically the finches you inhabit already know how to fly, of course, but in the past, students have overridden that knowledge due to their fears of jumping unsupported off of a perfectly good branch." There were a few titters of nervous laughter that sounded like a spring day. Professor Crane went on, "Some of you were with me last year when we became white-tailed eagles, after which I received a number of complaints from the eagles who sustained injuries from students who refused to obey the eagles' muscle memory, and panicked mid-flight. In hopes that we may avert similar accidents and leave the finches in the same state in which we found them, I will give you a little crash course." He paused, and chuckled, "No pun intended!

"Now, the thing to do is to spread your wings and give a little hop first before you start to flap. Once you flap a few times you'll catch a bit of wind. Then you tilt your center of gravity forward so that you can push the air behind you, like paddling an oar in the water. Got it?"

There was a little chatter of chirps in response, which sounded like a chorus of "Yes!" Then the students began to hop into the air. A few were brave enough to flutter a couple times before lighting safely back on the branch below them. Anthony, who was now a plump brown finch with a prim little beak that made him look like he was wrinkling his nose, managed to soar for a few seconds before the others, when one of his classmates tackled him accidentally and they both plummeted to the forest floor. Several others managed to catch a bit of wind, and began to awkwardly beat their wings towards the canopy above. The obnoxious black-haired boy was appropriately arrayed with a scarlet panache, and he lazily caught the wind and began to soar, making it look effortless.

Peter gritted his teeth and imitated him. He caught the breeze, willing himself not to look down. To his great surprise, once he managed to lift off, maintaining it was not difficult at all.

"Stop trying so hard!" he called to the others, who desperately attempted to avoid plummeting to the forest floor. "You don't need to work that many muscles. Just let the air carry you!" After a moment he realized that he didn't even have to flap constantly: he could glide on the lift from the previous flap and conserve more energy. "It's like swimming, but with less friction!" he called.

"Peter, look at me, look at me!" cried Cole, and he tilted his wings sideways carelessly. He narrowly avoided colliding with a black finch with a tuft of feathers protruding from its forehead.

Peter laughed again, thrilling at the sound.

"Higher then, higher then!" called Professor Crane. "I need to teach you all how to land!" Once he was within reach of a branch, Professor Crane tilted backwards and thrust his tiny little claw-like feet out in front of him, and then lighted on the branch from above. Then he called out instructions to the class of what he had just done. "Tilt your center of gravity behind you, then beat the air to hold you aloft before you reach for the branch below!" Several of the others careened into their branches, swinging complete circles around them with their feet hanging on precariously, laughing all the while. A rose-colored finch like Lily's crashed into uptight little Ms. Kwan, and several of her yellow feathers rained down upon the forest floor.

Somehow, Peter intuitively understood that all he had to do was change the angle of his wings in order to control his direction and velocity, and he lighted upon his branch gracefully. He watched Cole try and miss the branch, then swoop back around for several more attempts.

"It's all about the geometric angles of force," Peter called out to Cole. "Think of the position your body would need to be in to create drag against the wind, and then use that to help you slow down!"

"Er," Cole called back, his face screwed up in intense concentration. "Sure. Right!"

"I thought I'd heard you were a bit of a science geek," drawled the bird with the scarlet panache as he landed easily on the branch beside Peter.

Peter thought about responding, but then decided it wasn't worth the effort.

Without preamble, the scarlet finch said baldly, "So is it true? Are you the Child of the Prophecy?"

"Sorry. Who are you?" said Peter shortly.

"Ashton. Kip Ashton," drawled the scarlet finch. "My father is the head magistrate in Carlion," he added unnecessarily.

"How nice for you," Peter said coldly, his opinion of the scarlet finch solidified.

"You didn't answer my question," Kip pointed out.

"That's because I don't know the answer."

Kip snorted, if a finch could snort, and said, "I knew it. Every generation somebody shows up who looks a little like the painting and the whole city freaks out. They always turn out to be nobodies in the end, though."

Peter bristled, envisioning every one of those smug little scarlet feathers spontaneously molting off of Kip's body, leaving him naked as a plucked chicken.

"Fantastic!" called Professor Crane to the rest of the class. "Now, I will stay here," he said, and hopped up to the highest branch of the tree directly above his ugly brocaded vest, still marking the open porthole below. "Go! Explore! Be free!"

Peter gladly took the opportunity to end the unpleasant conversation with Kip, but just as he hopped off the branch, he risked a look down and felt a distinct sense of vertigo. A variegated pattern of different colors carpeted the forest floor. The ferns that had glowed at twilight were brightly colored by day, though muted slightly with the filtered light of the green canopy.

"Be back here no later than half past!" Professor Crane reminded them.

Ms. Kwan looked anxiously up at the sun, and a

look of relief flitted across her narrow face that they could, in fact, read the position of the sun as birds.

"Come on!" Lily called determinedly to Cole, Brock, and Anthony, and she clumsily leapt off her branch, furiously beating her wings toward where Peter waited, hovering in the air. There was a look of intense effort on Lily's little bird face as she tried to clear the top of the canopy.

Cole hesitated to relinquish his perch, but at last he leapt upward. The white-breasted finch beside him took off at exactly the same moment and tackled him accidentally. He plummeted to the forest floor, but just managed to grab onto a branch with his talons about halfway down. When he'd righted himself, Cole called out to the others, "Wait for me, wait for me! I can do this!" He began to beat his wings before he even let go of the branch, working up his confidence.

"Your body already knows how to fly. The key is to just stop trying so hard," Peter called back helpfully.

"Yes, that is the key to most everything in life!" cried Professor Crane, still close enough to overhear, and he nodded at Cole encouragingly as he said it. "Let go, let go, let go!"

Cole gulped and let go.

"That's it, you've got it!" whooped Peter, and flew back towards him, calling, "Tilt forward a bit!"

When Cole did this, he caught the breeze, and his wings stroked the air like paddles. "I'm doing it! I'm doing it!" he cried, exhilarated.

Peter waited while Cole, Brock, and Lily tried to catch up. Lily concentrated on staying aloft, and she looked like she was treading water.

"Didn't you hear what Professor Crane said?" asked Anthony, sidling up to Lily. "Stop trying so hard."

"Easy for you to say," Lily muttered.

"Tilt forward, it'll make it easier," Peter advised Lily as she huffed and puffed. She spared a glance in his direction, and looked rather skeptical but obeyed. When she picked up speed, she called breathlessly, "Thanks!"

When everybody caught up, Peter took the lead. He nearly forgot all about the others, distracted by the beauty of the Enchanted Forest below. It looked like a freshly mown lawn, with its impossibly thin and completely green stalks of trees. Towards the periphery he could see where the bizarre vegetation blended into more recognizable beeches and larches and firs.

"Wow! Wow! I feel like I'm looking at one of those relief maps that you can trace your finger over, with all the ridges on the mountains… except I'm in it!" cried Cole.

"Hold on," said Peter, peering below him, "Do you see that?"

"What?" Cole chirped.

"The waterfall," Peter said. "Where is it even coming from? It doesn't look like it's connected to a body of water. It just sprang up out of nowhere."

Anthony, who joined him on his other side, answered, "Sure, that's where Arthur pulled Excalibur out of the stone."

"What?" Peter and Cole both exclaimed together, and Peter said, "How can they know that?"

"Well, they don't for sure, but since according to the legends, he found it at the top of a waterfall in the Enchanted Forest, and since this is the only waterfall *in* the Enchanted Forest, everybody just assumes… hey, wait for me!"

Peter began to descend with concentric circles. Cole followed too closely behind and nearly collided with him twice, while Anthony dove straight after them to catch up.

"Oh, seriously?" Lily called behind them in exasperation. She had only just managed to catch up. She tried to imitate Peter, but alternately floundered like she was drowning and dropped like a stone.

Peter perched on the boulder at the very top of the waterfall, beneath which a cascade of water flowed over the smooth stones and into the cool spring below, trickling off through the forest beyond with a cheerful gurgle.

"This is so surreal," said Peter to no one in particular. Then he turned to Cole and said, "I used to dream about this place at night when I was little, after my dad told me the stories of the sword in the stone. In my dreams, it looked exactly like this."

"Probably because your dad had been here," said Cole.

"I suppose," Peter agreed.

Anthony alighted beside them. "So back to tonight," he hissed, glancing up at Lily and Brock, who were still much too far off to overhear. "I don't see why you two have to come at all. I can get Newton and be back before you know it."

Peter shook his head. "Newton will never come

near someone he doesn't know. He'll hide and you won't even see him. I have to come with you." He didn't feel like telling Anthony his real reason… but Newton really was skittish around strangers. That much was true.

"Have it your way then," Anthony shrugged. "Too bad I'm not a space specialist; I could just warp directly to your house. We'll have to use a porthole. I'll meet you both after school at the hitching post, and we'll ride into Carlion to the space specialist's shop. There's a porthole there that goes to the Grandfather Tree."

Cole chimed in, "We'll have to be there at about five till the top of the hour, to catch the 5:00 bus. Are you sure you can follow the map Pete drew to find his house from the bus stop?"

"And the car keys?" Peter added, a little apprehensively. "They're hanging on the key ring just inside our front door. Are you sure you can break into the house to get them… and drive the car? You're sure you know how?"

Anthony groaned. "You two sound like nervous old ladies! I'm telling you I can do this. Before you know it I'll be driving up to the Grandfather Tree to pick you up." He ruffled his feathers nonchalantly. "And don't worry about the bus fare either—I know a guy in town."

Peter laughed. "You 'know a guy'?"

"Yeah, he goes into Norwich all the time; he'll have a couple of pound coins lying around that he'll give me. Stop worrying!"

Seeing Brock and Lily flying toward them, Peter mused, "How are we going to ditch Lily and Brock?

Lily would try to stop us, and I still don't trust Brock... ah, sorry, Cole."

Cole shrugged. "That's okay, I don't trust him either, honestly. Let's push them to go to the drama tryouts. Brock is just enough of a ham to fall for it, and I think Lily already wants to go check it out anyway."

Brock landed finally, but he was still far enough away that he couldn't hear their conversation over the splash of the waterfall. Lily almost landed several times, but every time she dropped a significant amount of altitude, she started flapping frantically to slow down and ended up regaining half of what she'd lost.

Anthony went on, "How long does it take to get from the Grandfather Tree to the bus stop near your house, Peter? And how long to walk from the stop to your place?"

"About fifteen minutes total," said Peter.

"Okay," said Anthony, as Lily nearly collapsed at the bottom of the waterfall, exhausted. Brock meanwhile hopped from boulder to boulder, climbing towards the other three at the top. "So I figure if all goes smoothly, it'll be around forty minutes total for me to get there and back with your car, depending on when the bus gets there."

"What... are you... talking about?" Lily huffed behind them, and all three boys stopped, startled. They hadn't seen her climb up. "What car?"

"We were just... um..." said Peter, racking his brain.

Anthony interjected without missing a beat, "There's a vintage car park in Carlion. Things like the Model T—old junkers that nobody misses in the outside world. Nobody drives here of course, it's more just a novelty thing. I was gonna go show it to them."

Peter and Cole exchanged a look, impressed.

"Oh," said Lily, uninterested. She turned to Peter and said, "You're into cars?"

"Oh, yeah!" Peter exclaimed, a little too enthusiastically.

"That's why we can't go to the audition," Cole added.

"But you should go!" said Peter. Lily looked at him suspiciously, and he blurted, "Because somebody should be there to see Brock read Romeo!"

At that moment Brock drew level with them after climbing the last stone of the waterfall. "I never said I was going to go," he muttered.

"But you are," Cole predicted.

"How come?"

"Because that blond girl who wants to read with you is really pretty," said Cole matter-of-factly. "That's usually motivation enough for you."

"Ashley," Anthony agreed, saying her name like he was savoring it.

Brock thought about this, and didn't disagree.

"Shouldn't we head back?" Anthony interjected. "Class is probably almost over. Sun says it's almost half past."

"Yeah! We should!" Cole exclaimed, hopping into the air beside Peter.

"Oh, for crying out loud," said Lily, hoisting herself back into the air.

Peter quickly took the lead again, exultant that he had finally found a physical activity he was good at. He was tempted to try a somersault, but thought better of it.

As soon as he breached the canopy, Peter saw a red speck in the distance perched like a signpost. He flew towards it, outstripping the others, distracted by the lacy green canopy and the cloudy sky.

When he got closer, he heard Professor Crane calling, "Come on, come on, it's time to go back!" Several other finches disappeared beneath the canopy just below where Professor Crane sat, and Peter followed them. Beneath the canopy he saw the collection of bodies, and he slowed his descent beside his own body, feeling peculiar as he stared at his unconscious form.

"Maybe this is what it's like to die," said Cole as he lighted beside his own body.

"That's cheerful," said Peter dryly.

Lily was the last student to rejoin the class, hesitantly hopping from branch to branch until she finally lighted beside her body.

"Trying to fly as little as possible?" Peter observed, smirking at her.

"Shut up, Peter."

Then Professor Crane said, *"Aigne ar ais don duine!"* Immediately his little red finch flew away just as the wild-haired professor sat up again, blinking and disoriented-looking. The professor peered down at the cluster of birds, and said something that sounded to Peter like gobbledy-gook, but the gesture of his hands suggested that he'd probably said, "Gather round."

"I guess we don't understand English like this, after all," said Lily.

"Course we don't," said Peter, trying to fight the instinctive urge to fly away to safety at the sight of a human towering down from above.

Suddenly Professor Crane swept his arms wide, and bellowed words that were foreign to Peter's finch ears. All at once Peter felt his flesh swell past the point of endurance. The forest shrank, the colors muted, and his peripheral vision diminished as his eyes snapped together towards the front of his face. He felt not quite dizzy, but disoriented, and he sat up, looking down at the brown and gray bird beside him. They made eye contact for one long, very strange moment, and then it flew off.

He looked around at the others. Lily stood up too fast, and clutched her head to try and stop the spinning.

"Through the porthole, come now! Haven't got all day!" called Professor Crane. One student after another stumbled towards the ugly brocade vest and disappeared.

"Can we merge with the fish in the moat next time?" asked Cole eagerly as he walked towards the porthole.

"We'll see, we'll see," said Professor Crane cheerfully. "But tomorrow we're merging with red blood cells!"

Cole's mouth fell open. "No. *Way!*" Then he disappeared.

Peter was right behind him. He felt the familiar sensation of a hook somewhere around his midsection, drawing him irresistibly forward, and then found himself back in the classroom. Last of all, Professor Crane leapt out of the photograph of the bazaar.

Cole, Lily, and Anthony waited for him, but Brock and the other students had already left.

"Anthony can show you to your next classroom for Ancient Tongues, right?" said Professor Crane, and Anthony nodded as he headed for the door. Professor Crane pulled Peter aside and whispered, "I'm glad that you are finding friends here, Peter, but be careful around Anthony. He can be a bit of a troublemaker." Then he added in a loud voice with a conspiratorial wink, "Tell your old man hullo from me, Peter! And *do* try not to blow up our school, won't you?"

Chapter 10

Ancient Tongues was a bit of a letdown after Natural Sciences, so Peter zoned out for the most part—they did worksheets of terms from the Arthurian legends with badly drawn cartoons, and the assignment was to fill in the word in the Ancient Tongue and then sound it out with their partners. His partner was Nilesh, and although he was preoccupied with the excursion to get Newton after class, Peter was surprised that Nilesh was as cool as Anthony. Also, to Peter's relief, after the initial two classes, most of the students had already seen him and had mostly lost interest in staring at him. Nilesh did pump him for details about the Fata Morgana in between sounding out words from the legends, but after Peter had told him about the explosion following the annihilation of his dad's photons with the dark matter of the castle, Nilesh changed the subject to the jousting competition a few weeks hence.

Considering Peter had never made a single friend at King's Secondary School besides Cole and his geometry teacher, Mr. Richards, Paladin High was thus far shaping up to be far better than he'd originally feared.

After Ancient Tongues came lunch. Peter and the others followed Anthony to the cafeteria, which Peter thought was more like the Great Hall than like the cafeteria at King's Secondary School. There were long tables with benches instead of chairs, and all the food was spread out on family-style platters. Anthony grabbed a plate, walked by and helped himself to rotisserie chicken, filling the other half of his plate with fries.

"What would Professor Vane say?" Cole teased him, eyeing Anthony's plate as he instead spooned plump strawberries and blackberries onto his own plate beside the chicken.

Anthony shrugged. "She'd say I'm gonna end up 'out of balance' because everything I'm eating is white and brown. Whatever." He poked his chubby belly and said with a dimpled grin, "Clearly it's working for me."

Peter looked up as he piled his plate high to see Brock surrounded by a cluster of students, one of whom was the pretty blonde named Ashley. He was talking animatedly, and the whole group oriented themselves around him.

"Well that didn't take long," Peter observed to Lily, gesturing towards Brock with his head.

She smirked. "Did you expect it to?"

The students and Brock went outside with their lunches, and when Peter finished loading up his plate, he followed them, mostly out of curiosity.

Outside in the artificially controlled sunshine (Horace's doing, he now knew), a cluster of students sat on the grass in a tight little circle around Brock, like primary school students around a teacher at story time. When Peter got closer, he heard Ashley ask, "Is it true that people in the outside are *all* controlled by one of the penumbra?"

"It's true," Brock said with an authoritative air.

"They're not all *controlled*, at least not entirely," Lily muttered, who walked up beside Peter. "They just all have one."

"What do they look like?" asked another student eagerly.

"Like everything you can imagine!" said Brock. "There are hags and ogres, giants and dragons and—"

"Trolls?" piped another student, shivering with delicious disgust.

"Like you wouldn't believe!" said Brock. "Some of them have fangs and claws, dripping with venom—" he mimed them with his own hands, leaning forward like a creature from a nightmare, "and every one of them has a voice perfectly suited to the person it's attached to, and they tell them things and the person does them, just like he's a puppet—"

"Did *you* ever have one?" asked a blond girl with pigtails.

Brock faltered, and Lily smirked. "Yes, he did," she interrupted, and everyone turned to look at her and Peter.

"What did his look like?" demanded Nilesh. "I

heard everybody's creature takes the form of what they find most appealing!"

Brock suddenly looked both embarrassed and trapped, and Lily said dramatically, enjoying his discomfort, "His was a stunningly beautiful siren with hair like the flame of a candle."

"Hair like a flame... does that mean you like redheads or blondes?" asked the blond with pigtails, and giggled.

Lily told the blond girl firmly, "She was redheaded." Ashley, too, looked crestfallen.

Peter sat down next to Cole and Anthony to eat as a Scottish boy added to Lily, "And what was yours?"

"She didn't have one," said Peter, and everybody turned to look at him. "Nor did I," he added quickly, to avert the question, "but I couldn't see them before we came here. Lily could, though. She's been a Seer her whole life."

"Not my *whole* life," Lily corrected quietly. The crowd turned from Peter back to Lily, wide-eyed. Brock scowled at her, crossing his arms over his chest impatiently.

"You're an *Imbas Forosnai* then!" said Heather Kwan admiringly.

Lily blinked at her. "A what?"

"It's a real Seer," Heather explained, "somebody who can see the penumbra before anybody told you they were there."

"That must've been so exciting!" said Ashley. "It's like an adventure, every day, all the time!"

"Yeah, tell us, what's it like to be a Seer out there?" asked Nilesh.

"Well," said Brock, before Lily could respond. All the students turned away from Lily and back around to face him. He added grudgingly, "It *is* true that most of my life I wasn't a Seer, but I left Carlion a little before the others here, and then the penumbra came and attacked me."

There was a collective gasp. "No!" said the Scottish boy.

"Yes!" said Brock with relish, leaning forward. "I fought them off, of course, but there were too many in the end, and that's how I ended up at the Fata Morgana…"

Cole put a hand over his mouth to stifle his laughter. Peter also had to purse his lips together to keep from laughing out loud, and he glanced over at Lily, expecting her to share their amusement. Her arms were folded over her chest and she glared alternately at Brock and at the little cluster of students around him, hanging on his every word. When Brock finished telling a version of the story of the Fata Morgana in which he was the hero, the crowd burst into spontaneous applause—everyone, that was, except for Lily, Cole, and Peter. Even Anthony clapped and whistled.

"Wow!" cried the Scottish boy, "I'd give anything to have an adventure like that!"

"It must've been that way for you all the time!" said Anthony appreciatively to Lily, and the crowd turned back to face her again. "What was it like, being an Imbas Forosnai?"

"Yeah, and how'd you become one, if you weren't born that way?" added another girl eagerly.

"Well, I'll tell you. My parents were shot and

killed right in front of me when I was six," Lily snapped.

There was dead silence, and the crowd stared at her with mingled shock and horror. Lily pushed herself angrily to her feet and stalked off, tears of fury welling up in her eyes.

Peter stared after her for a long moment, until Cole jostled his shoulder.

"Are you going after her or not?" he hissed. "Because somebody should!"

"Um," said Peter, watching her retreating figure. He thought about protesting that she was scary when she got upset, but he realized Cole was right, he should at least try. "Fine. Wish me luck," he muttered, and pushed himself to his feet, trotting after her.

***

Lily sat on an uncomfortably pointy boulder on the otherwise grassy banks of the Winding Waterway. She'd taken off the sandals that went with her brown frock and dangled her big toes in the cheerfully gurgling, frigid water, wiping tears off her cheeks and sniffling.

She wasn't sure why she said it—only that she couldn't let them go on thinking that life on the outside was pure glamour. In Carlion, everybody had a family, and a home, and friends who didn't think they were crazy, and the opportunity to refine their gifts and no influence from the penumbra whatsoever... and yet, they romanticized *her* life.

They're the most ungrateful, spoiled, shallow

little... She racked her brain for a noun harsh enough to describe them and came up dry, so she trailed off, staring miserably into the water. Every few seconds she imagined that she heard footsteps, but it was just the splashing of the water against the rocks.

In her mind's eye, she saw Peter approach behind her cautiously. She would turn away for the first few minutes of course, insisting that she wanted to be alone; but he would persist, reaching a hand to one of her her shoulders and then snaking his arm around both of them.

When she finally did hear footsteps, she stopped breathing for a second to make sure they were real. But they grew louder. She set her jaw, determined not to turn around. She was going to make him work for it.

"Hey," said Peter, his voice uncertain. "You okay?"

Lily sniffed and shook her head no, hiding her face.

"Okay," said Peter, shuffling his feet behind her. They were silent for a long minute. Then he said, "You want me to go away?"

Lily hesitated. She wanted to say yes, but she had the impression that he would take her at her word if she did. So instead she said, trying to sound as indifferent as possible, "You can stay if you want."

"Okay," Peter said again, and sat down on the boulder next to hers. In another moment he said, looking at his makeshift chair, "This is surprisingly uncomfortable."

"It's a cold, pointy rock, Peter."

He thought for a minute and said, "Okay, so… not so surprising, then."

After another long pause, Lily said, "I just didn't want them to think my life was so easy in the outside world. You know, it's not the most glamorous thing, being an orphan with no friends."

"I never said it was."

Lily fell silent for a long moment, waiting for him to try to comfort her or ask her more questions. When he didn't, she heaved an exasperated sigh.

"What?" said Peter, seeing her expression.

"*Nothing.*"

"Are you mad at me now, too?" Peter protested. "What did I do?"

"Oh, Peter!" she huffed, pushing herself to her feet, tears springing into her eyes again. She hurried away before he could see them.

Peter called after her in frustration, "Hey! Whatever happened to 'cutting through the crap'?" When she didn't reply, he shouted again, "You're the mind reader, not me, remember?"

***

Peter avoided Lily's eyes during English Literature, which wasn't hard to do because she sat on the other side of the room from him, arms crossed. Peter sat next to Anthony and Cole again, and discovered that in Carlion, literature was almost always written in the style of the documents they found in the Secret Library—the Ancient Tongue enabled readers to merge with the text, living the story through the eyes of one of the characters.

"It is a huge responsibility!" Professor MacGregor said sharply, speaking over the whispered laughter. Her gray hair was pulled back into a severe bun, and the lines around her mouth resembled a prune. "Stories become like memories, as if the story happened to you. This means that stories have the power to shape you, almost the way real events do."

Peter was mildly interested only until he discovered that Professor MacGregor intended to lecture for the entire class period, and that they wouldn't be reading any stories in the Ancient Tongue that day. He tuned out then, glancing at Lily only when he knew she wasn't looking at him. Upon occasion they both looked at each other at the same time, and then turned away just as quickly.

"Didn't go so well, huh?" Cole whispered sympathetically.

Peter shook his head. "Girls," he whispered back, as if that was explanation enough.

Chapter 11

The Watchers in Ibn Alaam left the main thoroughfare and rode their camels through the arid sand in virtual silence. Presently, in the distance a structure the same color as the sand rose almost organically from the earth. Instead of the angular, manmade spires and buttresses of an ordinary castle, the structure was rounded, like the haunches of a crouching lion poised to spring. It glistened in the sun such that it looked like a mirage, particularly because it was surrounded by palm trees and preceded by a pond. At the very top, a flag fluttered in the breeze whose crest they could not make out.

"What is *that*?" asked Bruce, squinting at it.

"It looks like a Picasso painting in three dimensions," Dan observed, tilting his head sideways like he was trying to get the measure of it.

Masika cast them a sidelong smile. "That is the Watcher castle. I realize we use the term 'castle' rather loosely, more by convention than by actual definition."

The camels moved swiftly as the strange structure rose before them. When they arrived, Masika led them to a permanent-looking tent and moved the flap aside with one hand, guiding her camel inside. There she dismounted and left the camel to drink from the trough.

"We can leave them here," she said to the group, but she focused on Dan as she said it. When Dan dismounted and led his camel to the same trough, Masika stood close enough that her hand brushed against his before she turned and walked away. "Come, this way," she smiled at him, leading the way inside the castle through a tunnel.

Jael saw her, and frowned.

A small door barred the entrance at one of the lion's stylized paws, and Masika ducked as she entered. "Watch your heads," she added over her shoulder.

"Are we headed to the library?" asked Bruce, once they entered the cave-like tunnel.

"No, the Great Hall," came Masika's voice, muted in the still, musty air. "I presume you are all hungry, and Bomani would like to meet you. Bomani is our leader."

The room in which they emerged after about five minutes or so was very light and open, and hot. A skylight stretched like a canopy over the top of it, which was lovely, but did almost nothing for insulation. In the middle of the room was a very large round table, the center of which was hollow. Bruce stooped down to investigate, and exclaimed,

"Look, there's a trap door!"

"The kitchen is one floor below this," said Masika. "If you will pardon me, I will go and ask them to send up some sandwiches, and ring for Bomani to join us."

A few moments later, a polite cough sounded from the tunnel-like entrance, and Bruce, Sully, Dan, and Jael looked up to see a bald and dark-skinned man in his late fifties, with thick lips that parted easily into a friendly grin.

"Bomani, I presume?" said Sully, walking forward and offering his hand. The man took it heartily.

"And you must be Isdemus's right-hand men that he's told me so much about. And woman," Bomani added, nodding graciously in Jael's direction. "I understand you are here to inquire of our library regarding the last known location of the Philosopher's Stone?" His words were polite, but his eyebrows lifted along with the inflection of his voice. It was clear that he thought this was a very curious request.

"Did Isdemus tell you any more than that?" asked Sully.

"He was very cryptic, although I had the impression that he felt the story would benefit from the telling in person." Bomani gestured to the seats nearest them at the round table and said, "Shall we? I am sure that Masika will have the servants send lunch momentarily. It is always better to chat over food, is it not?"

"Everything's better over food!" Bruce declared, obediently pulling out a chair. The others followed suit.

At that moment Masika reappeared, and without hesitation, she took the seat between Dan and Jael. Jael arched an eyebrow at her, but Masika did not seem to notice. Bruce, however, started to cough-laugh.

Sully gestured to Bruce as they all took their seats. "Bruce, you're the best storyteller of the group. Why don't you fill Bomani and Masika in."

Bruce looked surprised and pleased by this distinction, and said modestly, "Well, I've had some practice. I *have* been telling the legends to the Child of the Prophecy since before he was old enough to understand me."

"The *probable* Child of the Prophecy," Sully corrected under his breath. "There is one other candidate."

"I presume you must be Peter Stewart's father then?" Bomani asked, raising his eyebrows.

"That's me," Bruce nodded. "Peter didn't believe in the Ancient Tongue or Carlion or the penumbra or any of our world until... well, last week, actually. I wasn't around for most of what happened after that because I got kidnapped by the Shadow Lord—"

"Wait, wait, wait," Bomani stopped him, glancing at Masika. "You got kidnapped by whom?"

Sully frowned, and Jael sighed, exasperated. "Don't tell me you don't believe in the Shadow Lord either!"

Masika narrowed her eyes at Jael. "Of course we *believe* in the Shadow Lord, but he said he was *kidnapped* by him," she gestured at Bruce.

"Well, not directly," Bruce amended, "The penumbra kidnapped me on his behalf. You probably heard the rest already." And Bruce told them the story of the car accident, his own subsequent abduction to the Fata Morgana, and Kane's disappearance into the Lake of Avalon, the final resting place of Excalibur.

Bruce skimmed over the topic of Kane without elaboration, so Sully added to the Egyptian Watchers, "Kane himself was a candidate up until that point."

Bomani's eyebrows shot up. "Was he really? There were three candidates?"

A shadow fell across Bruce's countenance, and the other Carlion Watchers tried not to look at him.

"Kane was my other son," Bruce said finally, in a very different tone than the one he'd used for the rest of the story.

Dan changed the subject quickly. "Our concern now is that the Shadow Lord will entice Kane to destroy Excalibur, setting the Shadow Lord free."

Masika and Bomani exchanged a skeptical look.

"At that point, he will be virtually invincible if he finds a human host, which is troubling enough in itself," Dan went on. "Once that happens, we believe he will seek out the weapon through which he may acquire an invincible army of penumbra: the Philosopher's Stone."

"I see," said Bomani, very quietly. Then he gestured at Masika. "In that case, you are quite fortunate to have Masika to assist you. She is our foremost expert on the legends surrounding the

Philosopher's Stone—"

"But I told them already that the legends are largely myth," Masika insisted, shaking her head. "There is no such thing as a treasure map to the Philosopher's Stone where X marks the spot, or we would have found it ages ago!"

"If all the references to its location have been kept *here* since the fall of Camelot, it's no wonder we've never found it," Jael muttered. "You don't believe in *anything* here."

"We would still be grateful for anything you could tell us," said Dan, shooting a warning look at Jael.

Just then, a trap door in the floor opened to reveal a perfect cutout of the round table, and the aroma that wafted up to them smelled of eggplant, onions, and tomato sauce. The table inched upward to where they sat.

"Mussaka sandwiches," Masika explained. When the sandwiches came in range and the inner part of the table locked into the outer, they each grabbed a plate and helped themselves.

Masika peeled the layers of her sandwich apart to let it cool. Then she looked at Dan, turning her back to Jael. "I will tell you what I can, even though I do not see how it can help you. The reason that many of the Watchers believe the Stone started out in Egypt is because there are references to it in our Pyramid Texts."

"Right. Isdemus told us that much," Jael interjected, peering over Masika's shoulder.

Masika glanced at Jael coldly before she continued. "The Pyramid Texts are profoundly astronomical in nature. Though they tell a story of the Egyptian pantheon, the gods and goddesses in the story are in reality symbols for their counterparts in the stars. For instance, the Egyptian god Osiris is represented astronomically as the constellation known as Orion, and the three pyramids along the Giza necropolis reflect the three stars in Orion's belt. The Nile is likewise the earthly counterpart of what the Pyramid Texts called the Winding Waterway, or what we call the Milky Way today."

"The Winding Waterway!" Bruce exclaimed. "That's the name of the river that runs through Carlion!"

"Probably not a coincidence. Somebody must have made the connection," Masika said. "One of the stories in the Pyramid Texts involves the Egyptian goddess Isis, who tricked the aging god Re into confiding his 'secret names' to her, and with that knowledge, Isis gained unmatched skills in magic and healing. That is as far as the story goes, but in the original hieroglyphic texts, I have been able to discern a few additional layers of meaning. It seems that Re confided to Isis one 'secret name' for each of the physical elements. The implication was that with those names, Isis was able to wield not just some control, but unlimited control over each element."

Bruce stared at her, forgetting to chew. "Unlimited control of the elements?" he repeated through his half-masticated sandwich. He looked at Sully, whose brow was furrowed in concentration, trying to follow.

"The secret names, of course, sound very much like the words of the Ancient Tongue were in the days of King Arthur," Masika went on. Jael snorted, but Masika ignored her. "Unlimited control, on the other hand, implies either that the story took place prior to the Great Deception, or that, in the story, Isis somehow got hold of the Philosopher's Stone, which could be used to transfer power of the Ancient Tongue to non-humans."

"Are you saying Isis really existed, and that she found the Stone too?" asked Dan, leaning forward.

"I do not know. That is just how the story went," said Masika. "My guess is that she was merely a symbol. As I said, the Pyramid Texts reflected a great deal of the knowledge of astronomy at the time, and the goddess Isis is traditionally associated with the constellation Virgo."

"Wait," said Bruce, "does that mean the Philosopher's Stone is inside the pyramids, then?"

Masika shrugged. "It may have meant that originally, but as I said, we hardly have a clear idea of the current location of the Stone. The pyramids have been excavated hundreds of thousands of times. I am positive that the Stone is not inside one of them now."

Bruce deflated into his chair, picking at the crusts on his plate. Sully watched all of this like a tennis match, his face creased in concentration.

"What else do the Pyramid Texts say?" said Dan. "Maybe they'll lead us to some clues to search elsewhere."

"That is all they say that appears to directly relate to the Stone, I am afraid," Masika said, and tilted her head to the side. "But I have always been fascinated by the fact that they also refer a great deal to the Great Rebel Apep, a mythical figure who takes the form of a dragon. The concept of a dragon as a representation of chaos is a common metaphor in European and Middle Eastern mythology, so in itself this is not surprising. What surprises me about it is the fact that King Arthur's symbol was also a dragon."

"A pair of dragons, to be exact," said Sully. "But what of it?"

"Does it not strike you as odd that our great hero would take for himself the symbol that has been associated with evil and chaos throughout history?"

"He didn't take it for himself," Jael pointed out. "It was on the hilt of Excalibur, and Excalibur chose him."

Bomani interrupted, "Was not that, too, a part of the prophecy?"

"What?" said Dan, confused.

"'Born under the seventh seven,'" Bomani quoted from the prophecy.

"Yes, that's Peter's birthday," said Bruce. "July 7th."

"And Lily's," Sully pointed out.

"July 7th of course bears the astrological sign of the cancer, which is the origin for the symbol of the Taijitu, or merging of darkness into light," said Bomani, and he lifted his hand to flash a golden ring identical to the one that Isdemus wore on his finger. The others in the room looked at him blankly, wondering where he was headed. "I know very little about the Pyramid Texts, but I do know a bit about alchemy. According to alchemical philosophy, each of the astrological signs is a symbol for an alchemical process. Cancer is the symbol for union through solution. Merging." He pointed to the ring again.

Bruce shook his head and looked at the others. "I'm sure you're making a profound point, but I don't follow—"

"Oh, I don't know if it's profound or not," said Bomani. "I am merely pointing out that this concept of merging in alchemy describes the symbol of the Child of the Prophecy, which shows the blend of darkness into light, though the two still remain distinct. The hilt of Excalibur depicted not one, but two dragons, and according to Masika, the dragon is the symbol of chaos and darkness."

"Wait a minute!" said Masika, as if something had just occurred to her. "I need to draw this. Does anybody have a pen?" Bruce, never without a pen, pulled one from his breast pocket and handed it to her. Masika grabbed a napkin and began to draw a series of arrows. "According to Hesiod in the 8th century BC—he was a Greek historian in the outside world, and incidentally also a Seer," she added, "Chaos," she wrote the first word with an arrow, "created Darkness," and then she drew two more arrows beneath it, "and Darkness gave birth to their opposites, Order and Light!"

Jael raised one eyebrow. "So you're saying before the Great Deception, Evil came first? That's totally backwards."

Masika shook her head, irritated. "My point isn't so much the order in which they emerged as the duality of two opposites: darkness and light." She pointed at Bomani's ring. "And both of the symbols of the Child of the Prophecy, the Taijitu and the Pendragon crest, imply the concept of a pair!"

Dan looked around at the others ominously. "Are you guys thinking what I'm thinking?"

Sully's brow cleared, as if he understood something at last. "A double dragon," he murmured. "One of darkness, and one of light."

"Like twins?" asked Bomani, turning to Bruce.

Bruce closed his eyes for a long moment, and swore.

Chapter 12

The next class at Paladin High was Historical Interpretations, taught by Professor Hunt, a straight-laced, no-nonsense Scottish woman. This time Cole sat between Peter and Anthony, which left a space open next to him. He glanced at Lily hopefully, but she brushed past him with cool indifference, settling in to the far side of the room next to Kip Ashton. Peter watched her, accidentally catching Kip's eye instead. He raised his black eyebrows at Peter and winked, his mouth curled into a sneer.

"What's up, Wonder Boy?" he called, waggling his fingers at Peter.

Peter looked away. "I hate that guy," he muttered to Cole.

Before the class actually began, he saw that the seat on his other side had been occupied by the redhead who wanted him to audition for *Romeo and Juliet* with her. Her name turned out to be Cassandra. She waved at him when he saw her,

124

even though they were sitting next to each other, and blushed and giggled again.

"This is my favorite class," Cassandra confided.

"Okay," Peter whispered back.

"It's where we compare what happened in the history books in the outside world with what really happened according to the Watchers."

"Oh." He paused and added, "Cool."

"Your dad is a Watcher, isn't he, Peter?"

He shifted in his seat. "You guys know all about me, I guess," he whispered.

She nodded enthusiastically. "Oh, yeah! I mean, not until a few days ago, but when you showed up in the city and looked just like the painting… and especially after the Fata Morgana, for sure!" She giggled again.

"Today we will continue to build on last week's discussion of the Great Deception," said Professor Hunt. She nodded towards Peter, Brock, Cole, and Lily curtly, but without gushing—for which Peter was grateful. "To our new students, welcome. You may find some of this discussion over your head, so please feel free to ask questions as they occur to you. For the rest, please take out your textbooks and turn to page 514."

"You can share with me, Peter," Cassandra whispered, shoving her textbook towards him.

He nodded thanks to her. "What's the Great Deception?"

"Oh," Cassandra said vaguely, "it's where… um… at the dawn of time everybody had power like you do, Peter. We could all do, like, anything. But then the Shadow Lord made a deal with the penumbra and we lost it."

Peter cocked his head to the side, lowering his voice as Professor Hunt wrote on the blackboard. "What do you mean? What kind of a deal?"

Cole leaned over to Peter and whispered, "She's telling you, listen." He pointed to the blackboard.

"The Shadow Lord…" Professor Hunt spoke slowly as she wrote, "was once a man, just like us. But he had great power. Who can tell me what kind of power he had?"

Heather Kwan's hand shot up in the air. Professor Hunt called on her and she said, "He was the first king of Mesopotamia!"

"Very good, Heather. But he wasn't satisfied with being a king; why not?" When no one raised a hand, Professor Hunt narrowed her eyes and scanned the classroom. She settled on Kip, who tossed a rubber in the air, caught it, and tossed again. "Mr. Ashton?"

Kip caught the rubber and tossed it again without pausing, but still managed to flash the professor a charming smile. "What's that, ma'am?"

Professor Hunt repeated her question. "What more did the Shadow Lord want, beyond the power to rule?"

"He wanted the power of the Ancient Tongue all to himself to prevent any rivals from taking his throne," Kip said finally.

"Correct, and what else?"

Heather strained to push her hand as high in the air as she could get it. Professor Hunt glanced at her and said, "Yes, Heather?"

"Eternal life," said Heather automatically.

"So what happened?" Brock blurted.

Far from immune to the attentions of the handsome newcomer, Heather continued with enthusiasm, "The penumbra wanted the authority to use the Ancient Tongue. Although they could repeat the words, the language held no power for them. The Shadow Lord wanted, as I said before, eternal life and to destroy the power of the Ancient Tongue for any man but himself."

"And how did the penumbra give that to him?" Professor Hunt prompted.

"They tricked him… they made him one of them," said Heather promptly, still speaking to Brock, "which meant that he would live forever, but only in spirit form. His human body died in the process. But unlike the penumbra, the Shadow Lord could inhabit human bodies and use the power of the Ancient Tongue through them."

Attempting to regain the students' attention, Professor Hunt continued the discussion. "As it turned out, neither party in the exchange got exactly what they expected. Evil has a way of cheating even its friends. The Shadow Lord lost his physical life and the penumbra discovered that they didn't have the power of the Ancient Tongue after all." Professor Hunt's eyes roved the classroom, trying to determine if anyone was confused. Her eyes settled on Anthony, who looked perplexed. "Mr. Hutchins?"

"See, I never really got this," Anthony replied as if he was continuing a conversation, "because both the penumbra and the Shadow Lord wanted control of the Ancient Tongue. I don't get how both of them thought they'd end up with control of the same thing in this deal."

Professor Hunt nodded, turning back to the blackboard. "Very good question," she said, and started writing. "The answer has to do with the concept of authority in the Ancient Tongue. The reason we can speak the Ancient Tongue to a particular element and it listens to us today is because we have authority over that element. It has to listen to us. But although we can speak the words for every other element as well, should we care to learn them, only our given element will actually obey us." She wrote a chart on the board, listing out the gifts: *Earth, Fire, Water, Space, Electromagnetism, Air, Mind, Eukaryotes, Muscle, Ideas.* Next to each one, she wrote the word for each of the gifts in the Ancient Tongue. "Before the Great Deception, our authority over the Ancient Tongue was complete, meaning we all had every one of the gifts, while the penumbra had none at all. But—"

"Ooh! Ooh!" squeaked Heather, waving her hand in the air, but with a sideways glance in Brock's direction.

Professor Hunt sighed. "Yes, Heather?"

"So the penumbra promised the Shadow Lord that they'd make him the only human with authority, as long as he promised to share his authority with them!"

"Correct," said Professor Hunt. Then she drew a symbol on the blackboard.

"Who can tell me what this is?"

Heather strained her arm into the air again, but Professor Hunt ignored her, instead calling on Cassandra, who stared at the symbol and shook her head blankly. Professor Hunt continued to scan the classroom, ignoring Heather's flailing arm. "Anyone?"

Peter flipped through the textbook, and raised his hand. "It says here it's called Squaring the Circle," he read, "and it's the symbol for the Philosopher's Stone."

"Very good!" cried Professor Hunt. "The Stone is the key; it's how the transaction was performed. What does legend say the Philosopher's Stone does?"

Forgetting that they weren't speaking, Peter exchanged a knowing look with Lily, who nodded once and looked away, acknowledging that they both knew this one. He raised his hand again and said, "It transmutes body into spirit. That's how the Shadow Lord gained his immortality, but he killed himself in the process." He paused and added, "But Professor? Why did that have anything to do with the Ancient Tongue?"

"Very good question, Mr. Stewart. Anyone?"

Heather looked like she was about to rupture a blood vessel in her forehead, she strained so hard.

"Yes, Heather?" said Professor Hunt, exasperated.

"Only because those were the terms the Shadow Lord gave it," she answered immediately.

"According to legend," Professor Hunt said, "the Shadow Lord was king with the authority to make treaties on behalf of his fellow men, just as kings and presidents and Prime Ministers have over their subjects today. The treaty he made with the penumbra transferred all the authority of the Ancient Tongue from humans to the penumbra, which meant the rest of mankind forgot how to speak the language altogether—in exchange for becoming one of the penumbra himself."

"Except that killed him," said Peter, forgetting to raise his hand.

Professor Hunt nodded. "And that's one reason why it's called the Great Deception. The penumbra didn't tell him that part until it was too late."

"So wait a minute," said Lily, her hand shooting up in the air only after she'd spoken. "The penumbra deceived the Shadow Lord, then? I thought he was their leader!"

Professor Hunt grinned widely. "That's right, Miss Portman—it was a double deception. Class, how did the Shadow Lord deceive the penumbra?"

Nilesh raised his hand and said, "Because he knew the Ancient Tongue would only work for humans. Even if he gave them authority, they couldn't use it unless they could inhabit a human body."

"Which only he could do," said Lily without bothering to raise her hand. "Because he was born a human, so even once he became a penumbra, his spirit could still inhabit a human body—"

"Like a lock and key," Peter finished.

Lily met his eyes and gave him a small smile. She had used exactly the same words to describe the process in the secret library of the Watcher Castle the week before.

Professor Hunt's face lit up. "Very good analogy, Mr. Stewart! That is exactly right—the Shadow Lord essentially got what he wanted, although not in the way he intended. He became the only human with the power of the Ancient Tongue when he inhabited a human body, and the penumbra enjoyed his power vicariously by aligning themselves with him."

Lily raised her hand and Professor Hunt called on her. "So what happened to everybody else? Once they didn't have authority anymore?"

Professor Hunt extended her arms to the side like a shrug and said expectantly, "Who can answer Miss Portman's question?" Then, flatly, "Yes, Miss Kwan."

Heather answered promptly, "Before the Great Deception, the Ancient Tongue was the only language on earth, so afterwards they no longer knew how to speak the Ancient Tongue at all, and they had to come up with new languages."

Professor Hunt nodded. "Precisely. The people became nomads since they could no longer communicate with one another. That was when hieroglyphics were born. From there, the Sumerian language evolved, and all the other languages of the earth arose from the disparate parts where the former inhabitants of Mesopotamia settled. People forgot that the Ancient Tongue even existed, and gradually they forgot that the gifts existed either. This was when they also ceased to see the penumbra, and the penumbra began to attach themselves to individuals in an attempt to control them."

"Then how come anybody can speak the Ancient Tongue now?" Peter whispered to Cassandra.

"Um," said Cassandra, and then she giggled and shrugged. Peter rolled his eyes, wishing he was sitting next to Lily.

"Mr. Stewart," said Professor Hunt, "did you have a question?"

"Yeah," he said, "how come anybody can speak the Ancient Tongue now, then?"

"Because of one man," said Professor Hunt, "the very first Imbas Forosnai. He retained the memory of the Ancient Tongue and remembered a few words, although it took him a long time to get them to work for him. Once he did, he discovered that the power was no longer unlimited like it had been, but instead he drained his own energy every time he spoke it. Because he remembered the time before the Great Deception, he also remained a Seer, when everyone else forgot. Who was that man, class?"

All at once, they chorused, "Merlyn!"

She nodded her approval. "Or at least that's what he came to call himself, but we know originally he had another name. At first Merlyn was ostracized as crazy and a bit dangerous, but he did finally manage to gain a few followers and taught them what he knew through the ages, which is why we can still speak it today. In the outside world, though, the concept of the Ancient Tongue became immortalized in legend as what they call 'magic,' and Merlyn as the greatest sorcerer that ever lived."

When the bell rang, Peter shuffled out of the class, dazed. Cole caught up with him, and Peter shook his head and murmured aloud, "I keep thinking I'm gonna wake up."

Cole nodded sympathetically and patted him on the shoulder.

"Merlyn must have been immortal too, then," Peter went on, looking at Anthony quizzically. "Because he was around all the way from the Great Deception to the time of Arthur, and that was what, like over ten thousand years?"

Anthony nodded. "I guess so. I'd never thought about that before."

Peter balked at him. "How did you not think about that? Wouldn't Merlyn still be around now, then?"

"Well, the whole thing is just a legend, isn't it?" said Anthony rhetorically. Then he added, "C'mon, PE is this way!"

Peter groaned. "You've gotta be kidding me. You guys have Physical Education class here?"

"Not kidding; we're in a fencing unit. I guess Lily can show us what she's got, then, huh?"

Reflexively Peter looked over his shoulder for Lily, who merged with the crowd some six people back. She caught his eye and didn't look away this time, which was progress, he thought.

Physical Education class was out on the lawn, and everyone had to dress out in uniforms of a sort of vibrant green cotton-like material tied with a sash at the waist.

Professor Walters, a portly man with a full, dark brown beard, blew his whistle and instructed students to line up as he passed out bokkens. He gave Peter his bokken last, and as he handed it to him, he whispered, "Delighted to finally meet you, Peter. I'd be more than happy to give you private lessons to get you up to speed with the rest of the class. I suspect sword fighting is something Isdemus particularly would like for you to learn."

Peter smiled at him, embarrassed. "Thank you, sir."

Professor Walters smiled at him approvingly. Then he turned to the rest of the class. "Pair up!" he barked. "You know the drill."

Anthony grabbed Cole, who was nearest him. Peter frowned and scanned the class; Brock, he saw, had paired up with Kip. *This should be interesting,* he thought. He wasn't sure which one he'd prefer to whip the other, but he'd take either. He noticed that Kip sized up Brock with an expression of envy, and Peter smirked.

Then Peter's eyes fell on Lily, who pursed her lips and beckoned him with her finger. He moved towards her, both relieved and slightly apprehensive. She took her stance opposite Peter.

"First, practice the simple vertical strike, on my whistle," said Professor Walters, and blew.

"Apparently this isn't their first lesson," said Peter, looking around with a frown.

"You do it like this, here," said Lily. She demonstrated with her own bokken on an imaginary opponent, driving it downward as if into the opponent's skull. "The defensive opponent blocks like this." She moved her bokken above her head, slanted to the floor. "That way the blow glances off of the defensive opponent's sword." She relaxed her stance and said, "Wanna be offense or defense?"

"You'd better be offense," said Peter. He felt awkward about attacking a girl.

Lily grinned at him. "You might regret that." She widened her stance and raised her bokken at Peter's head.

"I already do," he muttered.

All at once, Lily covered the distance between them and swung her bokken at his skull with a force that could easily knock him unconscious. He swung his own bokken above his head to parry, but not with enough resistance, hitting the top of his head with his own stick under the force of hers. Without a second's pause, Lily whipped her bokken around in horizontal strikes to his left arm, followed by his right leg. Peter's eyes widened and he flailed, just barely blocking her. But he left himself wide open; Lily thrust her bokken towards his gut with most of her weight behind it. Peter fell to his knees, winded, just as Professor Walters blew his whistle. Peter gasped for breath and realized the whole class had stopped to watch them.

"Sorry," Lily whispered guiltily, dropping to her knees beside him. "You all right?"

Peter didn't have breath to reply, but he scowled at her. *Maybe she didn't forgive me after all,* he thought.

"Apparently we have an expert among us," said Professor Walters, and a ripple of laughter passed through the class. "Do try not to kill the Child of the Prophecy, Miss Portman, won't you?"

Peter glanced up at her and saw her eyes flash, but she pursed her lips and said nothing.

"Actually, Lily's a candidate for the Child of the Prophecy too," Cole piped up.

A hush fell over the class, and Professor Walters looked at Lily as if seeing her for the first time. "Is that true?"

"Yes," Peter gasped, staggering to his feet. "And frankly I'd rather… she face… the Shadow Lord… instead of me." He panted, hands on his knees. "Wouldn't you? Are you sure that one of the gifts here isn't the gift of bokkens?"

Professor Walters began to laugh appreciatively, and some of the other students joined in. He clapped Peter on the back and then glanced back at Lily, whose cheeks were flushed with pleasure. "Well how about that! Two candidates at Paladin High! I can't believe *that* hasn't leaked out yet!"

Peter caught Lily's eye, and she held it for a second before sidling up next to him. "Sorry for beating you up," she said grudgingly.

Peter smirked at her. "Liar."

Chapter 13

As soon as Kane spoke the words of the Ancient Tongue to Excalibur, he heard a muffled sound, like the crack of concrete beneath something soft, like a pillow. Then everything went white, even though Kane did not lose consciousness. The colors vanished, and...

He was standing on the bank, in the exact spot where the penumbra had transported him and Peter what seemed like infinite ages before. Back then there had been a ribbon-like footbridge leading to the monstrous and cartoonish-looking Fata Morgana in the distance. But now there was nothing there at all—just an endless sea of glass that showed no sign of having regurgitated a human and a fractured sword on the shore moments before.

Kane's body felt oddly dry after immersion in the water, and he felt solid ground beneath his soles again. He tried to pick up his feet in order to test them out, tried to wiggle his fingers to make sure they were all really there. But his limbs would not respond to him. For a second he panicked.

Am I paralyzed?

Then he heard the voice, laughing. It sounded exactly like it had inside the Fortress and inside his mind, except it was infinitely worse now... because he realized that it was coming out of his own mouth.

Do you think I would choose to occupy a damaged body? said the voice. Suddenly Kane felt his own body turn a cartwheel at Sargon's command. To his utter horror, he began to whoop and holler, dancing on the banks.

"Kane!" cried a familiar voice behind him in a strained, hoarse whisper. Kane whipped around to see the enormous, luminescent form of Achen running towards him with an expression of mingled panic and relief. "Oh, thank goodness—you're safe—"

On the ground between Achen and Kane, the scattered shards of Excalibur glinted with gold on the shore. Kane tried desperately to lunge towards them, but to no avail.

None of that, Sargon *tsk tsk*'ed him exultantly.

Achen abruptly stopped running towards Kane then, staring at him in horror. Kane knew why, without having to consult Sargon.

My eyes. He knew they must be inky black now, and not his usual feral brown. Achen would know that those eyes meant he wasn't dealing with Kane at all.

Before Kane could do or think anything else, he heard his own voice shout, "*Scriosann a scamhóga*!"

Achen suddenly clutched his throat and collapsed to his knees, his breath reduced to a hollow rattle.

Achen! Kane screamed. *Achen!*

"*Slisne oscailt a cófra,*" said Sargon lazily.

A wide gash opened in Achen's chest, and his blood spurt upon the ground in a pulsing arc. Achen's eyes grew wide with shock and betrayal.

NOOO!

But Kane could not make a sound. He could do nothing at all, except watch Achen die.

After a few excruciatingly long moments as Sargon enjoyed both Achen's suffering and Kane's torment, abruptly Sargon lost interest and turned away. Behind him, Achen's rattling attempts to suck in air grew feebler. It would not be long now.

Sargon commanded Kane's legs to walk towards the thick forest behind the banks. Kane's arms extended and he heard his own voice cry, "*Crainn stoitheadh!*" Instantly, with a great rumble of the earth, all of the trees in his immediate line of sight pulled themselves up by the roots. As they began to fall back down, Sargon shouted, "*Ainliú!*" and the trees hovered over the ground, awaiting his command. "*Sruthán suas crainn!*" Kane watched in anguish as every one of the trees went up in flames, still suspended in the air until they were consumed, and their ashes began to fall to the ground.

Sargon cackled, lifting his arms in the air victoriously.

You lied to me! Kane roared. *You lied to me!*

"Did you really think I'd tell you how to kill

me?" said Sargon aloud. His voice—Kane's voice—made Kane nauseous, but he couldn't make himself retch. He couldn't do anything at all.

How could you lie to me? I am in your head!

"No, I am in *your* head," Sargon pointed out. "I've occupied the minds of men for untold ages of the earth."

I would have done it. I would have killed myself and taken you with me!

"I know you would have done it. You *are* very brave," said Sargon dismissively. He walked through the thicket now, pushing aside branches with hands that still seemed semi-transparent in this halfway point between worlds. Sensing Kane's question, he answered aloud, "And incidentally, we are headed to Carlion."

You can't find it! You don't know where it is! Kane cried with an edge of desperation. Behind him, Achen had gone completely silent. An immortal being had just died, and he, Kane, had killed him. It was too horrible to think about.

"Of course I don't know where it is. But you do."

I'll never tell you! Never!

Sargon abruptly stopped walking, as if to focus all his attention on the other person inside of him. Kane braced himself, knowing what was coming. In his mind's eye, he hunkered down in a protective ball around his thoughts, turning his mental energy away from the battering ram that was Sargon.

The aggression Sargon launched against him felt very much like physical pain. Kane felt something in him breaking, like his mind becoming unhinged.

He wasn't sure how long the attack lasted, only that the whole time he crouched in resistance, it felt as inevitable as destroying the sword of Excalibur had seemed in the Lake of Avalon. It was like torture, but it wasn't. He could have resisted physical torture, if only he had motivation enough to do it. But *this* was more like trying to resist truth serum.

Or, said Sargon as Kane fought another wave of nausea, *like trying to resist moving your limbs when you are no longer in control of your nervous system.*

It was impossible. Finally, exhausted and defeated, Kane was overcome.

"That's right," Sargon cooed. "We work together now. Isn't it delightful? There are no secrets between us. Everything you have is mine, and everything I have is yours." He added softly, "We're a team, you and I."

I will never be part of your team! Kane thought, but he could scarcely muster the fury needed to deliver the words.

Sargon laughed out loud scornfully and did not bother to reply. Then he stopped walking and looked around at the clearing. "I suppose this will do."

Kane knew he was looking for a place to create a porthole. *I'm not a space specialist,* he thought resentfully. *Sorry.*

Sargon raised an eyebrow. "I am the Shadow Lord," he said imperiously. "I'm a specialist in everything."

Without warning, Kane felt another penetrating blow from Sargon's mind. It left him with a sense

141

of being winded. Helplessly, he watched as visions of the secret passages inside the castle flooded his mind's eye, leading eventually to the door to the Secret Library. He even saw himself tapping out the sequence on the bricks to allow the passage to open.

Kane's stomach turned over, and he felt waves of sickening fear and despair. Though Sargon didn't think it in so many words, Kane knew exactly what he was planning to do. *No. No, no, no. You'll never get in,* Kane tried to say. *There's no way you can get in without someone seeing you…*

"No, but it won't matter. They will think that I'm you."

Kane thought desperately, *Isdemus will know! He'll have told all the Watchers. He saw this coming, I'm sure of it—he knew you'd return as me the moment I jumped into the lake, that's why he sent Achen! Nobody will trust you!*

"Hmm. Perhaps you are right." After a pause, Sargon added in a soft, brooding voice, "But there *is* one person in that castle of yours who would be willing to go to any lengths to help *you*… and who would have her own reasons for keeping her assistance a secret."

Nobody will do that! You can bet that there isn't a person in the castle now who doesn't know what happened in the Fata Morgana. And besides, most of the Watchers don't even trust me, *even if they don't suspect that I'm you. They—*

Kane stopped. He saw the face of the person whom Sargon meant swimming before his mind's eye, and he fell silent in utter bewilderment.

Gladys? The maid?

But before he could probe Sargon's mind for further explanation, Sargon held out his arms in front of him, preparing to speak the words of the Ancient Tongue.

It won't work! Kane thought, desperate for any means to stop him. *They'll kill you!*

Sargon *tsk-tsk*'ed again. "You really should stop telling me half-truths when I'm inside your head, Kane. You can't lie to me. You *know* it will work. You are hoping they will kill me, but you don't think they will. Even if someone other than the maid comes across us, no matter what they think of you, they won't try to kill you unless they are absolutely certain that you are really me—at which point they could not touch me. They wouldn't have a prayer.

"Face it, Kane," he said softly. "We are unstoppable."

Before Kane could attempt another protest, Sargon cried with ringing authority, *"Dlúth le cúl an chaisleáin!"*

In another second, Kane felt the sensation of a hook somewhere behind his innards, followed by a violent jolt forward... back into the world of men.

Chapter 14

After Physical Education class, Anthony, Cole, Peter, Lily, and Brock all headed to the hitching posts when Anthony suddenly tripped and faked a sprained ankle.

"Oh, oooh, ow!" he moaned. Peter noticed, impressed, that beads of sweat even appeared on Anthony's forehead. "Oooh, can you guys," he looked at Cole and Peter plaintively, "help me to the school healer?"

"I can heal you!" said Cole brightly.

Anthony shot him a look of daggers, which Cole completely missed. "No, no," Anthony insisted, "I think it's more complicated than what you can heal." He tried stepping on the foot again and winced. "Ouch! No offense, Cole."

Cole did look a little crestfallen, but he looped one arm under Anthony's shoulder while Peter took up the other. Lily frowned at them skeptically, crossing her arms over her chest.

"What was it you said you needed to do after class today, Peter?" she asked.

"Take Anthony to the healer, apparently," Peter replied quickly. "Go on without us; we'll catch up."

Once they rounded the corner and were out of sight, the Winding Waterway meandering in front of them on the outdoor path to the healer's separate building, Anthony dropped the pretense and started to walk normally again, letting go of Peter and Cole. Cole blinked at him, confused.

"Wait…" he said. "You didn't sprain your ankle?"

Anthony laughed. "You *are* gullible, aren't you? Come on, let's double back around the back side of the school so they can't see us. We've got to get to the porthole shop in Carlion."

Peter shook his head at Anthony with an expression of immense respect. "You *do* realize this means I'll probably never trust you," he remarked.

"As well you shouldn't!" Anthony returned easily, his dimples pronounced.

Peter had only seen the porthole shop from the outside before, but inside it was even odder than the Commuter Station. The collection of photographs and paintings was a mishmash of fine art and cheap posters. Some hung on the walls, some hung from the ceiling, and some were plastered to the floor with "caution" tape around them to keep unsuspecting shoppers from straying into their event horizons on accident.

"Excuse me, Mr. Kreutz," Anthony said to the shopkeeper, a man with extremely pointy eyebrows in at least four different colors, "but which of these portholes goes to the Grandfather Tree?"

Mr. Kreutz raised the colorful brows even higher. "Does yer mum know yer goin'?"

Anthony paused, and cocked his head ever so slightly to the side. "Mr. Kreutz," he replied with an air of delicacy, "Let's just say that if you do me this one *teensy* little favor, we'll call it square between us. Will that be all right?"

Mr. Kreutz narrowed his eyes at Anthony and shook his head, muttering under his breath, but he heaved himself up from his perch and shuffled around to the other side of the counter. The boys could just hear him saying, "…up to no good, mark m'words… 'll have m'head for this…"

They followed behind him eagerly, though, and Mr. Kreutz gestured at an unlabeled portrait of a young Jewish mother and her child, done in a late Victorian style. "Anybody asks 'n I never saw nothin', never *said* nothin', y'hear?"

Anthony made an elaborate bow. "On my honor," he promised.

"Not worth much, I'll wager," Mr. Kreutz muttered.

Anthony ignored this and glanced back at Peter and Cole. "See you two in forty minutes!"

When he had gone, Cole snuck a glance up at Mr. Kreutz, and then at Peter, nudging him pointedly and gesturing at the shopkeeper.

Peter cleared his throat. "So sir," he said, "We, um… we'll have to follow him in forty minutes."

"Yer not waitin' here," grumbled the shopkeeper. He gestured at the porthole where

Anthony had just disappeared, and then at the porthole shop door. "Get in, er get out."

Peter glanced at the portrait of the Jewish mother apprehensively without really seeing it, remembering the last time he was in the Enchanted Forest near the Grandfather Tree. He knew it was irrational, but he didn't much want to linger where only a week earlier he'd fled for his life. But he didn't want to risk wandering around Carlion for forty minutes either, just in case Lily or Brock or anybody else happened to see them and detain them.

"We'd better go, then," he whispered to Cole, who nodded at him in a wide-eyed reply.

Reluctantly, Peter approached the event horizon. He felt the unpleasant sensation around his navel that he still hadn't quite gotten used to, and the next thing he knew he was at the edge of the forest in the late afternoon. Some distance ahead, he saw Anthony's silhouette waiting at the bus stop, and he heard the rumble of the approaching purple and teal bus as it turned the corner and slowed to a stop.

Cole appeared next to him in the dappled light of the waning day with a grimace. "I hate that feeling."

"Tell me about it," said Peter. He pointed at Anthony's figure up ahead, just to show Cole that he was there as Anthony boarded the bus and it drove off. Vaguely, Peter thought he heard another rustle behind them, but when he looked around there was nothing there. *Must've been Cole,* he decided.

"So now we wait," said Cole, hunkering down in the undergrowth. "Do you think the penumbra can see through leaves?" he asked apprehensively.

"How should I know? Last week I didn't even know there were penumbra."

Cole fell silent at this. Then he ventured quietly, "We almost died here, you know."

Peter was silent for a long moment. "Yeah."

"I guess you're right, it *is* kinda crazy how much has happened in a week."

Peter snorted. "Kinda," he agreed.

They fell silent for what seemed like almost twenty minutes. Peter was starting to shiver as the daylight waned.

"Hey Pete?"

"Yeah?"

"If you don't want to be the Child of the Prophecy… are you hoping it's Lily, then?"

Peter bit his lip and thought about this. "No," he said at last.

"Why not?"

He shrugged. "I don't know. I just really don't like that idea."

"She can be a little scary sometimes," Cole agreed, in a tone that implied he thought this was what Peter was saying. "But maybe the Child of the Prophecy *should* be a little scary, if she's gonna win in the end. And you're not scary at all."

"Thanks," said Peter dryly.

Cole backpedaled, "I just mean… well, she whipped you in PE today, didn't she?"

Peter waved him off. "I know what you mean. She *is* scary, but not for that reason."

"Because she can read your mind, then?" asked Cole knowingly.

Peter felt his cheeks burn, but his back was to Cole, so he knew Cole couldn't see him. "Yeah. I'd say that's pretty terrifying."

"You two *do* get on really well, though," Cole observed.

"Not as well as we did at first," said Peter without thinking.

"What do you mean?"

Peter shook his head. "I dunno." Suddenly he felt a flood of frustration that he didn't totally understand. "She complains she can't read *me*, but I can't read her at all! One minute she's normal and the next she's all upset about something, but she won't tell me what it is. And she's only happy again once she's beaten me at something. She's like… she's like…" he searched for the appropriate word.

"Into you?" Cole finished knowingly.

"No!" Peter protested, horrified. His cheeks burned again. "No, she's not 'into me,' she's like, jealous of me or something!"

"You sure she's not into you?"

"Shut up, okay? I don't want to talk about this."

Cole fell silent obediently, and Peter felt guilty for snapping at him. But before he could apologize, Peter saw the ugly brown Suburban he knew so well barreling towards them. His heart leapt oddly in his chest at the familiar sight. Its driver seemed to have very little concept of his side of the lane, but as they were well outside the city and there was no one else on the road, it didn't matter much.

"Come on, get ready to jump in!" Peter whispered unnecessarily. Cole crept up beside him and they waited as Anthony screeched to a stop, right in the middle of the road. "Blimey, get out of the way!" Peter cried frantically, running towards him and simultaneously gesturing to Anthony to pull over. But Anthony just grinned at them through the window and leaned over to unlock and open the door to the backseat, apparently so pleased with himself that he was oblivious to Peter's whispered shouts.

"So far, so good!" Anthony announced when he'd pushed open the door.

Cole dove in first, keeping his head down and immediately stuffing himself below the far seat, and Peter jumped in on the other side. But he felt resistance as he tried to pull the door handle shut.

It took him a moment to understand when he saw the shock of red hair on the other side of the window. Its owner yanked the door open again and dove into the back seat almost on top of Peter, forcing him into the middle in stunned surprise.

Peter, Cole, and Anthony all gaped at him for a moment, before Peter finally found his voice, and shouted angrily, "*Eustace!*"

"Hi, Peter!" said Eustace hesitantly. "I'm here to help… with… whatever you're doing! What *are* you doing? Are we having an adventure? Are we gonna go fight some penumbra? I can help keep you safe, I can, you'll be dead glad I came along, not that I know what my gift is yet but I'm fast, and I hide really well! I bet you didn't even see me, did you, Peter?"

Anthony looked at Peter helplessly. "Should I drive then?"

"No!" said Peter firmly, "He's going right back

where he came from!"

"But do get out of the road, maybe," Cole added, biting his lip.

Anthony started the engine and crept to the side of the road in a jerking fashion.

Meanwhile Eustace straightened himself and said with as much gusto as he could muster, "If you send me back, I'll go straight to Isdemus and tell him what you're doin', that's what I'll do!" Then he thought for a minute and his expression faltered. "Well, I don't *know* what you're doin' exactly. But I'll tell him where you are! Unless you let me help, and then I'll never say a peep!" he added hopefully.

Cole and Peter exchanged a look, and Cole whispered, "He's not gonna hurt anything, Pete. Let's just take him."

Peter sighed roughly and turned his scowl on Anthony. "Fine. Drive."

"Are you mad at me?" said Eustace in a tiny voice, curling up low in the backseat and gazing at Peter with enormous eyes.

"Yes!" Peter snapped. "Don't you know it's dangerous for you to be outside the castle walls? Especially with me!"

"Well, then, why are you out?" Eustace retorted, and then added eagerly in a voice barely above a whisper, "Is it something to do with th' Shadow Lord? Are you getting top secret information that's gonna help defeat him? Or maybe you're gettin' a weapon! Are you gettin' a weapon?"

"No, Eustace, if you must know, I'm getting my cat, all right?"

Eustace started at him blankly. "Your… cat?"

Cole started giggling, and as soon as he did, Anthony cracked up too, at which point the car began to swerve into the oncoming lane.

Peter snapped at Anthony, "Keep your eyes on the road! We've had enough accidents on this road to last a lifetime!"

They lapsed into tense silence after that. Every few minutes Eustace turned enormous doe eyes on Peter, who refused to look at him. Cole fidgeted apprehensively.

At last Anthony warned, "We're entering the city. Keep your heads down. There are people and... *oh*!"

"Saw them, did you?" said Cole knowingly.

"Saw what?" demanded Eustace, perking up eagerly.

"Head down!" said Peter crossly, pushing Eustace's head back to the seat. "He means the penumbra!"

If possible, Eustace's eyes went even wider. "Th' *penumbra*!" he breathed. "Oh, let me look! Can I look, Peter? Can I?"

"No!" Peter and Cole shouted at once, and Peter added, "If you pop up and look around, they'll wonder why you were hiding in the backseat. Stay down!"

"There were a few on the bus too, but they weren't as bad as these. They're *hideous!*" said Anthony in shock.

"They're not always," said Peter, thinking of what Lily had said about Brock's siren, and of Guinevere. Then he added, "Reverse into the driveway when you get to my house so we're closer to the door."

Anthony snorted. "Yeah, right. I learned to drive less than an hour ago. Now you want me to do it backwards?" But several minutes later when Peter could sense by the car's motion that they had turned down the drive that led to his house, he felt Anthony halt right where his driveway ought to be, and begin to reverse very inexpertly. There was a sudden loud crash and clatter of metal.

"Sorry!" said Anthony, and then added crossly, "What are you doing putting your bin right by the driveway, anyway?"

"I'll go first to make sure th' coast is clear!" Eustace piped up.

"Anthony can tell us the coast is clear. We don't need you to do that," said Peter irritably, and Eustace's face fell. Peter sighed, and felt a twinge of guilt. "Well, all right. You can go with him, but just get out long enough to make sure there's nobody around!"

Eustace brightened again. Once Eustace and Anthony jumped out of the car, Cole turned and smirked at Peter.

"What?" Peter demanded waspishly.

"Nothing, nothing."

A few seconds later, Eustace's head popped up outside the backseat window eagerly, and he motioned Peter and Cole forward. Peter got out and dashed over to the side of the house.

As they crept into the front garden, Eustace prowling as if hunting some skittish creature frightened away at the slightest noise, Peter glanced with a rush of nostalgia at the white wicker furniture on the porch. He had spent hundreds of hours studying there during the summer months just for pleasure, wiping sweat off his brow from the sweltering humidity and drinking lemon squash. He spared a thought for what would happen to the porch now, and the house. He supposed his dad would sell the place eventually. Perhaps that had been his plan all along, once Peter found out about... *well, everything.*

Anthony waved Peter aside with an air of machismo and produced the set of keys he'd used for the car, inserting the house key into the lock.

"So you picked the lock all right earlier, then," said Cole, admiringly.

"Not like it was my first time," Anthony winked, and pushed the front door open.

A fat, long-haired white cat streaked out of nowhere and through the open door.

"Newton!" Peter exclaimed in relief, though he kept his voice to barely above a whisper. Newton wound himself between Peter's legs, purring, while keeping watchful eyes on Anthony and Eustace. Peter scooped up the cat and buried his face in his fur. "I know, I'm so sorry!"

"All right, come on, let's get out of here!" Cole interrupted.

"In a minute," said Peter. "I wanted to grab a few things out of my room while I'm here..." With one last squeeze, he unceremoniously dumped Newton back onto the floor and bounded up the stairs. Cole and Anthony followed closely behind while Eustace brought up the rear, still crouching and pivoting one hundred eighty degrees with each step like a spy.

Once in his room, Peter pulled a suitcase from beneath his bed and tossed things in at random. He yanked open two dresser drawers and pulled books from the shelves by twos and threes.

Anthony looked around at the walls, covered with posters of nebulae except for a white board with dry wipe markers, filled with half-erased equations in various colors.

"Geek through and through, aren't you?" he observed rhetorically.

There was a noise downstairs, and Cole froze.

"What was that?" he hissed.

"Probably just Eustace. Where is Eustace anyway?" said Anthony. "He was behind us a second ago."

Then Peter heard a sound that made his heart drop into his toes: it was the sound of the front door opening. He realized then that what Cole heard had been a knock.

"He *can't* have opened the door!" Peter moaned, but sure enough, they heard voices downstairs, one of which was Eustace's. The other, Peter realized, sounded like his next door neighbor, Mrs. Hodgkins. "It's my neighbor. She probably saw the car and came over to see if we were home," he whispered, his hands frozen over the half-filled suitcase.

"But she's not a Seer, is she?" Anthony hissed.

Peter hesitated. "I'm not sure, but probably not. Her penumbra won't recognize Eustace though. As long as we stay up here, we should be fine..."

"But *she* won't recognize Eustace. That's the problem, isn't it?" Anthony whispered. "She's probably here to see if someone's breaking in!"

"Eustace is like eight. She's not going to think he's a burglar—"

"Peter?" came a distinctly female voice down below, followed by the sound of footsteps on the stairs.

Peter looked at Cole, stricken. "We've got to hide!" He grabbed Cole and dragged him towards the closet before Cole could protest.

"Peter, is that you?" came Mrs. Hodgkins' voice, much closer this time, just as Peter pulled his closet door shut. He and Cole blinked at each other in the filtered light beneath the door, and could hear that she had just entered the room and found Anthony standing, apparently, over a half-packed suitcase.

"Where is Peter Stewart?" they heard a different voice hiss, and Peter and Cole looked at each other, horrified. Cole mouthed unnecessarily, "That's her penumbra!" just as Mrs. Hodgkins' voice repeated with pleasant nonchalance, "Where is Peter? And who are you?"

"I'm assuming Peter is the kid who lives here?" said Anthony without missing a beat. "I don't know him, I was just paid to come here and pack up some of his stuff and take it back to the agency."

"Who paid you?" hissed the penumbra, and Mrs. Hodgkins said suspiciously, "Who paid you? What kind of an agency? I've never heard of anything—"

"I dunno who pays me," said Anthony indifferently. "It's just my after-school job, they pay the agency and the agency pays me to show up and do whatever odd jobs people want me to do. Usually it's to clean up and do gardening and things like that, but I don't ask questions, long as I'm paid on time."

"*You don't know Peter then?*" demanded the creature, and she said, "You don't know Peter then?"

"Never met him," said Anthony smoothly. "Don't worry, I'll be out of here in a few minutes. I can give you the phone number of the agency if you want to check my story."

That seemed to convince her, and she said, "No, no, that won't be necessary. I'm just looking out for the place while the Stewarts are gone. Wanted to make sure they weren't being burgled!"

Anthony laughed easily. "No, I'm not even taking anything valuable, see? But I will be taking the cat."

"To the agency?" repeated Mrs. Hodgkins.

"Yeah."

"*Find out where Peter is,*" said the penumbra, and Mrs. Hodgkins pressed, "So you're taking all this to wherever Peter and Bruce are staying now?"

"Or where they told us to drop it off, anyway," said Anthony with a tone of finality, and Cole and Peter could hear him rustling clothes from Peter's drawers and into the open suitcase, signaling that the conversation was over.

After a pause and another pair of footsteps, Mrs. Hodgkins said, "Who is this, then?" Peter knew she meant Eustace. "You're a little young to have an after school job, aren't you?"

"That's my little brother," said Anthony before Eustace could reply. "I picked him up from school on my way here. I drag him along sometimes when it's convenient."

"Yeah, I'm his little brother!" Eustace piped up immediately, with too much enthusiasm. Peter groaned silently and sunk his head into his hands.

"Oh," said Mrs. Hodgkins, sounding vaguely uncertain again. "How did you both get here? I only saw the Stewarts' car in the drive…"

"We took the bus," said Anthony. "Stop's not very far away."

She seemed satisfied. "Well, all right then. If you see Peter when you drop off his things—"

"I won't," Anthony interrupted blandly, and Peter could hear the shrug in his voice. "Not part of my job description. Somebody else delivers."

"Oh," she said again. "Well, I'm… glad there's nothing here to be concerned about… I'll just be heading home then…"

"Good idea. Goodbye!" called Anthony. Peter and Cole listened as a pair of footsteps retreated out of the room and down the stairs until they could no longer hear them. A few seconds later, Peter heard the front door open and close again with a creak down below.

As soon as the windows stopped rattling from the force of the front door, Peter threw open the closet door and leapt out. "That was a close one!"

"You were brilliant!" Cole echoed, grinning at Anthony admiringly.

"And I was good too, wasn't I? Wasn't I, Peter?" said Eustace hopefully as Peter resumed tossing clothes and books into his suitcase as quickly as he could.

Peter turned to glare at the little boy, who shrank

back as soon as he saw Peter's fierce expression. "*You* could've gotten us all killed, do you understand that? What did you open the door for?"

Eustace's lower lip trembled just a bit. "She... but I thought she was your neighbor. She said she'd known you all her life..."

"And it didn't disturb you that she had a giant black raven sitting on her shoulder?" Anthony demanded.

"Is that what it was?" repeated Cole, frowning. "It sounded scarier than that."

Eustace quailed and said in a very small voice, "I thought it was her pet..."

"Her *talking* pet?" said Anthony.

"It didn't say anything downstairs..." Eustace protested meekly.

"He's never seen a penumbra before," Peter sighed. He looked away so he didn't have to see Eustace's trembling lip, and tossed the last pair of jeans into his suitcase. He zipped it shut, and gave silent thanks that the thing had wheels for all the books he'd thrown in as he lifted it to the floor.

Eustace said glumly, "I'll just go wait in the car, then, so I won't be in the way anymore." He started towards the stairs, but Anthony pulled him back by the collar.

"Oh, no you don't. We're not letting you out of our sight," he said firmly.

Newton waited at the foot of the stairs, and Peter scooped him up again, letting Cole drag the suitcase while Anthony checked via the back door that Mrs. Hodgkins hadn't waited around to make sure Anthony's story checked out.

159

Once they all safely dove into the Suburban, Cole whispered to Peter, "How're you going to explain Newton to Isdemus, then?"

Peter opened his mouth and closed it again. He hadn't thought of that. "Huh," he said.

Anthony gave a low whistle. "Somebody's gonna be in *trouble…*"

Chapter 15

The body that was Kane's appeared inside the Commuter Station, right beside the picture of the Grandfather Tree. Sargon's mouth curled into a slow, cruel smile. At last, he was here—the very place that was most off-limits to him, hidden for millennia, protected by the best of the nimbi, and all but impenetrable to the penumbra. And now he, the chief of the penumbra, their Shadow Lord, was here—with no one the wiser.

Gloat, then, Kane snarled inside his head. *I dare you.*

Sargon smiled. *Poor sportsmanship does not become you, Kane.*

Kane willed his vocal cords to obey him with all his might. *Bellator!* he tried to shout. *Verum! Fides Dignus! Isdemus!* But the words never crossed his lips.

Kane sank into momentary despair before trying another tack.

161

How exactly do you plan to avoid being seen? he demanded. But as soon as he asked the question, he knew the answer. He saw Sargon head towards the blank wall at the far end of the Commuter Station, and Kane felt his mind being bombarded once again. He tried to withstand the onslaught, but only halfheartedly. He already knew it was useless.

Thank you, said Sargon courteously when he had extracted what he wanted to know, and he began to tap five blocks to the left of the edge of the wall and twelve blocks up from the floor. He tapped three times rapidly, two long, one rapid, three long. In response, the wall revolved inward, admitting them into the secret passageway where they were not likely to encounter anyone else in the castle. But the moment it rotated closed again, not a moment too soon, Sargon and Kane heard voices on the other side.

"Where do we even start to look for them?" said one voice, anxiously.

Bellator! Kane longed to cry out. But Sargon stood silently on the other side of the wall, his ear pressed against it to catch every word.

The second voice was comparatively serene and calm. "I suspect Peter will choose to go somewhere familiar. His father told me this morning that he was having some difficulty adjusting to life here in Carlion." The sound of that voice tied Kane's stomach into knots. *Isdemus.* "Incidentally, Bellator, do you notice anything?"

A pause. "Sir?"

"My detection is poorer than yours, but does it not seem as if there is a ripple here, as if someone only just left?" Another pause, and then he added thoughtfully, "Or just arrived?"

"You are right, sir," said Bellator, surprised.

Kane somehow knew that Isdemus was looking right at him, as if he could see through the blocks on the wall. Nevertheless, Isdemus changed the subject. "Gather the nimbi who are available. Send half to search the city and the other half to the Enchanted Forest and the Grandfather Tree. Come and report to me the minute you know anything."

In response, Kane heard a *crack*, followed by a very quiet sound that Kane recognized as the rustling of Isdemus's robes. Kane knew in a flash what was about to happen, and he could not keep Sargon from knowing as well. They could either retreat further down the secret passage in an attempt to outrun Isdemus, or they could follow the revolving door to the other side when Isdemus opened the secret passage seconds later. Sargon chose the latter.

Sure enough, there was a deep rumble in the wall, and as the door revolved, admitting Isdemus inside the secret passage, Sargon snuck around to the now-deserted Commuter Station on the opposite side.

Got any other brilliant ideas? Kane snapped, once they were alone in the Commuter Station.

Yes, said Sargon, with irritating nonchalance. *The herb garden.*

The—? But before Kane could ask any more questions, they slipped out of the Commuter Station, keeping to the shadows as they rushed towards the spiral staircase, and fled down one more flight of stairs. They were in the third basement then. On one side of the castle the third basement was completely underground, but on the other the ground outside the castle sloped such that there was a door leading out to the herb garden, where they could be nearly assured of running into only one person. She was the only servant who ever ventured out that way, and she did it every day, around twilight.

You think she'll be able to get to the secret library, even with Isdemus patrolling the passage? Kane demanded, trying not to sound as panicked as he felt.

Yes, said Sargon. *Yes, I do. Not because she's particularly clever, of course, but because she will be so very motivated.*

Kane could sense what Sargon meant, but it didn't make any sense. Sargon believed Gladys to be racked with guilt over something she had done... something she had done to *him, to* Kane. But what? He couldn't recall that Gladys had ever paid much attention to him one way or the other. She seemed to stay out of his way as best she could, but he never had the impression that she was particularly fond of him, nor had she ever acted guilty that he could recall.

You'll see, said Sargon smugly.

They were on exactly the opposite side of the castle from the main entrance, hidden from view by the castle itself on one side and by the dragon-shaped garden on another. The herb garden could not possibly be more secluded, which was probably why Gladys always volunteered to gather herbs for the kitchen. She never had seemed to enjoy spending time around people very much.

Sargon slipped around a corner such that he was all but hidden by the hedge and the castle, and waited. He did not have to wait long; the late afternoon sun suggested that it was about time for the kitchen servants to begin preparing supper for the Watchers.

Ten minutes later, a harassed-looking woman with a gray bun exited the same door through which Sargon had come. She wore a full and very unflattering skirt in a brown rosebud print, gathered at the waist beneath her stained apron, and she had an empty basket over her arm as she hurried purposefully towards the little garden.

"*Psst!*" Kane heard himself hiss.

Gladys froze, but did not turn around.

"Don't be scared!" Sargon whispered again, creeping out from his hiding place. Then he added quickly as Gladys turned around, "And don't scream!"

He'd said it not a moment too soon: Gladys clapped both hands over her mouth and looked as if she couldn't decide whether to scream or swoon. Sargon caught her before she could do either, but she did drop the empty basket.

"They… they said you were dead!" she breathed, her eyes wide as saucers. "You were at the bottom of the lake…"

"I escaped, as you can see," Sargon said, and grinned Kane's most charming smile. "But I need it to be a secret that I'm back for now. Just between us."

Gladys began to shake her head vigorously, as if trying to wake herself from a dream, or a nightmare. "Why? Why wouldn't you want everyone to know?"

Sargon ignored this question, but the winning grin melted as he took a deliberate step closer to her, and spoke in a very low voice. "Gladys, I know what you did to Penny Stewart."

Gladys went white.

Peter's mother? Kane wondered, now completely confused. *But how did she even* know *Peter's mother—?*

Sargon continued, his voice deadly calm, "You killed my mother, Gladys."

Kane froze. *No. That's wrong. Penny was Peter's mother.*

In answer, he saw the symbol floating in Sargon's mind—the symbol he had seen so many times in his waking hours. It was the Pendragon crest, of the two entwined dragons. All at once, Kane finally understood with sickening clarity why there were *two* dragons in the symbol—not just one.

Peter is my… twin brother?

"I didn't mean to!" Gladys begged. "I didn't know what would happen, I—" and then she dissolved into tears, her body racked with sobs. Kane was revolted to feel his own arms wrapping around her, his voice soothing her as she collapsed against him.

It's her fault! Kane screamed soundlessly. *She killed my mother!*

"It's okay, it's okay," Sargon cooed. "You can still atone for what you have done."

"How?" Gladys wailed. "How can I ever atone?" she exclaimed, her last words garbled with emotion.

But why? Why did she do it? How did she do it? Kane knew that if he'd had control of his own stomach, he would have felt bile rising to his throat right about then. *And how can Peter be my...* Kane couldn't even think the word again. He couldn't. It was too awful.

All in good time, Sargon replied with infuriating calm.

Aloud, he said to Gladys, "I will tell you how. I need you to do something for me, and I need you to do it without question."

"Anything," she gasped, and buried her face into her hands again. "Anything!"

"Good. There is a secret passageway inside the castle."

For a moment Gladys gaped at him, confused. "There's a... what?"

"I'll explain to you how to get there, never mind that for now. Inside the passageway there is a library—"

"I know the library!" Gladys interrupted eagerly. "I've cleaned it many times—"

"You're thinking of the main library," Sargon shook his head patiently, verifying this with Kane's memory in a flash. "You have never been to the secret library. There is no other way to get there except through the secret passageway."

Gladys stared at him for a moment, and then hastily wiped her lined face. "Oh..."

"I will draw you a map if you have a piece of parchment—"

"I do! From my recipe!" she exclaimed, and retrieved a quill and scrap of parchment from inside the pocket of her apron. It had a short list of ingredients scribbled on it already. "Here!"

"Brilliant," said Sargon, and wrote out the tapping sequence to enter the passage. "I'm drawing you the map to the library from the Commuter Station. Now, you *must*, and this is very important, you *must* enter only when no one is looking. Have you got that?"

"Yes, Kane, yes, anything you say!" said Gladys, choking back another sob.

Her face nauseated Kane, and he wished he could look away.

"Good. Now here's where I want you to go..." Sargon drew out the map from Kane's memory, and added, "Bring a torch, because the passage is dark until you get to the rooms."

"Bring a torch," Gladys echoed.

Sargon regarded her for a moment, and marveled. *Could this be any easier?* "What I need you to do is to bring me a book. There's one particular book that I need. It's just here—" He drew out the wall of books that Kane knew to be facing the immediate entrance of the secret library, and drew the rows; he counted seven rows up and three shelves across, and then Sargon closed his eyes to visualize exactly which book it was. Kane, who had a photographic memory, desperately sent Sargon the signal that the book he wanted was on the opposite end of the library, but Sargon saw through it so easily that he might as well not have bothered. "It's the fifth book from the left of this shelf here." Sargon drew a star where it ought to be. "Its binding is of faded black leather. It's about this thick," he held up his thumb and index finger a few inches apart, "and it has this symbol on the cover." He drew first a small circle within a square, a triangle around that, and another larger circle around the whole.

"What is that?" said Gladys, her brow creased with concentration.

"Never mind," said Sargon, "it's on the cover. Bring me this book. I need it to help the Watchers defeat the Shadow Lord, Gladys."

She gasped. "Is he..." she lowered her voice to a whisper, "is he *back*, then?"

Kane could feel his face arranging in its most somber expression. "This is just between you and me right now, but... yes."

She gasped, and one hand fluttered to her throat.

"If you bring me this book, Gladys, you can atone for everything you have done, do you understand?"

"Yes," she said in a very small voice, and a sniffle. "Yes, of course, Kane."

"Good," said Sargon. "I will wait for you here.

And remember that if you meet anyone on the way, you are to tell *no one* about me. No one!"

"No one, of course, Kane, no one!" She gave a little jump and hurried towards the door, her empty basket forgotten on the ground by Sargon's feet.

The map in that book doesn't lead anywhere, Kane snarled. *It's useless! If it wasn't, we'd have found it thousands of years ago!*

It's useless to you, *because you don't know what you're looking at,* Sargon corrected with infuriating calm.

And you do? Kane challenged. But he felt a twinge of fear.

You haven't been able to find the Stone, Kane, because it was hidden from *you, not* for *you.*

By whom? Kane demanded. *It was hidden by the original Watchers!*

Kane could feel his face curl into the smirk that had made people loathe him all his life. *Is that what they told you?*

If the map wasn't written by the Watchers, then how did it find its way into the secret library in the first place?

Don't you remember the old stories, Kane? Sargon crooned. *There was a time when one of the penumbra lived inside the castle itself! She did everything I told her to do, and she had access to everything—even your precious secret library.*

Kane felt a sensation like a stone drop in the pit of his stomach as he instantly understood who Sargon meant. Of course.

Queen Guinevere.

Chapter 16

"**S**hould we just ditch the car by the side of the road, then?" said Anthony. He slowed the Suburban as they approached the Grandfather Tree.

"Guess so," said Peter. "Not like we'll be needing it anytime soon anyway." Peter felt the crunch of gravel beneath the tires as Anthony pulled over to the shoulder of the road, and then he heard Anthony begin to groan.

"Ohhhh…"

"What?" said Cole, exchanging a perplexed look with Peter.

"We've got a welcoming committee," said Anthony ominously.

"What do you mean?" Peter demanded sharply. "The penumbra?"

"Worse," said Anthony. "The Watchers."

"What?" Peter repeated, this time confused. His head bobbed up from the backseat to look around, Cole and Eustace right behind him.

"Ohhh…" Cole echoed Anthony, and Peter's stomach did a backflip. A veritable army waited on the side of the road, most of them looking especially radiant in the waning light of the approaching evening. There were centaurs, satyrs, elves, leopards and enormous, bare-chested warriors. Every last one of them was outfitted for war, and though they still glowed, Peter could not see the trees on the other side of them.

That meant they were solid.

"They took physical forms," Cole murmured. "Even outside Carlion…"

"Yeah," Peter croaked.

In the midst of the army, Peter could see the one face that he dreaded more than any other: Isdemus. Despite his age and his lusterless form, he looked as fearsome as any of them, his robes black as night and his white hair reflecting the glow of his companions. Around him were several other Watchers whom Peter had met once or twice since his arrival at Carlion, but he could not remember most of their names. Isdemus's eyes locked on Peter's as Anthony drew the car to a complete halt, and for one wild second, Peter wondered frantically if there was any way he could avoid getting out of the car and having to face him. But he knew there wasn't.

Isdemus pushed the nimbi aside as he strode forward to meet Peter. As he approached, Peter could see the lines of his face etched with relief mingled with disappointment, which, as far as Peter was concerned, was far worse than anger.

"Where have you been?" said Isdemus quietly.

Peter clutched Newton to his chest so tightly that he meowed and began to claw at Peter's shoulder. Peter briefly considered passing the question off to Anthony so that he could weave one of his wild stories, but he knew there was no point. Isdemus would see right through it, and Peter felt too ashamed to lie anymore. But instead of admitting his fault right off, Peter found himself saying defensively, "Newton was starving! We'd just left him all by himself; somebody had to rescue him—"

"Do you think we are so heartless as to allow your pet to starve to death in your absence?" Isdemus cut him off, his voice still calm and even. "Vanessa has brought Newton food daily since you and Bruce arrived in Carlion. Her instructions were to bring him to you as soon as she could gain his trust enough to capture him." He gestured to the middle-aged Watcher behind him with nut brown hair streaked with gray. "I told Bruce so this morning when he asked me about sending someone to retrieve Newton. I would gladly have told you as well, but you did not ask." Isdemus focused entirely on Peter, though the others shuffled uncomfortably behind him.

"I—" Peter faltered, and then hung his head in shame. "I'm sorry, sir."

Isdemus did not seem to hear the apology. "When Miss Portman told us you'd disappeared after school, we sent out search parties to all of the places we thought you most likely to go. We focused at first on Carlion itself. Unfortunately it never occurred to any of us that you would be so foolish as to go back to your house, especially after what happened at the Fata Morgana. When I heard that Mr. Hutchins was with you, I feared the worst," Isdemus glanced at Anthony sternly, "as his reputation for trouble precedes him. Once we were forced to conclude that you were no longer in Carlion, all the Watchers we had available outfitted for battle, and the nimbi took bodies, as you see. If the penumbra had so much as caught a glimpse of you, Peter, they certainly would have taken physical form in order to kill you, despite the risk to their own immortality. The nimbi knew that they, too, would have to become physical in order to defend you. They were prepared to risk their lives to save yours, as were all of the Watchers. All this for a cat, which in all likelihood would have been back in your arms by nightfall, regardless!"

Peter didn't bother to venture another apology. It seemed far too feeble. He felt the combined glares from all of the assembled Watchers and the nimbi around Isdemus, and very much wished he could disappear.

"Anthony," said Isdemus unexpectedly, and Anthony jumped.

"Yes sir!"

"Give Vanessa the keys to the Suburban. She will drop it back at Peter's house."

Wordlessly, Vanessa moved forward to obey, and took the keys from Anthony. The rest of the Watchers and nimbi moved into a single-file line before the Grandfather Tree and began to disappear when Peter heard Cole approach with his suitcase on his other side. He wished that Cole had left the suitcase in the car. Its presence seemed shameful to him now, considering what it had nearly cost.

Isdemus strode towards the Grandfather Tree without looking at Peter. It was too much.

"Sir," Peter said finally, "I know it doesn't help, but I really am sorry. I should have trusted you."

"Yes, Peter. You should have."

Suddenly Cole blurted, "Don't be mad at Pete, sir; it's all my fault! It was my idea to get the car—"

"But I'm the one who actually drove!" Anthony interjected. "It's my fault! You guys were just along for the ride—"

"No, it's my fault!" Eustace piped up eagerly.

"Oh? How is it your fault, Eustace?" said Isdemus, waiting their turn as the last of the nimbi and Watchers before him disappeared into the Grandfather Tree.

"Well, I… dunno, but I'm sure it is!"

"Don't listen to Eustace, sir, he was only following me," Peter sighed. "He was hoping to get in on an adventure."

"And he did at that," Anthony muttered.

"I don't know why you're all covering for me; it really is my fault," Cole insisted, almost angrily. Then he added in a tone of self-flagellation, "I'm a terrible person, sir. You should lock me in my chamber with only bread and water for a week!"

The corners of Isdemus's mouth twitched, and he favored Cole with a very brief glance of acknowledgment. "I will be sure to keep that punishment in mind for future offenses."

It was Isdemus's turn through the porthole next, and he stepped forward calmly as if taking a casual stroll down a lane. His body warped for a split second and then disappeared. Only the four boys, Verum and Bellator were left behind.

"Get going with you then," said Bellator roughly. "We're bringing up the rear."

"Trust us that much, eh?" said Peter weakly just as Eustace disappeared next.

"You've earned it, wouldn't you say?" Verum shot back, and Peter flushed.

As he stepped forward towards the Grandfather Tree, Newton gave a frantic meow at the unpleasant sensation. The next thing he knew, Peter lurched forward on the carpet in the Commuter Station, trying not to stumble to the ground from the sudden deceleration.

"To the side, Peter," said Isdemus, who waited for him a few paces down the hall, though most of the rest of the Watchers, Eustace, and the nimbi seemed to have cleared out already. He hastened to Isdemus's side.

"Supper is ready in the Great Hall," Isdemus said shortly. "After you have taken your supper, Peter, I request that you join me in my office on the third floor."

"Yes sir," Peter mumbled.

He turned to see Cole, Anthony, Verum and Bellator emerging behind him. Peter nearly turned back around towards the corridor when he saw another person emerge from the Commuter Station, whom he was quite certain had not been present in the forest moments before.

"Gladys?" he said, confused.

"Oh!" The maid hastily extinguished the torch she clutched in one hand and dropped it unceremoniously on the cold stone where the red carpet ended. She looked quite terrified at the sight of such a reception.

Isdemus heard her, too, and turned around in mild surprise.

"What are you doing here?" Peter persisted, "Did you just come back from somewhere?" He gestured at the other photos in the Commuter Station.

"No!" she said quickly. "No, of course not, I was just cleaning... I... excuse me!" she said, hurrying past them into the hallway. When she brushed past, Peter noticed that she walked very strangely, stooped over, and there was an irregular bulge beneath her apron. But before he had a chance to ask her about it, she was gone.

Cole frowned. "What was that all about?"

"Yeah, what is there to clean in here, anyway?" said Anthony.

Then after a pause, Isdemus said abruptly, "Please excuse me." He brushed past them and headed deeper into the Commuter Station, towards the blank wall. Peter longed to find out what he was doing, but the nimbi ushered the boys along such that he could not even turn around to look.

"I should head on home," Anthony mumbled. "My mum will be wondering where I am."

"Back here, then," Bellator said gruffly, redirecting Anthony again into the Commuter Station. "There are portraits to take you anywhere you like in the city." Anthony turned helplessly to Cole and Peter. Peter wanted to thank him, but it seemed inappropriate under the circumstances.

Once Peter, Cole, and Verum were in the

corridor again, Peter said, "I'll just go and drop Newton and my suitcase in my chamber. I'll be downstairs in a minute."

Verum grunted suspiciously, but nodded his consent.

"And... Verum?" Peter added, fumbling for words. "Thanks. For er, well..." he gestured at Verum's physical form.

Verum nodded. "I would die for you, Peter Stewart," he said, with no emotion.

Peter blinked at him, feeling extremely uncomfortable and even more ashamed. "Er, well... yeah. Thanks," he said again. Then he hurried towards the spiral staircase with Cole, anxious to get away.

When they turned onto the corridor where Peter's chamber was, they heard a frantic female voice exclaim ahead of them, "Peter!"

Lily ran towards him and before Peter knew what was happening, he dropped Newton instinctively as Lily threw her arms around his neck, nearly knocking him backwards.

"Whoa, there!" he said, surprised and pleased that at least someone wasn't mad at him. But she wasn't listening.

"Cole!" Lily exclaimed, pulling him too into a hug without releasing Peter. Then just as suddenly she let go of Cole and planted both hands on Peter's chest, shoving him away as hard as she could. "What the *hell* were you *thinking*?"

Before Peter had a chance to answer, another voice from behind them cried, "Cole!" Peter heard two more pairs of footsteps approach from the stairs, and the next thing he knew Mrs. Jefferson had thrown her arms around her younger son. Brock, who was with her, patted Cole on the shoulder, which was the only part he could reach. Mrs. Jefferson spoke to her son a mile a minute in near hysterics, but Peter wasn't listening.

Peter turned back to Lily and hastened to explain, "We went to get—"

"We *know* where you went, the other Watchers just told us," Lily snapped. "Of all the stupid, selfish…"

Through her diatribe, Peter could hear Mrs. Jefferson's sobs, which made him feel even worse.

"…and all for this?" Lily continued, kicking Peter's suitcase, arms still folded over her chest. "Really, Peter—!"

"I'm sorry, all right?" Peter yelled back, frustrated. He looked at the Jeffersons, running a hand through his unkempt blond hair. "You guys go downstairs; I'll meet you there in a minute." He deliberately turned his back on the group, and heard at least Cole and Mrs. Jefferson still talking and sobbing, respectively, as they headed back towards the staircase.

Once the other footsteps retreated and Peter shoved his door open, Lily persisted, "What got into you, anyway?"

Peter glared at her over his shoulder as Newton slipped between his legs and leapt on his four poster bed. "Did you just hang about to harangue me some more?" he snapped. "I don't know what else you want me to say."

"I want you to make sense! Why would you take

such a stupid risk with your life—never mind everybody else's!—just for a suitcase and a cat, who would have arrived safely within a few days anyway?"

"What are you always on my back about for, anyway?" Peter exploded, rounding on her. "One minute you're friends with me, then you're mad but you won't tell me why, then you're nagging me—I can't keep you happy no matter what, so why even bother?"

Lily looked like she'd been slapped, and Peter saw tears filling her eyes again. But this time he was having none of it.

"Oh, no you don't! That's not working on me this time!"

But it was too late; hot tears slipped over Lily's cheeks, and she sniffled and brushed them away with the back of one hand, wrapping the other arm around her waist and looking away from him, out the frosted windowpane to the dark grounds of the castle.

Peter turned away from her and unzipped his suitcase roughly, as if it had done him a personal insult. He began tossing clothes and books aggressively into his wardrobes, determined to ignore her tears. But it was hard, when he heard her sniffling every few seconds. He gritted his teeth. For one wild second, he heard Cole in his head. *Are you sure she's not into you?* But he dismissed the thought. He had no explanation for her behavior, but the idea that she might actually fancy him seemed the most outlandish of all.

Suddenly he felt a pair of arms snake around his

midsection from behind. Lily hugged him tight, pressing her face against his back. Too surprised to do anything else, Peter dropped the pair of jeans he was holding, turned around and wrapped his arms around her too. All the anger drained out of him at once, and he tried to ignore the strange fluttering in his stomach. Her hair smelled like vanilla, and his heart beat faster.

At last Peter admitted quietly, "I just wanted some sense of normalcy." He added, more gruffly than he'd intended, "Of all people, I'd have thought you'd understand that."

She looked up at him, her face flushed and her eyes still rimmed with redness. Suddenly embarrassed, she stepped back from him and wiped her face with the back of her hand again. "I do understand that."

"I didn't know it would be such a big deal," Peter added defensively, his anger flaring again for some unknown reason. He crossed his arms over his chest again, suddenly feeling very self-conscious and not sure what else to do with them. "I know I should have known, but I didn't, and I won't do it again. Happy?"

Something like a curtain fell over Lily's countenance. "You'd *better* not do it again," she said crisply. Then she turned on her heel and marched out of his chamber.

Chapter 17

Bruce was still absorbing the revelation of the Double Dragon at the round table in the castle of Ibn Alaam, the half-eaten mussaka sandwiches long since forgotten on the plates in front of the Watchers. The room seemed to grow hotter by the minute as the sun rose higher in the sky and beat down through the skylight up above. Beads of condensed sweat gathered and rolled down Bruce's sideburns, but he didn't bother to wipe them away. In his mind's eye, he saw a Kane who was really Sargon, his eyes black and ageless, pressing the blade of Excalibur against Peter's throat.

Bruce knew who would win that fight. They were hopelessly outmatched. He sank his head into his hands. If the Child of the Prophecy turned out to be Lily, at least she could fight. He had seen her at the Fata Morgana, and she was more than capable of holding her own. But Peter? He would certainly be a gonner. *And then I'd lose both of them.*

Abruptly, Sully pushed back from the table and stood up.

"Where are you going?" Bruce croaked.

"Back to Carlion to tell Isdemus about the Double Dragon."

"Don't you think he's already guessed?" Dan put in. "I expect that was what he was hinting about when he said Kane wasn't really dead, right after we all got back from the Fata Morgana."

"He probably suspected it the moment he found out they were born twins," Bruce murmured, a little nauseated. "I don't know why I didn't realize it myself. Didn't want to, I guess. But until a few days ago, I thought Jason died with Penny years ago." He used Kane's birth name, and his name cracked as he said it. Dan sat on his other side and reached out to pat him on the shoulder sympathetically. "This…" Bruce struggled to choke out the words. "This means in the end, it will be Peter who has to face Kane, doesn't it? Not Lily?"

"We don't know that," Dan said softly.

"But probably," said Jael. Dan shot her a withering look, and she widened her eyes and shrugged at him as if to say, *What? It's true!*

"You know," Bruce murmured as if he wasn't listening, "I had wondered why Isdemus didn't seem to be acting like Lily was a serious candidate even when we found out she fit the prophecy too. I'll bet this is why… because of the Double Dragon. He… he knows it has to be Peter, doesn't he?" He looked up at the other Watchers, desperate to be contradicted. But they all shifted uncomfortably, unsure how to comfort him.

"Even if Isdemus did think of that already, I think he ought to be told. Just in case," said Sully at last. He stood up and moved to the center of the room, as if heading for the door.

"Just a minute!" cried Bomani. "I think I should come with you. A message like this should also come from me, as the ranking Watcher in this room!" In reply, Sully extended a hand. Bomani took it warily, looking perplexed. "What… are we doing?"

"Warping," said Sully matter-of-factly. Before he could ask questions, Sully added, "You'll find out what it is in just a second." He began to mutter the Ancient Tongue under his breath, and they vanished.

Masika gaped at the spot where Sully and Bomani had been seconds before. "What just happened? Where did he go?" Masika demanded. "Did he go through the trap door?" She crouched on the floor as if to check.

"Oh, for heaven's sake. He's a space specialist!" Jael snapped.

"That's…" Masika swallowed. "That's not possible."

Dan breathed a warning, "Have some patience, Jael. This is new to them."

"Wait a minute," Bruce interrupted, staring off into the distance. Everyone turned to look at him. "There's another angle to this. Dragons represent chaos, right?" He looked at Masika for support.

"Yes," she said carefully, still half-glancing at the spot where Sully had been standing.

"Well, there's something in physics called the

Chaos Theory," Bruce went on slowly.

"Oh, brother," Jael rolled her eyes, but Masika leaned across the table, interested.

"Go on," Masika encouraged.

Jael muttered, "Don't worry, he will."

Bruce ignored her. "In Chaos Theory, you don't match strength for strength. The smallest amount of force, correctly applied, can subvert the most powerful of systems. It's called the Butterfly Effect."

"Like in martial arts, when you use your opponent's strength against him?" Masika nodded.

Bruce agreed, "Precisely. The Butterfly Effect is a reference to the idea that a butterfly flapping its wings on one side of the world can create a disturbance that can become a hurricane on the other side of the world. But you're right, the same idea applies to martial arts. A single hand thrust without even a great deal of force can kill your opponent if it's delivered in exactly the right spot—"

Jael interrupted, "Bruce, this is terribly interesting, but it's not getting us any closer to finding the Philosopher's Stone. I vote we go to the library now."

"I disagree, Jael," Bruce insisted. "This theory is critical to discussing the strategy by which the war against chaos is to be fought! We can't just match strength for strength!"

"So we'll talk about that when we're actually *fighting* a war against chaos. But right now we're trying to find a stone. So let's get going," said Jael, pushing back her chair.

"No!" Bruce said sharply, and everyone turned to him in stunned surprise. Bruce was ever the easy-going one; no one could remember him asserting himself like that before. "We're talking about my kids here," he said finally, his voice quavering.

Masika laid a hand on Bruce's shoulder gently, but it was Dan who spoke.

"We all love Peter and Kane too," he said quietly. Jael shot him a look and raised her eyebrows. Dan understood that she was accusing him of bending the truth a little with reference to Kane, but he ignored her. "But for now, finding the Philosopher's Stone *is* our strategy. It's what Isdemus sent us here to do. If we can get it before the Shadow Lord does, we won't have to worry about Chaos Theory."

Bruce looked away, breathing in and out, trying to banish the awful image from his mind. "And if we can't?"

There was a long pause before Dan answered, "Well... this conversation will be relevant then."

"But let's hope that never happens," agreed Masika.

After a long silence, Bruce nodded.

"I will show you the way to the library," said Masika, delicately pushing back from the table. She led the way, with Dan on her heels.

Jael caught Dan's collar and pulled him back roughly.

"Ow! What?"

Jael waited until Bruce and Masika were far enough ahead that they wouldn't be overheard. Then she hissed under her breath, "I don't trust her."

Dan blinked at her, confused. "Why not?" They trailed behind the others inside the semi-darkness of the tunnel, which was rough looking, as if it had been hewn out of the side of a mountain.

"She doesn't believe in the gifts. As a matter of fact, she doesn't believe in anything!"

"Watch it!" said Dan, putting his hand over Jael's forehead just in time to protect her from colliding with a protruding bit of tunnel, and scraping the flesh off his knuckles in the process. He instinctively put his fingers in his mouth to tend his injury and whispered, "You were the one who said we shouldn't worry about that right now because we have bigger fish to fry, remember?"

Jael shook her head. "I know, but I'm not sure I trust the interpretation of any ancient documents by a woman who doesn't even believe in the Ancient Tongue!"

"Jael, she knows what she's talking about. She can cut our investigation time in half. End of discussion." Jael opened her mouth to protest, but Dan quickened his pace to outstrip her before she could, passing Bruce as well and eventually falling into step with Masika. Jael huffed at his retreating figure indignantly.

Presently Jael joined Bruce, forcing herself to forget the disagreement with Dan. "You okay?" she whispered gruffly.

"I've been preparing myself for this for Peter's whole life," he said. "But now it turns out I might lose both of my sons."

Jael thought for a minute. "I know," she said.

187

"But you already thought Jason died when he was four, until a week ago."

Bruce sighed roughly, and ran a hand through his cowlicked brown hair. "It's like going through it all over again."

"Even though none of us ever exactly *liked* Kane," Jael went on, and then added quickly, "No offense."

Bruce laughed shortly, his laugh echoing through the halls such that the others all turned around to look at them. Masika turned sharply to the right and Dan disappeared behind her.

"None taken," said Bruce. "Honestly I was never fond of him myself. I just wonder how different our relationship might have been, had I known..."

"Isdemus knew what he was doing," Jael cut him off firmly.

"I'm not questioning Isdemus," said Bruce, annoyed.

They fell silent for another few paces. Then Jael muttered with a bit of an edge to her voice, "I'm not good at this sort of thing. Comfort."

"Well," said Bruce. "At least you're trying. Besides, your gift is strength. Those two probably don't mix."

Jael gave a little snort, as the ground sloped down steeply, forcing them to walk on the balls of their feet to keep from sliding forward. "I'll bet Masika would be good at comfort. She seems like the gushy type."

Bruce arched an eyebrow at her. "If I didn't know better, Jael, I'd say you were jealous."

Jael was silent.

"You know," whispered Bruce, like he was changing the subject, "when a system is confined to a certain predictable pattern, the way to break out of it is to open it up to new possibilities. In Chaos Theory this is called adding 'degrees of freedom.' Once the degrees of freedom reach a certain critical point, different outcomes become possible, where they were impossible before."

"That's great, Bruce," Jael murmured, rolling her eyes.

Bruce regarded her for a moment and then said bluntly, "Why do you keep refusing Dan?"

Jael blanched. "*Shh!*" Reflexively her eyes darted to Dan and Masika, up ahead.

"Oh, they can't hear us," Bruce waved a hand at them offhandedly. Sure enough, neither of them had missed a beat. Then he prompted again, "So? How come you keep turning him down?"

"Because, Dan is... well, *Dan*," she whispered back helplessly, like that explained it. "Don't get me wrong," Jael persisted, "I'd die for him. I just can't imagine..." She shook her head and stared absently at Dan's back, and she wiped a bead of sweat off her forehead which had condensed in the stagnant, sweltering air.

Up ahead, Masika stopped beside a recessed door and withdrew a key from beneath her blouse. Jael stopped walking to keep enough space between them, and lowered her voice even further as she confessed, "Honestly, I'm not sure I can imagine being with anyone again."

Bruce shrugged, and cautioned, "Just make sure that's really what you want."

Masika giggled at something Dan said and he put his hand on the small of her back to guide her through the open door. Jael bit her lip and looked away.

Chapter 18

Isdemus had not been in the Great Hall for dinner, for which Peter had been both relieved and dismayed, since he knew that later that evening, he would be alone with him. It would have been much better to ease the awkwardness beforehand in a public setting. Lily, at least, seemed to think Isdemus intended to reprimand him further in his office that night. Peter assumed so too, but Lily was irritatingly smug about it.

After dinner Peter walked slowly up to Isdemus's office, lost in painful thought. He winced as he recalled Verum's vow: *I would die for you, Peter Stewart.* For a moment, he wondered what had happened to Achen. Was he back from Avalon yet? Peter had almost forgotten that the nimbi could be killed if they took physical form. He hoped Achen was all right.

Peter took a deep breath, his knuckles hovering over Isdemus's deep cherry wood door before he found the courage to make contact with it.

"Come," said the voice from within.

Once Peter pushed open the door, he blinked for a moment in the half-light of the flickering torches. The study was large and bizarre, filled with plush velvet armchairs and a mahogany desk, which was stacked with texts of very ancient-looking manuscripts. Every inch of wall space was likewise covered with bookcases and books, labeled things like "Alchemy and You: How to Get the Most from the Elements of the Earth," "Everything You Ever Wanted to Know about Hyperspace," and "101 Ways to Unlock the Potential of the Universe." There were a pair of brass eyeglasses with coke bottle lenses, lying next to an open text on Morse code, a bright copper kettle on its side next to a chipped porcelain cup of half-drunk tea, an entire wall of jars stuffed with herbs, a slide ruler, protractor, abacus, and a globe of the earth that still showed a land bridge between Alaska and Asia.

For a moment Peter forgot his dread of the confrontation with Isdemus and blurted, "I know this place!"

Isdemus looked up from his desk and peered at Peter over his steepled fingers. "Oh?"

"I mean, I haven't been here before, but it looks just like how my dad used to describe Merlyn's study... except it was supposed to be in the Tower Room." Silently, Peter added, *where Kane used to live*.

Peter was surprised to see Isdemus smile, though it did not reach his eyes. "Indeed," he said. "You are right that Merlyn owned these things, and also that he used to live in the Tower Room in Arthur's day. He loved astronomy, you see, and the Tower Room naturally provided the best view of the stars. Just after the fall of Camelot, Merlyn became the head of the Order of the Paladin, and his study has been considered the official headquarters ever since. However, in 1500 years, you must allow for the rearrangement of furniture."

"You didn't prefer the Tower Room to the third floor, sir?"

"Oh, no, I certainly do prefer it," said Isdemus, smiling more genuinely this time, "but I did not want to force my visitors to climb all 492 steps to the top every time they wished to speak with me."

Peter nodded, suddenly feeling awkward again. He shuffled his feet, wondering whether he should take a seat or wait to be offered one. Finally he said, "Sir, about tonight—"

But Isdemus held up a hand to silence him. "We have already discussed it. It is in the past now. Please." He gestured to one of the plush velvet chairs, and Peter took it gratefully, even as Isdemus stood up and began to walk around the study, idly fingering his strange instruments and inadvertently drawing Peter's attention to them as he moved. "You are probably wondering why I called you here, Peter. There are things that you specifically need to learn which I do not believe Paladin High can teach you, as marvelous as the rest of its education may be. For instance," he let go of the abacus, which he had been thumbing a moment before, and turned to face Peter, "the fact that you can reverse entropy, and that you are, as Bruce put it, like a 'battery pack.' You are capable of tapping into an unlimited resource, but unless I am much mistaken, you do not yet know how to do it on command."

Peter's heart beat faster, and he leaned forward. "You mean you can teach me?"

"I *may* be able to teach you," Isdemus corrected. "After all, nobody like you has existed since before the Great Deception, so there is no curriculum designed for a person of your talents. However, there is a great deal of theory that we have never before had the occasion to test." At this, he rested his hand on a stack of very worn-looking books on his desk, most of them hand-bound and falling apart, in varying shades of brown and black. "For many centuries, the Watchers had hoped that when the Child of the Prophecy came along, he would discover his or her gifts on their own and would have no need of instruction. However, it now appears that we may not have the luxury of time to enable that to happen." Isdemus looked away, his expression troubled.

"But it could still be Lily, right?" Peter asked nervously. "Sir?" He still wasn't at all sure he wanted it to be her either, but the idea that she was completely out of the runnings and it was him for sure made him queasy.

Peter's unanswered question hung in the air. Isdemus turned back towards him and changed the subject. "After the fateful accident which brought you and your friends here, Peter, you described a Meadow. Tell me about that Meadow again."

"Yes sir," said Peter. He described again the still

water and the trees, unruffled by a breeze of any sort. He told him how the rainbow emanated from the surface of the water, and each color showed a different version of reality.

"And what's beyond the rainbow?" Isdemus prodded.

Peter blinked. "What do you mean, sir?"

"Do the colors just continue out forever once they emerge from the pool, or do they all merge together at some point?"

"I…" Peter paused. "I don't know. I never looked."

"I suppose I can understand that. You've always been in crisis when you've been in the Meadow before." Isdemus rubbed his chin through his long white beard.

"Why do you think the colors would merge, sir?"

Isdemus stood once more and began to pace as he mused aloud. "This is only a guess," he said. "But what you describe sounds as if the colors represent the possible outcomes for the present moment. When you choose one, I expect the colors might merge into a white line."

Peter blinked at him. "Because when the quantum wave function collapses, all of the colors of the rainbow would condense to a single outcome!" he declared, wide-eyed. "And the entire spectrum of visible light combined forms pure white!"

Isdemus nodded, still pacing. "If there is such a line—and there should be—then inside of that Meadow, you would be able to relive your past."

Peter could hardly breathe. He gripped the sides

of the upholstered chair so tightly his knuckles were white.

"I think it is time to test this hypothesis." Isdemus walked around to the front of his desk and leaned on it, facing Peter. "Here is what I want you to do. Do you see my lenses there?" He indicated the coke-bottle lenses that Peter had noticed on first entering. "I want you to lift them. Using the Ancient Tongue."

"I haven't learned the Ancient Tongue for air manipulation yet, sir." *I haven't learned the Ancient Tongue for anything,* he added to himself.

"Ah, quite. The words are *spéaclaí eitilt.* But when you say it, I want you to take my hand. Then when you get to the Meadow, before you choose any of the colors in the rainbow and dive into the pool, I want you to speak my name, out loud."

Peter looked at him quizzically but did as he was told, fastening his hand around Isdemus's bony fingers.

"Now, repeat after me, Peter. *Spéaclaí eitilt."*

"Spe-a-cli ee-tilt—" Peter repeated slowly, watching Isdemus's face.

"Focus on the lenses, Peter, not on me. Try again."

Peter sounded out the vowels a number of times, but after the third try he felt Isdemus's grip tighten on his hand, and then suddenly—

Daylight filtered through the trees though it was nighttime in Carlion, and Peter could not see any direct source of light. The trees were eternally still, and there was the pool, drawing him, reflecting the cheerful colors of the rainbow from its surface.

Isdemus stood beside him, blinking in wonder with an expression much like a small child discovering the world for the first time. "Magnificent," he murmured, letting go of Peter's arm and looking around. "Truly indescribable…"

"I can bring other people here?" said Peter in wonder.

"I suspected you could," said Isdemus, still distracted as he moved back towards the pond in the clearing, "but I did not know whether it would be by touch, as at the Fata Morgana, or by using one's true name in the Ancient Tongue. It seems that by touch one may access your power in more ways than one." As he said this, Isdemus waved his hand through the colors of the rainbow as easily as through the image of a projector. He shook his head in amazement.

Peter turned around to see if there really was a white line.

There was. His mouth fell open.

Isdemus turned with him, and smiled. "So it is true. This *is* the Space of Possibilities…"

"Space of Possibilities?" Peter repeated, still staring at the white line.

"You call it the Meadow, for obvious reasons, Peter. But in the literature, previous members of the Watchers have referred to this place as the Space of Possibilities, because to them it was just an idea, a strange kind of physical reality just in the middle between a possible and an actual event. Bruce tells me that scientific theory describes it as Superspace."

Peter blinked at Isdemus. "That can't be."

Isdemus raised his eyebrows at Peter. "I wonder that you are capable of pronouncing the word 'can't' in a place like this."

Peter shook his head again and said, "But look! The images in the rainbow only show the lenses, because that's what I just spoke to, and they only show them flying in various directions, because I told them to fly. But Superspace is meant to be a place of *infinite* possibilities. I mean, if such a place exists, I could…"

Isdemus smiled at him. "You could what, Peter?"

"I could turn the lenses into a lump of lead if I wanted, or gold, or water, or anything else! I could condense them so tightly that they'd form a black hole, and suck the entire castle into oblivion! In Superspace you're not bounded by ordinary rules—you can rearrange atomic structures, you can—"

"Perform alchemy?" said Isdemus, twinkling at him. "Transmute one form of matter into another?"

Peter's mouth hung open but he didn't reply.

"This," said Isdemus, stretching his arms wide and turning in a slow circle, drinking everything in, "*is* the Space of Possibilities, Peter. Here, you are limited only by what you can conceive of. The night of the accident, you were fortunate to have studied entropy, such that you knew it *could* be reversed, however unlikely. The idea occurred to you, and you chose it. Because you had already seen entropy reverse once, when the mirrors ruptured in the Fata Morgana, you thought of it again, and reversed entropy a second time. But there were in fact an infinite number of ways that the same scenario might have resolved in your favor. Can you think of no others?"

Peter blinked at him. "I suppose… I could have turned the mirror shards into drops of water…"

Isdemus nodded. "Or you could have introduced a strong breeze to blow them off course, so that they fell harmlessly into the Lake of Avalon. You could even have caused them to dissociate spontaneously in a puff of smoke!"

"But if it's not in the rainbow…" Peter began.

Isdemus smiled at him and Peter had a sense that he had just said something very silly. "What you see in the rainbow is nothing more than what you expect to see, Peter. Some of that is determined by the words you already spoke—you told the lenses to fly, and so you see the lenses flying. But you could have told them to heat up, or to condense, or to do anything else you liked. All of those possibilities exist, all the time. The difference is whether or not you see them."

He shook his head slowly. "I don't under—"

"You think there are only seven colors in the rainbow?" Isdemus interrupted, pointing again at the colors emanating from the pond. "Look closely."

Peter obediently leaned forward. Sure enough, he saw that as he focused on each individual color, infinite variations expanded before him between each different shade.

"In the accident and in the Fata Morgana, you saw variations of force, Peter, and reversal of entropy, because that's what you were looking for. That's what you expected to see. Think of something, anything you can imagine, that might happen to my lenses. But keep in mind that I *like* those lenses, so I'd rather they weren't destroyed," he added, with a hint of a smile.

Peter bit his lip. "They could... erm... get bigger?"

"Certainly they could!" Isdemus beamed at him. "That can happen in one of two ways, of course. Either you can add matter to them by taking it from another article in the room, or you can simply increase the size of the molecules that comprise the lenses already."

Peter thought of Professor Vane's sponge-like cheekbones and his mouth twitched.

"Now, with that in mind, look into the images of the rainbow and see if anything looks different," said Isdemus. Peter obeyed, and gasped. This time, he saw slightly different shades of color but the same rainbow, and in each image, the lenses (which still hovered over Isdemus's desk, as commanded) had swelled to look rather like a balloon.

"Those options were there all the time?" Peter demanded.

"It is all a matter of where you place your focus," said Isdemus, nodding with approval. "You cannot select from possibilities that you are not aware of."

Peter turned back to stare at the rainbow, imagining this time that the lenses spun in the air like a top. The images suddenly changed, as did the shades that depicted them, such that the lenses spun obediently. Next he imagined that the molecules turned to liquid and spilled hot brass and silica fluid on Isdemus's desk, eating a hole right through the mahogany.

"Very good, but I'm afraid I like my desk too," said Isdemus, amused. "We can practice this more later." Next he took Peter by the shoulders and turned him away from the pond and towards the trees, in the direction of the white line. "Now if you don't mind, I am quite curious…"

Peter still felt dazed. Isdemus was already walking on ahead of him and Peter stared after him, following almost unconsciously. "I can do… *anything*…" he murmured to himself, trying to grasp the concept.

"Come, Peter!" called Isdemus, hurrying through the trees and leaping over roots like a man half his age. The white line to their right persisted as they followed it through the trees, which all seemed strangely similar to one another. Peter had an uncanny feeling that they were running through an infinite loop, and would never reach the end because there was no end…

"I'm not out of breath!" Peter cried out after some time, noticing that he was capable of running without the unpleasant sensation of exertion for the first time in his life.

"Of course you're not, Peter. This is the Space of Possibilities, not of Reality!"

"But," Peter rushed to catch up, "Sir—"

"Here, Peter," said Isdemus, holding up a hand to stop him.

Peter blinked at the spot on the white line that Isdemus had indicated. It seemed indistinguishable from every other point, and the line seemed to stretch onward for as far as the eye could see, through an endless forest of identical trees. "Why here?"

Isdemus smiled at him, his eyes reflecting the singular white gleam. "Why not?"

"But how do we… you know… get in there? There's no pool to dive into…"

"I would guess—and this is only a guess, Peter—that the purpose of the pool is to select an outcome. But this is the past. You cannot select for the past because it has already happened, so there is no need for a pool. But that should not hinder you from viewing it, in the same way you were able to view the possibilities in the rainbow just now…"

"So… this is like the movie theater of my life?" said Peter, suddenly feeling uncomfortable. He wished he could privately preview the spot Isdemus had chosen, just in case he happened to have been on the toilet or something.

"It may be," said Isdemus, "but I must admit that I'm hoping it's more than that. Go on, give it a try."

Relieved that Isdemus gave him his privacy at first, Peter stepped forward and peered as hard as he could at the white line. It expanded obediently, but it did not change. It was still as white and as blank as ever. "I don't see anything." When Isdemus did not reply, Peter looked back at him over his shoulder and saw, to his surprise, that Isdemus was smiling triumphantly. "Is… that a good thing?"

"Maybe," said Isdemus. "Were you expecting to see yourself?"

"Yes," said Peter blankly. "I figured this was a timeline of my life…"

"Try something different this time. Try thinking

of your father instead."

Peter was still confused, but he did what he was told. "I—I see him!" he stammered, stunned. "He's—blimey, he looks about twenty, and he's in a shabby little dormitory—" Peter stopped and pulled back, the full weight of what he was seeing beginning to click. "The reason I didn't see myself when I looked the first time was because I wasn't born yet!"

"Precisely," said Isdemus, sounding as if he were trying to control his excitement. "Peter, this is... stupendous. Do you realize what we have here? In theory we can watch *all of history* unfold in this space of yours! Granted, finding any particular moment in time from this homogenous line may be like finding a needle in a haystack..."

"But isn't that just like reading books written in the Ancient Tongue?" said Peter, remembering his first experience in the secret library, in which he had entered King Arthur's mind. "Were those not memories from history as well?"

"No, those were merely interpretations based on our best guess of what happened from the memories we have been able to collect," said Isdemus, his voice still trembling. "But this, Peter..." He turned away from him and began to muse aloud. "I wonder if there is a way to parse through in order to quickly find a particular moment in time?"

"You mean, could we find out what happened to the Philosopher's Stone?" said Peter shrewdly. Isdemus looked stunned for a moment before a knowing smile crossed his face.

"I see that once again I have given you too little

credit."

"That *is* what they're after, then? My dad and the other Watchers?"

"Yes, Peter, that is what they're after. And I'm afraid they're not the only ones."

"What do you mean?" Peter said quickly.

"I am not certain yet, but I can say that tonight I discovered the first bit of hard evidence that someone else may already be on its trail. Both fortunately and unfortunately, both sides are at this time forced to decipher clues left through the ages that have never yet yielded results. But perhaps this place of yours may tip the scales in our favor." Isdemus pursed his lips, and then frowned. "The problem is, how to find what we want to know?"

"Could you just speak the name of the person you want to watch?" said Peter.

"I could," said Isdemus slowly. "The problem is that I do not know who to watch. And if I did, most likely it would be a penumbra. I cannot speak the true name in the Ancient Tongue of one of the penumbra or I would risk inviting him here, much like speaking the name of the nimbi serves as a summons."

"We could try it with someone who's dead first," Peter suggested. "Like... well, the last person we know of who had the Stone was Arthur's sister Morgan, right?"

"Yes, but Morgan was her common name, and not her name in the Ancient Tongue," said Isdemus in the same half-distracted tone of voice, as he began to walk further down the white line. "Additionally, from the memories we have collected, she died in the process of converting the Castle of Avalon into the Fata Morgana, and the Stone remained in the field she left behind. But it is not there now."

Peter followed him, beginning to feel frustrated. "Well, I'm out of ideas."

"Peter, take my hand," said Isdemus suddenly, holding his arm out to Peter, who was too surprised to do anything else. Then Isdemus said very loudly and clearly, *"Sibhialtacht an chéad!"*

Peter couldn't have described the sensation if he'd tried. It wasn't like going through a porthole exactly, because that implied movement through space, and he knew they weren't actually *in* space. The scenery didn't change at all—he was still surrounded by what appeared to be exactly the same trees, with exactly the same infinite white line to his right that had been present before. And yet, he knew in some way he couldn't explain that they had moved.

"What did you just say?" Peter asked.

"I said 'Great Deception,'" said Isdemus, releasing Peter's hand. "We know that the Shadow Lord, when he was human, was the first king ever to rule on the earth. But unfortunately, because he ruled prior to the Great Deception, his human name and his true name were the same. And of course, now that he is a spirit, you know what happens if you say that name aloud."

"Yeah," Peter said quickly, remembering the swarm of penumbra descending upon him and Kane on Monte Alban, moments before they had found themselves on the banks of Avalon.

"But moments ago, when you only thought of Bruce as you looked into the white line, he was the one you saw. So what I want you to do now is to concentrate on the Shadow Lord, but do not speak his name. I will do the same. Are you ready?"

Peter nodded, feeling his heart begin to race once more. He pictured the bloodless, disembodied face he had seen reflected in the surface of the water in the Fata Morgana, feeling a cold chill race up his spine as he did so. Then he looked at Isdemus, whose deeply lined face regarded him with childlike eyes glimmering with anticipation. He was the very embodiment of timelessness, and seemed to belong in this place of the infinite. "Ready when you are, sir."

And then, together, they stepped forward.

Chapter 19: circa 10,500 BC

Peter and Isdemus were transported to a primitive forest. The water flowed quietly over rocks along the creek bed, beneath the canopy of a thousand enormous trees. Crickets chirped softly and the wind rustled the leaves. Ahead of them stood three figures in a little triangle. Two were obviously penumbra, transparent, and they stood with their backs to Isdemus and Peter: a siren and a hag. The other was a man, whom Peter could see plainly. He looked barely twenty-five, with deep-set eyes, a sunken chest and a surly expression. Peter could tell they were all speaking the Ancient Tongue, and yet in this place, he understood them anyway.

"Go on now, what are you waiting for?" hissed the hag to the human. "Make the vow!" It leaned towards him, hands outstretched like he was ready to pounce.

But the man did not look threatened in the least. His beetle-black eyes glinted back hungrily. "Very well," he murmured, his voice trembling. "I, Sargon, King of Mesopotamia, grant you, the penumbra, the power of the Ancient Tongue on behalf of all my subjects—in exchange for absolute power and eternal life!"

Peter shuddered as if he had a chill, and looked at Isdemus, who was too riveted upon the scene to pay him any notice.

Then Sargon's face clouded, as if something was wrong. He clutched his throat. Then he began to squawk.

The siren started to laugh musically. "Excellent!" she cried. "Most splendid! Quick, Vortigem," she turned to the hag, "Command something! Command the stream to dry up; try that!"

Happily, the sallow hag focused upon the stream and cried in a resounding voice, "*Sruth tirim suas*!"

But nothing happened.

He blinked, and looked at the siren, perplexed. Then he tried again.

"*Sruth tirim suas*!"

But he got the same result.

"You try!" he demanded of the siren as he turned a seething expression on Sargon. Sargon continued to squawk, glaring back at Vortigem dangerously.

The siren turned her gaze upon a rock instead, and commanded it, "*Eitilt*!" But nothing happened.

Sargon roared in frustration, and Vortigem stomped the ground. "How is it that it isn't working for either of us?" he demanded of the siren. But she did not look back at him. She began to pace, thinking. It was then that Peter got a good look at her: she was tiny, with black hair, violet eyes, and skin like porcelain. Something about her manner demonstrated that she was clearly the leader.

"Sir," Peter whispered to Isdemus, "who is she?"

Isdemus wrenched his eyes away long enough to reply. "That," he said, not bothering to speak in a whisper, "is the future queen of Camelot."

"Guinevere?" Peter gasped. But Isdemus put a finger to his lips to indicate that they should keep listening.

"Because," Guinevere said at last in reply to the hag's question, "we have only completed half of the bargain. Come, Vortigem!"

She tore off through the forest at a breakneck pace, Vortigem following after, and Sargon had no choice but to run along behind them, wheezing asthmatically through his concave ribcage.

"Where are you going, Your Viciousness?" called Vortigem after Guinevere, irritably. He passed right through a large tree root without stumbling. Behind him, Sargon tripped on it and let out an angry, unintelligible cry.

"Taking him to the Stone!" came Guinevere's reply. "He will know what to do when he sees it!"

They emerged at the top of a hill still thick with trees, where a clearing was marked with several large, flat stones erected in a small stone circle.

Vortigem grinned. "I never knew this was here! Did the Venerables put it here?" he asked. When Guinevere nodded, he asked, "Where does the vortex connect to?"

"You'll see."

The two creatures stopped moving to give the stumbling lad a chance to catch up to them, and then Guinevere gestured him forward. He looked at them both warily, and the hag's smile stretched wide across its face.

"After you," it said. Sargon grunted in reply, but stepped into the center of the circle. And then—

The scene melted into a broad grassy platform, like an ancient observatory. Guinevere and Vortigem walked to a particular spot facing the eastern horizon and stopped.

"We. Want. You. To. *Dig*," said Vortigem with a grandiose shoveling motion, "Right. Here!" He pointed to the ground with several large sweeping motions.

In response, Sargon lashed out, his fist swinging right through the hag's transparent body. Guinevere laughed scornfully, and Sargon howled with rage. Once he calmed down, though, Sargon seemed to understand what the penumbra wanted him to do. Since he had no alternative, he crouched down on his hands and knees and scooped the moist soil out by fistfuls. Presently his breathing slowed to a more regular rhythm, and his brow began to relax.

Sargon went on digging until the hole was large enough that he could stand in it, and it covered him to his waist. Once or twice he stopped altogether and shook his head vigorously, indicating that he refused to do any more, but the penumbra regarded him with infuriatingly superior smiles and motioned for him to continue.

Suddenly Sargon froze, and his expression changed from a vague scowl to an almost hungry gaze as he stared down into the bottom of the pit. He bent down, snatching something out of the earth.

"Let's have a look, then!" wheezed the hag greedily. He moved around to Sargon's other side to gaze at the small prize from above. It was blood-red and semi-transparent, reflecting and refracting the light of the sun off its perfectly spherical shape.

After a long moment, while Sargon just stared at the stone, Vortigem's expression changed from greed to a scowl. "How can he use it without any language?" he demanded.

"The Stone will make sure he understands what it requires," Guinevere murmured again with bated breath. She leaned forward eagerly.

Sargon crouched motionless in the pit for what seemed like an eternity. Then, unexpectedly, he withdrew a dagger from a sheath around his waist. He held it above his own chest for a moment, a fleeting expression of terror in his sunken black eyes.

Then he plunged the dagger straight into his heart, and crumpled into the earth with a soft cry.

"…You see?" Guinevere whispered. "He knew exactly what it required."

Seconds later, a new figure rose from the mouth of the grave, ethereal and bloodless. It resembled the Sargon from moments before, but it seemed not so much immortal as undead.

"Where is my body?" it demanded. The voice was different now, much higher and colder than it had been before. It sounded exactly like the one Peter remembered from the Fata Morgana, and it sent chills down his spine.

Guinevere grinned at him sweetly. "You told the Stone you wanted to become immortal. But in order to perform the transaction, you had to give it something to work with."

Sargon's specter floated upward and hovered over the ground without bothering to climb out of the pit.

"You lied to me!" he hissed.

"We did not lie," Guinevere returned pleasantly. "You told us you wanted immortality with ultimate control. Through you, all mankind lost their power, along with their language. Through us, you alone have gained back both... or you will have done, once you find a willing human host."

Sargon clenched his semi-transparent fists. "First you stole my language," he whispered. "Then you stole my life!" He moved ghost-like towards Guinevere, his ethereal nose nearly touching her nose of flesh and his words dripping with hate. "I shall make you another vow. The only power you will ever enjoy through me shall come at the price of your total allegiance. You and your kind shall serve me for all eternity!"

***

Peter felt a hand on his arm first, and then the grassy plain dissolved into the Meadow. He blinked for a moment, disoriented by the peaceful trees in stark contrast to the scene he had just witnessed.

"That... that was the Great Deception!"

"Yes, Peter," said Isdemus.

"We just saw... *him*. Before he was ever, well... *him*!" Peter was surprised at how normal Sargon had looked. He was not at all the disembodied face

Peter remembered from the Fata Morgana, until he became the shadowy specter.

"We also saw the original location of the Philosopher's Stone, Peter." Isdemus's voice was soft, but his blue eyes danced with excitement.

Peter blinked at him uncertainly. "But it was just a grassy field. It could have been anywhere!"

"No, it could not. Not anywhere," Isdemus corrected. "Only a handful of landmarks on the earth have terrain exactly like that."

"Where could it have been then?" Peter demanded, and Isdemus looked down at him archly, so he flushed and added, "Sir."

"I hesitate to bring up your behavior tonight, since I've already told you that it is forgiven," said Isdemus, moving back towards the trees with a swish, "but not forgotten. In our relatively brief acquaintance you have proven to me twice that you have a certain tendency towards recklessness."

"I won't go after it on my own!" Peter blurted hastily.

Isdemus stopped walking and turned to Peter with a look so intense that Peter felt completely exposed. It was as if the lie flashed in neon lights on his forehead. Peter finally dropped his gaze from Isdemus's in shame. Then Isdemus turned his back on Peter again and headed through the trees, towards the pond.

Well, I wouldn't, Peter told himself, a bit defensively. *Not unless there was a really good reason.*

But there *was* a really good reason. If he turned out to be the Child of the Prophecy, then he would need that Stone. It would virtually guarantee that his side would win… and that he, Peter, would not fail them.

But of course, Isdemus wanted to find the Stone quite as much as Peter did, and his dad was already on the case. *Why should I get involved?* Peter asked himself, more to convince himself he shouldn't than anything else.

He knew the answer, though. As much as Peter wanted everything to just go back to normal, he knew it couldn't. So if Isdemus told him where the Stone was, he would have to go after it. *And I'd probably bring Anthony, too,* he added to himself. Who knew when Anthony's elaborate lies might come in handy?

When they arrived, Isdemus gestured at the images of the molten lenses in the rainbow. "I'm fond of this particular shade of lavender," Isdemus mused. "I once had robes in that color. Also, the lenses are not utterly destroyed in the lavender image. Come, Peter." Without waiting for Peter's reply, he leapt into a spry swan dive and disappeared into the water with barely a splash.

Seconds later, Peter was back in Isdemus's office, and Isdemus began to pace as if they had never left the room. Abruptly, he said, "I'm afraid I must cut this meeting short now."

"Why?" Peter asked, although he knew that he was unlikely to get an answer.

As Peter expected, Isdemus did not reply, but only held open the door for Peter to exit. Peter hesitated, weighing his curiosity for what Isdemus planned to do next against whether he dared to challenge Isdemus's wishes again, considering what had happened earlier that night.

Finally he decided not to push his luck. He left the study without another word, and Isdemus closed the door behind him.

Chapter 20

The next morning, Lily tried everything she could think of to convince Peter to tell her what he and Isdemus had talked about the night before, barely hiding her smirk of satisfaction. She was sure that Isdemus had punished him in some way for his foolish trip into Norwich. But Peter disappointed her by evading her questions. He still wasn't sure what he should and should not tell her.

Peter was still lost in thought about the Philosopher's Stone, the white line of history, and the fact that he could invite others to the Meadow with him as he rode to Carlion with the others for school the next day. Cole and Lily rode a bit ahead of him, while Brock straggled behind. Brock seemed quiet too. Cole, meanwhile, kept up a steady chatter with Lily about the upcoming lesson in Professor Crane's class—Professor Crane had promised they were going to merge with one another's red blood cells that day.

"Will you *please* stop talking about this?" Lily finally begged Cole.

Cole raised his eyebrows. "Why?" he asked, amazed. "Aren't you excited?"

"No! I don't like blood."

Cole started to laugh, incredulous. "How can you be squeamish and also fight like you did in the Fata Morgana?" Peter heard a twinge of admiration in his voice.

"Well, that's different, isn't it!" she insisted, "that was life or death! This is just... blood for the sake of blood." She shuddered.

Brock tuned in at this point, and informed Lily importantly, "You wouldn't last a day at football practice back at King's, then. Somebody always needs stitches or loses a tooth or ruptures a spleen..."

Cole scoffed. "That's such bunk, Brock. That barely happens once a season."

"He's just trying to seem macho. Aren't you, *Romeo*?" Lily added scornfully.

That jarred Peter out of his thoughts. "Romeo?" he looked at Brock, amused. "You actually went to the auditions yesterday? She cast you as *Romeo*?"

Brock flushed. "I don't know yet. The list gets posted today," he muttered. When all three of them burst out in derisive laughter, Brock snapped, "I'm just trying something new, shut your faces!"

Cole snickered quietly to Peter. "Should we tell him that the men in Shakespeare's plays wear tights?" he whispered, just as Lily simpered in a breathy, affected tone, "Oh, Romeo, Romeo, wherefore art thou Romeo?"

"As if I'd ever play Romeo opposite *you*!" Brock shot back furiously.

"As if I'd ever audition in the first place!" Lily retorted, laughing.

Cole managed to choke out through his laughter, "What would Richard and Harry say if they could see you now?"

"They'd spread the word that drama was cool, because everything I do is cool by definition!"

Cole was about to fall off his horse he was laughing so hard, and Brock turned almost purple with anger. Peter only smiled rather vaguely, still distracted. But the part of him that attended to the conversation felt almost sorry for Brock. He thought he understood how Brock must feel, because it was very much the way he felt himself: like a fish out of water. At the same time, Peter marveled that he was even capable of feeling sympathetic towards Brock Jefferson, of all people.

Maybe Isdemus is right, Peter thought. *Maybe anything* is *possible…*

Anthony met them in the hallway when they arrived at Paladin High, and escorted them to the Natural Sciences classroom.

"All right, everybody, buddy up!" Professor Crane said as they entered the classroom. "No doubt many of you have already heard about today's lesson: it's gotten to be rather famous, which is quite saying something for my classes, if I do say so myself. The objective of this lesson is to learn about the circulatory system—"

Following that declaration, a little cheer went up

from the classroom followed by whispers of excitement.

"I *could* do this by lecture, of course..." Professor Crane went on, looking at the class slyly, and he was rewarded with groans of protest. Nilesh called, "Oh, come on!"

The professor went on cheerfully, "But, despite the risks involved in this number of inexperienced students merging with red blood cells, in thirteen years I've never had a student fail to return to his or her body. Eventually, anyway," he added with a wink to the class in general.

"Psst!" Lily hissed at Cole. She whispered, "Maybe you and Brock should work together, then. After all, you have the same blood already!"

Peter glanced at Brock, who looked nauseated despite his machismo on the ride to school. He tried not to laugh again, feeling another bizarre twinge of sympathy.

"... Most of you are already aware that this is how most medical imaging is done in Carlion," Professor Crane was saying.

"Really?" Peter whispered to Anthony, who sat in front of him.

"Sure. Who needs x-rays and stuff when the healer can just go in and see what's wrong for himself?" he whispered back, and then amended, "Well, actually it's not usually the healer who goes in, since they're eukaryote specialists. The imaging specialist does that. But you get the idea."

Heather Kwan's hand shot up in the air and she glanced at her partner Anthony with trepidation. "How exactly do we get back out again, Professor?"

"The same way you get in! You'll find lancets on your lab benches, one for each partner. All right, pick who's going first…"

Lily grabbed Peter's sleeve, looking a bit white.

"Does this mean we're partners?" he asked.

She nodded, declaring under her breath, "I trust you more than anybody else in here." Peter grew a bit warm at this, but Lily didn't notice, extending her finger towards Peter, shielding her face with the other. "You can go first."

"On your marks!" cried Professor Crane. "Get set! POKE!"

"Ow!" said Lily, and Peter said hastily, "Sorry!" He looked up at Professor Crane and asked, "Why is this necessary anyway?"

"Because you're beginners. Seeing the blood cell you are going to merge with helps the first time out when you don't know what you're doing. All right, Lab Partners B, I want you to squeeze a drop of blood to the tip of your finger. Lab Partners A, I want you to concentrate *very hard* on that drop. As soon as I finish speaking, think with all your might of diving into a pool, and then just… go with the flow! One more time, on your marks, get set, *chumasadh leis braon fola*!"

Peter dove. It was remarkable how much the sensation actually felt like diving—as if he'd just leapt off a high rise towards a swimming pool which, as he fell, expanded into an ocean. He landed without a splash and the force of the waves pulled him under.

The world he entered into was like nothing he could have even imagined. He tried to compare it to something he'd seen before: it was like being in a crowd, except surrounded by round aliens with multiple heads inside their bodies. Some had what looked like two heads inside of them, and some had four. Then there were little shredded looking bits floating along beside them, like sea kelp. Some inexorable force compelled him to move forward, like a current. He looked in front of him and behind him, and realized that the current came from the thrust of little doors that slammed shut just as he went through them.

The valves, Peter thought vaguely, trying to remember what he'd learned about the circulatory system. He'd studied it only briefly, several summers before. He tried to identify the aliens around him as other red blood cells and white blood cells of various types. He flashed back to the page of the textbook that had depicted them as they looked under a microscope, and marveled at how different they were now that he *was* one of them.

He found himself wishing that Lily could be here with him so that he could explain to her everything they were seeing... not that she would care to hear it, but he'd still like to have her there to listen all the same. Then the strange idea occurred to Peter that Lily couldn't come with him because he was *inside* Lily's bloodstream. Despite the fact that they were in science class, the idea seemed... awkward. And somehow inappropriate.

The valves slammed harder, and the stream got wider, moving faster and faster. Presently Peter saw that he was headed for a waterfall (*or, a blood-fall?*), and there was absolutely nothing he could do about it. He felt a brief flash of terror, and then he fell, along with all the other red blood cells and white blood cells and platelets that looked like pieces of kelp. For a split second, he saw what lay at the bottom of the blood-fall: it was a gaping mouth with three enormous teeth chomping rhythmically.

That's her heart! he realized, a split second before the pressure catapulted him through the teeth.

The rest was a blur. It was like he'd been on a toy boat in a storm, long since capsized, and the undertow dragged him down to a watery grave. But then, beneath the water's surface, there was another vicious-looking mouth with three more teeth. He'd barely seen it before he burst through, propelled with dizzying force much greater than that of any of the valves.

The flow of her bloodstream slowed after that, diverted down multiple paths until it was only a trickle. If Peter could have breathed, he would have sighed with relief. He was in what looked like a Zen garden: it was made entirely of lace—lucent, effervescent, and peaceful.

I'm in her lungs now, he thought, amazed. He knew this was where red blood cells were oxygenated, and as he trickled through the lace, he had a sensation sort of similar to the way he felt after eating large meal, like he was being fueled for the rest of his journey.

The lace garden began to merge again and the pace picked up, and a wave of dread passed over Peter, knowing what was coming next. He plummeted once again into the turbulent sea of blood, back into the other side of Lily's heart, and then towards two gaping jaws. He passed through the jaws, and they expelled him *out*, with such dizzying force that for a moment, he thought he'd lost consciousness.

Then the stream slowed. Peter marveled as the bloodstream narrowed, diverting down various side paths. He tried to picture where in her body he had to be now based on how long it had been since he'd been ejected from her heart. *Her fingers are coming up*, Peter thought anxiously. He figured the artery would start to loop around like a bend in the stream when it got to her hand, since it'd have nowhere else to go, and then he should get off at the first capillary bed he saw… But what if it was the wrong finger? How was he supposed to know? He imagined Lily frantic with his body slumped next to hers, and himself lost in her bloodstream indefinitely. But before he could fully contemplate this possibility, he saw daylight, and—

"Peter!"

He sat up and gasped. For a few seconds he couldn't get enough oxygen. "Wasn't I breathing while I was in there?" he managed to choke out at last.

"Of course you were," Professor Crane said, who happened to be passing by their section of the classroom just then. "Breathing is a brainstem function, and merging only acts on the conscious level. But it's a reflex—anytime you merge with something that doesn't respire on its own, the body gasps for air upon return. And congratulations, you are the first back!" He beamed at him. "How was it?"

"It was…" he looked at Lily, who if possible looked even whiter than she had before. "Incredible."

"Was it?" she smiled at him weakly.

"And confusing," he admitted, still trying to reorient himself to the classroom as all over the room, other students began to come to. "I could sort of figure out what things were as I went, but it all happened so fast, I was afraid I'd never find the right exit."

"You make it sound like it's an exit off the motorway!" Lily almost scolded him.

"That's sort of what it felt like, except under water."

"Do I have to do this?" Lily begged the professor, holding a lancet over Peter's finger with trepidation. "Can't I just… learn it out of a book or something?"

"Nope!" said Professor Crane cheerfully, and plucked the lancet from her hand, pricking Peter's finger for her. He winced. "Everybody's got to participate!"

"But what happens if I faint? In there?"

"You can't faint. Your body's already unconscious and red blood cells don't have consciousness of their own. You're stuck being fully aware, I'm afraid. On your mark…"

"Wait, wait!" she cried desperately.

"It'll all be over before you know it!" he persisted doggedly, and he spoke the words of the Ancient Tongue. The next thing Peter knew, she fell limp on the table.

"I really don't like that part," he muttered to Professor Crane, eyeing Lily's lifeless body. Professor Crane gave him a merry smile and continued his turn about the room.

It took nearly an hour for everyone in the class to have a turn, and poor Heather Kwan ended up bleeding from all of her fingers before Professor Crane was able to successfully extract Anthony. But eventually everyone was conscious again, and feeling somewhere between exhilarated and nauseated. Cole looked more thrilled than any of the rest of them: having found himself at a blind-ended finger, he had (even as a red blood cell) somehow managed to invoke the Ancient Tongue and cut his own way out. Brock was heavily bandaged and rather irritated by this, but Professor Crane seemed quite impressed, and praised him loudly.

"You're a natural healer!" he crowed, which made Cole beam all the more.

Meanwhile, Peter noticed with satisfaction that Kip Ashton looked more on the nauseated end of the spectrum. *Not so smug now, are you, 'Ashton, Kip Ashton'?*

By the time the lab was over, Professor Crane only had ten minutes left at the end of the class to actually lecture about the circulatory system before the bell rang.

"You all right there?" said Peter, holding his arms out as if to steady Lily in case she toppled over when she tried to stand.

"No, no, I'm fine," she said. "It… it wasn't as bad as I thought it was going to be. I mean, it was sort of terrifying, but not in the way I expected. It didn't really look like blood once I was in there. But I did think your heart was going to eat me."

"Yeah, it looked that way, didn't it?" said Peter. He was surprised, pleasantly, that he'd had almost no thoughts to spare for what he'd seen the night before in the Space of Possibilities in all the excitement. But he figured he'd have plenty of time to think in Ancient Tongues, since it had been shockingly dull the day before.

He was surprised again.

"Awesome! We're having lab today!" Anthony said when they entered the classroom, pointing at the signs throughout the room printed on poster board, each of which proclaimed the name of one of the gifts of the Ancient Tongue. Anthony turned to Lily. "I've never had a partner to practice with before!"

She raised her eyebrows in surprise. "Oh, are we partners, then?"

"We will be, yeah," Anthony said. "Everybody breaks up into their gifts, and they all practice together. But I've always been by myself—there aren't any other electromagnetic specialists in our year."

"Not so fast, Mr. Hutchins," said Professor Lambert. She was an overweight bespectacled woman dressed in a ghastly purple cape, a pair of boots that zipped up the front and looked like they might cut off the circulation in her calves, and a lime green dress with ruffles down the front. "First I will be collecting your homework," she announced as the rest of the students filed in. When she finished doing this, the students stood up and sorted themselves according to their gifts.

"Wait!" said Peter as they all dispersed around him, "What about me?"

"What about you?" said Lily.

"I don't know what my gift is." It seemed absurd, considering how much had happened, but it was true nevertheless. "Where am I supposed to go?"

Professor Lambert overheard this and beckoned him towards her, looking rather pleased. "I thought you might not know yet, Peter. This will be a treat for all of us! I wander amongst the groups, so why don't you just follow me and try your hand at each of them in turn?"

Peter tried to think how to resist this invitation; he wanted to avoid having the entire class focused on him if he could help it. Meanwhile the professor grinned at him expectantly, revealing pink lipstick stains on her teeth.

"Thanks, but... I think I'll just go with Lily and Anthony," Peter said quickly. Cole's group included Kip, who leered at him, and he didn't want to join Brock's group either.

"Aww," Kip cooed from the eukaryote specialist group. "Is Wonder Boy afraid of disappointing us with his mediocrity?"

Peter narrowed his eyes at Kip, and decided that perhaps there were worse things than making another enemy. He opened his mouth to retort, but Cole did it for him.

"Pete fought the Shadow Lord and lived to tell

the tale. Who cares if he doesn't impress *you?*"

"Boys!" said Professor Lambert sharply before Kip could reply, "That's enough! Peter, join the electromagnetic specialists then, and no more disruptions." Her tone sounded clipped, as if she felt rather put out that he had refused her invitation.

When Peter got to the electromagnetic specialist corner of the classroom, Anthony was already sitting down cross-legged facing Lily, holding out his hands. Lily sat beside him, but she looked at his hands warily.

"What are you doing?" she asked.

"C'mon, sit down. I'll read your mind."

"Uh," she looked at Peter and raised her eyebrows. "I'll pass. Thanks."

"Okay. Peter?"

"What's with the hand-holding?" Peter asked, sitting down reluctantly.

"Just makes it easier to focus on your subject if you're touching," he said. "After that it gets easier or harder depending on how close or far away you are."

"Just please don't start singing Kumbayah," Lily muttered when Anthony grabbed Peter's hands, and they both laughed, a little embarrassed.

Anthony murmured the words in the Ancient Tongue, and Peter listened so he could copy him later. Then abruptly Anthony dropped his hands and looked up at Peter in amazement.

"Whoa!" he exclaimed. "Where was *that* place?"

"What place?" Peter asked, taken aback.

"The one in your mind! It was some kind of meadow!"

"You *saw* that?" Peter said. "It's... um... it's where I go when I speak the Ancient Tongue."

"Every time?" Anthony demanded. "Seriously?"

"Why were you thinking of it now, though?" Lily asked Peter shrewdly.

"Oh," Peter said vaguely, "I went there last night again. In Isdemus's office."

Lily raised her eyebrows at him and started to ask again what they'd talked about, but Anthony crowed, "Wow! I wish I went there when *I* speak the Ancient Tongue!"

"What happens when you speak it, then?" Peter asked. He had actually been curious about this.

"Either what you say happens or it doesn't," Anthony answered with a shrug. Then he added after a minute's thought, "Usually it doesn't. Not for me, anyway."

Lily added, "But you can walk around and change what you said before it actually happens if you don't like it, can't you?"

Anthony blinked at her. "Uhh..." He looked back at Peter, then at Lily again. "Can't say I know what you're talking about."

Now Lily looked confused. "So... so time doesn't stop for you?"

"No!" he declared, goggling at her. "Are you kidding me? Time *stops* for you? That's freaking awesome!"

Peter stared at Lily like he'd never seen her before, his heart thumping oddly in his chest. Lily met his eyes, and they held each others' gaze for a long moment.

"What do you mean, time stops for you, Lily?"

Peter asked at last.

Lily bit her lip and shrugged. "I thought... I thought that's what happened to everybody."

Peter looked at Anthony, who still gaped at them both, and then turned back to Lily. "Apparently not."

The rest of the lesson went by quickly enough, but Peter was barely conscious of it, still puzzling over what Lily's experience when speaking the Ancient Tongue. When the bell rang, Lily grabbed Peter's elbow as they made their way to the cafeteria.

"So time stops for both of us when we speak the Ancient Tongue, but not for anyone else," she said under her breath, without preamble. "What do you think that means, Peter?"

"The prophecy says nothing about that either way," Peter pointed out, evading her question.

"Maybe not, but it's weird that it's just *us,* don't you think?" She paused, and wedged her way through the crowd sideways. When Peter rejoined her she added, "I wonder what happened to Kane when he spoke it..."

"Huh," Peter murmured, and lapsed into thought, still feeling a bit strange. Then he said suddenly, "Lily, do you think..." he trailed off and she looked at him expectantly. "Do you think it's possible it hasn't been decided yet?"

"What do you mean? Is it possible that *what* hasn't been decided yet?"

"Well, maybe it isn't like it's already one of us and we just don't know which one yet," he reasoned

230

slowly. "Maybe it really *could* be either one of us in the end."

Lily pursed her lips. Peter had the impression she was making an effort to look indifferent, but it wasn't working. "It's possible," she said, her voice even. She paused for a long moment, not meeting Peter's eyes. Then she said tentatively, "Do... do you think that's likely though?"

"Search me; I don't know how prophecies work," Peter said, though he couldn't keep the edge out of his voice. But he couldn't stop himself from adding, "Isdemus seems pretty sure it's me, though."

"Of course he is," Lily snapped.

Peter narrowed his eyes. "What's that supposed to mean?"

"You're a boy, aren't you? And... and *look* at you! You're the one they've protected all this time, you're the one with the unlimited power, *you're* the one—"

"Come off it!" Peter cut in, exasperated. "That's not even why he thinks it's me, it's nothing to do with how I look, or with being a boy! It's because—"

"I don't even care why, I don't want to hear it!" She turned smartly on her heel, exactly like she had done in his chamber the night before, and started to dash away.

Peter shouted after her, "You *do* care, obviously!" He was so frustrated he could hardly stand it. "You—used to make sense! Why are you so mental all of a sudden?"

Lily wheeled on him again, eyes flashing

dangerously. "*What* did you call me?"

Peter took a step back, realizing his mistake. *Mental* was the one thing he should never, ever call Lily. He'd learned that almost the first day he'd met her. He said defensively, "Well, you *are* acting mental, aren't you?"

"I hate you, Peter Stewart!" Lily hissed through gritted teeth. Then she tossed her curly brown ponytail over her shoulder with righteous indignation, and marched away.

Peter stood there, mostly furious, but also a little hurt.

He didn't want to be the Child of the Prophecy, he knew that much for certain. So why didn't he want it to be Lily instead?

Because... because that means she'd have to fight the Shadow Lord, Peter realized. *And the prophecy says 'both shall fall.'*

He didn't want it to be Lily, he suddenly realized, because he didn't want to lose her.

He sighed, irritated, and muttered under his breath, "But she hates me anyway, so what do I care?"

Chapter 21

Ibn Alaam's secret library was surprisingly warm and inviting, compared to the dank secret library in Carlion. Several plush velvet chairs surrounded a large octagonal table, and each chair had a doily in front of it, as if it were waiting for a cup of masala chai to complete the picture. Books filled the walls from floor to ceiling in all directions, except for one, where a fireplace thankfully sat empty and stone cold. Another source of heat might have rendered the room uninhabitable.

"I think it would be best to start at the beginning," said Masika, once all four of them had entered the library. "And I mean the *very* beginning." Before anybody had a chance to respond, she moved towards a shelf about at her eye level, and pulled a book down. Bruce scrutinized it.

"Shat Ent Am Duat?" he read, confused.

"Shat, isn't that the past tense of—" Dan began, smirking.

"It means, *The Book of What is in the Duat,*" Masika interrupted, missing the joke. "The Book makes multiple references to Zep Tepi, or the First Time," she went on, settling into one of the velvet chairs and pushing aside the doily as she opened the text. When this assertion met with silence, she explained, "The First Time to Ancient Egypt was supposed to be the time when the gods came to earth and established the kingdom of Egypt. To the Watchers, though, it represents that epoch of time prior to the Great Deception."

"Ah!" said Dan, sitting down in the velvet chair beside Masika. "And the Duat is?"

"Sky-ground duality," said Masika as if that were obvious, thumbing through the pages distractedly. When this assertion also met with silence, she looked up and said, "I am sorry, I forget that people outside my anthropology circle do not understand these things. Ancient Egyptians, as with alchemy, believed quite literally in the adage, 'as above, so below.' Many of our most famous structures were profoundly astronomical in nature. They were meant to mimic the layout of the stars."

"Such as?" said Jael.

"Such as the Pyramids at Giza," said Masika, still distracted. "They are constructed as a mirror of the three stars of Orion's belt, in precisely the correct orientation to the Nile as to mimic the position of the Milky Way in the sky, the Nile's celestial counterpart."

Jael snorted, and Dan shot her a withering look. "What?" she protested. "That sounds like a stretch to me!"

Masika leveled her gaze at Jael and said evenly, "You will forgive me if I am uninterested in debating your ignorant opinions."

"So what is the connection between the Philosopher's Stone and this Duat?" Bruce interrupted, ignoring the tension between the two women.

"Well," said Masika, still glaring at Jael, "the legends suggest that at the time of the Great Deception, the Stone was hidden in Ancient Egypt, which was of course one of the first great civilizations in the known world. The best interpretations of our manuscripts also imply that after the Shadow Lord was banished, the Stone was returned to its original location."

"By whom?" said Jael. "It couldn't have been a member of the Watchers, or we'd know exactly where it was."

"We don't know who put it there, and we don't even know for sure that they *did* put it back in its original location," said Masika. "But if *someone* did, then in order to find where they put it, we'd have to go back to Ancient Egyptian philosophy, such as the Duat. So no matter how 'ridiculous' you think their theories may have been, as long as the ancients believed them, they are still relevant to our search," she finished acidly. "Would you not agree?"

Jael pursed her lips and said nothing.

"So what we need to find out is which structures in Egypt have been around since right after the Great Deception," Bruce finished, and Masika nodded.

"Or in Zep Tepi, in their philosophy—exactly. I brought up the Pyramids not because they fit into that category—scholars believe they were built around the time of Pharaoh Khafre in 2500 BC— but because the site itself is extremely old. Traditional Egyptologists believe that the Sphinx, too, was the work of the Khafre dynasty... but we believe differently."

"We, as in the Watchers?" said Dan, and Masika nodded again.

"There are a few scholars in the outside world that believe the same, but they are in the minority and are largely ignored, which baffles me because the evidence is overwhelmingly on their side. First, there is a great deal of water damage on the Sphinx which does not appear on the pyramids. Rainfall of that magnitude did not fall on Egypt in 2500 BC; Egypt was already a desert by that time. We would have to go back to at least 5000 to 7000 BC in order to account for it. Second, if you consider the sky-ground duality of the Pyramids at Giza, you cannot help but notice that the Sphinx gazes at the exact position of the sunrise at dawn on the spring equinox."

"So?" said Jael.

"So, in 2500 BC, the spring equinox would have risen against the background of the constellation of Taurus, which is traditionally represented by a bull. For a site that is clearly intended to mimic the heavens, if the Sphinx had been constructed in Khafre's day, one would have expected the equinoctial monument to have taken the shape of a bull, or at least to represent a bull in some way. But it's not a bull—it's a Sphinx, which symbolizes a lion."

"So, the constellation of Leo, then?" said Bruce, leaning towards her across the table.

"Yes," said Masika, "and the Age of Leo, when the Sphinx would have gazed at its astronomical counterpart on the spring equinox, would have put its construction around 10,500 BC." Bruce and Dan both gasped, and Masika went on, "That also happens to be the date when the Nile and the Milky Way would have lined up perfectly, as would the position of the three stars of Orion's belt and the three pyramids, even though they had not been built yet."

"10,500 BC! That's exactly when the early Order of the Paladin estimated that the Great Deception took place!" Dan exclaimed.

Masika beamed at him. "Yes. Now do you see the connection?"

"Wait, wait a minute," said Bruce suddenly, and he pushed back his chair and began to pace as he thought aloud. "The equinox happens twice a year, at the shortest and the longest days. It's when the earth is broadside-on to the sun, and so daytime and nighttime are of equal length."

Masika tilted her head to the side. "Go on."

"It's the moment of perfect balance of day and night, light and darkness—like the Taijitu!" Bruce finished excitedly, "So it's the symbol of the Taijitu, not literally but astronomically!"

Dan's jaw dropped as he looked from Bruce to Masika. "So the Philosopher's Stone might be hidden somewhere in the Sphinx, then?"

Masika tapped her fingers against her lips. "Not *in* it, because it's solid of course," she murmured, "but around it perhaps…" She stopped suddenly, looking as if she'd had an epiphany.

"What? What?" said Dan.

Her eyes danced. "Of course! The Temple!" When all three of the others stared at her blankly, she said, "There are two temples in the complex at Giza. One is called the Valley Temple of Khafre, and it is still largely intact. But the other is called the Temple of the Sphinx. It lies to the east of the Sphinx. It has no roof, because on the equinoxes, the sun streams right through the Temple at sunset, capturing the moment when day and night are in perfect harmony!"

"The physical symbol of the Taijitu, where light merges into darkness," Bruce finished in awe, as his mouth hung open. "Well, what are we waiting for? Let's go!"

Just then they heard a knock at the door, and another Watcher from Ibn Alaam admitted Sully to the library. Sully nodded his thanks as the other Watcher departed. He looked flustered.

"What is it? What did Isdemus say?" said Dan, frowning at Sully's expression. "Where's Bomani?"

"Peter was missing," said Sully, ignoring the other questions.

"What?" cried Dan, Jael, and Bruce all at once.

"They found him again," Sully added hastily. "Trust me, you don't want to know." He shook his head at Bruce and said dryly, "That kid of yours could use a beating, that's all I'm gonna say."

Bruce sank back into his chair in relief. "Pretty

sure beating a kid who can reverse entropy isn't a fantastic idea," he said weakly.

Sully went on, "Anyway, I couldn't really get much of a reaction out of Isdemus in all the confusion, but we did tell him about the double dragon symbol and what that might mean about Kane. I think you were right, Dan, he'd already thought of it."

"Nice of him to tell *us*," muttered Jael. "What about Bomani?"

"Bomani stayed behind to help Isdemus with… whatever it was he was working on."

"Well, perfect timing, Sully," said Bruce, still sounding shaky. "We think we know where the Philosopher's Stone is."

Sully's eyebrows shot up into his white hair. "That was quick!"

"Now, wait a minute!" Masika protested, "I hardly think we have enough to say—"

"But we have a solid lead, don't we?" Bruce cut her off. "And we have a space specialist, so it won't waste that much time to go and check it out. All we need to do is locate the spot in the Temple of the Sphinx where the light streams in at sunset on the spring equinox…"

"Is somebody planning on filling me in here?" Sully interrupted, frowning.

"We will when we get there." Bruce looked expectantly at the others. "So? What do you say?"

"But it's not the equinox!" said Dan, "how are we going to find the right spot?"

"We'll just have to hope it's marked somehow," said Bruce, and then turned to Sully again. "So do you think you can get us to the Giza plaza?"

"I've never been there," Sully frowned again. "I'd have to see it on a map to estimate distances…" He looked at Masika.

Masika looked puzzled, but she pulled an atlas from another shelf and handed it to Sully, who thumbed through and scrutinized the appropriate page. They could hear him muttering to himself, "Let's see, the scale is a centimeter per one hundred meters, and we're here, so…"

"What's he doing?" Masika whispered to Dan.

"He's got a photographic memory," Dan explained, "so if he's been to a place before he'll know exactly how far to go. Even if he hasn't been there, if there's someone else there with an entangled coin, he can get a read on their location and warp there anyway." He read Masika's expression and said, "Blimey, I forgot you don't have entangled coins here either. If he's never been to a place before and doesn't have a coin to track, then he's got to estimate distances."

Sully nodded. "Looks like about 220 kilometers to Giza from here."

"And we can all warp with him?" Masika said, looking distinctly uncomfortable with the idea.

"Yep! Long as we're touching him at the same time," said Dan.

"What happens if he misses?"

"Then we all end up in the Nile," said Jael dryly. "Hope you can swim."

"He never misses," said Dan, with another sharp look in Jael's direction. "The gift of space comes with a built-in navigation system. Better than any of those satellites they use in the outside world."

"I wouldn't brag about me too soon," said Sully, but he put down the atlas and said, "All right, I think I've got it. Grab on."

They all obeyed, Masika last of all, hanging back until she was absolutely certain she had no other choice.

"I'll count to three for the newcomer," said Sully, looking at Masika. "One, two—"

They all felt an unpleasant lurch, and then heard Sully's muffled, "Three!"

*

Bruce blinked. "Nice job, Sully!" he said appreciatively. They were standing in the causeway between the Sphinx and the crumbling structure that must have been its Temple, with the pyramids to their backs.

"Quick, into the rubble!" said Sully. "Get down!" He took off at a run and the others followed behind, bewildered. When they caught up, panting and crouched beneath the low walls that were once the Temple of the Sphinx, Sully explained, "I doubt the penumbra in these parts will recognize us, but you never know."

"Right! Good thinking!" said Bruce, his eyes round. "Lucky the Temple isn't exactly a tourist attraction."

"Yes, most of the tourists are over there," said Masika, pointing back towards the ramps leading up to the Sphinx. Then she looked around at the rubble of their present surroundings and said rhetorically, "This does not look like much, does it?"

"So," said Sully, leaning his head against a

massive block, hidden from view from the tourists, "*now* are you gonna tell me what we're doing here?"

Bruce explained quickly. When he finished, Sully still looked unconvinced.

Dan said, "So will there be a dividing line of light and dark or something? Perhaps it runs right through the center on the equinox?"

"Well," said Masika, still crouched beneath her block, "the spring equinox was in March, and it's October now. So wouldn't the point be right about… well, further…" she pointed to a section of the temple cast in shadow, and drew her finger in a line to the opposite wall.

"I'd think the spot we were looking for would be in the corner, furthest from the Sphinx," Bruce mused aloud, "so if Masika's estimation is right, it should be right about…" he stopped and gasped, crouching against the far wall with his nose only inches from a piece of rubble that made up the floor.

"What? What?" Dan demanded, half-running and half-crawling towards the point.

"Hey!" called a voice behind them. It was male, some distance away, but they froze. "You there in the Temple!"

"Hurry up, Bruce!" Jael hissed.

"Look here! Etched in this block—"

"Blimey," Dan gave a low whistle, and even Masika's mouth fell open when she saw it.

"Hey! You there!" The voice was getting closer.

"It is not as if this area is off limits," Masika frowned. "People just do not normally bother coming in."

"I don't think it was *his* idea to come after us," said Jael significantly, eyeing the penumbra in the shape of a serpent draped around the guard's shoulders like a cape.

"Isn't that the glyph for the Philosopher's Stone? Squaring the Circle?" said Sully, peering over Bruce's shoulder at the symbol of a circle with a square around it, then a larger triangle, and then a larger circle around the whole.

"Yes, that is it," said Masika in amazement. Then she added thoughtfully, "It looks weathered, but somehow... newer, yes? I cannot see a symbol that shallow surviving from 10,500 BC..."

"Well, don't just stand there looking daft; dig it up!" Jael hissed at Bruce, looking over her shoulder at the security guard, who was by then only a stone's throw away.

"That's your territory, you're the one with the muscles!" Bruce countered, getting out of the way, as Sully shoved Jael towards the block.

"Get ready, Sully," said Dan anxiously, gauging the guard's distance. "Soon as she digs it up, get us out of here..."

Bruce, Dan, and Masika all grabbed on to Sully's forearms in preparation as Jael heaved the enormous stone block out of the earth, sending sections of the adjacent wall crumbling down.

"*Hey!* Whadda ya think you're—"

"It's empty!" Jael huffed, as the guard and his serpent were just about to leap on top of her. "Nothing there!"

"All right, grab on!" said Dan. But he didn't wait for her to obey. With one hand firmly attached to Sully's wrist, Dan grabbed on to Jael's forearm with the other. At the same moment, the guard dove as if he meant to tackle her. Jael's eyes widened as the transparent red eyes of the serpent locked onto hers. She could have sworn she saw a flash of recognition, and in the same instant she felt the guard's hands just brush the flesh of her ankle. She felt the beginnings of the weight of his body, but before she could feel the full impact, instead there was the sensation of a hook behind her navel, and she slipped right through his grasp, vanishing into thin air.

"That was close!" said Masika back in the library of Ibn Alaam, trembling all over as she let go of Sully.

"Oh please," Jael scoffed. "It was one guard. I could have taken him with my hands tied behind my back. Besides, there were five of us and only one of him."

"Yes, but had the guard's serpent recognized us and realized what we were after, it could have alerted all the other penumbra," said Sully quietly.

"Then we *would* have had a mess on our hands."

Jael felt a twinge of discomfort at the memory of the serpent's eyes locked on hers, and wondered if it *had* recognized her. But she decided not to mention it. Nothing they could do about it now.

"There was really nothing there?" said Bruce to Jael, crestfallen. "I was so sure…"

"Yeah, you were also sure about that chaos nonsense too, though, weren't you?" said Jael, dusting off the rubble from her hands.

"I still think the Chaos Theory will have some integral part to play…" Bruce protested, and then added, "But the Squaring the Circle symbol *was* on that block. That had to mean something! Do you think the Stone used to be there and somebody moved it?"

"If they did, then they did it thousands of years ago," said Jael. "That block hadn't been moved anytime recently."

"I feel like we're overlooking something obvious…" Bruce insisted, pacing. "So, wait a minute. What *did* you see down there?"

"Nothing of consequence. A dirty little hole."

"Nothing beneath the hole?"

"There were a couple of geckos, if that's what you mean."

"But it doesn't make any sense!" Bruce exploded in frustration. "Isdemus said the original location of the Stone was in Egypt. How could the Stone be here, but not in the one place that bears its symbol? Was he absolutely certain that the Stone had been moved back to its original location?"

"I had the impression he was," said Sully.

Jael frowned. "I thought he seemed pretty sure too. But let's just suppose for the moment that the Stone *has* been moved somewhere else. Do we have any leads on that at all?"

Everyone stared at one another, waiting for someone to have an idea. Suddenly there was a *crack*, and a glowing elf-like creature stood among them. Masika let out another cry.

"You have nimbi in Ibn Alaam!" Jael snapped at Masika.

"Yes, but they don't do *that*!"

"Verum, what news?" said Sully.

"Isdemus sent me," said Verum. "He says he received definitive intelligence that the Stone is indeed in Egypt, and he is nearly certain it is somewhere in the Giza plaza." Nobody spoke for a moment. Verum read their expressions and said, "You act like this is bad news."

"It is!" said Bruce in frustration. "We've just been to the Giza plaza…" He recounted the episode for Verum in detail, and finished, "but Jael says there was nothing there. So unless Isdemus is suggesting that the Stone is buried in a random unmarked location…"

"Or it could have been deeper beneath the blocks of the Temple, could it not?" Masika interjected.

"Yes, but that could go on forever!" said Jael. "How would we know when we'd dug deep enough or wide enough to say for certain that the Stone wasn't there?"

"If we hit molten lava, I'd say that's a good indication we'd gone too far," Dan joked.

"Why did Isdemus say he was sure it was in

Giza?" said Sully, turning back to Verum. "That might tell us whether he's got new information or only what we've already investigated."

"Did he say anything about the Temple of the Sphinx or the equinox?" Bruce added eagerly.

"No, he said he saw it," said Verum.

Bruce and Sully exchanged a look of confusion. "He saw what?"

"He said he saw the place where the Stone was originally buried, and it was in Giza."

There was a long pause. Everyone exchanged a look, but nobody vocalized the question. Isdemus seemed to know all sorts of things that he should have no way of knowing. Then Bruce said finally, "Well, I'm flummoxed, because that sounds like the Stone ought to have been exactly where we just were!"

"We still haven't tried the digging until we hit lava idea," said Dan, only half-joking this time.

"Yes, and I'm sure the guard who nearly tackled me would stand passively by while we excavated right next to one of the Seven Wonders of the World," said Jael, "and none of the tourists or their penumbra would give us any trouble at all."

"Well, do you have a better idea?" Dan muttered.

There was another long pause, and all of the Watchers stared at each other in frustration.

"You may as well go and ask him if he can give us any more direction, then," said Sully to Verum at last. "Explain that we've already been to Giza. The only thing I can figure is that the Stone was moved since the time that Isdemus thought it should have been there."

Verum bowed low and disappeared.

It was Bruce who finally vocalized what everyone was thinking. "Without any further clues… it appears we're at a dead end."

Chapter 22

Peter ate lunch at Paladin High lost in thought, while Cole and Anthony chatted. Brock was off eating with his new co-star Ashley, who had been cast as Juliet to his Romeo, and his new club of admirers. Lily had gone down to the Winding Waterway to eat alone, which was just fine, as far as Peter was concerned.

Every now and then Cole and Anthony glanced at Peter to see if he wanted to jump in, but his expression was so glazed and faraway that they eventually gave up on him. He was still chewing on what it meant that time stopped for Lily when she spoke the Ancient Tongue. *What if it* is *her, in the end?* The idea of him being responsible for saving the world still made him want to retch… but when it came down to it, he knew now that he'd prefer it to be him rather than Lily. Even if she did hate him.

But what I want's got nothing to do with it, of course. That won't change facts, he told himself. *So*

249

I've got to understand the facts.

When he finished eating, Peter announced that he was going for a walk down by the Winding Waterway, though purposely in the opposite direction from where he knew Lily was sitting.

"Want some company?" said Cole, polishing off his sandwich.

"No," said Peter. He hastened to add, "Sorry. I just need to work something out in my head."

"I'll talk it through with you if you like," Cole offered.

"Thanks, but I want to be alone," Peter said bluntly. He didn't even look at Cole's expression before he turned away. It was the truth, after all.

Peter hunched his shoulders against the slightly chilly autumn wind and tucked his hands in his pockets. When he was far enough away that he could no longer hear the other students, he absently listened to his footfalls against the grass as he thought.

He remembered Isdemus grabbing his shoulder in the Fata Morgana, and saw the previously diminishing flames suddenly shoot straight up to the sky. (That was how Isdemus and Bruce decided it "must be him" after all.) But Lily had nearly collapsed with the effort of maintaining her force field. So she didn't have unlimited power, like he did.

He paced. He recited the prophecy in his head, twice, just to be sure he hadn't missed anything. But nowhere did it say anything about unlimited power.

Then again, it didn't say anything about being able to freeze time either, and they both could do *that*, apparently.

Suddenly he exclaimed "Hey!" to himself aloud, and he stopped walking. He looked at his watch, the one he'd grabbed from his room in Norwich the night before. He still had twenty minutes before Historical Interpretations started; maybe if he was lucky, Professor Hunt would be there early. He turned back in the direction of the school and ran towards her class. It was odd how often he ran now, he thought. Prior to the last few weeks, he couldn't remember ever considering anything important enough to warrant physical exertion.

When Peter entered the classroom, Professor Hunt turned around in surprise as she erased the blackboard in preparation for the next class. "Peter?"

"Professor, I just had a question," he said breathlessly. "About the Great Deception."

"Oh!" she said, obviously pleased. "It's rare to see such dedication in new students, Peter. What can I help you with?"

"Something's been bothering me, Professor. The first night I was here, Isd—er, someone," he stopped himself, not sure how much he should and should not say, "told me that nobody had done what I did—use more energy than he had in his own body—since before the Great Deception. So I assume that must mean that prior to the Great Deception, everyone had unlimited power over their elements."

"Yes, that's correct, Peter, although not just over 'their' elements," the professor corrected, setting her eraser down and pulling up the chair to her desk. She gestured for Peter to sit down opposite her, which he did, although he hovered on the edge of his chair. "The concept of individual elements did not arise until well after the Great Deception. Before, everyone had unlimited control over every element, not just the one."

Peter's heart sped up. He, so far, had shown aptitude for the gift of air, and also for the gift of metal, which he supposed was a subdivision of earth.

He had at least two, then.

"Professor," he said, trying to keep his voice even, "can you tell me why that changed? Why did people have unlimited power before the Great Deception, but afterwards they became limited to the energy in their own bodies, and only had one gift apiece?"

Professor Hunt looked impressed. "That is a very advanced question, Peter. Unfortunately I am not the most qualified to answer it... you might have more luck with Professor Crane. All I can tell you is that it has to do with the link between Quantum and Newtonian physics. I understand they are currently separate systems with no connection between them that we know of, but that was not always the case."

Peter stood bolt upright, and Professor Hunt's eyebrows shot up at his enthusiasm. "Thank you Professor! I'll see if I can catch Professor Crane before the lunch hour ends."

He ran back out of the classroom, and Professor Hunt laughed with delighted incredulity. "Good luck!" she called after him.

Lily was in the hallway walking to Historical Interpretations early, just as Peter ran out of Professor Hunt's room, bolting in the opposite direction.

"Peter! Where are you going?"

"To talk to Professor Crane really quickly! I'll be back in a few minutes!"

She started to jog after him. "What are you trying to talk to Professor Crane about?"

Peter scowled to himself as he ran, although Lily couldn't see him, and he grew winded. "Why are you following me? I thought you hated me." But he slowed to a walk, and she closed the distance between them.

"I… got carried away," she said stiffly. "I'm sorry."

"You're sorry because you don't mean it, or you're sorry you said it?"

Her anger flared again. "Well, you shouldn't be calling me mental!"

"Lily, I've got just a few minutes before the lunch hour ends, can we please have this conversation later?"

"Not until you tell me what you're talking to Professor Crane about. If it has to do with the prophecy, I should probably hear it too, don't you think?" She added this last bit with a slight bite to her tone, slowing to a walk beside him.

"What makes you think it has anything to do with the prophecy?" Peter knew he sounded guilty even as he said it.

"Peter. Please." Lily crossed her arms over her

chest.

Peter didn't bother to protest again. He opened the door to Professor Crane's classroom.

Professor Crane ate alone at his desk, thumbing through a science magazine from the outside world and squeezing together two slices of bread on either side of a sandwich at least four times larger than the size of his mouth.

"Peter!" Professor Crane's words came garbled through the half-masticated sandwich. He gulped and smiled brightly. "And Lily! What a pleasant surprise. Come in, come in!" He gestured to the desks at the front of the class. "What brings you to my humble abode at this most glorious time of day? I should have thought you both would have better places to be!"

"I had a question to ask you, sir. It's about the connection between Quantum and Newtonian Physics," said Peter, casting a sidelong glance at Lily to see her reaction. She raised her chin just a bit to show she resented the glance, but didn't reply. Peter went on, "Professor Hunt told me I should ask you about it."

"Oh?" said Professor Crane, raising his eyebrows. "I'd have thought you'd just ask your dad, Peter!"

That caught Peter off guard. "Well, I would, sir, but my dad is off on business."

"Bruce. Isn't he always?" said Professor Crane, chuckling to himself. He took another bite and kept talking anyway, much like Bruce did. "Well, you're in luck, because physics is one of my favorite subjects. It's one of the reasons that Bruce and I get along so well. I am absolutely fascinated by his research in the outside world! To think that he has the cheek to use the Ancient Tongue as a research method and to try and get projects like that through a review board!"

"He does?" Lily asked, glancing at Peter, who nodded wryly.

"Dad's been trying to do that since long before I believed there even was such a thing."

"Even the outside world seems to be catching up, though, don't they?" said Professor Crane, winking at Peter. "Even *they* realize, if only on a microscopic scale, that scientists can and do alter their own experiments by the very act of observation!"

"Sir, Professor Hunt just told me that before the Great Deception, the Ancient Tongue was connected to some original source of unlimited power. It was only afterwards that we became limited to the energy in our own bodies."

"But *you* have unlimited power even now, I heard," Professor Crane mused.

"Well… yes. It would appear that way," said Peter, trying not to look at Lily. "But the prophecy doesn't actually say anything about that."

"I wouldn't know," said Professor Crane, ripping the crusts off his bread. "I'm not a Watcher so I've never read the prophecies. I can't tell you one way or the other whether the reconnection of the Ancient Tongue and its power has to do with the Child of the Prophecy. But it would seem to make sense, wouldn't it?"

"Peter goes to this place whenever he speaks the

Ancient Tongue," Lily cut in, casting a sidelong glance at Peter. "It's a meadow, and it has a pool with this rainbow coming out, and a bunch of possible outcomes of whatever it is that he said."

"…And then I pick the one I want from the rainbow and dive into the pool," Peter finished, adding hurriedly, "But Lily says when she speaks the Ancient Tongue, time stops and she can walk around in it and change things, too."

Professor Crane raised an eyebrow, and although he still eyed Peter curiously, suddenly he regarded Lily with more interest as well. "She does, eh?"

Peter went on, "My theory is that the reason I see lots of options is that the rainbow represents my probability wave. Then my choice determines which one happens, and it doesn't matter how much or how little energy it takes. So it's like what happens in the Copenhagen interpretation of quantum mechanics, except on a macroscopic scale." Then he added, "I don't know how to explain what happens to Lily, but I suspect it's a variation of the same thing."

Professor Crane had stopped eating now. His bug eyes, already magnified by his reading glasses, seemed to take up at least half his face. "So you think…"

Peter didn't wait for him to finish, but turned to Lily and explained excitedly, "Newtonian physics is the set of laws that describe what happens on the macroscopic scale—big stuff we can see—"

"I know what macroscopic means, Peter," she said impatiently.

"—but quantum mechanics describes what

happens on the quantum scale, which is unimaginably small. Remember I told you about the Double Slit Experiment? That's the quantum scale, and tiny particles like that abide by a completely different set of rules; they don't follow Newtonian physics at all. Einstein spent the latter part of his life trying to find the connection between Newtonian and Quantum Physics, but he never did—"

"And you think it's because of the Great Deception!" finished Professor Crane in wonder, and Peter nodded, his eyes wide and eager. "That is a very interesting theory, Peter."

"Whoa, whoa, wait a minute!" Lily interrupted crossly. "You're saying that before the Great Deception, at the dawn of time..."

"Macroscopic stuff, big stuff, obeyed quantum laws!" Peter finished. "That meant everyone could basically do what I can do in that Meadow, regardless of its size or the nature of the element. But when the Shadow Lord gave the power to the penumbra—"

Professor Crane cut in, "We lost the connection. So even once we recovered the language, now we're all limited to the power in our own bodies." He shook his head. "You've done your father proud, my boy..."

Peter blushed just a bit, but pressed on. "So you think it's true then? And if it is true, *how* did it happen?"

"The Shadow Lord vowed to give his power to the penumbra in the Ancient Tongue, on behalf of all mankind," Professor Crane said. "And vows in the Ancient Tongue cannot be broken."

"Hold on!" Lily insisted louder than necessary, annoyed. "So if the quantum whatever gets reconnected to the bigger world, that means what?"

"Two things," said Professor Crane excitedly, his sandwich forgotten. "First, one would expect that if the laws were rejoined for a particular individual," his eyes rested on Peter, but from time to time he glanced at Lily too, "then one might expect time to slow down, even stop, at that point. When that happens, what occurs afterwards is no longer bounded by the laws of probability."

Lily swallowed hard, trying to control her voice as she pressed, "You said it means two things. What's the second?"

"One might also expect that for the individual who is capable of existing in that infinite space, the possibilities might be equally endless."

"Meaning unlimited power," said Lily quietly.

"Meaning unlimited power," affirmed Professor Crane, now looking at Peter only.

Peter bit his lip as the bell rang, signaling the end of the lunch hour.

Lily was quiet as they left Professor Crane's office and walked down the hall. Instead of swinging her arms at her sides, she wrapped them around her stomach.

"You okay?" asked Peter.

"Sure," she muttered.

"Lily—"

"So it's you. Congratulations," Lily cut him off with a bite to her tone.

"Don't be thick," Peter shot back. "Weren't you listening? One of those conclusions applied to both of us!"

"But both of them apply to you, don't they? Just like all the other signs. I've only got one gift, *and* I've got limited power!"

"What do you want me to say?" Peter demanded, really angry now.

The other students in the hallway stopped to stare, but neither of them seemed to notice.

"What I want," Lily shouted back, planting a hand in the middle of his chest, "is for you to stop patronizing me!" Her eyes flashed, and she stalked off to Historical Interpretations alone.

Chapter 23

Lily avoided Peter's eyes for the rest of the day. In the void she left, Cassandra tried repeatedly to get Peter's attention, but Peter was much too distracted to care. Cassandra, discouraged and pouty, instead joined Brock's entourage.

"We're gonna go to the first *Romeo and Juliet* rehearsal just to watch," Cole snickered to Peter after classes had ended for the day, indicating himself and Anthony. "Wanna come?"

"I think I'll head back to the castle," Peter said. "I've got a few things I want to talk to Isdemus about." He said it stiffly, aware of Lily's presence right behind them. Privately, he was also afraid that Professor Vane might still manage to force *him* to play Romeo instead of Brock. He wasn't sure which would be worse: to be the Child of the Prophecy, or to be Romeo.

Cole shrugged. "Suit yourself! Although I really don't know why you *don't* wanna watch Brock try and read Shakespeare…"

"I'll go with Peter," said Lily, to Peter's surprise. She fell into step beside him as he headed to the hitching post.

"Thought you weren't speaking to me," Peter said coldly once they were out of earshot of the others.

"You're not talking to Isdemus without me," she informed him. "Whatever you have to say, you can say in front of me—"

"Fine," Peter cut her off, "But you don't have to bother me about it all the way there!"

"Well I just won't talk to you at all then!"

"Fine with me!"

The silence between them grew unbearable after that, but Peter stubbornly refused to break it. It was hard to believe that just the night before, she had hugged him in his room. *She can be so… so…* he trailed off, unable to think of an adequate word to describe what Lily could be. But he knew it was something really foul. *If she was a bloke, I think I'd punch her in the face,* he thought savagely.

Lily broke the silence first. "So what *did* Isdemus say to you last night, anyway?"

"Wouldn't you like to know," Peter muttered.

"Well I'm going to find out as soon as we talk to him so you might as well tell me now! That way I won't have to stop you every five seconds with questions!"

Peter sighed. It was a reasonable point. "All right, fine. He wanted…" Peter hesitated. "He wanted me to take him into the Meadow."

"Take him?" Lily demanded, lowering her voice

as the crowd thickened into a queue to retrieve their horses. "What do you mean, take him?"

"Apparently…" Peter sighed again. He knew she wouldn't like this. "Apparently he says there's been speculation that the Child of the Prophecy will go to a specific place when he or she speaks the Ancient Tongue." He added both gender pronouns on purpose, keen to avoid yet another row. "In terms of the legends, they call it the Space of Possibilities, but in physics they call it Superspace. It's essentially a space where anything is possible. It's also a place where you can see into the past."

Lily was silent for a moment. They reached the front of the queue and Lily untied Candace and mounted, while Peter did the same with Charger. When they fell into a canter, Lily said, "So that's what you meant when you said Isdemus has reason to think it's you and not me."

Peter nodded, but didn't dare agree aloud.

Lily didn't say anything for a long time. Peter thought he heard her sniffle. Finally she said, "If it's you, then I'll have to teach you how to fight. You looked like a complete idiot in the Fata Morgana, not to mention in PE yesterday."

"I'm aware of that, thanks," said Peter. But he did feel a bit lighter.

She sniffled again. "So how can you take someone else into the Meadow with you?"

Relieved that she'd let the subject change, Peter said, "Turns out I can take anybody with me as long as I'm touching them at the time."

"Huh," said Lily. "So what's this about seeing the past?"

"The rainbow collapses into a white line—" Peter began.

"Once you've made a choice, you mean?"

"Yeah, and the white line is like a timeline. It's not just a timeline of *my* life, though," Peter added. "It's a line of... history. It means we can go back and see events as they happen, if we know what we're looking for."

Lily looked at him sharply. "So you carry your own secret library around with you wherever you go?" The note of envy in her voice was unmistakable.

"Basically," Peter admitted.

"So what did Isdemus want you to show him?" Then she stopped and said, "Let me guess. He wanted to know where the Philosopher's Stone was?" Peter nodded, and Lily gasped. "Well? Where was it?"

"It was buried in an unmarked location in the middle of a big grassy plain."

She stared at him. The horses' hooves clopped on the sod. "That's it?"

"Apparently it meant more to Isdemus than it did to me." When Lily didn't answer right away, he added, "I guess it was in something like 10,500 BC, so it's probably not a grassy plain anymore."

Lily said presently, "That's probably what your dad and the other Watchers are after, then, Peter. The Stone."

"It is," said Peter. "Isdemus told me."

Lily fell silent for most of the rest of the journey, but it was not an uncomfortable silence this time. She was obviously lost in thought.

When they were almost at the stables, Lily said finally, "So you want to ask Isdemus about what Professor Crane said. Right?"

Peter nodded.

"You want Isdemus to confirm that it's you."

Peter sighed. "Lily, it's not like I'm after glory here. I'm not, truly. I never wanted any of this." He paused. "But—*please* don't take this the wrong way—I don't want it to be you, either."

She stopped short, and seemed to be caught off guard by his manner. He wasn't defensive or malicious at all, but instead seemed rather earnest. "Why not?" she asked cautiously.

"Remember the second to last line of the prophecy?"

They both dismounted and led their horses by the reins to the stables as Lily dropped her voice and quoted, "You mean, *'Both shall fall, but the one who holds the blade that was broken shall emerge victorious'*?"

"Right," Peter whispered back. He didn't want Eustace to overhear them. "I don't very much like the bit about 'both shall fall,' do you?"

"But *somebody* wins in the end!" she hissed back.

The other stable hand, the skinny boy with black hair and a perpetually stunned expression, came out to lead the horses away, staring at Peter unabashedly. Peter and Lily both muttered their thanks to him.

"I honestly don't know how to interpret that line," Peter whispered back as they headed across the courtyard with the double dragon fountain. "But it doesn't sound good, whatever it means."

"So you don't want to be the Child of the Prophecy because you're afraid of dying?"

"I'm not *afraid*," Peter corrected her, annoyed.

"It's okay if you are," Lily said.

"Well I'm not!"

"Then what *are* you afraid of?"

Peter sighed, scowling. "Never mind." He knew the answer to this now, but he wasn't about to admit it to Lily, not after all of her tantrums that day. "Why do you want it to be you so much then? What could possibly be so appealing about that?"

Lily stopped walking towards the entrance and lingered by the fountain instead. "I dunno, Peter," she murmured, absently dipping her fingers in the water, "I guess I just want it all to count for something."

Peter sat down on the ledge and frowned at her, trying to understand what she meant. He shivered as a few droplets of water splashed him. "You mean being a Seer and alone most of your life, and all that?"

She nodded. "In a weird way, I feel like all of that can be redeemed, if I went through it for a reason." She sighed. "That probably doesn't make any sense to you."

Peter bit his lip, suddenly feeling foolish for the row they'd been having earlier. "No, it makes loads of sense," he said quietly. He met her eyes for a long moment. "Lily, I don't know how to say this…" he trailed off, and took a deep breath.

He noticed that her cheeks grew pinker than they'd been a second ago. "What?"

"Well," he hesitated. "Just remember that… the reason Kane almost got us killed, the reason my dad was abducted, the reason he jumped into the Lake of Avalon—all of it was because he was jealous of me, because he thought I was the Child of the Prophecy and he wasn't."

Lily blinked at him, and her face fell. That wasn't where she'd thought he was going with this at all. A curtain fell over her features again, and her tone grew cold. "What's your point, Peter?"

Peter fidgeted. "Just… let's not let that happen to you and me, all right? We have to stick together. It's the only chance we've got."

Lily pursed her lips, and softened. She nodded abruptly, and then as if she were thinking about his words still, she nodded again. "You're right. Of course you're right."

Peter relaxed and gave her a tentative smile, which she returned somewhat halfheartedly.

"Come on," she said abruptly, "we want to find Isdemus, don't we?" And she stood up and walked towards the entrance with that purposeful stride of hers without waiting for him to reply.

When Peter caught up with her, they passed by the kitchen on their way to Isdemus's office. The servants were just beginning to prepare supper, and Gladys suddenly rounded a corner and collided with Peter.

"Blimey! Sorry about that," said Peter. He frowned down at his jeans, which were covered with white flour from the bowl that Gladys carried.

Gladys turned as white as the flour in the bowl.

She tried to duck around them, but just as she did, Peter moved out of the way in the same direction, and then they both moved in the opposite direction.

"Please let me pass!" Gladys blurted desperately.

"Well, I'm trying—" said Peter, and Gladys ducked her head and streaked past him into the store room behind the Great Hall so quickly that it seemed she hardly moved her feet.

"What was *that* all about?" said Lily, staring after her.

"I have no idea..." said Peter, trailing off. Then he dropped his voice and confessed, "I used to think she was just a nervous person, but now I'm not so sure. She had a strange bulge beneath her apron last night, like she was hiding something. During our lesson afterwards, Isdemus mentioned that we don't have the luxury of time... like he thought the Shadow Lord was coming back sooner than we think..."

"What's that got to do with her, though?" whispered Lily.

"Maybe nothing," Peter shrugged. "But maybe something. I can't explain it, I just have this feeling that she's involved somehow." He suddenly became self-conscious and said, "I guess that sounds silly— 'I have a feeling.'"

"Remember who you're talking to," Lily reminded him, with a half smile. "So what do you think we should do?"

"Do?" Peter repeated, surprised.

"About Gladys. Don't you want to know why she's acting so strange?"

"Sure I do, but I don't see how, unless you want

to break into her chamber or something."

"We could ask her," said Lily.

Peter blinked at her. "You mean like, 'Excuse me, Gladys, but why are you so mental?'"

Lily raised one eyebrow. "With perhaps a bit more tact, but that's the general idea, yes."

"Couldn't you just read her thoughts?"

Lily frowned. "I could try, but I doubt it would work. Anthony says it's hard if you're not right next to the person, and better if you're touching them, remember? It's hard to touch someone without being noticed."

"We could find a pretext for it, though," said Peter. "Admittedly I can't think of one at the moment, and besides, I want to talk to Isdemus…"

"Second," Lily went on, as if she hadn't heard him, "I noticed today that I can't read anything except what the person is thinking about at the time. I can't dig into memories or ask specific questions or things like that."

Peter's eyebrows shot up. "When did you find *that* out?"

Lily's cheeks reddened again just a bit. "I was practicing… well, most of the day, whenever I had an excuse to touch someone. I just silently asked questions about their childhoods or things like that, to see what I could find out. But most people were thinking about food, or what they were going to do when school let out, or about somebody they fancied."

Peter's heart sped up, and he tried to remember when she'd touched him that day. Then remembered she'd been inside his blood vessels for a good half hour. *Can't get a whole lot closer than that,* he thought, his stomach in a knot. "Who fancies who?" he asked, trying to keep his voice even.

"None of your business!"

"Well, none of yours either!" Peter retorted, feeling his cheeks burn again and refusing to meet her eyes.

"I had to practice, didn't I?" Lily shot back.

"Back to Gladys," Peter said pointedly. They reached the stairs that led up to the third floor then, where Isdemus's office was, but they both paused to reach a consensus.

"Right," Lily hissed, lowering her voice to a whisper and refusing to meet his eyes. "My point was, I'll only be able to tell you why she's been acting so odd if she's thinking about the reason at the time I happen to be touching her. I suppose we could give it a go, but I'd guess that if we had to contrive some reason for me to touch her, it'd seem so odd that she'd only be thinking about what I was up to. Which brings us back to my original suggestion—"

"Just ask her."

"Yes." She shrugged. "Never know until you try, right?"

"We'll have to get her alone," said Peter slowly, "and most of the time she's in the kitchen with all the other servants…"

"I have an idea about that. I've watched her a bit since we got here, not for any reason, but just because she's so strange. She goes off by herself every day down the west wing corridor around five o'clock or so."

"Perhaps that's where her chamber is?" Peter suggested.

Lily shook her head. "I don't think so. I saw her go all the way to the stairs, and I had the impression that most of the servants' sleeping quarters were on the first basement."

"Well," said Peter, looking at his watch again, "we've got about twenty minutes or so until five. Any ideas where we could wait for her?"

"Do I have to think of everything?"

Peter suppressed a smile. "This *was* your idea."

"Come on, I'm sure we'll find something on the way."

Presently Peter pointed out a hallway, which made a right angle with the Western corridor.

"That's not a hiding spot, that's a hallway," said Lily.

"Yes, but you said she goes all the way to the stairs—"

"I *think* she does. I was never watching that closely."

"Well, if you're right, then if we flatten ourselves on the wall closest to the main part of the castle here, she won't see us unless she turns around after she passes by. Then we can watch where she goes."

"And if I'm wrong? What if she doesn't go all the way to the stairs? What if she does turn around?" Lily asked.

Peter shrugged. "Then we'll improvise."

"That'll be tricky, trying to explain what we were doing alone together in a dark abandoned hallway, not saying a word to each other—" she stopped when suddenly the obvious excuse occurred to both of them.

"Er, right," said Peter awkwardly. "I… expect we'll think of something."

"Shh! Are those footsteps?" Lily pushed Peter against the wall and flattened against it on his other side. The footsteps were muffled on the running red carpet through the center of the hall, but they could hear them grow closer and closer. Finally they saw a silhouette with a frumpy-looking frame and hair tied back in a frazzled bun pass by with a basket over her arm. Lily mouthed counting to three and then crept out behind her, motioning to Peter to follow.

They tiptoed at a far enough distance that they could blend into shadow if necessary, but not so far that they lost sight of her.

At last, they saw Gladys disappear through a door that led out to the grounds. The last orange-red rays of daylight filtered into the hallway for a moment before the door sealed itself again.

"What now? If we follow her out there, she's bound to see us!" Lily whispered.

"Well, of course she'll see us, but the point was to confront her, wasn't it?" Peter whispered back.

"Oh. Right."

Peter pushed the door open and blinked as his eyes adjusted to the bright sun. Lily stepped out beside him. Gladys stooped down to pick some herbs from the ground and place them in her basket. Peter cleared his throat, and Gladys jumped, dropping the contents of her basket all over the ground again.

"Peter!" Gladys exclaimed. He couldn't help but notice the fear in her voice when she said his name.

Lily looked at Peter as if to ask permission, and then stepped forward and said boldly, "Gladys, we're sorry about sneaking up on you like this, but we wanted to ask you a question and thought it best if we asked you when you were on your own."

Gladys spared a glance in Lily's direction but did not reply. Then her eyes immediately reverted back to Peter.

Lily glanced at Peter again, trying to determine whether he wanted to jump in, and went on, "You've been acting very strangely towards Peter ever since he arrived at the castle, and it seems to have gotten worse in the last few days. We want to know if there's anything you'd like to tell us." She looked at Peter again for backup.

"Yeah," said Peter, trying to nod with gusto.

Gladys blinked at him, looking much like a cornered animal. "I have nothing to say!" she declared breathlessly.

Peter raised his eyebrows and looked at Lily.

"So… why have you been treating Peter like he's carrying the plague or something?" Lily pressed.

"Thanks," Peter muttered to her.

"Well?" Lily raised her hands in the air.

Then to both their surprise, Gladys broke down and began to cry.

"Um," said Peter. He looked at Lily and hissed, "What do we do now?"

In response Lily stepped forward and reached a hand towards Gladys's shoulder; Gladys did not attempt to move away.

"I'm… so… sorry!" Gladys sobbed, mopping her face with her stained apron.

"Sorry for what?" Peter asked blankly.

"About your mum. I didn't even know you were twins! Kane's always been such a rebel, and… and everyone assumed it was because he hadn't any parents… but I didn't know it was my *fault* that he didn't…!" She dissolved into tears and could not go on speaking for a few moments, until she collected herself again.

"What on earth are you talking about?" Peter demanded. "What about my mum?"

Lily exchanged another look with Peter. "You did something to Peter and Kane's mother?"

Gladys did not answer for a long moment but suddenly began to tremble all over. "I never meant to hurt anybody."

Peter looked too thunderstruck to continue the conversation, so Lily pressed on. "Gladys, last night Peter saw that you had something under your apron when you left the Commuter Station, and Isdemus seemed to think that was significant. What was it?"

Gladys's mouth went into a perfectly round *o* and she fell silent.

Suddenly, with a sickening sense of cold dread in the pit of his stomach, Peter understood.

He knew why Isdemus suddenly felt the urgency to find the Stone, and find it fast.

"He's back," Peter whispered. "He came to see you."

Gladys didn't reply but went on shaking all over, looking as if she were still sobbing except there were no tears and no noise. Lily stood rigidly beside Peter in shock. At last Gladys whispered, "He told me not to tell."

"I'll bet he did!" Peter roared. "Do you know who that *was*?"

"Peter," Lily breathed, putting her hand on his arm, but it was enough that he stopped talking. She turned back to Gladys and said, "Gladys, did Kane ask you to do anything for him?"

Gladys did not answer, but her expression was as good as confirmation.

"What did he ask you to do? Please, this is important. You have to tell us."

After a long moment, during which tears streaked out of the corners of Gladys's eyes and she did not bother to wipe them away, she finally said again, "He told me not to tell. He… he said it would help to defeat the Shadow Lord."

Peter saw Gladys in his mind's eye again, scurrying out of the Commuter Station away from a blank wall, carrying a torch and clutching something beneath her apron that looked rather rectangular…

"He sent you to the secret library, didn't he?" Peter interrupted. Gladys's eyes widened and her lower lip quivered, but she said nothing. "What did he make you take? What did you bring to him?" When she quailed under his blazing eyes but did not reply, Peter shouted, "Tell me!"

"I don't know what it was!" Gladys burst out at last. "It was just a book with a symbol on the front; I didn't know what it meant!"

"*What symbol?*" Peter roared.

"This, this!" the unfortunate Gladys wailed, thrusting her hands clumsily into the pockets of her apron and withdrawing a crumpled piece of paper. She held it out to Peter, sobbing as if her heart would break and hiding her face in the crook of her opposite elbow. Lily took it and smoothed it so she could see what was written there.

"Peter," Lily said quietly, "It's the symbol from class yesterday."

Peter tore his eyes away from Gladys and looked down at the symbol drawn on the paper, of a circle with a square around it inside a triangle, which was inside another circle.

"He's after the Stone, too," Peter whispered.

Chapter 24

Lily took the lead on the way to Isdemus's study, Peter pounding behind her. They ran down the carpeted main hall, past the suits of armor and the tapestries, then ducked around to the stairwell, taking them two at a time all the way to the third floor.

Isdemus and an older Egyptian man with a large belly and a shiny head were both speaking to Verum when Peter and Lily burst into the room. Isdemus sighed heavily when he saw who it was. Meanwhile Bomani whispered to Verum, "Is this the Child of the Prophecy?" He was looking at Peter when he said it.

Verum waffled his head side to side, noncommittal. "Technically it could be either one of them."

Lily, who ordinarily would have bristled at that, burst out, "Sir, we have something to tell you."

Isdemus did not reply, but turned to Verum and

said in a lower tone, "Please tell Sully and the others what I have told you. I will be in contact soon."

Verum bowed and disappeared with a *crack*. Then Isdemus turned his attention to Peter and Lily. But Peter looked at Bomani uncomfortably, and Lily said for both of them, "Sir, we'd prefer to speak to you alone."

"I understand," said Isdemus. "This is Bomani, the head of the Watchers in Ibn Alaam. Anything you need to say to me can be said in front of him." He sat down behind his desk, looking at Lily expectantly. "Well?"

Peter blurted out before Lily could answer, "Kane is back, sir. Gladys saw him."

Bomani looked shocked, but something in Isdemus's expression gave the impression that this was not entirely news to him. "She told you this?" Isdemus asked at last.

"That's not all, sir," Lily went on. "He's looking for the Philosopher's Stone. Gladys gave him a book out of the secret library with the Squaring the Circle symbol on the cover."

Bomani's eyes widened, and Isdemus pushed back his chair and got to his feet. "I knew she had taken a book, but I hoped it was not that one," Isdemus murmured. "I was afraid it would come to this." Then he cried, "Fides Dignus!"

With a *crack*, the ugly little creature appeared in the middle of the room.

"Fides Dignus, Gladys should be downstairs preparing supper with the other servants. Please ask her to come to see me."

Fides Dignus bowed, amplifying the rolls of flesh adorning his abdomen, and disappeared again with another loud *crack*.

"Er," said Lily, looking at Peter, "should we stay here and wait for her then?"

"Yes, I think so," said Isdemus quietly. "She will be less likely to deny the conversation if you are present."

Everybody fell silent, and Peter felt Bomani scrutinizing him. He thought of the red baseball cap Kane had given him the first time they were in Carlion and wished he had it now. Bomani gave a low whistle.

"My my, you *do* look like King Arthur," he murmured at last.

Lily bit her lip, and Peter knew she was biting back something scathing.

Presently there came a knock on the door, and Isdemus said, "Enter."

Gladys's cheeks were blotchy and red, and her eyelashes clung to one another. It was obvious she had still been crying since she had left the herb garden.

"Close the door behind you, if you please, and sit down," said Isdemus, gesturing at the chair opposite his desk, the one in which Peter had sat the night before. Gladys glanced at Peter and Lily furtively before turning her back to them.

Once she'd sat down, Isdemus went on, "These two tell me that they just had a very interesting conversation with you." Gladys said nothing, and so Isdemus prompted, "Do you confirm or deny?"

She was silent for a long moment. At last she

whispered, her voice barely audible, "Confirm."

Lily took a step closer to Gladys from behind, and when Gladys did not look up at her again, she took a few more.

Isdemus went on, "They tell me Kane has returned from the Lake of Avalon, and has come to the castle to see you. Is this true?"

Gladys said nothing.

"Gladys," said Isdemus again, his voice more stern, "You must tell me what you know. If Kane has returned, it means the Shadow Lord has been freed, as well."

Gladys averted her watery eyes, and she said nothing.

"That being true, it is possible," Isdemus went on doggedly, "that the Shadow Lord is still looking for a willing host. But what Peter and Lily tell me about the manner of Kane's behavior when he spoke with you leads me to believe that this is not the case. The very fact that Kane returned to the castle and did not announce his presence to the rest of us is in itself nearly proof that the person you were dealing with was not, in fact, Kane, but the Shadow Lord himself."

"Which we all assumed would happen anyway," said Bomani under his breath.

Gladys gave a startled cry, but refused to make eye contact with Isdemus. She began to rock back and forth very slightly.

Isdemus seemed to take her reaction as confirmation, because next he said, this time in a much gentler tone, "I know why you did what you did, Gladys. I suspect that Kane, or the creature who appeared as Kane, told you that if you were to help him, you would atone for what you did all those years ago, did he not? He told you perhaps that you could undo the damage you had done to him if you aided him and kept silent about it. Even that your aid and your silence would help to defeat the Shadow Lord."

Gladys burst into tears again, her limbs half curled as her body spasmed with sobs.

Peter looked at Lily anxiously, trying to get her attention, but her hands were stretched towards Gladys's back, her eyes half-closed in intense concentration.

"What did she ask you to take for him, Gladys?" Isdemus asked quietly.

Unable to speak, Gladys reached again into her pocket and thrust the piece of paper at Isdemus on which Sargon had drawn the map to the secret library, the exact location of the book, and the symbol. When Isdemus saw it, he showed it to Bomani and they both nodded once, their expressions very grave.

"This is it," Isdemus murmured. Then he looked at Gladys and said loudly enough to be heard over her sobs, "Thank you, Gladys. You may return to your work."

Gladys stared at him through watery eyes mistrustfully, but at last she stood to her feet, approaching the door by stops and starts until she fairly fled out of the study.

When she had gone, Peter began, "Sir—"

"Thank you for bringing this to our attention," Isdemus cut him off. "I'm afraid we have work to do now. It is urgent," he added, when Peter almost interrupted again.

Peter looked at Lily, frustrated. "Yes sir." He was beginning to resent Isdemus's abrupt dismissals.

When Peter closed the door softly behind them, he wheeled on Lily. "What did you find out when you touched her?"

"Loads. Come on." She motioned him away from the door to Isdemus's office. Once they were a safe distance away, near the spiral staircase, she whispered as they ran, "Apparently Gladys grew up in Carlion, and she came to work as a maid in the castle when she was a teenager. Isdemus is very controlling of all the servants in the castle, I guess, because of all the secret information that flies around in here."

Peter tilted his head to the side, rounding the corner and climbing the stairs two at a time. "Huh. That's interesting. Controlling how?"

"He won't allow any of the servants outside the city. He thinks the servants in the castle know just enough to be dangerous."

"Okay…"

Lily led the way to her own chamber on autopilot, and when they arrived she slipped the key out of her pocket and ushered Peter inside. She went on, "Anyway, the citizens of Carlion all think the outside world is glamorous and exciting because of all the tragedy and crime and drama." She didn't allude again to her outburst the day before over her parents' deaths, but Peter remembered, of course, and nodded, sitting down on the velvet chair next to her bed, while Lily settled herself on the window seat opposite him. "The natives here tend to think they're missing out on something. Gladys felt the same way, apparently. She begged Isdemus for decades to let her go to the outside world and at least visit and see what it was like, but he refused. She grew to resent him for it, and finally she ran away about ten years ago."

"Ten years…" Peter did the math in his head quickly. "So I would've been four, which was when Dad and Isdemus said Mum was killed."

"Right. Because Gladys was raised in Carlion, she was really naive. She knew that the Watchers go out and try to make people into Seers, tell them about their gifts and bring them to Carlion if they're willing to come. So she just started talking freely about Carlion and the Watchers to anybody who would listen. She was a Seer of course, but she'd never actually seen a *penumbra* before, she'd only seen the nimbi. So when the penumbra started to question her, through their hosts, about what the Watchers were watching *for*—"

Peter groaned. "Oh, she didn't!"

Lily nodded gravely. "She told them about the prophecy, although she didn't know much of it. But she cleans the entire castle, even the nooks and crannies, so at some point I guess she must have seen your mum's picture and learned enough about her—"

"Because after she ran away with Kane, Dad emptied the house of all the pictures of both of them," Peter finished, looking ill. "He must have given them to Isdemus so I wouldn't come across them."

Lily nodded sympathetically. "But Gladys didn't seem to know that your dad was Dr. Stewart, or that it was really you and Kane that the Watchers were protecting. She didn't even know your mum had kids at all. All she knew was your mum's name, what she looked like, and that she was connected to the prophecy somehow. She shared your mum's identity innocently of course; she had no idea mentioning her name to the penumbra would lead to her death.

"A few days later her car exploded," Lily finished, quietly. "That's how the Watchers found out where she'd taken Kane four years earlier, because it was all over the papers that she was dead, mostly because they couldn't figure out how it happened. The flames were so hot that she was incinerated, so the Watchers all assumed that Kane must have been with her when she died."

Peter covered his mouth with his hand, feeling like he might throw up.

Lily murmured, "Turns out Kane was with a babysitter, but Isdemus didn't find that out until four years later, after he tracked him down in the orphanage. It was the orphanage that named him Kane, by the way, but I don't know why they changed his name. Maybe they didn't know what his real name was or something. But it was Jason. Jason Stewart."

Peter's mouth fell open. "So that explains it!" he exclaimed. "I'd been wondering why, with a name like Kane, nobody figured out he had to be my brother…"

Lily nodded. "Isdemus never told any of the other Watchers who he really was, including your dad. Isdemus told your dad that Kane was really Jason only when your dad told him about meeting me." Lily swallowed.

"So right before Dad was abducted then," Peter nodded numbly. "That explains why I never noticed him acting odd about it… Dad never was any good at hiding things."

"The rest of the Watchers found out only after the Fata Morgana, and Gladys only discovered Kane was your brother yesterday morning, at breakfast."

"When Cole blurted it out, and she dropped the plates," Peter remembered in a whisper.

Lily leaned forward sympathetically. "Not done yet," she said. "You want me to keep going?"

Peter swallowed hard and nodded.

Lily pressed on, "After your mum's death, Isdemus tracked Gladys down and dragged her back to Carlion, because he figured out what must have happened and he was afraid she'd also endanger you and your dad. But when he found her and started questioning her, he realized she didn't even know you or Kane existed. Isdemus told her what happened, and he even told her that now the Child of the Prophecy was without a mother—"

"They didn't know about you yet," Peter cut in, smiling weakly. Then he remembered that the same statement of motherlessness was equally true of her.

Lily nodded. "Isdemus thought Kane was dead too, so at that point I think you really were the only candidate they knew of. Anyway, as soon as he told

Gladys what she had done, she was horrified and returned with him, of course—"

"And became the pathetic creature she is today," Peter finished. He sank his head into his palms.

"That's why she acts so weird around you," Lily finished. "She knows she's responsible for the fact that you have no mum."

Peter looked up again, out the frosted glass windowpane behind Lily. "She isn't totally responsible for that," Peter murmured. "She's the reason Mum is dead, but not the reason she wasn't in *my* life. She'd already been gone for like six and a half years before that. She wasn't coming back."

Lily was silent for a moment. "Then yesterday morning she found out that Kane, whom she'd known for years, was *also* orphaned because of her…"

"And then he came back and asked her to help him..." Peter groaned.

"So of course she could do nothing else," Lily finished, nodding sympathetically. "She felt like she owed him. She didn't know he was the Shadow Lord."

Peter closed his eyes. "I never thought I'd say this, but I actually feel sorry for her."

They both watched the condensation roll down the windowpanes for a moment.

"So what are we gonna do now?" Lily asked.

"What do you mean?"

Lily stared at him like she didn't know him. Then she ticked off on her fingers one by one, "Uh, let's see. The Shadow Lord is after the Stone. The Watchers, as far as we can tell, don't know where it is—"

"They know more than we do, though!" Peter pointed out.

Lily ticked off a third finger, "And you carry a secret library around with you wherever you go." She then lifted both hands in the air and flopped them down on her legs again, like she'd just made an unassailable point.

"I'm not sure what more you think I can learn in there, though—"

"Um, we!" Lily corrected sharply. "You said you can bring other people in!"

"But Lily, I literally watched the Great Deception *as* it happened. What more do you think I can find out in there besides that?"

"Well, but that was just the first time the Stone was found. Right?"

Peter stared at her, not sure what she was implying. "Yeah…"

"But we know it was moved only one other time, because Morgan le Fay used it to create the Fata Morgana, didn't she?" When Peter didn't reply right away, Lily persisted, "Which means someone put it back there again right after that. You said that grassy plain probably looks a lot different now than it did in 10,500 BC, so…"

Peter stared at her with awe. "You're bloody brilliant, Lily."

She beamed at him. "Glad you finally caught on."

Chapter 25

Lily looked around her chamber and informed Peter, "We've got to find something you can command in the Ancient Tongue."

"I have to read your mind," Peter announced.

She looked taken aback. "What?"

"I don't remember how to say that many things, and if I screw up, you can help me because you know the words too. It's just faster!"

"I can remember other things you can say in the Ancient Tongue besides that!" Lily protested, although her expression was unconvincing.

"Oh yeah, like what?"

"Like…" Lily racked her brain, and suddenly remembered Cole repeating the same phrase over and over. "Like *stad fola*, for instance!"

Peter rolled his eyes. "'Stop bleeding'? I'll be glad to use that if you want me to draw your blood instead of read your mind."

Lily looked like she couldn't quite decide which

she'd prefer, but at last she sighed heavily and held out her hands. "*Fine*. If you must."

Peter scooted his chair closer to her perch on the windowsill and grabbed her hands. "Let's see, I'm trying to remember what Anthony said. It was something like... *brisead is-teach in-a aig-ne...*"

Lily muttered, somewhat against her will, "It's *briseadh isteach ina aigne.*"

Peter tried a few more times, varying his pronunciation slightly and speeding up until the words flowed off his tongue.

He was almost startled by the peacefulness of the green grass, the still, sparkling pool, and the blue skies, with the rainbow emanating from the pool's surface. He could tell at a glance that every image in the rainbow was of a primate that looked a good deal like a raccoon, only slightly smaller.

Lily released his hand and gasped. "It worked! Peter, this place is incredible!"

"What's with the raccoon?" Peter asked, pointing at the rainbow.

"It's a wombat."

"Oh-kay..."

She looked embarrassed and said a bit defensively, "It's what I was thinking about."

"Right," said Peter dryly. "Makes perfect sense, with everything that just happened to us, that a wombat would be foremost in your mind." He pointed towards the white line. "That's the history line. We've gotta figure out something to say in the Ancient Tongue to get us to the part we want to see." His face fell and he added, "Oh."

"What?"

"We've had exactly two classes in Ancient Tongues, Lily," he said. "And today hardly counted, because I already said the only thing I learned how to say a few seconds ago!"

"But yesterday we did worksheets in class," Lily pointed out.

Peter perked up again. The worksheets had been almost entirely words and phrases related to the legends. "And one of the answers was the Battle of Salisbury Plain! Somebody who was there must have buried the Stone shortly afterwards, right?"

"That could work…" Lily agreed.

Peter closed his eyes, trying to visualize the words. He grabbed Lily's hand again and pronounced very carefully, "*Cath seo caite Artur!*"

As soon as he spoke the words, Peter felt his stomach lurch as they hurdled forward.

There was no clearing, no pool, and no rainbow in the place where they landed, but only a thin white line amid myriad trees.

"Now what?" asked Lily.

"Now we have to picture the person we want to see and step forward, and then we'll get sucked into the white line so we can watch what happened. Let's think of… Morgan, maybe?"

"But she was already dead by this point, wasn't she?"

"True." Peter fell silent.

Presently Lily said, "We should think of Guinevere!" Peter looked at her, puzzled, and she said, "What other penumbra would've been in a position to know everything about Arthur's family? Don't you think it's as likely to be her as any of them?"

Peter considered it and said, "Worth a shot, I guess." He took Lily's hand and said, "Ready? Just think of her and only her, and step forward."

As soon as they stepped forward, the white line expanded; then it seemed to swallow them. The next thing they knew, both of them saw a tiny black-haired woman darting through the shadows of the desolate field where the Castle of Avalon had been.

"That's her!" Peter whispered.

Debris and rubble marked the flat expanse of peat moss and heather. Guinevere moved like a cat, her hair flying behind her as she leapt from place to place, investigating various bits of rubble.

"Aha!" cried Guinevere triumphantly. She seized something from beneath the peat moss, and held it high in the air like a trophy. The sky was overcast, but still the stone glittered like shards of glass. Somehow, in Guinevere's hands, the reflected glory of the Stone made her even more beautiful.

Peter crept closer to get a better look. The stone was irregularly shaped; it looked as if the bottom was spherical but the top was flat, and a bit of it hung off the edge, like a sheet that had been stacked on top. Upon second glance he realized that they were two separate pieces.

"It has a lid!" Peter hissed to Lily.

"Yes, and do you see how the lid is shaped? It's a triangle!"

"The circle, with the triangle in the middle..." Peter began.

"And I'm guessing that means that inside the

triangle there's an empty cube…" Lily added.

"And inside the cube is a hollowed-out circle," Peter finished. "The symbol of Squaring the Circle. It's literal!"

"So what's inside the final circle, I wonder?"

"I'll bet it's hollow, to leave space for the sacrifice of the person who finds it," said Peter, remembering what Guinevere said when Sargon saw the Stone. *He will know what to do.* Even the color of the Stone seemed symbolic. "So the etchings on the outside of it must be words in the Ancient Tongue, explaining how to use it?"

"I guess," Lily whispered.

Finally Guinevere tired of admiring her prize and pocketed it inside the folds of her tunic, running back into the woodland behind the clearing.

Peter took off running behind her, leaping over branches and brambles, though he realized he needn't have bothered when he didn't leap soon enough for one of them, and his foot passed clean through it.

Then suddenly he and Lily both stopped abruptly, and Peter cursed.

"Where did she go?" Lily gasped.

"There must be a porthole here," said Peter. "Just keep thinking of her and we'll follow wherever she went!"

The peat moss melted away into a vast expanse of desert, punctuated by three enormous pyramids and the Sphinx with its face half-eroded away.

"Is this the *Giza plaza*?" Lily gaped.

They stood only yards from a roofless structure clearly meant to be a temple. A few people wore tunics tied with camel's hair and packs strapped to their backs, trudging along like downtrodden animals. A few rode such animals, camels mostly, but they paid very little notice to Guinevere, or indeed to any of their surroundings.

"She's inside the temple! Hurry!" said Lily, pointing, and she and Peter dashed in, right up behind her, just in time to see her disappear.

"Wha—?" Peter began. But then he understood. An enormous block in the base of the temple had been removed, and while it looked at first like it had left only a hole in its place, a second glance told him that he had this impression based on the position of the shadows left behind. The block had clearly obscured a passage.

Peter leapt into the hole behind Guinevere, and Lily followed him. It took them both a moment to adjust to the pitch blackness, but no sooner had they done so, they heard the sound of flint striking stone, and a moment later a torch blazed in Guinevere's free hand.

"I'll bet this place would be sweltering if we were here for real," Lily whispered. They had to jog to keep up, and the tunnel curved and dipped, which, combined with the flicker of firelight and Guinevere's pace, made it seem as if it had been designed to confound.

"We're headed towards the Sphinx; the back of it, I think," said Peter, his words keeping time with the noise his trainers would have made, if he'd had any weight in that place.

Suddenly the tunnel seemed to widen, like an antechamber, and then the flicker of the light danced on the walls of a hollowed-out cave, at the center of which was a single stone table. The light illuminated Guinevere's features in a ghostly way, making her beauty seem even more terrible than it had by daylight. A triumphant grin spread across her features and she withdrew the nearly spherical gemstone box from beneath her tunic. She laid it on the very center of the table.

"My precious *chloch an fhealsúnaí,*" she whispered. "None but I shall ever find you now. And because of you, I will be second in command when the fool king of Mesopotamia returns!"

Guinevere caressed the surface of the Stone with a fiercely delighted expression on her unbearably lovely face, and extinguished her torch.

Peter and Lily stepped back, and the white line shrank back to its pencil-thin form. Lily turned to Peter, wide-eyed, still in the thick of the forest.

"It's underneath the Sphinx," she breathed.

Chapter 26

Sargon didn't know where he was.

The only time he had ever been to Egypt had been well over ten thousand years earlier. He relied partially on Kane's memory to guide him, but Kane did not know Egypt very well either, so that was not especially helpful.

The sheer number of bodies shocked Sargon: fat ones, thin ones, tall ones, short ones, those dressed in rags, those wearing long shapeless tunics that fell to their feet, or those in styles of fitted clothing that he had never seen before. There were scarves, hats, gloves, high heels and purses, all dyed with vibrant colors. Sargon gleaned the words for all of these items from Kane's memory, but he was baffled that even common humans wore dyed fabrics.

They're easy to come by now, Kane told him, answering Sargon's mental questions automatically. He hadn't the strength to resist.

Sargon arched an eyebrow. *In my day, we had to*

crush thousands of sea snails in order to produce one purple garment!

It's not like that now, Kane told him. *There are machines for everything.*

You mean to tell me there are machines that crush thousands of snails, available to the public?

No. We don't need snails anymore. We can mass produce the dye. Kane's thought had the defeated quality of a sigh. He wished Sargon would stop asking him questions and leave him alone.

Whether you like it or not, you will aid me in anything I wish to know, Sargon told him imperiously.

Kane did not reply. He had been stunned to apathy ever since he found out that Peter was his twin brother.

Which meant the prophecy had applied to him too all along.

He'd always believed it could have been him because no one knew who his parents were, but it turned out he was Bruce Stewart's *other son.* Had he not dived into the Lake of Avalon, had he just allowed Peter and the others to rescue him... had he just held on long enough for Achen to rescue him even afterwards...

But now it all amounted to nothing. Now he was the enemy.

Touching, sneered Sargon. *Now pay attention.*

Every human being had a penumbra, but because there were so many of them, it was nearly impossible to tell which creature belonged to which human. The world Sargon remembered had had far more space than people, but this place was quite the opposite; it was as if there was no more land left, and the only thing to do was to build up. Dilapidated buildings rose from a few to thirty stories high or more. Almost as many animals roamed the streets as people: mostly cats and dogs, though there was the occasional stray cow or goat. Laundry hung from metal rungs bolted to the walls of the buildings just outside the windows, or on the uncovered bits of the buildings, which protruded from the sides of them. Kane's memory automatically identified these as *balconies*.

Sargon looked down at his feet, and uttered a cry of contempt. Cockroaches crawled out of a crack in the road, eating the crumbs of some sort of food that had been nestled in a red and white paper wrapper. He looked up to see a street vendor selling the food in the red and white wrapper several yards away.

Smells of human waste and sweat and refuse combined with spices like cardamom and a strangely aerosolized version of fruit (*hookah*, thought Kane, and Sargon saw the image in his mind of an elaborate sort of pipe for smoking), and each breeze carried the scent of balmy sea air and the aroma of fish.

Thick black smoke emanated from the backs of the strange metal beasts (*cars*, Kane thought) that made a cacophony of noise like a dreadfully dissonant symphony. The beeping of so many cars formed a sort of accidental rhythm.

Fifteen hundred years, Sargon thought in amazement. He had seen millennia come and go, but never had such a short period of time produced such staggering change as this. This did not even resemble the world as he had known it. He'd had thousands, even millions of humans under his subjection, spread out over the European and African continents, on into the Near East—but this place looked as if there were millions in the span of a few city blocks.

Sargon stepped in front of a man dressed in a gray tunic, his head covered with a cloth. His penumbra was a faun, which fixed its eyes upon Sargon's, narrowing them suspiciously.

"I demand that you answer me, citizen. What is the name of this place?"

Sargon saw the man's eyes flicker warily to the side of his face.

He's staring at my scar, Kane told him. *I always get that reaction. Although never in my life have I deserved it so much...*

"The city? It is Alexandria," stammered the man, in clipped English. He tried to sidestep Sargon, but Sargon blocked his path.

"Alexandria?" Sargon repeated. "*The* Alexandria? The one founded by Alexander the Great?"

"Yes," said the man, now looking downright alarmed.

"*Are you a stranger here?*" hissed the man's faun, staring at Kane's face with shrewd curiosity. No sooner had it finished speaking, the man echoed, "Are you a stranger in these parts?"

Sargon smiled tersely. "You might say that I am both very strange and very familiar."

The man blinked at him, and then hurried away as quickly as he could, while his faun craned its neck to stare at Sargon even as his host ran away. Sargon let him go, and stepped in front of a woman with a wicked-looking elf clinging to her back by its claws. He grabbed her by the elbow. "Woman!" he boomed. "Which way is Ibn Alaam?"

The woman looked alarmed, and her gaze also flickered to the scar on Kane's face. "Never heard of it," she stammered. "Let me go!"

But instead of releasing her elbow, Sargon decided to change his tactic and address himself directly to the elf. "Creature," he said, "I am your lord and master. You know me as the Shadow Lord. I command you to acknowledge me at once!"

The woman screamed, and the crowd nearby stopped moving in order to stare. The people in her direct path moved aside as she ran towards them, more in surprise than anything else. But before she disappeared, the elf leapt off her back, looking more fearful than suspicious. The crowd slowly returned to its business, but most of them still diverted their paths away from Sargon.

"M-my Lord?" stammered the elf uncertainly. "Forgive me, my Lord, but…h-how do I know it is really you?"

With a casual flick of his wrist and a mutter of the words under his breath, the sixteen-story building behind them went up in flames—not as a fire catches from a match, slowly creeping up the edges, but instantly ablaze from ground to rooftop.

Suddenly the sounds of screaming drowned out all the other noises of the city, and the heat of the fire pulsed and pounded against Kane's skin, though Sargon made no attempt to move away. People began to stream out the single exit in the front of the building, tripping over one another. It was obvious, to Kane's horror, that many of them would never make it out alive.

Put it out! Kane shouted, but Sargon ignored him.

"Do you doubt now?" Sargon said to the elf lazily.

In response, the elf turned to Sargon, its eyes shining, and it fell at his feet, planting kisses all over Kane's filthy boots with its transparent lips.

"My Lord and my Master," it murmured reverently. "If by my life or my death I may serve you..."

Firemen arrived on the scene, and most of the crowd had stopped moving in order to watch as the building slowly imploded on itself. Sargon did not spare a glance back to see how the situation would resolve, but the place where he stood became unbearably warm, so he sauntered into the crowd and disappeared. The elf leapt to its feet and moved alongside him. A small crowd of penumbra abandoned their hosts and gathered around Sargon amid the chaos of the fire.

Sargon said to the elf, "You desire to share in my power?"

"My Lord, you know my every thought, I see!" said the elf obsequiously. "Perhaps I might suggest the park for our initial council?" He extended a finger and pointed at a small, grassy but still very dirty enclosure only a stone's throw away, where teenagers barely older than Kane basked in the sun. They were either too far from the fire to take much notice or too apathetic to care.

Sargon took this advice, walking towards the park and bellowing, "Everybody OUT!"

It took most of the teenagers a few moments to decide whether or not to obey, but most of them eventually sauntered off, shooting Sargon looks of mingled fear and indignance.

Triumphant, Sargon stepped onto the base of a statue so that he could be seen as well as heard. Then he shouted, "Fellow penumbra! I am searching for the Philosopher's Stone, which is as much to your advantage as to mine—though it should not matter if it wasn't, since you have all sworn your allegiance to me!"

There was a general cry among the crowd of transparent creatures, a cry that sounded like jeers and barkings and neighings.

"The Stone is in its original location, the very place I found it ten millennia ago. I know this place to be in Egypt, which is why I am here now. But alas, I know not which part of Egypt it was in then, and even less would I recognize it in its present condition." He gestured at the city of Alexandria, and went on, "Few of you can perhaps appreciate how vastly the world has changed in the last fifteen hundred years, having been privileged as you were to watch it happen. But I have been shut away and am only now becoming acquainted with modern society.

"But no matter. We must, by any method we may devise, discover the location of the Philosopher's Stone. If it is in Egypt, I know of only one place to go to find it, and that is the Watcher city that was established here. It was created long after my time, but according to my reference—"

I am not your reference, thought Kane bitterly.

"—it is called Ibn Alaam, and it is a coastal city. There will be barriers around it in your dimension, put in place by the nimbi such that you cannot locate it—of this I am certain. But if there is a Watcher city in Egypt, then there are Seers among the people. Go, comb the entire country until you find a human being without a penumbra. When you do, you may be sure that he will know how to find Ibn Alaam. It is your task to extract that information from him, any way you can."

"But how?" said the elf in a wheedling tone. "Seers will see *us*, of course, and will not respond to our questions…"

"You will have to use force, then," Sargon boomed. "You will have to cross over to the world of men!"

There was a general gasp of shock, and one very brave gnome cried, "You are asking us to commit suicide! If the Seer is a Watcher then he will certainly carry weapons. I've heard what happens to those of us who take on bodies. We become mortal! If they kill us, we actually *die*!"

There was a murmur of unrest among the crowd, and whispers of dismay.

"Silence!" Sargon cried. "Do you want to continue to live your immortal lives simply keeping mankind from discovering his power? Restricting him to a mediocre life until he dies, and then finding another host, only to repeat the process forever and ever? Do you?" Nobody replied. "Or do you instead want to take their power and use it yourselves?" There was a small murmur of assent, but it was hesitant. "Nothing worth having can be obtained without risk. Are your lives now so fulfilling, so precious to you that you will not put them in some small measure of jeopardy in order to gain eternal glory, the kind of power of which you have only ever dreamed? Be bold now, my fellows! Take your rightful place in the order of the earth!"

Now his speech met with cheers, and Kane could feel his own heart racing and a shiver of fierce pleasure ran through his body.

You gave yourself goose pimples; well done, Kane sneered.

You see how I managed to hold captive kings and conquer nations for thousands of years, Sargon returned smoothly. *I am irresistible.*

Once the cheer died down, the penumbra began to disappear in order to carry out their mission.

And now? Kane demanded when the last of them had gone. *What are you planning to do now? You'll never find any of the Watcher cities, you know, not even if you send every penumbra in the world to try and find them. They're too well protected.*

"Excuse me," said a musical voice. It sounded like the tinkling of crystal. Sargon turned around to face her, and when he did, his whole body gave a start of recognition.

The owner of the voice went on, her perfect, full lips parting as she did so and baring her perfect white teeth, "That was a very stirring speech you just gave, although I don't know if it was quite up to your usual standards. But of course, allowances must be made. You have been at the bottom of a lake for the last fifteen hundred years. Your oratory skills are understandably a little rusty."

Sargon's eyes narrowed. "Do not forget," he said acidly, "however circumstances may have been at the beginning of all things, you are now my subject. You will speak to me with respect."

"Oh, most certainly, I am your subject, and a more faithful one you will never find!" returned the marvelous woman, though Kane thought there was a hint of sarcasm in her tone. "In fact, I will be your second-in-command when you again rise to power. I shall be your Queen once more."

Sargon's eyes smoldered. "You *dare*...!"

"Yes, I dare," returned Guinevere boldly, taking another step closer to him, her violet eyes fixed upon his black ones, "because without my help, you will never find the Philosopher's Stone. The map in the secret library of Carlion got you only this far, but you will never get closer than this. You know as well as I do that Ibn Alaam is closed to you, and even if you were to find it, there is no guarantee that you would be any closer there to discovering the location of the Stone than you are now. If the Watchers themselves knew where it was, they would have removed it centuries ago. But I know for a fact that they have not done so."

"And how do you know that?" Sargon demanded.

"Because I am the one who put it there," she said softly. "I led you to it in the first place, Sargon of Mesopotamia, and I put it back where it belonged after you fell in the Battle of Salisbury Plain. I knew that when you returned, as soon as the Sword was destroyed, the very first thing you would do, before you ever dreamt of fighting Arthur's heir, would be to amass an army so spectacular that no power on earth would have a prayer of resisting you. But in order to do that, you would need to find the Stone. And in order to find the Stone, you would need me."

"You dare to blackmail me?" Sargon hissed dangerously.

"Oh no!" laughed the delightful creature. "You are perfectly free to refuse, of course. But if you do, you will never find the Stone, and you will never defeat the Child of the Prophecy." She grinned wickedly. "When you have wearied yourself trying to discover its whereabouts on your own, you know how to find me." She made like she intended to walk away, but she did it in such a way that it was clear to both Sargon and Kane that she knew he would never let her go.

"All right!" said Sargon at last, angrily.

All merriment went out of Guinevere's face, and she demanded in a deadly tone of voice, "Swear it. Swear it in the Ancient Tongue."

"Haven't you tricked me enough with vows in the Ancient Tongue?" Sargon roared, but though he gritted his teeth as if he could crush her fragile body between them, he knew he had no choice. "Very well, then. When I find the Stone, I vow to make you my second-in-command. *Nuair a bhfaighidh me an Cloch, beidh tu mo dara igceannas.*"

"Splendid," Guinevere purred. "As always, it's a pleasure doing business with you, Sargon."

Sargon thought about striking her dead then and there, but she knew he would not dare—and indeed, now, he could not.

"The pleasure is mine. Guinevere," he spat.

Chapter 27

Bruce looked around at the other Watchers in the library of Ibn Alaam, hoping that someone could offer another clue about the location of the Stone. The silence stretched on for an interminable few minutes, when Sully started to fumble with his pockets.

"Sully?" said Bruce, sitting forward hopefully. "What is it?"

"Isdemus," said Sully, frowning as he pulled the entangled coin from a drawstring pouch in his pocket. "He's calling me."

Bruce exchanged a worried look with Dan and Jael.

"Be back as soon as I can," Sully murmured, and vanished with a *crack*.

Not five minutes later, he reappeared with Isdemus and Bomani at his side.

"Isdemus!" cried Jael in surprise, and stood up immediately.

Isdemus wasted no time. "Our worst fears are confirmed. The Shadow Lord has returned." All of them gasped in shock. Then he added even more reluctantly, "And he has taken Kane's body."

Bruce clenched the sides of the table until his knuckles turned white. Everyone turned towards him instinctively, and Masika reached out a hand and put it on top of his.

"Then it's true," Jael murmured. "The Taijitu... the Pendragon Crest... two dragons, one light and one dark..."

"There is more," Isdemus continued, looking at Bomani gravely. "As Kane, the Shadow Lord has returned to Carlion—" There were more cries of shock, until Isdemus silenced them with his hand— "but he did not arrive openly. Instead he approached one person, alone, and convinced her to sneak into the secret library and steal a book. That book will lead him to the critical conclusion that the Stone has been returned to its original location."

"Who?" Jael demanded, her fists clenched. "Who did this?"

"That I cannot and will not tell you," said Isdemus quietly.

"It's the mole!" said Sully through gritted teeth. Then he added to Isdemus, "You know who it is, then?"

"I have my reasons for keeping her identity private," said Isdemus. "She is quite repentant, and would, I believe, do absolutely anything to expunge her guilt—"

"So she showed it by helping the Shadow Lord steal the Stone?" Jael demanded, pounding her fist into her hand.

"Jael," said Isdemus firmly. "That is no longer the critical piece of the story. What is done is done. I have sent several of the nimbi to alert the Watchers in other sister cities. Now we must find the Stone before the Shadow Lord does."

"What happened to Achen, then?" Bruce asked Isdemus quietly. The others all looked from Bruce to Isdemus, their eyes widening as well.

Isdemus bowed his head gravely. "I do not know for sure. But at the moment, as I cannot summon him and there is no further reason for him to remain in Avalon, I must assume...he is dead."

There was a moment of silence at this. Dan clenched his jaw, and Bruce went whiter still.

"But the Shadow Lord won't be able to travel quickly, if he's in Kane's body," Dan pointed out shakily. "Kane isn't a space specialist."

"*Kane* was not," Isdemus agreed, and they all started at his use of the past tense. "But unfortunately, the Shadow Lord has no such limits."

Masika interjected, "But even if the Stone was replaced in its original location, how would he know where that is?"

"He was the one who found it the first time, of course," said Bruce, swallowing hard like he was trying not to vomit.

Bomani added, "Also, at least some of the penumbra knew where the Stone was in the beginning. They were the ones that led him to it."

Isdemus nodded. "Yes. I am nearly certain it was one of the penumbra who replaced it somewhere in the Giza Plaza after the Battle of Salisbury Plain.

She will know precisely where it is now."

"She?" asked Jael shrewdly.

Isdemus nodded. "Our success depends on whether or not the Shadow Lord knows that too. If he simply summons her and asks her to lead him to it..."

"What can we do, though?" Bruce interrupted. His voice was flat and his face pale. "We already looked in the only place in Giza the Stone was likely to be. It wasn't there!"

Isdemus looked grim. "Tell me."

Bruce looked away, unable to continue. So Dan explained the symbol in Giza and Jael's encounter with the guard's penumbra.

When he was finished, Isdemus frowned. "That is very strange." His frown deepened and he turned to Jael. "Is it possible that you simply didn't look hard enough?"

"It's possible," said Jael doubtfully. "I was distracted by the guard, but I got a pretty good look down there. And I'm telling you, it was empty."

Dan turned to Masika and raised his eyebrows.

"Why are you looking at me?" she said, taken aback.

"You're the one who figured out the first symbol. What else have you got?"

She blinked at him for a moment. "Well..." she began hesitantly, and bit her lip, thinking hard. "There *is* another piece to the sky-ground duality that I didn't mention before, but I don't see how it is relevant..."

"What is it?" Dan interrupted eagerly.

Masika moved towards the books on the wall

and traced the titles with her finger until she found what she was looking for. She pulled it from the shelf and sat down in one of the velvet chairs, plopping a large, dusty volume on top of one of the lace doilies. As she opened it, she explained, "The Venerables, or the Ancients of Egypt, believed that the stars told a story. They believed it told The Story, in fact, about their two primary deities, Osiris and Isis. Both are referenced in the Pyramid Texts. The counterpart of Osiris in the stars is Orion, of course, which is why the ancients built the pyramids in line with Orion's belt. The counterpart of Isis is the star Sirius, which is the brightest star in the sky. . . "

Dan lunged forward, scanning the pages over Masika's shoulder. "So what does Sirius correspond to on the ground?" he demanded.

Masika blinked at Dan for a moment, and the whites of her eyes grew wider. She flipped through the pages until she exclaimed, "Yes! This is it!" She pushed the book away from her and explained hurriedly, "At Zep Tepi, the First Time, the position of Sirius in the sky would have lined up perfectly with the rear paws of the Great Sphinx. But that makes no sense; the Sphinx is solid. Nothing can be hidden inside."

"And besides," Jael added, "Why was the Squaring the Circle symbol in the Temple, then?"

"The Temple and the Sphinx are likely connected somehow…" Bomani murmured, "just as Isis and Osiris were in the story…"

"It's a celestial treasure map!" Dan cried. "The Stone must be *underneath* the Sphinx. Let's get going!"

Chapter 28

The shimmering white line cut like an arrow through the still trees in the forest, pointing Peter and Lily towards the clearing, the rainbow, and the pool. Peter had a queer feeling of déjà vu as he ran past the still trees, as if the scenery was on a never-ending loop.

"Can we just say 'rainbow' and skip all this?" Lily huffed.

"Sure," Peter huffed back. "You know how to say that? Be my guest."

Lily didn't answer. They kept running.

Suddenly they burst through the trees and into the welcome sight of the clearing, but they did not slow down. Peter raced past Lily to where the rainbow emanated from the pool.

"Dive in!" Peter shouted behind him.

"What?"

"That's how you get out; you have to dive into the pool!" He didn't specify that they needed to choose a particular color, since every image was of the same wombat Lily had conjured before he'd read her mind. He dove in first, and the next moment sat blinking on the floor of her chamber.

A few seconds later, Lily sat up and blinked at him too, disoriented. Peter didn't wait for her to return to full capacity, but leapt to his feet again, pulling her to hers and bolting out of the chamber.

"Isdemus is probably still in his office—"

"Peter, that was hours ago!"

"No it wasn't. No time goes by in the Meadow, remember?"

Lily didn't have a chance to reply. She was too busy sprinting after him. Peter took the stairs two at a time, grabbing the banisters to propel himself upward. In minutes they were back outside of Isdemus's door, Peter pounding with the flat of his hand.

"Why isn't he answering?" Peter panted.

"Are you sure no time goes by…?"

"Yes!" he cut her off. "Remember the accident? That wouldn't have been possible if time had elapsed! You said time stops when you speak the Ancient Tongue too," he reminded her.

"Well, maybe he and Bomani went somewhere—"

"I thought they had a lot to discuss!"

"It doesn't matter," Lily cut him off sharply. "The fact is he's not here now."

Peter's hand, which had been just about to knock again, came to rest against the door, and he pounded his forehead against the back of it a few times in frustration. "I don't know where else to look for him!"

"*We* may not," said Lily slowly, "but don't you think one of the nimbi could find him? At least they could search the area faster than we can."

Peter's forehead was still flattened on the door, but he turned his face just enough to look back at her, one cheek squished against his hand. "Why didn't I think of that?"

Lily arched an eyebrow at him, but before she could retort, *I have good ideas sometimes too,* Peter pushed back from the door and said the first name to pop into his head.

"Achen!"

There was no reply. Peter exchanged a concerned look with Lily; that had never happened before. Then he remembered that Isdemus had sent Achen to Avalon to look for Kane, and thought maybe that was it.

"Um, Verum!" he tried again.

Nothing.

"I have a bad feeling about this…" Lily murmured.

"Fides Dignus!" Peter shouted, fighting panic now. "How can *none* of them respond? Bellator!"

"Fides Dignus said they didn't *have* to come when we called, remember?" Lily pointed out. "Isdemus must have sent them all away after we left on a mission or something…"

"But we know where the Stone is!" Peter shouted in frustration.

As soon as he'd said it, Lily lunged at him in alarm, clamping a hand over his mouth. "Not everybody in the castle needs to know that, Peter!"

she hissed, releasing his mouth.

"But *somebody* does," he argued, wrenching himself away from her, "and apparently we'll have to take whomever we can get!"

"Pete!" cried another voice behind them. "What are you yelling about?"

They both whirled around to see Cole and Brock walking towards them. Even they were a welcome sight.

"You look kind of—strung out," Cole observed to both of them when they got close enough.

"We found out something important, and there's no one here for us to tell!" Peter burst out.

"Well, what do we look like?" Brock scowled at him, and muttered, "Just because there's no prophecy about *us*…"

"Peter," said Lily, ignoring this and grabbing his arm. She said significantly, "If there's nobody here for us to tell, then you know what we'll have to do."

His stomach turned over, but he nodded, swallowing hard. "Yeah," he croaked. "I do."

"Well, that makes two of you," Brock cut in irritably.

They both looked up at Cole and Brock, and then Peter looked down at Lily, her hands still clutching his forearm tightly enough to leave white indentations where her fingers were. Peter said, "We *did* need their help last time." Then he sighed and turned back to the brothers. "We've gotta make this quick, though, and we can't talk here. Come on, my chamber is closest." He let go of Lily and set off at a run back towards the spiral staircase.

A few minutes later, all four of them burst into

Peter's chamber. It was dark outside by then, lending it a somber atmosphere for their council.

"Now," Brock growled, fixing Peter with his sharp blue eyes. "Talk."

Peter glanced at Lily, and they both said in unison, "We know where the Philosopher's Stone is."

Chapter 29

Peter and Lily finished telling Brock and Cole what they discovered in the Meadow, and the brothers stared at them for a few moments without speaking.

"And now you can't find Isdemus or any of the Watchers," Brock summarized.

"And none of the nimbi are responding either," Peter added.

"We could wait until someone comes back," said Cole hopefully. "I mean, that can't be too long, right?"

"Maybe, maybe not," said Peter, "but the Shadow Lord is back, he's on the trail of the Stone, and theoretically he's got a map that could lead him right to it. We don't exactly have a lot of time to play with."

"Well, what are we waiting for?" said Brock, a bit too loudly. "Let's go!"

"Hold on!" said Cole, his eyes round and his face white. "There's got to be someone we can tell! I mean, this is pretty drastic, don't you think?"

"Cole," Lily scolded, "you were the one who insisted Peter and I not go to the Fata Morgana without you!"

"That was different; my brother was in there!" Cole protested.

Brock blinked at him in surprise and for a fleeting moment, he looked almost touched.

"This is much bigger than that now," said Peter, and added as an aside, "No offense, Brock." Brock shrugged to show he didn't take it personally, and Peter pressed on, "Cole… I mean, it's up to you, of course. Lily and I can both fight, but I think… I mean, I suspect we'll need a healer with us."

"You know how to fight, huh?" Lily muttered to Peter rhetorically, raising an eyebrow at him.

"I know how to say a grand total of three words!" Cole was almost hyperventilating now.

"Yeah," said Lily, "but those words are 'stop bleeding' and 'heal,' and that's enough to cover the basics!"

"Hold on," said Brock suddenly, and they all turned to look at him in surprise. He glanced at Cole and asked the others, "Whom did Isdemus leave in charge of the castle?"

"What?" said Peter, confused.

"You know, when he leaves. There has to be a second-in-command, right? Who is it?"

They all looked at each other blankly for a moment. Peter said, "I'd have thought it would be Jael, Sully, or Dan. Probably Sully I guess, since he's the oldest. But he's not here either; at least I don't think he is…"

"He *is* a Space Specialist, though," Brock pointed out. "We just have to find a way to call him back. Or we could go to him, if we knew where he was."

"Only if we knew the Ancient Tongue for creating portholes," Peter pointed out. "Which we don't…"

"I have an idea!" came a voice from underneath Peter's canopied bed. A little redheaded boy popped his head out eagerly in the midst of their little circle.

It took Peter a moment first to process his presence, and then another moment to find his voice in the midst of his fury. "*Eustace!*"

Cole groaned, and Brock gestured at Eustace but looked at Peter and Lily, like this was their idea. "What the bloody hell is he doing here?"

"Get out!" Peter shouted at Eustace, punctuating his words with a pointer finger to the door.

"But—"

"*Now!*"

"But," Cole began in a small voice, "Don't you think we ought to hear what he has to say?"

"No!" said Peter, through gritted teeth.

"I'm so confused," said Brock, turning to Lily, who shrugged at him as if to say, *don't look at me.*

Eustace took advantage of the moment, crawling out from under the bed as he piped, "I really can help this time, Peter! You just said yourself that you dunno how to contact Master Sully, or how to locate Isdemus neither, but I been spyin' longer than you an' I know things about th' castle, an' about th' Watchers… you didn't know I was here, did you? Did you, Peter? But I was, and I hid, and I'm quiet, and I hear things! But, if you don't wanna know what I know, then I'll just go away, me and my secrets, and let you figure out what you're gonna do all on your own…" As he said this, he made a ridiculous show of walking towards the door in slow motion.

Peter sighed in exasperation, and glanced at Lily, who shook her head incredulously.

"Fine, Eustace," said Peter finally. "Tell us your idea, but make it quick!"

"Really, Peter? Really? You won't regret this, honest you won't—"

"I regret it already," Peter muttered.

"Okay, it's like this. I happen to know that th' Watchers went to Ibn Alaam!" He said it with a flourish, as if he expected *oohs* and *ahhs*. Instead all he got were blank stares.

"What's that?" said Brock finally.

"It's another sister city in Egypt!"

"Egypt!" Lily exclaimed. "So the Watchers already know the Stone is there?"

Understanding dawned on Peter's face. "Of course! Isdemus said there were other cities all over the world like Carlion, for people who became Seers or discovered their gifts and needed a safe place to learn how to use them…" He trailed off and looked back at Eustace. "How do we get there?"

"Oh," said Eustace, and looked quite smug. "Well, I can tell you that, but for a price."

"Why, you blackmailing little…!" Brock began, standing up to his full height.

"I'm not blackmailin'!" Eustace protested, trembling. "I just mean I wanna come with you!"

"Absolutely not!" Peter roared, and stood up too. Lily and Cole, who were now the only ones sitting, exchanged a look with one another and also stood up, because it seemed the thing to do. "Eustace, do I need to remind you what happened the *last* time we let you come along? We all could have been killed!"

"I'll do what you say this time, Peter, I promise! If you let me come along, I'll obey any order you give me, right away, no questions asked…"

"Why is Peter suddenly in charge?" Brock grumbled.

"Because it was Peter's Meadow, that's why," Lily retorted.

Peter spared her a grateful glance, and asked her under his breath, "Well? What do *you* think? Should we four just go try to find the Stone, or should we try to find Sully and tell him first?"

Lily pursed her lips. "I really don't think we can afford to wait, but if we have a chance of getting help then we can't pass it up—"

"In that case," Brock cut in authoritatively, "I say half of us go to this Ibn Alaam place, and half go straight to Giza and try to locate the Stone."

Peter nodded. "I think that's a good plan," he said, glancing at Lily, who nodded too. "Cole?"

Cole still looked a little nauseated, but he nodded once. "I guess…"

Eustace watched this discussion, perplexed. "So… so I can come?" he insisted, as if he had only been listening for the answer to this all-important point.

Peter sighed irritably. "Well, if half of us are

going to Ibn Alaam, and we don't know where it is unless you show us, then I suppose you'll have to. But you *must* do exactly as you're told!"

"Oh! Oh, I will, Peter!" cried Eustace, jumping up and down. "Not a peep from me, not a word, I'll be so quiet you won't even know I'm—"

"Fabulous, how about you start now," Peter growled. Then he turned to the others. "The next part to work out is who is going where."

"I'm going to Giza," said Lily immediately.

"Me too!" said Brock, and Eustace said, "Me three!"

"*You* are going to Ibn Alaam," said Peter to Eustace severely, "because that's the whole point of your coming at all!"

"I'll go with Eustace," said Cole quickly, and turned big pleading eyes on his brother next.

"Nope. I'm going to Giza," Brock said stubbornly.

Peter looked between Lily and Brock. "Neither of them can fight," he said. "One of you has to go with them."

"How come not you?" Brock growled.

"I'd love to," said Peter, grimacing. "But I've *got* to go to Giza, because I've seen where the Stone is and if the Shadow Lord shows up, I'm the only one who can match him." He thought of what Isdemus had shown him in the Meadow. *Anything is possible,* he reminded himself. But his heart still threatened to leap from his chest.

"Your own brother," Cole murmured to Peter, shaking his head. Impulsively, he dove at Peter and hugged him. Peter clapped him on the back in

321

awkward surprise before disentangling himself.

"All right," said Lily decisively, "we'll draw straws for who goes with you, me or Brock."

"Who's got straws, though?" said Cole.

"Well… hmm," said Peter. Then he jumped up and ran to his wardrobe, pulling out a pair of jeans he'd grabbed in Norwich and rifling through the pockets. "Here we are," he said, withdrawing a 50 p coin.

As soon as she saw what it was, Lily declared to Brock, "Heads I go to Giza, you go to Ibn Alaam. Tails, other way around."

"How come? I want heads to Giza!" Brock protested.

Peter shook his head, exasperated. "What Lily said. Heads, she's with me."

It was heads. Lily smirked and Brock scowled.

"All right then. How are we supposed to get to Ibn Alaam?" Brock muttered.

"That's a good question," said Peter, and turned to Eustace. "It's time for you to earn your keep. How do they get there?"

"Easy! There's a portrait in the Commuter Station that takes you straight there!" said Eustace.

Peter narrowed his eyes at Eustace dangerously.

"Peter," said Lily with a warning note in her voice, putting a hand on his forearm.

"You mean to tell me…" Peter began, as Eustace's eyes grew wider, "that it was that obvious? We could have figured it out without you?"

"But you never would have known they were in Ibn Alaam without me!" Eustace pointed out, shrinking his head into his shoulders until his neck seemed to disappear. "You promised I could come along, don't forget, you promised!"

"I know I promised," Peter muttered, glancing at Brock and Cole. "Sorry in advance for whatever trouble he's going to cause you."

Chapter 30

When the Watchers all let go of Sully and stood blinking in between the three pyramids and the Sphinx, Bruce had the immediate instinct to duck and run for cover.

"This isn't dark at all! It's like we're in floodlights or something!" Bruce exclaimed.

Bomani explained, "Yes, the pyramids and the Sphinx are lit all the time because they're tourist attractions." He didn't bother to keep his voice down to a whisper because there were no tourists around. It was three in the morning.

"Nice of you to mention that now," Jael grumbled.

"It does not matter," said Isdemus. "We had no choice but to come."

Masika added, "As long as we stay out of the direct beam of the lights and keep to the shadows, we ought to be all right. The base of the Sphinx is not lit up, see? And anyway, for the next two hours there will be fewer people around than at any other time of the day or night."

"Only two hours?" repeated Bruce incredulously. "You mean people start showing up here at five in the morning?"

"That is when Cairo starts to wake up," Masika explained, "because that is when the first mosque call sounds. So for the next two hours, we have the best chance of remaining undetected."

They all hurried into the shadows of the pyramids at a crouch except for Isdemus, who carried himself in his usual regal and unhurried manner. As soon as they were under the cover of darkness, they all relaxed into their normal gaits, though suddenly feeling the humidity and wiping beads of sweat from their brows. Bomani fell into step with Isdemus at the head of the party.

Jael blearily ran a hand through her lank brown hair, glancing at Dan. Her eyes were bloodshot and she yawned every few minutes. She became even crankier than usual on lack of sleep. "Too bad we don't have an earth specialist with us."

"Because?"

"Because they could move dirt easier than I could. And at any rate, if *they* moved it, then I wouldn't have to."

"Stop whining, Jael," Sully said sharply. "We can help you dig." Despite his white hair, his shoulders were broad and strong, and so the offer was not insignificant. "I'm not sure what we'll do for shovels though."

"We'll do it the old-fashioned way," Isdemus returned. "We'll use our hands."

Masika looked down at her clean white blouse and khakis. "I will pass on digging."

Jael muttered under her breath, "You would." Masika did not seem to hear her, but Dan glanced up at her and pursed his lips.

Isdemus and Bomani led the way, but Jael followed closely behind. Dan caught up with her and fell into step, far enough away that the others could not hear. "I could reroute some of the water from the Nile to help you dig," he offered.

"Isn't the Nile many kilometers that way?" Jael said, pointing in the distance.

Dan shrugged. "If I really focused I could do it, though. I could command high pressure water to tunnel through the earth within seconds."

"Then everything would be under water, so even if there is anything down there, we won't be able to see it," Jael yawned.

"Good point. I could siphon it back out again of course, but it would still be all wet and muddy."

"And likely to draw attention," she added. "The Nile spontaneously flooding Cairo might cause a bit of a stir, even at three in the morning."

"True." They were silent for another few minutes, and Dan said abruptly, "Jael, I have to ask you something."

She raised her eyebrows at him and waited. "Well then?"

He took a deep breath and plunged on, "We might not make it out of here alive, so it seems like this might be my last chance—"

"What is it, Dan?" Jael interrupted blearily.

"Are you jealous of Masika?"

Jael stopped walking for an instant, but she caught herself and kept moving. "Why would I be jealous—?"

"Because she's flirting with me. And you don't like that."

Jael was stunned to silence for a moment. "Dan," she said quietly. But she didn't say anything else.

"You disliked her from the minute you met her, because you saw how she was looking at me. Try and deny it."

Jael sighed and shook her head. "Dan, I really don't think this is the time or place for this conversation—"

"Hence my original statement! We could die out here!" Dan protested heatedly, grabbing her elbow. "So I want to know! Call it a dying man's last request if you want, but I want to hear you admit it!"

Her eyes flashed back at him now. The others outstripped them on their way to the Sphinx, and Sully eyed them both curiously, but neither paid any attention to him. "What are you really asking me, Dan? This isn't about Masika, is it?"

Dan hesitated only a moment. "I want you to admit that you're in love with me, Jael. I know you are, but I want to hear you say it."

Jael closed her eyes for a long moment, and then opened them again, drawing a shaky breath.

"I can't," she whispered.

Dan blinked. "You can't, or you don't?" He let go of her elbow.

"Can't." She shook her head. "I can't... go through it again." She looked away at the receding figures of the other Watchers. They would now have to jog to catch up.

"Because of what happened to your husband, you'll never take another chance again," said Dan finally. "Is that it?"

Jael sniffled and turned her face away from Dan. "We've got to catch up; come on." She jogged back towards the others before Dan could say anything else.

Jael caught up first, leaving Dan too stunned to move for a few moments behind her. When they both rejoined the group, Isdemus was saying, "That one is the brightest star," pointing up at the sky. Then he looked at Masika and said, "Sirius, yes?"

"Yes," Masika called back. "And those three are Orion's belt." She gestured first at the three stars and then at the three pyramids.

A stone sand wall blocked the Sphinx from tourists. Isdemus vaulted himself over it and dropped to his feet below as if he were a much younger man, heading towards the back of the Sphinx without missing a beat. One by one, the others copied him, landing in the same place and following in his footsteps.

When Isdemus reached the rear paws, he dropped to his knees in the hard-packed sand. Despite his midnight-blue robes and seemingly frail body, he scooped the earth with his hands into piles behind him. The others followed suit. For nearly twenty minutes, nobody spoke, and nobody paused except to wipe the sand out of their eyes or the sweat from their brows. When they had hollowed out a significant volume of sand, enough that Jael could stand in it waist deep, she said, "At what point exactly are we going to give up and look somewhere else? There's nothing down here."

"Many ages of the earth have come and gone even since the Stone was last returned in its final resting place," said Bomani. "At one time the Sphinx was covered in sand all the way to its neck. That is the reason for this wall here."

"Yes, but that was not in Arthur's day, nor since," Masika pointed out, brushing the dirt stains off her trousers with the effect of grinding them even more deeply into the fibers. Apparently she'd decided to help, after all. "However," she added, "the conspiracy theorists say that there is a secret chamber beneath the rear paws of the Sphinx, and estimate a depth of roughly thirty meters."

"Thirty meters!" Jael echoed, and looked below her in horror. "How are we going to dig that far with our hands? We won't even be able to scoop the dirt back out pretty soon!"

"Why hasn't anybody ever excavated down here before if they thought something was there?" asked Bruce.

"Because it is the *Sphinx*," said Masika haughtily. "It is one of the Ancient Wonders of the World. They are not just going to let someone dig it up, particularly not conspiracy theorists held in low esteem among Egyptologist circles."

"Well, if it's supposed to be that deep," said Sully, "we really had better go and get an earth specialist. We won't be able to do without one."

"How about Harris?" said Dan. "He won't relish the thought of being roused in the middle of the night, though—"

"Some things are more important than sleep," said Sully, his mouth set in a hard line. "I will go and fetch him."

"Should we all go?" said Masika, hopefully.

"No!" said Jael, as if the suggestion were personally offensive to her. "What if the Shadow Lord shows up while we're gone?"

"What if the Shadow Lord shows up while we are *here*?" Masika countered, her eyes round. "We would not stand a chance!"

"Maybe not," said Dan, "but perhaps we can delay him, at least a bit."

"Right," said Bruce solemnly, and stepped closer to Dan and Jael. "And so we wait?"

"And so we wait," Dan confirmed.

"We wait," Jael repeated, looking at the others in solidarity.

"I am proud to join my brothers and my friends," Isdemus agreed, smiling at them gravely. Then he looked at Masika and Bomani and said, "But we cannot ask you two to stay. You *do* have gifts, but you have not been taught how to recognize or use them. It would be cruel to ask you to fight the Shadow Lord with no weapons at all. It would be best if you both went with Sully."

Masika's relief was evident, and she crossed the distance to Sully and took hold of his arm at once. Bomani frowned, but bowed his head to Isdemus obediently and followed her.

Sully hesitated, gazing at the faces of each of his friends in turn as if it may be for the last time. Finally Dan moved forward to embrace Sully, who hesitated only a moment before returning the crushing hug. Jael swallowed hard and looked away.

Sully released Dan, pursed his lips, and nodded curtly to all of them. Then he, Masika, and Bomani disappeared.

Chapter 31

Peter and Lily parted ways with Brock, Cole, and Eustace on the staircase, as the latter party continued on their way to the second basement and made for the Commuter Station. There was an awkward moment where Cole choked up and threw his arms around both Peter and Lily, and Brock shook Peter's hand before Eustace urged them on, so Brock only had time to wave goodbye to Lily.

Peter and Lily ran on, taking the long route to avoid the Great Hall, where the rest of the Watchers were eating dinner. Peter steered them towards the sitting room where he'd met with his dad the morning before, just before they left for school. His heart pounded, and he wasn't sure if it was from exertion or nerves.

"It's just here," he panted, pushing open the double doors to the cozy little room with velvet chairs under the large arched window. Books lined the entirety of the two adjacent walls, except for the cheerful fireplace, which was currently lit. Peter spotted what he was after on a little round table beside one of the chairs: the globe. He hurried towards it and picked it up.

It was the most beautiful globe either of them had ever seen, and also the strangest, depicting the sister cities as well as those cities known to the outside world. Every country was set with a precious or a semi-precious stone, labeled in ebony, and cheerful aquamarine and midnight-blue stones represented the ocean. Peter traced his finger from Carlion to Giza, looking perplexed. Meanwhile, Lily pulled a dictionary of the Ancient Tongue off of a nearby shelf, thumbing through it and mouthing the words as she came to them. Her hands trembled as she flipped the pages.

"This is what Sully does, I think," Peter murmured, inspecting the globe for his destination. "Except I don't know the scale." He turned the globe upside down to see if it was written anywhere. To his surprise, it was. "Ah! One to forty million!"

Lily looked up from the dictionary and raised her eyebrows. "That can't possibly be helpful to you!" Both their voices were pitchy with nerves.

"It is," Peter insisted. "Now I can get more of a mental picture of how far this is." He drew a line with his finger from Carlion to Giza, concentrating hard.

"I hope you're right, or we might end up in the middle of the ocean," she murmured apprehensively, and went back to the dictionary. "Okay, I think I've got it. It looks like you can say *a iompar chuig...* and then Giza, I guess?"

Peter frowned. "Giza, just in English?"

"Well, I don't know, I don't see another word for Giza in here. You could just say Ancient Egypt, but who knows where that would take us?"

"All right, come here," said Peter, holding out his hand to her. Lily closed the dictionary, set it next to the globe, and put her hand in his. "*A iompar chuig Giza!*" Peter commanded. Both of them felt a lurch, as if from a porthole, but it released when Peter said the word *Giza*.

"Hm, I guess there must be another word," said Lily, frowning. She released his hand and thumbed through the dictionary for a few more seconds, biting her lip as she read. Then she reached out her hand to Peter's again and said just as she was setting the dictionary down, "Let's try *A iompar chuig sean Éigipt!*"

The lurch returned, and suddenly the castle warped and disappeared.

In the next moment, they found themselves on a beach. There was what looked like ocean in front of them, with boats in harbor some distance away. A few of the boats were out on the water, and while there probably had been sunbathers earlier that day, it was already dark.

Lily turned to look at Peter, wide-eyed.

"What just happened?" she demanded, still clutching the dictionary in her other hand.

Peter swallowed hard. "We warped," he said.

"But I'm not a space specialist!"

"Well, apparently you are!"

Lily suddenly realized she was still holding his hand and let go. "But…" her mind spun. "But I barely even glanced at the globe. I mean, I looked, but I don't know what forty million of *anything* is…"

"Let's find out where we are then," said Peter, his voice tight. He started to move towards the harbor and refused to look at her, his jaw set in a hard line. He was upset, but he wasn't sure why. Presently, he said, "Giza isn't anywhere near the ocean, so this has to be either the Mediterranean or the Red Sea."

"Assuming I was even that accurate," said Lily. They fell silent again, and Peter picked up his pace. Lily matched him.

Lily pointed and said, "That looks like a port city that way."

"Super. Come on." Peter started off in that direction.

"Wait, Peter; it'll take us forever to walk that far. Why don't we just warp closer?"

"Oh. Right." Peter stopped walking and looked at her. "Well. Go on, then."

"Don't you want to try this time?" Lily asked timidly.

"Oh. Um, sure," said Peter. "Can you look up how to say 'port city'?"

She did, and she told him, careful not to string the whole phrase together in the Ancient Tongue this time. Peter took her hand, but she noticed he held it a bit more loosely than he had before.

A moment later they found themselves standing in a very industrial-looking city, with brown square-shaped buildings several stories high. Many green bushes lined the water, trimmed to look homogenous.

Lily wanted to say something, but she didn't know what. "It must be very late; there's nobody here."

"That way," said Peter suddenly, "I hear noise. Maybe that's the direction of downtown."

They walked through streets of hot asphalt and concrete buildings closely packed together. Although they hadn't seen any people yet, as they got closer to the area Peter had pointed to, they saw more and more cars. Most of them were hatchback and beat-up looking, which had to mean they were approaching a more populated area.

At last they came upon a street fish market vendor, closing up for the night, and Peter dashed towards him.

"Excuse me!" he said.

"Yes?" said the vendor in clipped English, turning around. He regarded Peter and Lily skeptically. "You want to buy fish?"

Behind the man was a transparent gray beast, built like a human but with features like a wolf. Its intelligent eyes fixed upon Peter's immediately, and its mouth fell open, revealing yellow fangs dripping with saliva.

"No, no," said Peter, shaking both his hand and his head for emphasis, eyeing the wolf warily. "Could you tell us what city this is?"

"This city?" echoed the man, now looking even more skeptical. "Are you lost?"

"*What is your name?*" demanded the werewolf.

"What is your name?" repeated the man, without waiting for a response to his previous question.

"Never mind my name; the city! This city, it's called—?"

"Port Suez," said Lily behind him, pointing to the sign on the awning of the fish shop which neither of them had seen before, written in both Arabic and English. Then she lunged forward and pulled Peter away. "Thanks very much, sorry to bother you!"

Once they rounded a corner, Lily hissed to Peter, "Let's go; come on!"

"I don't know where to go, though, do you?" Peter snapped. "I have no idea where Port Suez is in relation to Giza! I could have asked how far it was and which way if you hadn't yanked me away!"

"Really, Peter? You wanted to announce to that werewolf where we were going?" Lily demanded. "We have only seconds before it figures out who you must be, and when it does, it's going to come after us!"

Peter stopped arguing then and broke into a jog next to Lily. "I vote we try southwest," he panted. "If we're at the Mediterranean, then Giza is south of us, but if we're at the Red Sea, then it's to the west. So we should split the difference. Look up how to say southwest in there, and I'll just picture the distance in my head!"

Lily flipped through the dictionary frantically just as they heard a voice behind them, and the heavy plod of footsteps. "Boy? Where did you go, boy?"

"It's *siar ó dheas*!" said Lily urgently. "Go!"

Peter grabbed her and warped them away, but they remained in place just long enough to see the fish vendor and his werewolf lumbering towards them as fast as his heavy legs could carry him.

*

They reappeared in miles upon miles of empty desert. The sand rippled around them in a corduroy pattern from the wind.

Peter swore.

"Let's try again," said Lily firmly, not letting go of his hand.

"Which way? We can't just keep warping at random…"

"We haven't got a choice!"

"We *do* have a choice; we can reason this out!" Peter shot back. "We were at the sea. We went southwest, and now we're in the desert. That means we have to go either north or east."

"Or northeast," said Lily. "But that'll take us right back to where we were!"

"Not if we don't go as far."

"Fine!" Lily snapped, whipping the dictionary open harder than necessary. "Northeast is *oirthuaisceart*. But it's my turn!"

Peter shook his head stubbornly. "No way, it was your lousy directions that got us in this mess in the first place!"

Lily fixed Peter with her nastiest glare as he grabbed her hand. She thought about yanking it away, or slapping him… and for a split second, for reasons she could not fathom, she also considered kissing him. But he spoke the Ancient Tongue before she could decide, and they disappeared.

Chapter 32

"**W**hat in the world?" said Brock, looking around as he, Cole, and Eustace emerged from behind the white sheet hanging in the downtown market of Ibn Alaam.

It was nighttime by then, and most of the shops and stands had shut down. A few people ducked into apartments or down darkened alleyways, but nobody seemed to be in the streets long enough for the boys to ask them any questions.

"Hey!" said Brock, seeing an old man in a dark blue gallebeya ducking into the stairwell to his apartment. "Excuse me, can you point us in the direction of the Watcher Castle?"

The man shook his head. "There is only one main road, and you are on it," said the man in clipped in English. He pointed down the road to indicate which way they should go.

When they got to the outskirts of the city, having met very few people along the way, they saw that the stables where they might have procured camels during the daytime were closed for the night.

"Now what?" said Cole, throwing up his hands.

"Leave it to me," said Brock, and marched over to the nearest door he could find, which looked like an apartment. He knocked.

A few seconds later a suspicious-looking, middle aged woman in a frumpy robe opened the door just wide enough to peer through, a chain barring the visitors' entry.

"It is very late," she observed without a greeting, frowning at Brock.

"Sorry to bother—" Brock began, but Eustace cut him off.

"We're trying to get to the Watcher castle and it's such a very long way off and th' stables are closed and we wondered if we could borrow a horse or a camel or anything that could get us there faster!" Eustace looked at Brock eagerly, as if for approval. "Right?"

"Eustace, hush," Cole whispered, not in a scolding tone but as if they were co-conspirators. "You're supposed to stay quiet, remember?"

Eustace's eyes grew as round as saucers and he mimed a zipping motion across his lips, throwing the invisible key over his shoulder.

The woman narrowed her eyes at the three boys and said, "Who are you? Why are you trying to get to the castle at this time of night?"

"We're from Carlion. We're, um, Watchers," Brock said, crossing his fingers behind his back.

"Where's Anthony when you need him?" Cole muttered under his breath. Eustace looked at him with wide eyes, pressing his hands together, begging to help. Cole shook his head at him. In response, Eustace bounced up and down like he needed a toilet, still fixing Cole with his pleading eyes.

Brock went on to the woman, "Listen, it would take far too long to explain and it's top secret anyway, but it's imperative that we get to the Watcher castle as soon as possible! Have you got horses we can borrow or something? Or, um… camels?" he added, remembering the stables.

"We'll bring 'em right back!" Eustace cried at once, and then clamped both hands over his mouth again.

The woman gave a short laugh. "You must be joking! Give you a camel?" She slammed the door in their faces.

Brock blinked, crestfallen. "It'll take us all night to walk that distance on foot!"

Eustace continued his eager little dance, extending a hand up in the air and fixing his stare on Brock this time.

Brock sighed. "What is it, Eustace?"

"I can break in to the stables!" he blurted, clamping his hand back over his mouth again.

Brock and Cole exchanged a skeptical look. "Oh yeah?" Brock said at last.

"Prob'ly! I locked myself out loads o' times, so's I know how to break open stable locks! Least I can if they're th' same as the ones in Carlion!"

Brock and Cole shrugged at each other, and Cole said, "Better than walking all night…"

"I hope they don't have prisons in this city,"

Brock murmured dubiously, as they set off in the direction of the stables, which were only some thirty meters away.

When they arrived, Eustace dropped to a crouch, looking over both shoulders theatrically as he tiptoed to the lock.

"He walks normally all the way *to* the stables…" Brock observed under his breath.

Eustace ignored this and flattened both his palms against the slats, peering through. They were wide enough that he could see the sliding metal piece on the other side.

"Somebody gimme somethin' long and thin!"

"Like what?" Cole frowned.

"Like a screwdriver!"

Brock laughed shortly. "Oh sure, just lemme pull out my portable toolbox."

"Shh!" Cole hissed at his brother disapprovingly, "He's trying to help us!"

Eustace meanwhile stuck his first two fingers between the slats and wiggled them around, letting out little grunts here and there. "Wood's too thick!" he said, "Can't get a grip…"

Brock sighed. "Can we just break the door down?"

Cole looked alarmed. "We'd get in so much trouble!" As soon as he said it, he stopped, watching Eustace attempt to break in at that very moment. "Well, we'd get in even more trouble," he amended.

"Priorities, Cole," said Brock, and waved Eustace aside.

"Wait, wait! Almost got it!" Eustace said,

sticking his tongue out and squeezing one eye shut as he wriggled his fingers.

"If you don't move," Brock warned, "I'm gonna kick the door down, and you're going with it."

"Have you ever kicked a door down before?" Cole asked skeptically, cocking his head to one side.

"Of course not," Brock returned. "When would I ever have kicked a door down?"

"I dunno, you just seem awfully sure of yourself…"

"Got it!" Eustace interrupted. They all heard the creak of metal, and he wriggled his fingers back out, wincing as he did it. "Tada! Ooh, splinter," he added, sucking on his fingers.

Brock pushed the door open doubtfully, but it swung open with no resistance.

"Eustace! You're amazing!" said Cole appreciatively, and Eustace pulled his fingers out of his mouth and beamed.

"Uh oh, one other problem," said Brock, once all three of them had stepped into the shadows of the stables.

"Ugh!" cried Cole. "It smells like a zoo?"

"They're camels." Brock turned back to the other two. "Do either of you know how to ride a camel?"

"Sure I do!" said Eustace, trotting over to one of them happily. He fitted the camel with a muzzle, reins, and a saddle, untied it and handed the reins to Cole first. Then he did the same with two more. Brock and Cole watched him, grudgingly impressed, and followed Eustace out into the night air as he led the way with his own camel. Cole inhaled the clean air with relief.

"Man, that was putrid!" Cole exclaimed, fanning his nose.

"Watch me!" Eustace declared, tugging his camel's reins to the ground until it obediently buckled its legs and Eustace climbed on. Cole and Brock exchanged a look and copied him, although it took Cole a few tries before his camel crouched low enough to the ground that he could mount.

"Where'd you learn to do this, anyway?" Brock asked Eustace.

"Sometimes when Watchers from other cities visit Carlion, Isdemus lets 'em ride whatever they want, like camels an' elephants an' stuff! Not all th' time, but enough that I figured out a thing or two! I'm dead useful, I am!"

"I won't disagree with you this time," Brock admitted, trying to convince his camel to obey his lead towards the vast expanse of desert.

Half an hour later, the leonine structure that was the castle of Ibn Alaam loomed before them. Despite the fact that they had never seen a structure that looked less like a castle in their lives, it was the only building around.

"That's gotta be it," said Cole doubtfully.

"It's like a cross between the Sphinx and an igloo," Brock murmured.

"Ooh, ooh!" said Eustace, "I read about igloos once, they're made of ice and people live in 'em in the outside world 'cause they don't have any weather specialists, and—"

"Can it," Brock barked, and then he pointed in

the distance. "Cole. Did you see that?"

"I… thought I saw something," said Cole uncertainly, "but it could have been a trick of the light…"

"No, there's definitely something moving up there!" said Brock, digging his heels into his camel's flanks. The camel spat upon the ground but did not move any faster. "Oh, come *on*!"

"Wait a minute, I think there's three somethings… they're people! They're going into the entrance!" said Cole, and then shouted, "Hey! You there!"

All three of the figures froze, and after a moment's hesitation began to move towards them. They came slowly at first, and then one of the three broke into a run.

"It's Sully!" cried Brock, and let out a whoop of joy. "SULLY! Sully, we came looking for you—"

"Brock! You're an earth specialist!" Sully exclaimed when he saw him, like it was the best news in the world. The other figures approaching behind Sully were a middle-aged man and a very pretty Egyptian lady.

Brock stared at Sully, confused. "Well, yeah—"

"We need your help!" Sully blurted. He caught his breath and went on, "The other Watchers are out in Giza—"

"Looking for the Philosopher's Stone, we know," said Brock hastily. "That's why we're here. We came to tell you that we know exactly where it is!" Sully's mouth fell open, and Brock glanced apprehensively at the strangers.

"They're friends," said Sully quickly.

Brock nodded. "The Stone is beneath the back paws of the Sphinx, but it's in a subterranean chamber, and you have to access it through the Temple!"

Masika's mouth fell open. "So that's why the symbol was in the Temple…"

"How do you know this?" Sully demanded.

"Peter," Brock, Cole, and Eustace all answered at once, and Cole explained, "He actually saw it in there."

Sully blinked at him. "He…?"

"You will still need an earth specialist to uncover the entrance," Masika said to Sully, cutting him off. "Jael did not manage to find the entrance to a subterranean chamber in the Temple. Assuming it is there."

Sully stopped arguing and said to Brock, "We left the others in Giza in case the Shadow Lord shows up to try and take the Stone. I'm here looking for an earth specialist." He fixed his steel blue eyes on Brock. "You're far from a perfect solution, kid— no offense. But I haven't got time to keep looking for someone else."

Brock set his jaw, pursed his lips, and dismounted, trying to look braver than he really felt. "I'm in," he declared, his voice steady.

Sully turned to Masika and Bomani. "Take care of these two," he indicated Eustace and Cole, "and I'll be back with the others as soon as I can."

"What?" Cole protested. "No way! If Brock's going, I'm going!"

"And me!" Eustace piped.

"Aren't you the stable boy?" said Sully, raising a

bushy white eyebrow at Eustace. "What are you, eight years old?"

"Come on," said Masika to Eustace in a sugary voice, crouching down so she was at his eye level, pointing at the leonine castle behind her. "Wouldn't you like to explore the castle with me? There are secret passages and trap doors, and all sorts of things!"

Eustace's eyes widened in excitement the minute she mentioned trap doors. "No kidding?"

"No kidding!" Masika promised, stretching out her hand, which Eustace took eagerly. She led him away, Bomani trailing after them, although he glanced back at Sully as if he'd like to go with them. Eustace looked back at Cole to see if he would come too. But Cole continued to watch Sully.

"Cole *is* a healer," Brock pointed out to Sully. "In the event of a fight, well... he certainly proved his worth last time."

Cole gave his brother a look of surprise and gratitude. Brock smiled back at him as if to say, *don't get used to it.*

"I don't have time to argue with you," Sully sighed. "Grab on." Both brothers seized one of Sully's forearms, and then the bleak desert around the castle of Ibn Alaam warped and disappeared.

Chapter 33

Peter and Lily lost count of how many times they warped, although Peter knew, thanks to his watch, that they'd been at it for almost four hours. They both would have collapsed a long time ago, if not for his unlimited energy... although now he wondered if Lily also had unlimited energy and they just hadn't discovered it before. After all, it turned out she, too, had more than one gift: she was both an electromagnetic specialist, and a space specialist. No one else had more than one, that he knew of... except for him. *Is it possible that it really is her?*

He hadn't any attention or energy to spare thinking about that again, although the fact that Lily was being so patronizing about it made it that much harder to take. He wished she'd just gloat outright and be done with it. They had stopped talking to each other almost completely.

"It's gotta be almost three in the morning," Peter said at last, pointing upward. The moon was well past its highest point in the sky. Lily nodded back at him, bleary-eyed and somehow jittery at the same time.

By the time they finally arrived in Cairo, which they recognized by the pyramids in the distance, it was even trickier finding a place where they could warp without drawing attention to themselves. Cairo remained fairly active even at night. Peter avoided recognition by the penumbra mostly by keeping his head down, sticking to the shadows, and walking behind Lily.

Once inside the city, they could no longer see the pyramids, so it was harder to get their bearings. The moon and stars were not especially clear either, between the thick smog and the brightness of the city lights.

"I thought I caught a glimpse of the pyramids that way," Lily pointed at the side of a building.

"I know; I'd estimate it's about ten kilometers from here." Peter locked eyes with her. He knew he could get them to Giza in one more warp, or two at the most. This was it. "It'll be quick and easy," he promised, more to reassure himself than her. "We know exactly where the Stone is. All we have to do is get in and get out."

"Right," said Lily, sucking in a breath and returning his grip tightly. Both their palms were clammy with sweat.

A moment later, the dingy alleyway in downtown Cairo vanished, and Peter and Lily reappeared in the desert oasis, with three towering pyramids before them. They were magnificent and more formidable-looking in real life and in darkness, though their exteriors were much more weathered than what they had seen in the Meadow.

"Peter? Lily?" cried a familiar voice behind Peter, followed by a chorus of groans. They both spun around.

"Dad!" Peter let go of Lily and ran towards his father and the Sphinx, and at the same time all the other Watchers started speaking and shouting over each other at the same time.

"What are you doing here?!"

"Get out of here, are you barking mad—?"

"No, no, you have to—!"

"*Peter and Lily!*" thundered Isdemus, silencing the others. "You both must leave. Right now!"

"But we know where the Stone is!" Lily blurted.

After a moment's stunned hesitation, Bruce said, "So do we, but we need an earth specialist to get at it. It's too deep for us to dig with our bare hands. Sully went back to Ibn Alaam to get one."

"And incidentally," Jael added crossly, "how do you two always manage to figure out on your own what it takes a whole team of us to work out?" She intended to sound irritated, but the admiration in her voice was obvious.

"Peter and Lily, go back to Carlion at once," Isdemus commanded again, his voice weary and tense at the same time. "As soon as Sully returns we will excavate the Stone and be on our way. We will not need your help—"

"Actually, sir, you will," Peter interrupted, and turned back to Jael, "because you're digging in the wrong place." Jael's eyebrows shot up, and he amended, "The Stone isn't buried in the earth. It's in a subterranean chamber."

Now he had their attention. "How do you know this?" said Bruce.

"Because I saw it in the Meadow!" He glanced at Isdemus. "The entrance to the passage is right over here…" he jogged in the direction of the Temple of the Sphinx, and Lily took off behind him, the others following reluctantly. Peter stopped short when he saw the crumbling ruins of the Temple, which had been so magnificent when he'd seen it in the Meadow.

"But that's where we were the first time!" Dan exclaimed.

Bruce said triumphantly, "The physical symbol of the Taijitu; I *knew* it! I *knew* it couldn't be a coincidence!"

"But it can't be!" Jael insisted, "I looked, there was nothing down there!"

"There's a secret tunnel," Peter explained, crouching down among the ruins and biting his lip. "It's got to be here…"

Crack.

Everyone straightened at once like they'd been shocked, looking around. They only heard a single crack, but the entire plaza between the Sphinx and the pyramids filled with penumbra. All of them were transparent… except for one.

Peter screamed, "Back!" Without thinking, he vaulted himself over the ruins of the Temple and back to the middle of Giza plaza, putting distance between himself and the other Watchers.

Behind him, Isdemus shouted, "Lily! The force field!"

Almost instantly, Peter heard a *wong* sound. He kept running without looking back, hoping she'd manage to protect all the others.

A boy with blond hair and a jagged scar across his right cheek approached Peter from the midst of his nightmarish army. He still wore the dark jeans and black overcoat he'd had on the night they stormed the Fata Morgana together. Sargon fixed his black eyes on Peter and smiled, looking him up and down in a way that made Peter shiver.

"Well, well, well," he said softly, in Kane's voice. "If it isn't my dear brother."

Chapter 34

"**Y**ou're not my brother anymore," said Peter to Kane in a low voice, as he unconsciously balled his hands into fists. "I know who you are now."

"Actually, I *am* still your brother," Sargon replied, his voice so calm it was almost melodic. Then he amended, "Well. *I* am not, but Kane is still in my head. At the moment, he is screaming, 'No, no, Peter, run, he'll kill you'—in case you would like to know."

"You're lying," Peter spat. Dimly, he heard the voices of the Watchers in the background, and the voices of the penumbra, but all of his attention was on Sargon. "Kane wouldn't care whether I died or not anyway. He never liked me."

Sargon laughed, cold and sinister. It made Peter shudder. "Well. *That* is certainly true."

Peter's vision throbbed with the hammering of his heart. He had no idea what to do next. Sargon walked towards him, casually, the long black overcoat swinging at his ankles. Peter flinched and almost stepped backwards; it took all the courage he had to stand his ground.

When Sargon was only a meter away, Peter briefly feared his knees might buckle… but then Sargon passed right by him, on his way to the Temple.

Where all the other Watchers were. Where his dad was, and Cole. And Lily.

"Stop!" Peter cried desperately.

Sargon obeyed, almost politely, turning to see what Peter had to say.

"Don't…" he hesitated. "Don't you want to fight me?"

Sargon raised his eyebrows, and laughed. "Fight you? Peter, Peter." He shook his head. "Aren't we all here for the same reason?" He opened his arms to indicate the Giza plaza. "You and I both know the prophecy. Without Excalibur, I see no reason for either of us to waste our energy. The time will come for that soon enough." He turned around and walked very deliberately towards the Temple again. Peter saw the Watchers freeze beneath Lily's force field. He spared a glance at her; she was pale and trembling.

She hasn't got unlimited power after all, he thought, and then shouted at himself, *Do something!* At the same moment, he heard his voice shouting in the Ancient Tongue.

Instantly he was in the Meadow.

He breathed again and approached the rainbow, not sure what he'd said. Each image showed Sargon swept off his feet and sprawled on the ground at various angles. Peter scowled and chided himself, "Come on, Peter, you can do better than that..." But he drew a blank. What else could he do, without creating energy out of nothing?

Finally Peter chose the image in indigo where Sargon was sprawled on his face, arms and legs akimbo, and he dove in.

Peter returned to the present just as a gust of air hit Sargon full in the back, knocking him forward before he could catch himself. Peter heard the *whoosh* as the fall knocked the wind out of him.

Uh oh, he thought.

Sargon climbed to his feet very slowly, facing Peter this time. His expression was unreadable.

"All right," he said softly. "Have it your way." His gaze drifted down to the sand below him. He murmured under his breath and beckoned a chunk of sand to rise and hover several feet in front of him. Slowly the sand morphed into a shapeless mass of silver... and then separated into hundreds of daggers.

"Think of your options, Peter!" Isdemus shouted. "Anything is possible!"

Sargon hurtled the daggers towards Peter with the speed of bullets. Peter heard screaming from the Watchers, and his own voice shouting unfamiliar words.

He was in the Meadow again. He looked at the rainbow to see what option he had come up with this time, and saw that he had turned the daggers into feathers. He nearly dove into the pool, but then he stopped.

"You can do better than feathers, Peter," he

murmured to himself. As he stared at the images in red, suddenly the feathers morphed back into daggers, and the daggers arced into boomerangs.

Peter dove in.

In the next second he was back in Giza, and Sargon's daggers course-corrected in midair, turning back towards Sargon.

Sargon transformed the daggers back into sand, commanding it in Peter's direction again.

Without knowing what he did, Peter commanded the sand around him to rise up also, and he found himself in the midst of a dust storm so thick he couldn't see a thing.

Peter panicked. There was a *crack crack crack crack crack* in the background; Peter wasn't sure if they were nimbi or penumbra or other Watchers.

Think, Peter!

Before he could do anything, though, a fist made contact with Peter's throat. He choked and spluttered, gasping for breath and inhaling dust, which made him choke even harder.

"Water!" he heard Dan's voice shout through the storm. "Turn it to water! *Deannach ar uisce!*"

Somehow Peter managed to copy Dan's words. The dust turned to water, drenching both him and Sargon. But he could see again—

The first thing he saw was a sword aimed at his neck. Peter hit the ground, missing decapitation by a fraction of a second.

"Somebody give him a sword!" Lily shrieked. "Somebody give him a—somebody give *me* a sword, *I'll* fight him!"

Sargon's chin-length blond hair clung to his

hollowed cheekbones, accentuating the obsidian eyes that were decidedly not Kane's. Peter jumped and scrambled away clumsily as Sargon advanced. Lily was right; he needed a weapon, but he couldn't think what substance to use, nor the words to command it—

"Peter! Here!" cried a voice behind him. He turned around to see Bellator, who tossed him a saber. He caught it by the hilt just barely, and in the next second managed to block Sargon's downward stroke enough to protect his head from being cleaved in two. But the force of Sargon's blow was too much for his weak grip, and Peter's sword collided heavily with his own shoulder, drawing blood.

"Horizontal slices to the limbs!" cried Lily, her voice trembling. "Remember, Peter!"

Bellator shouted to Isdemus, "Let me help him!"

"No, Bellator," Isdemus shouted back. "You cannot speak the Ancient Tongue. Sargon would kill you in seconds!"

"But Peter doesn't know how to fight!" Bruce cried desperately.

"*I* know what I'm doing, let me fight him!" Lily gasped again. She was on the ground now, trembling with the effort of the force field. Peter and Sargon were at it hammer and tongs, but Peter was flailing.

"Sargon's playing with him!" Dan cried. "He could finish him off anytime—he just wants a fight!"

"Well, then, let's give him one!" Jael shouted fiercely.

Lily moaned, unable to speak. Her face was white, her arms stretched above her head in an effort to keep the force field in place.

"We're standing by, boss," said Bellator to Isdemus with a small host of nimbi just outside the force field, keeping their eyes on the still-transparent penumbra.

"What are they waiting for?" said Verum, scrutinizing the penumbra.

Sully gritted his teeth. "I suspect Sargon told them to stand down until he kills Peter."

Verum shook his head. "Most of them aren't even watching Sargon and Peter. I think they're waiting for something *else*..."

Lily moaned again. "How... much... longer?" she gasped. Then she strained to turn her head. "Peter?" was all she managed to get out.

"He's alive, barely," said Bellator, his voice taut. "But he's not even using his power anymore."

"He cannot fight and use his power at the same time," Isdemus observed gravely. "He's not skilled enough."

"Let us out, Lily, let us out!" Bruce begged. "At least we can distract Sargon long enough for Peter to—"

A voice behind them shouted something in Arabic, and they all turned to see a man in a black police uniform running towards Peter and Sargon. His penumbra, a jaguar, deserted him and joined the rest of the penumbra around Sargon. The man stared at Sargon and Peter, still shouting and waving his gun in the air.

"The tourists are arriving," Jael moaned. Beyond

the policeman, a few people dressed in shorts and t-shirts pointed at Sargon and Kane, who probably looked like a couple of teenage boys rehearsing a choreographed duel from a distance.

Peter gasped for air. He hadn't fully recovered from the blow to his wind pipe, and he certainly wasn't conditioned for endurance. He noticed a few beads of sweat on Sargon's brow as well; at the moment Kane's body restricted him, and it was scarcely more physically developed than Peter's.

That has to be a key somehow, Peter thought. *Kane.* What did he know about Kane's physical weaknesses?

"What—are you waiting for?" Peter gasped. "Why haven't you killed me yet?"

Peter saw Kane's familiar gap-toothed smile, and Sargon looked away from him purposefully. Peter followed his gaze, and felt his stomach drop out beneath him.

Tourists.

"No. Don't—" Peter managed to gasp. "NO!"

A jet stream of ice hurtled towards the tourists. There was nothing to protect them, not even a tree.

Peter began to shout something. The next second, he was in the Meadow again.

He'd conjured a ring of fire around the tourists to melt the ice, but the ice was too thick: in every image in the rainbow, a javelin of ice eked through, impaling a balding, middle-aged man with a camera slung about his neck. A little girl still clutched his hand. She, too, was riddled with hundreds of tiny ice daggers.

Peter bit his lip, thinking hard. He could turn the

ice back to water, or into vapor…

Or I could dig a hole.

His eyes flew open. He knew the tourists would have a nasty fall at first, but it was the best he could do. In the image in bright green, he saw the earth split open and the ice javelins pass over the tourists harmlessly.

Peter dove in.

He heard the screams as the tourists fell; at the same moment, an involuntary scream ripped from his own throat. Sargon slashed his right arm, and Peter's sword fell uselessly to the sand. He heard the nimbi rushing forward, even as he fell to his knees.

Everyone was shouting. The pain was unbearable. In the midst of the unintelligible clamor, Peter heard Bruce's scream, "Lily, let GO!"

Then there was pandemonium. All of the Watchers and the nimbi rushed at Sargon, trying to get between him and Peter. But Sargon conjured a wall of fire, cutting Peter off from the Watchers. Peter heard Dan frantically trying to douse it on the other side, but then he cried out, "There's no water in the air here; he's burning it all up!"

Sargon pressed his blade against Peter's throat. It was already wet with Peter's own blood.

"You asked me why I haven't finished you off."

Peter writhed in agony.

Sargon went on, "I needed to distract you and your friends long enough to accomplish my purpose." Peter's eyes began to roll back in his head, but Sargon's smiling face swam over his, even as darkness threatened to take him. He saw

Sargon's lips form the words, "Relax, Peter. The moment has come."

The ring of fire vanished, but before the Watchers or nimbi could move, there was another *wong,* louder and more powerful than the one Lily had conjured. Bruce lurched forward, pounding against Sargon's force field that imprisoned the Watchers away from Peter once more.

"I want you all to see this," Sargon said, loudly enough for all to hear. He gestured behind the Watchers, to the Temple ruins.

Everyone turned to see a beautiful woman, her black hair whipping wildly around her face. She grinned maniacally and thrust one arm to the sky. In that hand she clutched a blood-red stone.

There was a moment of silence, and then the plaza erupted with cheers, grunts, neighings, stompings, and groanings, immediately followed with a succession of *crack, crack, crack* as the penumbra took physical form. Instantly the plaza teemed with the solid forms of hags, satyrs, giants, ghouls, werewolves, centaurs, and creatures without name.

Sargon stooped down, and as he did so, he pressed the blade so tightly against Peter's throat that he drew fresh blood.

"Behold," he whispered, sweeping his other arm around in a gesture to the penumbra. "My invincible army."

Chapter 35

Sargon grinned at Peter, but Peter's vision went in and out of focus. All he saw were black eyes, teeth, and a scar. Sargon straightened, retracting his blade for the final blow.

Peter heard his own voice shouting, and he was in the Meadow. He dove into the pool without even looking at it.

Sargon's blade burst into a sunflower, flopping harmlessly against Peter's neck.

Peter tried to hobble to his feet, just as Sargon conjured hail the size of golf balls. They pelted him relentlessly. He scarcely had the strength left to shield his head.

Then he heard another *crack*.

"Sully!" Peter heard Bruce cry out. Vaguely he heard Brock's and Cole's voices too. Welts bubbled up on Peter's forehead, all over his shoulders and his back as he crouched against the ground, waiting to be stoned to death.

"Lily, quick!" Isdemus shouted.

Peter felt a hand on his back, right where the last hailstone had landed.

Wong.

The onslaught stopped as Lily's force field enveloped him, and Peter collapsed. He rolled over to see Lily's face smiling at him weakly as she wrapped her hand around his bruised shoulder. As she did it, Peter watched the color return to her ashen face.

Cole lunged at Peter a second later, his face screwed up in concentration as he chanted with all his might, "*Stad fola!*" He clutched Peter's other arm as tightly as he could. "*Leigheas!*"

Peter felt the pain leaving his body, like it was being sucked out with a straw. He wiggled his fingers once the nerves were reattached, and inhaled an unlabored breath.

"Thanks," he gasped. "How did you all—" Peter gulped for air again, "—get out of the other force field?"

"I think Sargon just forgot about us in all the confusion," Lily murmured.

Peter sat up, and his jaw dropped as he looked around. The hail pounded the ground all around them, the earth quaked, and the wind whipped into twisters: all the result of the penumbra testing their newfound powers. The hail slid off of an invisible dome above Peter and the Watchers, and the ground beneath them remained silent and still. It was an oasis… but they knew it could not last for long.

Bruce shouted, "Jael! Would you say *now* is a good time to talk about the strategy of a war against chaos?"

One by one, everyone turned from the rampage of the penumbra towards Bruce as his words sunk in.

"I think," Dan declared, "we are all listening now!"

Peter sat up, and Lily clutched his arm tighter, stretching the other one overhead to maintain their sanctuary.

"We can't defeat the penumbra using a stronger, or even an equal and opposite force, because we don't *have* an equal and opposite force!" Bruce shouted, speaking only to Peter now, his eyes lit with urgency. "So we have to use the Butterfly Effect! Turn the strength of the chaotic system back on itself!"

"Bruce, talk sense, what are you saying we should *do*?" Jael demanded.

"Use our gifts creatively," Sully said as it dawned on him. "Create a diversion—"

"While I get the Stone back from Guinevere," Peter finished.

Bruce's eyes widened. "Well, now, wait a minute—"

"I *can* match her," Peter said shortly. "None of you can."

Isdemus nodded. "We will have to move now; she could disappear at any moment!" Then he turned to Bellator and the small army of nimbi with him. "You all must leave."

"You can't be serious!" Bellator balked, but Isdemus cut him off.

"Our only chance is to use our gifts against them,

and you do not have any. You would die in the attempt. Therefore, you must leave. That is an order!"

The nimbi looked mutinous, but they obeyed, disappearing with a great simultaneous *crack*.

Next Isdemus looked at Lily, who understood and let go of Peter's shoulder at once.

The elements assaulted them, but Dan turned the hail to rain, at least where they stood.

A giant aimed a kick in their general direction, but Bruce cried, *"Fhótóin i súile!"* There was a flash of light near the giant's face. His foot landed amiss and he stumbled and fell.

At the same moment, Isdemus leapt over the giant's arm and shouted at the three penumbra behind him, *"Dóiteáin chun ae!"* Nothing happened at first, but then one of them, a hag, fell to its knees, its eyes bulging and smoke flowing from its mouth. Then it collapsed, followed by the others within seconds.

"Brilliant!" cried Dan to Sully. "He's cooking them from the inside out!"

Bruce had already begun to weave his way through the army, blinding the penumbra as he went. It didn't last long, but it was enough of a distraction that at least he stayed alive long enough to dodge them.

Isdemus left a wake of dead creatures behind him as he moved, each crumbling to its knees.

Jael launched herself into the crowd, but for once, her strength did not help her at all. A satyr nearly gored her with its horns, but Bruce blinded it as he ran by, causing it to gore a dwarf behind her by mistake. Jael fell in behind Bruce after that, and in the split seconds after Bruce blinded one of the penumbra, Jael made noise nearby, temping it to lunge towards her. Then she dodged, and, with luck, the two nearest penumbra tore each other limb from limb.

Dan shouted, "Quick! Lily!"

"What?" she shouted back in alarm.

"Seventy percent of their bodies are water! I can polarize it, but then I need you to magnetize it afterwards!"

"What?" she repeated, both frantic and confused. "What good will that—"

"They'll stick to each other! Ready?" Before Lily could respond, he was already speaking the Ancient Tongue fluently to the five penumbra running towards them.

"But I don't know how to say that!" Lily shrieked.

"*Bheith ina gcomhlachtaí maighnéid!*" Dan shouted back.

Lily repeated after him, extending one arm towards the charging army and using the other to cover her face, as if bracing for a car crash. But when it didn't come, she peeked over her arm and saw that, sure enough, all five creatures were entangled with one another, an enormous mass of sallow flesh, fur, teeth, and blood. She blinked in amazement.

"Nice thinking!" she shouted to Dan.

Sully warped between two of the penumbra long enough to get them to swing at him, disappearing at the critical instant. Several of them killed each other before the others caught on to what he was doing.

Only Brock and Cole remained. Brock pointed at Bruce and Jael, who seemed to be quite the team, felling nearly as many of the penumbra as Isdemus. "Let's copy them! You be the distraction! Go!"

Cole nodded frantically, and ran straight at a centaur and the jaguar that had belonged to the policeman, shouting and waving his arms like a war cry. When they turned to attack him, Brock commanded the ground to open up and swallow them whole.

Meanwhile, Peter ran straight at the Temple, unhindered at first. But in a strange moment of intuition, he ducked, just in time to see a ball of fire pass over where his head had been only seconds before.

Sargon.

Before Peter even had a chance to think, the ground beneath his feet split open. Peter leapt into the air clumsily, and he nearly landed several feet away. But the ground split open there too. Peter shouted something in the Ancient Tongue, and suspended his body above the gaping jaws.

He didn't see Guinevere anywhere.

The earth all around Peter rose up in a mountain of sand, which transformed into water and became a tidal wave.

"*Uisce go haer!*" Peter shouted instinctively.

In the Meadow, he saw the wave spiral in on itself and move towards Sargon like a tornado. He dove in.

When he returned to the present, Peter fell into the crater Sargon had left in the ground beneath him. Sargon warped out of the way and let Peter's tornado propel on by, towards the two penumbra behind him.

"It's over, Peter," said Sargon calmly, sliding into the crater with him. "You cannot win."

All around them the battle raged. Peter staggered to his feet as Sargon advanced. He knew Sargon's words were true. He *couldn't* win. He was only prolonging the inevitable.

"Kane," Peter croaked, fixing his pleading eyes on his brother. It was his last hope. "If you really are still in there… fight back. Please. *Fight back*!"

It was only a fraction of a second, but Peter saw it: the obsidian eyes faded to a feral brown. Then the blackness descended again, and Sargon burst out laughing.

"Let me tell you just how little control Kane has now. I killed Achen—slowly and painfully—and I made him watch. He could not do a thing to stop me!" He turned back to Peter, his expression calculating. "But you are right," Sargon murmured, as if speaking to someone inside himself. "There would be no glory in a mundane death for your dear brother, such as decapitation or breaking his neck. I can do much, much better than that."

A deep and rumbling *crack* made Peter spin around. His jaw dropped in horror.

One of the pyramids dislodged from its foundation. It soared up, up, up in the air. Blocks easily weighing several thousand kilos each fell to the earth as the pyramid climbed higher. Then, once it was directly over the battle raging in the plaza, the pyramid inverted… and fell.

"*Sully*!" Isdemus shouted.

Peter saw everything in slow motion. The Watchers, Brock, Cole, and Lily all ran towards Sully, but Sully disappeared alone. Instead, Lily grabbed on to Cole, Dan, Jael, Bruce, Isdemus, and finally Brock—and they disappeared.

Peter was alone. He had no idea where Sargon was anymore. All he could see was the pyramid, shedding several thousand kilo blocks as it hurtled through the air, close enough now to blot out the early morning sky. One great block broke off before the rest, directly above where Peter stood.

Then he heard another *crack*, right next to him.

"*Clocha a deannaigh*!" he heard his own voice cry—but too late. He felt the impact for just a split second before—

The Meadow. The trees. The pool. The rainbow…

But every image inside of the rainbow was horrifying. *Every* one. Peter's legs were crushed in all of them. He couldn't reverse the pyramid's trajectory anymore—at least not the bits that had already made contact with his body and the ground. But he could still transform the rest of it into something else…

In the rainbow, the pyramid had turned to dust. But at that close range, the dust would still weigh thousands and thousands of kilos. *Conservation of matter,* Peter thought desperately. Was there anything he could turn the rest of it into that would *not* kill him?

Then he saw something else in the rainbow that made his blood run cold.

Sully.

He was grabbing hold of Peter's ankle just at the moment of impact—the moment the block had crushed Peter's legs beyond recognition.

Peter searched the images frantically for one where Sully was not underneath the weight of the blocks. He found none.

He tried turning the pyramid to dust, and then water, and air—but he knew even air at that density and momentum would hit them with enough force to kill them both.

He tried photons, but he knew before he even attempted it that that wouldn't work. Photons had no mass. He couldn't just make matter disappear.

In the end, dust seemed to be the best he could come up with. He hoped the tourists were far enough away from the impact that they would not be buried alive.

Peter blinked at the peaceful trees, the still pool, and the warm light. All he could think of was how glad he was that the others had gotten away. Lily, his dad, Cole... at least they were safe.

At least they still had Lily. She was their only hope now.

He placed a hand on his chest, and felt the throbbing of his heart for the last time.

Then he dove in.

There was a sound like rushing wind, agonizing pain, collision... and darkness.

Chapter 36

Lily appeared with the rest of the Watchers in front of the castle in Carlion, right next to the fountain of the Pendragon crest. They all nearly collapsed in a heap, gasping.

The last they had seen, Sully had had only instants remaining to rescue Peter. Nobody spoke. They hardly breathed.

Suddenly two more bodies appeared, lying on the ground a few yards away. All of them ran towards the two prone figures on the stone patio with exclamations of relief. But the exclamations turned to gasps and screams as soon as they got close enough to see what had happened.

Peter's upper body was intact, but he was unconscious. His legs were so badly mutilated that they barely looked human anymore.

Sully still clutched Peter's heel, but he had been completely crushed. He was dead.

All of them stopped running at various stages,

too horrified to move.

It was Jael who broke the silence first.

"No," she whispered. She wrenched herself away from Dan and lunged forward. "He can't be, he can't be..." she gasped over and over, and then looked at Cole, hysterical. "*Do something!*"

Cole stepped back in alarm, and Brock wrapped his arms around him from behind.

"There is nothing he can do, Jael," said Bruce, his voice hoarse and trembling. "If there is even the slightest probability of a given outcome then it can be selected. But once the pyramid landed... once someone has been killed... probability goes to zero..."

Jael collapsed into Dan's arms, sobbing uncontrollably, her rigid exterior crumbling all at once. Bruce rushed to Peter's side. If it hadn't been for the injuries to his legs, he might have been sleeping.

"What about Peter?" Lily whispered to no one in particular. "Can... he be saved?"

Instead of answering, Isdemus called out, "Fides Dignus!"

The ugly little nimbus appeared and made a bow, and at first he only looked at Isdemus's face. But he took one look at his expression and turned around, where he saw Sully and Peter, with Jael sobbing and Dan clutching her tightly, rocking her back and forth. Fides Dignus's mouth fell open and he whispered, "No..."

"Fides Dignus, Peter requires the attention of Dr. MacDouglas immediately," said Isdemus, business-like. "His legs have been crushed, but as long as blood flow can be reestablished before the tissue dies they can be restored."

Fides Dignus nodded swiftly and disappeared, too overcome to speak.

"How long does he have before the, er, tissue dies?" said Cole anxiously, staring at his friend's unconscious form in shock.

"I do not know the answer to that," said Isdemus, looking away.

"This is all my fault," Bruce whispered, stroking Peter's hair off of his forehead. "If we'd just warped away the minute they got the Stone…"

"None of us expected to make it out alive," Isdemus interrupted. "It was a sacrifice we were all willing to make."

Lily fixed Isdemus with a shocked, accusing glare, her eyes brimming with tears. "Don't you even *care*?" she whispered.

Isdemus turned his face towards her with a heartbroken expression. "Lily. Do you know why the rest of us survived?"

Lily didn't trust herself to speak, so she said nothing, her lower lip trembling.

"The penumbra did not work together. They only looked out for themselves. But to each of us, the survival of our companions was worth the ultimate sacrifice." He paused, tears misting his blue eyes. "So in response to your question, yes, Lily. I care desperately."

Lily looked back at Peter's ashen, unconscious body and covered her face with her hands.

"Can't I help him?" Cole whimpered.

"You're not a healer yet, Cole," said Dan tightly,

still rocking Jael back and forth. "This will require exact diagnosis and the appropriate words in the Ancient Tongue."

"But don't *you* know the words? You can teach them to me!" Cole insisted.

"I may have the words in my vocabulary, but I don't know which ones to use," Dan croaked. "That's what Dr. MacDouglas is for."

Peter suddenly stirred, and Bruce froze, one hand hovering over Peter's forehead. When everyone else saw movement, they too held their breaths.

"He's alive!" Bruce cried anxiously. "He's alive!"

"Peter?" Lily shrieked, kneeling beside Bruce. "Peter, can you hear me?"

Peter started to moan.

Just then, there was a double *crack* as both Fides Dignus and Dr. MacDouglas appeared. The latter rushed towards Peter and Sully.

Dr. MacDouglas looked very grave but not surprised. Fides Dignus had evidently already prepared him for what he would find. The healer inspected Peter quickly, checking his pupils and assessing for pulse and respiration. Bruce stepped back to make room for him, but since he could no longer stroke Peter's hair, he had taken to chewing his fingernails instead.

Dr. MacDouglas looked up at Bruce and announced, "The crush injuries are nearly complete. I will need to speak to each of the bones individually, as well as to all the nerves and blood vessels. I won't bother repairing the muscle until all the rest is done because they wouldn't be able to get any blood supply until then anyway."

"Fine, good, do it!" cried Bruce.

"I will not be able to heal him completely in one session," Dr. MacDouglas warned.

"You will if you touch him while you do it!" Cole interjected.

Dr. MacDouglas looked briefly confused, but then his expression cleared. "Of course," he said, "He has unlimited power. I forgot." He gently touched Peter's shoulder as he began to speak the Ancient Tongue fluently, his hands hovering over Peter's legs as he did it.

As Dr. MacDouglas continued to speak, Peter's legs resumed their normal shape and appearance. When he finished, Peter looked basically normal from the outside, aside from his blood-stained clothing. But he was still unconscious.

"What else is wrong?" Bruce demanded. "Why isn't he awake yet?"

Dr. MacDouglas frowned. "I don't know," he murmured.

"You don't *know*? What do you mean you don't *know?*"

"Bruce," said Isdemus quietly.

Bruce stopped arguing then, but began ripping off his fingernails with his teeth in earnest.

"I think he must be bleeding internally," Dr. MacDouglas said slowly, "but I need to know where in order to fix it. And for that, I need a mind specialist."

"Wait, what does that mean?" Cole demanded.

"Fides Dignus!" Isdemus ordered. He didn't need to say anything else; with a curt nod indicating that he understood what Isdemus wanted him to do, Fides Dignus disappeared.

Dr. MacDouglas shook his head. "He won't find him. I already tried to bring my imaging specialist with me, but I don't know where he is this morning."

"What's the imaging specialist supposed to do?" Bruce demanded.

"He'll merge with one of his blood cells," said Lily, stricken.

"Why, yes," said Dr. MacDouglas, surprised. "How did you—"

"We did it in class yesterday. I was Peter's lab partner, I've done it already!" Lily cried. "Send *me* in!"

"No, send me!" said Cole stubbornly, "I'm a healer! Or I'm gonna be..."

"The words won't work for you," Brock murmured to his brother. "Professor Crane did that for us, remember?"

"But they'll work for me; I have all the gifts!" Lily declared loudly. Everyone turned to look at her; it was the first time she'd said this out loud. "Well, I do!" she insisted.

"She *did* warp us all here," Bruce pointed out. "So she's got at least two gifts..."

Dr. MacDouglas shook his head at Lily. "But even if you managed to find something, you won't know what you're looking at." He wiped a bead of sweat off his forehead. "If you don't know what you're looking at, you won't be able to describe it to me, and we'll be no better off than we are now."

"I'll figure it out!" Lily almost shouted. "This is

Peter we're talking about! What were the words again? Tell me!"

Dr. MacDouglas raised his eyebrows but told her the words she needed, and Lily repeated them as she stared intently at the blood still drying on Peter's legs. Then she collapsed.

"Careful!" cried Bruce, and lunged forward to catch Lily's body so she didn't fall on top of Peter.

"What if she gets caught in the bleed she's trying to find?" Cole asked anxiously.

"Then chances are she'll never make her way back out to tell us anything," said Dr. MacDouglas, his face ashen. "That's why the imaging specialists do this. The more intricate their knowledge of anatomy, the more likely they can find their way back out again."

A few eternal minutes later, Lily gasped for air and sat up. Bruce let out a little cry of relief.

"What did you see?" Dr. MacDouglas demanded.

"Well, I don't know exactly... after I got to the waterfall with the three enormous teeth at the bottom, which I guess was his heart—"

"Those would be the heart valves," said Dr. MacDouglas with a furrowed brow, nodding.

"After that I slowed down, but it looked different than last time. I went into this..." Lily searched for words. "It was almost like a marshland, spongy—"

"Marshland?" said Dr. MacDouglas sharply. "It wasn't more like a Zen garden?"

"No," Lily shook her head firmly. "It was the first time, but not anymore."

"His lungs are full of blood," Dr. MacDouglas

declared. He spoke the Ancient Tongue again, his hands hovering just over Peter's chest. Something about Peter's countenance improved, but he still didn't wake.

"One more thing. I've got to tell his body to make more blood. He's lost a lot of it." Dr. MacDouglas looked at Bruce as he said this, seeking approval. "It's a tricky process. It might go wrong. If it does, I could accidentally give him a blood dyscrasia, and those can be hard to treat. But if I don't do it, I don't know whether he'll—"

"Do it!" Bruce shouted.

"You don't know if he'll what?" Lily asked anxiously, but by then the doctor had already gone to work again. "You don't know if he'll *what?*"

"Ever wake up," said Brock, his voice very soft. Lily and Cole both looked at him. He was watching Peter with an unreadable expression... almost like remorse.

Peter's eyelids fluttered at last. Encouraged, the doctor spoke louder and faster, hands moving at a hover all over Peter's body. For a few seconds, nobody breathed.

Then Peter opened his eyes.

Jael burst into fresh tears and buried her face in Dan's shoulder once more. Everyone else released their breath with a collective *whoosh*, followed by weak, giddy laughter from Cole and Lily. Isdemus wiped his wet cheeks. Bruce closed his eyes as if offering a silent prayer.

The first thing Peter saw was Lily, who gazed down at him with a tender expression he'd never seen from her before. He tried to smile back.

"This young lady may have saved your life," said Dr. MacDouglas, laying a hand on Lily's shoulder.

"Sully," Peter croaked, and instinctively turned to look down at his feet.

All of the smiles evaporated. Peter stared at Sully's broken form, uncomprehending for a minute or two. Nobody spoke and nobody moved.

Peter turned aside and retched.

When Peter relieved his stomach of its contents completely and stopped dry heaving, he was trembling and sweating all over. Bruce put his arms around him from behind, but Peter did not return the embrace. He couldn't speak at all. He couldn't think of anything worth saying.

Isdemus approached Peter and Bruce, kneeling down beside them, his blue eyes wide with compassion.

"There was nothing you could have done, Peter," said Isdemus quietly.

Peter didn't reply, nor did he look at Isdemus. He stared off into the fields beyond the castle, so green and still and pristine, as if nothing had happened at all.

"Peter?" asked Bruce timidly.

Isdemus sighed. "He's in shock. Give him time." Then he turned to the healer. "Dr. MacDouglas, would you be so kind as to fetch a few of the Watchers from the castle, and assist them with Sully's body—"

"No," Peter interrupted, looking up for the first time. "I can heal him. I can fix this—"

"No, Peter. You can't," Bruce interrupted softly.

"I can! He died—" Peter choked on the words, "—saving me, and it's my job to reverse it!" He whirled on Isdemus accusingly. "You said I could do anything! You said anything is possible!"

Isdemus bowed his head but did not reply.

"You can only select from possibilities that still exist, Peter," Bruce murmured, sniffling as he wiped his face. "I wish it wasn't so. But it is."

Lily tiptoed to Peter's other side and slipped her arms around him, laying her head on his shoulder. As soon as she did, Peter's lower lip started to tremble. He hugged her back, releasing a few involuntary sobs.

With much caution and many tears, four other Watchers from the castle along with Dr. MacDouglas lovingly wrapped Sully's body in a white sheet. Jael nearly didn't let them go, but Dan told her in a low voice, "Jael, it won't do any good not to bury him. He's gone."

Jael's chin quivered. She brushed her damp cheeks and nodded. Dan tried to draw her close again, but she pushed him away. He looked at her quizzically.

"You see?" she whispered. "That could have been you."

Dan opened his mouth to protest, but Jael clutched her arms around her midsection and walked away from him, to the other side of Isdemus. She didn't look at him again.

"What now?" Brock murmured once Sully's body was gone, his tone dull and flat.

Peter, still tangled in both Lily's and his dad's

arms, looked up. "I have to go back to Giza," he announced. An eruption of voices protested, but he shouted over them, "What about the tourists? We have to make sure they're okay!"

"We will send one of the nimbi to check on them, in their own dimension and not in ours," Isdemus said firmly.

"But what if they're buried alive?" Peter argued, flushed and trembling all over. "I turned that pyramid to dust, and before that I put them all in a big hole! Somebody who can help them has to go back, somebody who can fight the penumbra if they're there. That's got to be me; you know it does!"

Isdemus ignored this and shouted, "Verum!"

The elf appeared. His stricken expression told the group that he'd heard what had happened to Sully.

"Sir," he said stiffly.

"Please return to Giza, in transparent form, and make sure the tourists are unharmed."

Verum bowed, shed his physical body with a *crack,* and then vanished completely.

"There were other tourists, too, though," Peter insisted angrily. "They arrived after the battle began—"

"I saw them too," Isdemus cut him off, "but I am certain that the second the penumbra crossed over into our world, any human who was able would have fled in terror. The penumbra, meanwhile, would have been much too occupied with us at that point to pay them any attention."

There was a lull for a moment. Peter deflated,

and his face reverted to the vacant expression he had worn before. Suddenly he remembered what Sargon had said about Achen, too: *I killed him, slowly and painfully, and I made Kane watch.* He swallowed hard.

So much death. Peter clutched Lily's hand on one side and his dad's in the other. Who would be next?

"So now what?" Dan asked at last. "The Shadow Lord and his army will terrorize the entire world within hours."

Isdemus shook his head, and said with quiet confidence, "I do not think so. That will happen eventually, but if I know the Shadow Lord, his next step will be to protect himself from all vulnerabilities before he publicly declares himself."

Brock looked up. "He's already declared himself pretty publicly, wouldn't you say?"

"Only in Giza, and that story will be hushed up quickly enough," said Isdemus. "The witnesses will be summarily ignored, or perhaps considered temporarily insane due to shock."

"And the pyramid?" Peter demanded. "How do you think they'll explain that away?"

"They will," Dan assured him gravely. "I don't know how, but they will. They always find ways. After all, the Shadow Lord sank an entire continent once, and all the history books unanimously insisted afterwards that it never existed in the first place."

Cole looked perplexed. "Which continent was that?"

"Atlantis," Dan replied. Cole's mouth fell open, and he exchanged a stunned look with Brock. Dan went on, "They'll probably say the pyramid was struck by a meteor and pulverized into dust."

"Without leaving a crater behind?" Peter asked, raising an eyebrow.

Dan shrugged. "Or something like that. Nobody ever thinks too critically about the explanations."

Peter turned back to Isdemus and challenged, "So what do you think the Shadow Lord is gonna do next, then, if he's not going to declare open war yet?"

"Well, we can assume that he now knows as much of the prophecy as Kane did," said Isdemus with a heavy sigh.

"Which is how much?" Jael sniffled, wiping her face and sitting up a bit for the first time.

"I was never able to determine that for certain, but for the moment we must assume that he knows the whole thing."

"What does it matter?" Peter muttered. "The bottom line is the same, isn't it?" He extricated himself from Lily's and his dad's arms, and wrapped his own arms around his knees. "He wants Lily and me dead."

Isdemus shook his head and said, "I am not convinced he knows that Lily is a candidate yet, so you might be safe for the time being, Miss Portman. But we must take all precautions." Isdemus paced as he spoke, more to himself than to the others. "I believe the Shadow Lord will develop a strategy for conquest first, rather than merely using brute force. He will do this partially because he is proud, and because he would feel that force alone lacks finesse. But in the meantime, yes, he will devote the remainder of his considerable resources to finding and killing the Child of the Prophecy—whoever he believes that to be."

Peter turned to look at Lily, and she returned his baleful gaze. Then she looped her arm through his again, laying her head back on his shoulder and closing her eyes. Peter pressed his cheek against her hair.

He felt so tired that he could have slept for days and days.

Chapter 37

It was very strange how life went on.

The Watchers from Carlion and from thirteen other sister cities throughout the world gave Sully a grand funeral outside the city gates, but just inside the edges of the Enchanted Forest. The only citizens of Carlion present were those whom Sully had recruited personally. Masika, Bomani, and Eustace were there, too: Isdemus had sent a space specialist to fetch them from Ibn Alaam once everything was over. Masika stood next to Dan, but Dan paid very little attention to her, since most of his energy was focused on comforting Jael. Even Eustace seemed subdued, and though he tried to get as close to Peter as he could, he said very little, for which Peter was grateful. He hadn't the energy to fend off Eustace on top of everything else.

Everyone who felt moved to do so said a few words about Sully and what he had meant to them. Isdemus had to cut them off eventually because there were too many who wanted to speak, and had they all been allowed, the funeral would have stretched well into the evening.

Peter was stunned to learn that the graveyard where Sully was laid to rest also contained the graves of all of the members of the Watchers who had gone before—all the way back to most of the original Knights of the Round Table, and even King Arthur himself.

Directly after the funeral, Mrs. Jefferson pulled both of her sons aside and spoke to them in rapid hushed tones. Peter overheard enough to know she was concerned that Carlion was no longer safe and perhaps they ought to go home to Norwich after all, but he didn't stick around to hear the outcome of the conversation. He was beyond caring about even that. Instead he wandered off by himself, not knowing where he was going until he found himself standing over King Arthur's grave.

The monument was so well-kept that it looked almost new. Arthur's first wife Cecily was buried beside him with a tomb just as elaborate, as if she had been the one and only queen of Camelot. Glowing flora and fauna filled the entire graveyard with vibrant colors, and the light of the sun filtered through the canopy above, dappling the ground.

Peter barely noticed when his dad put an arm around his shoulders.

"This is really him," said Peter dully.

Bruce pursed his lips. "It really is."

"And I've got to finish what he started."

Bruce didn't reply right away. "The Council is starting right before the feast. You ought to be there."

Peter looked up. "Council? What council?"

Bruce raised his eyebrows. "The International Council of the Watchers. Isdemus called them together as soon as we got back."

"What for?"

Bruce gaped at him. "What *for*?"

"Dad, the Shadow Lord is back and he has an invincible army. What hope do we have?"

"What hope did the ragtag lot of us have of fighting against them all a couple of days ago and living to tell about it?" Bruce countered. "But we did it."

"Not all of us," said Peter quietly. He turned back in the direction where Sully's casket still stood above the ground, waiting to be lowered.

The castle looked dilapidated from their vantage point. Peter knew that once they crossed the drawbridge, it would change in a twinkle back to the majestic splendor of Carlion. But none of it dazzled him now. It seemed surreal to think of how much had happened in the span of just a few days.

"Isdemus and I spent a long time last night discussing Chaos Theory," Bruce went on. "The smallest amount of force applied in exactly the right place can make all the difference, even when we are hopelessly outmatched."

"So the purpose of the Council is to decide what constitutes 'exactly the right place,' then," said Peter. "Don't tell me that I wasn't told about this Council because Isdemus thinks it's more important that they 'keep me safe,' because that is the biggest load of—"

"No," Bruce interrupted. "You and Lily both need to be there, now."

Something in Bruce's tone of voice made Peter stop walking and turn to look at him. Bruce wouldn't meet his eyes.

"I knew this day would come all along," he went on, sounding rather strange. Then he amended, "Well, not *this* day exactly, but something like it. The day when I couldn't protect you anymore." He paused, sniffed, and then gave a hollow laugh. "Although let's be honest; I haven't really been protecting you for some time now, have I?"

Peter didn't reply. He turned back to Arthur's grave, knelt down and pressed his hand against the cold stone, as if it foretold his future.

The Council was already in session by the time Peter, Lily, Brock, and Cole approached the castle gates. The fields were empty, and the stable boys had been given the day off.

Lily and Peter hung back behind Brock and Cole. Neither of them spoke, lost in thought.

"So," Lily said finally.

"So," Peter returned.

"What are you thinking about?"

Peter shrugged. "What are you thinking about?"

Lily pursed her lips. "I'm thinking about what's going to happen now."

Peter nodded slowly. Truthfully he wasn't thinking of anything. His mind felt like muted white noise.

Lily went on, "I can only think of two possibilities. Either we try to steal the Stone back, or…" she trailed off.

This roused Peter from his stupor, and he looked up at her. "Or what?"

"You remember the prophecy?" said Lily carefully.

Peter snorted.

"I'll take that as a yes. You know how the very end of it says, *'The one who holds the blade that was broken shall emerge victorious'?*"

Peter stared at her for a minute, processing her implication. "You're thinking they're gonna go after Excalibur?"

Lily nodded. "And then they'll have to re-forge it, I would assume."

"Of course," said Peter slowly. He lapsed into silence, lost in thought.

Presently Lily ventured, "Peter, you know they aren't going to want us involved in whatever they have planned."

"No," Peter agreed. "They definitely won't."

"They're gonna want us out of harm's way somewhere. So if we want to be involved…"

Suddenly Peter's anger flared. "If we *want* to be involved?" he repeated incredulously. "Lily, what if we *hadn't* gone to Giza? What if we'd stayed out of it like we were supposed to? Sully would still be alive!"

Lily gaped at him at first, and then she swallowed, like she was gathering the strength to respond. "That's not true, Peter—" Before she could get any further, though, Peter broke away from her. He couldn't stand to talk to her any longer.

"Peter!" he heard Lily call after him, frustrated. He could feel Cole's and Brock's eyes on them both, but he didn't care.

He didn't know where he was going, but found himself veering towards the dragon-shaped garden instead of the castle gates and slipped inside. He felt desperate to be alone, even if only for a few minutes.

At the center of the garden, a scalloped stone bench sat before a fountain spilling over a glass orb. A breeze rustled the leaves of the bushes around him, and rustled Peter's hair too. He sat down on the bench, staring at the orb without really seeing it.

In the last two weeks, he felt like he had lived three lifetimes. Peter wanted to think about Sully's death, he wanted to process his part in it... but he couldn't. He just couldn't.

So instead he thought about Lily. He wished, not for the first time, that she was a bloke, so he could punch her in the face. But then he remembered the way she had looked at him the moment he woke up, so tender and vulnerable. He felt himself grow warm, and his stomach gave a not-entirely-unpleasant lurch.

Dad and Cole might have been right, he admitted to himself. Maybe she really did fancy him. Maybe that was why she'd been acting so bipolar lately.

Maybe it's why I have too, he admitted to himself at last.

But how Peter felt about Lily, and how she felt about him, seemed moot at this point. After all, one of them was going to be the Child of the Prophecy.

Which meant one of them would most likely end up dead. Probably sooner rather than later.

He thought of the cemetery. He had just left the grave of a man who had walked the earth 1500 years ago, and who had looked exactly like him. Sully's death crept into his thoughts again, but he shut it out before the memory could fully return. He'd have to be at the Council in a few minutes, and he couldn't afford to go there.

And yet, he couldn't help it. He pictured the cemetery earth, soft and wet, where they interred Sully's body less than an hour before. One minute he'd been so vibrant and alive, then cold and buried a few days later.

Would that be him?

Would that be Lily?

He thought of his own funeral. Lily would be sobbing. Cole would be comforting her, Peter was sure. His dad would be...

He couldn't think of that.

He tried to imagine himself at Lily's funeral, and found he couldn't think of that either.

"Peter?"

He looked up to see Lily approaching him from behind. He sighed. She sat down next to him, but did not say a word, drawing her arms around her and shivering as the wind cut through her black dress. They sat like that for what seemed like hours, as the wind grew colder still and chill of the bench seeped through their clothes. Through his numbness, Peter felt a pricking awareness of her presence. He knew he needed to apologize for snapping at her. He didn't know how much more time they had left together, but it probably wasn't much—certainly not enough to waste by being angry with each other.

"Lily?" Peter said finally.

She looked up at him expectantly. He saw that her cheeks and eyelashes were wet with tears. "Peter?" she replied, with a hint of a smile.

"Whatever happens, I just want you to know…" As she waited, Peter choked on the words he'd intended to say. "I'm… really glad I met you," he said at last.

He saw a brief flash of disappointment cross her face. But she nodded, the tears slipping onto her cheeks again. She wiped them away with the back of her hand.

"Peter, you have *no* idea," she whispered.

Peter closed his eyes and nodded that he understood what she meant. Without second-guessing himself for once, he reached out and took her hand. She squeezed it gratefully.

Isdemus had told him anything was possible.

But Isdemus had been wrong. Everything Peter really wanted seemed forever outside his reach.

**Sneak Preview: *Impossible*,
Book 3 in the *Piercing the Veil* trilogy**

Prologue

Sargon stood on the edge of a precipice. He was somewhere in the Andes mountains, thick fir trees at his back and sheer rock descending to a ravine below. He could not even see the bottom.

In one hand, Sargon held the Philosopher's Stone. It was blood-red, and cut in a spherical shape. In the other, he held the fragments of a golden sword: Excalibur. He closed his eyes, a blissful smile curling his cruel lips, creasing the jagged scar across Kane's right cheek.

You're going to lose, Kane snarled. *Peter will destroy you.*

You know that is a lie, Kane, Sargon replied calmly. *I have the Philosopher's Stone, and the fragments of Excalibur. I am invincible.*

But you don't know how to reforge Excalibur. As long as they are fragments, you have no hope of fulfilling the prophecy!

Sargon shook his head, still smiling. Kane was

right, of course: he did not know how to reforge the sword. Yet. But he knew how to find out.

In a ringing voice, Sargon cried out, *"An sprioc, inis dom do speisialta!"*

Instantly the Andes disappeared, and the world became silent and luminous. Kane felt himself locked in a rigid lattice structure of purest, deepest red, the light of the sun bouncing all around and through him.

A thousand flashes of the Stone's memory bombarded Kane at once: the impossible, dizzying, unimaginable heat from the inside of a volcano; the crushing pressure; the explosive force, propelling him down the edges of a mountain amidst running lava.

Excalibur must be reforged, Sargon told the Stone. *How can this be accomplished?*

Kane felt, rather than heard, the Stone's answer. He watched without eyes as men slaughtered one another, their blood running like the lava had done seconds before. It was both a memory and a reply.

Blood, thought Sargon with satisfaction. *Of course. It is so simple.* Had not the Stone required him to spill his own blood in exchange for his immortality?

The red luminescent world disappeared, and Sargon blinked, again standing on the edge of the precipice. *Of course,* he thought again. He consulted Kane's memory of the prophecy with a flash: *Both shall fall, but the One who holds the blade that was broken shall emerge victorious.*

In order to reforge Excalibur, someone must die.

There are three candidates, Sargon thought. *I*

have already taken the body of one; only two yet remain. One will serve the blood sacrifice. Then, with Excalibur restored, I shall kill the other.

Sargon felt Kane's quiet despair. A cruel smile curled his lips once more.

It is a beautiful symmetry, Kane. Is it not?

Afterword

It took me almost a year to research the "Piercing the Veil" series before I actually started writing. For those who are curious, here's a breakdown of some of the concepts I *didn't* make up, appearing both in *Intangible* and *Invincible.*

From *Intangible:*

General plot structure:
•*Penumbra:* the word technically means eclipse, but it also can be translated "shadow."

•*Nimbus:* the word nimbi means ring of light, or halo (and the plural is indeed nimbi). I chose the word to contrast them with the penumbra, as light to darkness.

•*The Taijitu:* Although this symbol is most popularly affiliated with Taoism, the symbol was also used in the Roman army's Notitia Dignitatum around the time of the fall of the Roman Empire.

However, the Taijitu has no relationship to the astrological symbol of Cancer other than the fact that they look sort of similar if you turn the latter on its head.

• *The Ancient Tongue*: it's actually ancient Irish.

• *Sargon*: Sargon was the name of the first ruler of Mesopotamia, living from 2296-2240 BC.

• *How the penumbra can "cross over" to our world*: According to legend, in the ancient Middle East there was a city called Gordia that would eventually be absorbed into the territory of Alexander the Great, and it was a place where the veil between the dimensions wore thin, held together only by a knot. The legend had it that if the Gordion Knot was ever untied, the veil would be torn entirely. Alexander the Great had also heard that the one to untie the knot would become king of Gordia. He tried to untie it, but eventually gave up and sliced the knot in two with his sword. (I intended to work this story into the first book to explain why the penumbra and nimbi can cross over into our world, but never found a good place to mention it.)

Concepts of alchemy:

• *Alchemy:* the pseudoscience of the middle ages in which alchemists (the forerunners of chemists) believed one form of matter could transform into another, particularly metal into gold. From a mystical standpoint, base matter could also achieve spiritual transformation.

The Tria Prima: these three symbols are the Three Primes of Paracelsus, and they represent sulfur, the omnipresent spirit of life, mercury (the fluid connection between High and Low), and salt (representing base matter).

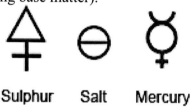

Sulphur   Salt   Mercury

•*The Punctum:* This symbol represents the sun, and was associated with the Egyptian sun god Ra. It is also the alchemical symbol for gold.

•*The Philosopher's Stone:* Alchemists believed they could transmute one form of matter into another, but it didn't actually work. So they theorized the existence of the Philosopher's Stone as the missing ingredient. (I intended to state that the Philosopher's Stone *was* the Holy Grail, since that object appears so frequently in Arthurian legends, but it never became relevant to the plot.)

Concepts from the Arthurian Legends: most of my research on the legends came from "The Arthurian Legends, An Illustrated Anthology," by Richard Barber; "Sir Gawain and the Green Knight," by Simon Armitage; "The Book of Merlyn," by T.H. White; "The Once and Future

King," by T.H. White; and the legendary "The Death of King Arthur," by Sir Thomas Malory.

•*The Fata Morgana*: According to legend, Arthur's evil half-sister Morgan (or Morgana, depending on the version you read), also called the Fairie Queen, created a castle in Avalon that was half part of our world and half part of another. Sailors claim to see the mirage of a castle off the banks of the Straits of Messina in Italy, but regardless of how long they sail towards it, it always hovers just out of reach, and they are said to drown in its pursuit. They call it the Fata Morgana.

•*Excalibur*: Famously, Arthur pulled this mystical sword from a stone, fulfilling the prophecy that the one to do so would become the rightful king of England. I chose to make the sword gold because of its relationship to alchemy (gold represents "spirit" or otherworldliness, which is why the sword can bar the Shadow Lord from his return into the world of men). After the Battle of Salisbury Plain where Arthur died and Camelot fell, one version of the legend has it that Lancelot and the last remaining Knight of the Round Table, Girflet, throw Excalibur into the Straits of Messina.

•*The Fall of the Roman Empire:* The Huns and the Visigoths (warring Germanic tribes) attacked the Roman Empire around 470 AD, displacing Roman soldiers to Britain. These soldiers intermarried with the native Celts, and that is how Britain came about. This is also around the time that historians estimate the real Arthur might have lived.

•*Guinevere*: Queen Guinevere (or Guenever, nicknamed Jenny in some versions) was Arthur's one and only wife—and she was human (there was no Cecily.) She had an affair with Arthur's best knight Lancelot, forcing Arthur to charge them both with high treason.

•*Mordred:* most versions have it that Mordred is Arthur's nephew, the son of his half-sister Morgan, rather than his son (although in some versions, Morgan tricked Arthur into sleeping with her, and she became pregnant by him). In either case, once Mordred grew to adulthood, Arthur left him in charge of Camelot. In Arthur's absence, Mordred set himself up as king, and Mordred and Arthur killed one another in the Battle of Salisbury Plain.

•*The Order of the Paladin:* the name was originally used to refer to Charlemagne's Twelve Peers in fourteenth century France, his best warriors. The word paladin is also associated with Arthurian legends in general to mean any chivalrous hero. (Isdemus tells Peter that this was the original name of the Watchers, and the name lingers in Carlion here and there—for instance, it is the name of their secondary school, Paladin High.)

•*Carlion:* Again according to "The Once and Future King" by T.H. White, the city of Camelot was situated in the greater region known as Carlion.

•*The Pendragon Crest:* Most versions depict only one golden dragon on a red background (or red dragons on a gold background), but for my purposes I made them two. This obviously became critical in *Invincible*—which was originally titled *Double Dragon.*

Concepts from Physics: I knew next to nothing about quantum physics before I began to write

Intangible. Most of my research came from the following books: "A Brief History of Time," by Stephen Hawking; "The Dancing Wu Li Masters," by Gary Zukav; "The Physics of Superheros," by James Kakalios; "Equations of Eternity," by David Darling; "Parallel Universes," by Fred Alan Wolf; and "The Philosopher's Stone," by David Peat.

•*Superstring Theory:* According to Stephen Hawking's "A Brief History of Time," string theory describes strings as the foundational matter of the universe—instead of particles, the smallest units are strings. (Isdemus's explanation of the strings as a trampoline are my attempt to get this picture across. Because the nimbi and penumbra exist outside of our universe, they are therefore outside of the "strings". This explains how the nimbi and penumbra can pinpoint bizarre activity.)

•*Quantum physics:* On a very small scale, at any given moment, a particle may move in infinite or near-infinite possible directions. This constellation of possibilities is called the quantum wave function (represented by Peter's rainbow). However, when an outside observer acts upon the particle in some way, the quantum wave function "collapses" into a single event. This interpretation of quantum behavior is called the Copenhagen interpretation, and it is the one I went with in *Intangible*. The other interpretation for the behavior of quantum activity is the multiple universe theory, which holds that every possible movement of every particle actually takes place in an alternate universe. (I thought about incorporating this into the plot, but it just became way too complicated.)

•*Entanglement:* the Watchers' entangled coins are based on the idea that two particles which were once connected remain in "communication" with each other regardless of where they later end up in the universe—for instance, when one electron spins in one direction, its entangled twin spontaneously spins in the same direction, even if they are light-years away.

Concepts from general science:

•*Peter's experiment:* At the beginning of the book, Peter performs a titration experiment in chemistry class in which sulfuric acid breaks down a chocolate bar into elemental carbon, repairing a leak in his damaged plastic tubing.

•*The "crack" with the appearance/disappearance of the penumbra:* the speed of sound is about 340 m/s. Any matter moving faster than that will break the sound barrier, and cause a sonic boom. Since the nimbi and penumbra (and also space specialists) spontaneously disappear and re-materialize, they move faster even than the speed of light—so they would break the sound barrier easily. However, when nimbi and penumbra appear in their own dimension, they have not taken a physical form in our world and therefore can do so silently.

•*The event horizon around a porthole:* The event horizon is the "point of no return" surrounding a black hole where even light cannot escape (which is why black holes are black). I use the same term for portholes (or wormholes): when a character or object comes within a certain distance of the porthole, he or she is compelled to pass to the other side.

•*Dark matter*: Some 85% of matter in the universe cannot be seen, though its effects can be demonstrated. One possible explanation for this includes multiple dimensions (several of which are explained by Superstring theory)—however, Bruce's literal interpretation of "dark" matter as the opposite of light (photons) was my own.

From *Invincible:*
General Plot Structure:
•*Squaring the Circle:* As mentioned in *Intangible*, the Philosopher's Stone was the legendary object connected with alchemy, necessary to convert base material (like a physical body) into a celestial body (like a penumbra). Squaring the Circle was the symbol associated with it in alchemical writings.

•*Newton and the Philosopher's Stone:* Many great scientists were said to have been obsessed with finding the Philosopher's Stone, including Isaac Newton and Nicholas Flamel.

Egyptology: The majority of my research came from "The Message of the Sphinx," by Graham Hancock and Robert Bauval, and "Ancient Egyptian Mysticism and its Relevance Today," by John Van Auken.

•*Zep Tepi:* the "First Time" (or the dawn of time), as referenced in *The Book of What Is In the*

Duat.

•*Isis and Sirius:* The Egyptian goddess Isis was represented by the star Sirius, the brightest star in the sky. Ancient Egyptians believed that the story of Isis and Osiris was played out in the stars.

•*The Age of the Pyramids and the Sphinx*: Most scholars put the date of the pyramids around 2500, and under Pharaoh Khafre. However, according to some more obscure Egyptology circles, the Sphinx dates back to 10,500 BC. First, the water damage on the Sphinx points to a very wet climate; however, in Khafre's day, Egypt was already a desert. Second, the Egyptians believed the heavens to be a reflection of the earth ("as above, so below," just like in alchemy), and so it made most sense for the Sphinx, which represented a lion, to mirror the position of the heavens during the age of Leo. This would indeed have placed its construction around 10,500 BC. This was the reason why I placed the Great Deception at that date.

Concepts from Arthurian Legends

•*Turning into finches:* In "The Once and Future King" by T.H. White, Merlyn teaches Arthur about the animal kingdom by turning him into various different kinds of animals (one of which was finches).

•*Vortigem:* Vortigem was an evil king mentioned in the Vulgate Cycle of the Arthurian legends. (I considered using this as the name of the Shadow Lord instead of Sargon.)

Concepts from Physics:

•*Quantum vs Newtonian physics:* Totally different physical laws govern the behavior of matter at the quantum versus the macroscopic level: while quantum particles have near-infinite possibilities available to them, in our world, if you drop a stone, it's going down. Einstein spent the latter portion of his life trying to determine how the two were connected and has never managed to do it, nor has anyone since. For the purposes of the trilogy, prior to the Great Deception, the macroscopic world obeyed quantum laws (controlled by the Ancient Tongue); it was only afterwards that the two became disconnected, and people's use of the Ancient Tongue became limited to the energy within their own bodies. For my purposes, the one who holds the Philosopher's Stone will reconnect quantum and Newtonian physics, for himself as well as for all who obey him (rendering him essentially invincible).

•*Chaos Theory*: According to Edward Lorenz, weather systems are so sensitive that the flapping of a butterfly's wings can change tomorrow's weather on the other side of the world (called the Butterfly Effect); small changes can amplify to have magnificent effects down the line. (For more on this, check out "Chaos Gaia Eros," by Ralph Abraham, and "The Seven Life Lessons of Chaos," by John Briggs and F David Peat.)

•*Superspace (Peter's Space of Possibilities, or Meadow):* According to "Parallel Universes" by Fred Alan Wolf, superspace is "an infinite space that contains all possibilities including other universes" (66). I didn't read much more about it to be honest—I just took it from there!

About the Author

C.A. Gray is a Naturopathic Medical Doctor (NMD), with a primary care practice in Tucson, Arizona. She has always been captivated by the power of a good story, fictional or otherwise, which is probably why she loves holistic medicine: a patient's physical health is invariably intertwined with his or her life story, and she believes that the one can only be understood in context with the other.

She still wants to be everything when she grows up. She moonlights as a college chemistry teacher (she has a degree in biochemistry, with minors in Spanish and Creative Writing), writes white papers for a supplement company, does theater when she gets the chance, and sings at her church. She is blessed with exceptionally supportive family and friends, and thanks God for them every single day!

Publication-ready formatting by:

Daisy Bank Editing Services

http://www.flyingferrets.eclipse.co.uk/Daisy Bank Editing Services/home.htm

CPSIA information can be obtained at www.ICGtesting.com
Printed in the USA
LVOW11s2248300914

406670LV00001B/35/P